REPETITION

CRYSTAL SIDELL

Published by Dead Fox Publishing
deadfoxpub.com

Editing: Lauren Woods, Liz Perrine
Proofing: Kelley York
Cover Illustration: Blaine Daigle
Interior Formatting: Kelley York

Digital 978-1-960322-33-3
Paperback 978-1-960322-34-0
Hardcover 978-1-960322-35-7

1st Edition April 17, 2026

Content Notes

Standard horror tropes apply. This includes but is not limited to: violence, blood, gore, death, and body horror.

For a full list of content notes, please visit our website.

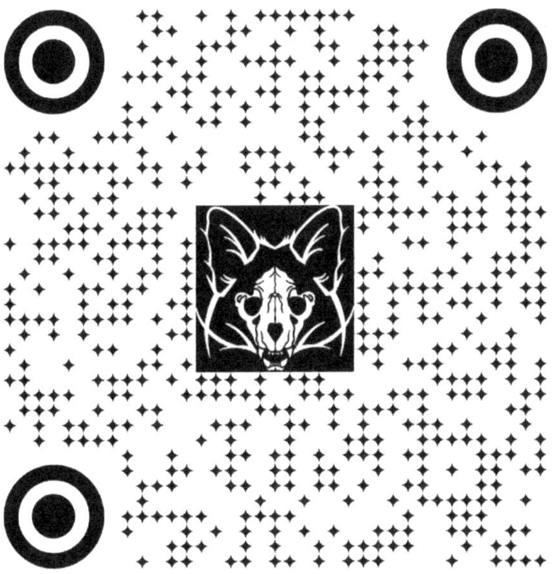

Dedication

For the women who are no longer in my life but regularly visit me in dreams:

Cyndi Jo (1987-2017)
my only sister, who lived up to the song she was named after – "Girls Just to Want to Have Fun."

Grandma K (1935-2024)
who introduced me to What Was I Scared Of? and Wynken, Blinken & Nod and the wonderful magic of storytelling.

Grandma Pat (1925-2017)
who always greeted us enthusiastically upon entering the house and yet always managed to slip out unnoticed.

Debbie (1964-2012)
a great stepmom who enjoyed life to the fullest while she could.

One

Out of place. Out of time. That's how the house at 919 Victor Street looked. But it was affordable and in a good location, and that made the property worth considering.

"At least it's not a dump," Marche Baker muttered, turning off the ignition. The previous house she'd toured had gutters swinging from the roof and mold running along the floorboards. The one before that had broken windows and a crack zig-zagging up one of the sides. In comparison, this house was a palace.

Someone had recently splashed a fresh coat of paint on the wooden frame. The color combination—dove gray paired with a snow-white trim—gave the place an air of old-time elegance. The windows had received attention, too; the spotless eastern-facing panes mirrored the late morning sky with sublime precision. If the house was an impressionist painting, its walls would represent the heavens and its windows, the clouds.

"Huh?"

Marche leaned over the steering wheel and squinted. Was it her imagination, or had something crossed in front of one of the upstairs windows just now? *But the real estate agent said the house was vacant. Could it be a squatter?* As she stared at the pane in the top left-hand corner, the glass reflected the image of a crow flying past.

"Mystery solved," she murmured.

Marche stepped out of the car and stood facing Victor Street, looking to her right. Traffic on Washington was light but steady, with a car or two passing every minute. She glanced left. Thick woods sat at the end of the street. She liked that. Egret Bay's population was denser than what she was accustomed to back in Haven Shores. At least a dead-end street provided the illusion of privacy. That was one checkmark off her list.

The street itself was another draw. Victor stretched out before her like a residential builder's advertisement of model neighborhoods. The yards, neatly kept, were spaced widely apart. The houses were clean and modern. Most of the shingled roofs came in varying shades of gray or white, but a few sported daring looks. One near the end of the street was maroon, another was avocado green, and her next-door neighbor's rooftop was azure. The road had been recently repaved, so there weren't any potholes.

As she considered the pros and cons of living in a house situated on the corner of a semi-busy street, a silver Corvette pulled into the driveway beside her compact car.

"Hope I didn't keep you waiting long?" Jemima Bright said, exiting the vehicle and extending a plump hand.

"Not at all." They shook. "I just got here."

"You find the place all right?"

"The directions were pretty straightforward, thank you."

"Good, good," Jemima said with a nod. "Well, what do you think of the neighborhood?"

"It looks nice. Respectable."

Jemima grinned. "Inviting, isn't it?"

"Hmm." Marche glanced down the street again. "Is this the only two-story house on the block?"

"Yes, I believe so. Multi-level homes aren't standard in the neighborhoods around here," Jemima said. "Most of the houses start out as a single-story and the owners add on later."

"So the second level isn't part of the original floor plan?"

"Let me see." Jemima pulled a red folder from the crook of her arm. She rummaged through the contents at a snail's pace, her right index finger scanning first one page and then another. "Oh!" she softly exclaimed. "I beg your pardon. The house hasn't been modified. It's older, you see..."

"How old?"

"Looks like it was built in 1932."

"Is it safe?" Marche asked, casting a skeptical glance at the house. "It won't cave in when you open the door?"

"Aren't you a funny one," Jemima said, chuckling. "Shall we go inside, then?" Tucking the folder back under her arm, she led Marche to the front door. Unlike the other houses on the street, this one had a stoop rather than a porch.

"Has it been on the market long?" Marche asked.

"I'll get that information for you in just a sec."

Normally, Marche would expect more from a realtor, but she'd hired Jemima on a whim yesterday. (She'd fired the other agent in a huff after he'd shown her one rundown property after another.) The woman seemed a little ditzy, and she hadn't quite done her homework, but she also hadn't had much time to prepare. Marche was eager to find a house as quickly as possible, so she was grateful the woman was willing to work her into her schedule on such short notice.

Jemima bent forward to fiddle with the combination lock fastened to the doorknob. "In today's market, the houses in this price bracket take an average of three months to sell. But it's not that uncommon to see a property listed for longer than that."

Jemima unlocked the door and Marche quietly followed her inside. The air smelled stale, like mothballs. This house, Marche could tell, had been empty for a long time.

The realtor paused inside the doorway and flipped through the listing sheet once again. Tapping a page, she traced a finger over its contents. "This one has been on the market for fourteen months." She dropped the folder to her side and surveyed the foyer.

"Is there something wrong with the house?" Marche asked, her skepticism returning. "Structural damage, maybe?"

"Nothing's been noted," Jemima said. "Now this *is* an old house, so it's bound to have some problems. The good news is that it seems to have a solid foundation. Though you never can tell. You won't know for sure until you have the house inspected."

"It does look like it's in pretty good shape," Marche admitted, her gaze sliding up the staircase. "At least there's no carpet."

"Floors and walls are trivial," Jemima said. "You can easily paint over colors you don't like and re-tile floors. But you can't fix a sinkhole."

Marche entered the room to the left of the foyer. The cream walls, newly painted like the exterior, offered no hints of its history. She saw no evidence of nail holes or fading from where picture frames might have hung in place for decades. The room was empty except for a television cable coiled like a snake on the floor. Light flooded in through the bare window.

"What's the square footage of this place?"

Jemima shuffled through her papers once more. "2,112. You're getting a lot of space for the money. Houses of this size—in this section of Egret Bay—generally run at least $275,000."

"So, what's the catch?"

"None that I can see. It just doesn't have some of the amenities that lots of other houses in the area have. There's no pool. The floor is vinyl, not tile. And, as you know, it has a wood frame rather than concrete block. Plus, it's been on the market for quite some time."

"Do you think we could get the seller to lower the asking price?"

"Depends," Jemima said with a shrug. "If they're eager enough, anything's possible. I recommend using caution with counter-offers, though. If you propose $175,000 for a $225,000 house, you risk insulting the seller. They might refuse to negotiate at all."

Marche nodded. The bank had pre-approved a loan for up to $195,000. Though she had Dom's life insurance payout in her pocket, she'd rather not touch those funds unless it was absolutely necessary.

Returning to the foyer, she headed toward the two doors under the staircase. The first opened upon a freestanding sink and toilet.

"This is your half bath," Jemima said, peering over Marche's shoulder. "Your full bath is on the second floor."

The other door revealed storage space for coats, shoes, and miscellaneous items. At the end of the hall, she discovered the laundry space, tucked between the kitchen and dining room.

"Are the washer and dryer included?" Marche asked.

"Absolutely. This house comes 'as-is,' so what you see is what you get."

"I'm not sure how I feel about having the laundry here," Marche mused, "but I could live with it." Closing the door, she inspected the room to her left. It looked identical to the den, except there weren't any cables lying about.

"This is your formal dining area," Jemima said. "It's a good size."

"It is," Marche agreed. "This house has almost more space than I know what to do with."

"Better too much than too little, right?" Jemima offered.

Marche gasped when she saw the kitchen. "Seriously?" she said, staring at the red-and-white checkered linoleum. "They repainted the whole house but left this eyesore?"

"The seller might have been on a tight budget."

"Or maybe they're colorblind," Marche added, opening a cabinet door. She winced at the yellow floral sticky paper covering the shelves. The cabinet's cream-colored interior glowed a dull yellow where the light landed on it. "I've seen more attractive kitchens in my time, but that's superficial, I guess."

"When it comes to real estate, it's all about location—"

"—location, location," Marche chimed in.

Jemima inspected one of the plywood cabinets above the stove. "This looks like handiwork from the seventies. But the doors aren't falling off the hinges and the shelves feel sturdy. They're functional."

"Functional," Marche repeated to herself. She didn't need something beautiful (she couldn't afford it, anyway); she needed something that worked.

Marche glanced out the window. The neighbor's yard offered a pleasant respite from the kitchen's nauseating color scheme. Pink and yellow flowers dotted the side of the ranch-style house. Between the two plots, a jacaranda tree sprouted from the earth, spanning its branches to create a stunning umbrella of violet. *It reminds me of...* And suddenly she was catapulted back to a time in her childhood when she'd sat with her mother under the honey-scented blossoms of a tree that looked just like it. Too often, her little sister was around, demanding all the attention. But this time, just Marche and her mother had sat together.

Though it was only a simple spring picnic, that afternoon had meant the world to her. She recalled giggling as her mother read a funny poem to her, and then her mother tugging playfully on one of her braids...

"Ready for the second floor?" Jemima asked.

Marche returned to the foyer and mounted the stairs located opposite the front door. She fully expected to hear a squeak or two, but the only noise to reach her ears emanated from the soft squishing of her rubber soles against the wooden surface.

"Sounds solid," she murmured.

Despite some elements of unattractiveness, the house already surpassed her expectations. *It's still nowhere near as nice as Bridget's place, though.* Bristling at the intrusive thought, she decided she liked the house even more. *It* is *a nice house. I could see us living here.* The sooner she got out from under her sister's roof, the better.

"In addition to the bathroom, you'll find three bedrooms up here," Jemima said over her shoulder. "Do you have any children?"

"A daughter," Marche replied.

"How nice! How old is she?"

"Five."

"Children are so sweet at that age, aren't they? My great niece just turned four, and I tell you, sometimes I just want to gobble her up!"

"What state is the roof in?" Marched asked. Pausing briefly on one of the steps, she glanced upward.

Jemima set her folder on the banister overlooking the first floor and sifted through the contents once again. "Um... The previous owner replaced it six years ago. You shouldn't have to worry about any repair work for at least a decade or two."

"Hurrah for that."

Marche reached the second floor and looked through the first door she passed. It was the bathroom.

"The toilet is high-efficiency compliant, and the sink and faucet are new. The fixtures, too," Jemima added, pointing her pen at the circular ceiling light with its brushed nickel finish. "What do you think of the tile?"

"Feels beachy." The aquamarine squares climbed halfway up the walls, at which point they gave way to beige stucco. With the outside light reflecting off the ceramic surface, she was bathed in a sea of blue. "The bathtub doesn't quite match though," she said about the mauve basin. She looked inside the medicine cabinet and examined the space under the sink.

The bedrooms came last. Two of the three rooms occupied a corner. They walked through the room overlooking the backyard first.

"There's your attic space," Jemima said, pointing to a square slab in the ceiling. She ran a finger over one of the two windowsills and peered through the panes. "You could use one of these rooms for an office if you like to work at home. A guest room is always nice to have as well."

"I suppose so."

The master bedroom—designated as such due to its size—occupied the front corner overlooking Victor Street and Washington Avenue. The third bedroom, located next to it, was the smallest.

Four walls and a closet didn't take much time to inspect; Marche finished her perusal of the second floor in less than ten minutes.

"I have two more houses I'd like to show you today," Jemima said as they descended the stairs. "They're both smaller than this one, but I think you'll like them. The neighborhoods are friendly and they're zoned for reputable schools."

"Actually, I think I'm ready to make an offer," Marche announced. She was tired of house shopping and even more tired of sharing a living space with her sister. And then there was the jacaranda tree. Every time she looked out the kitchen window, it would be there—a comforting reminder of her mother.

"Are you sure?"

"It's got everything that I'm looking for. And I really do like the location."

"Would you like to tour the other houses on the list, anyway?" Jemima asked. "It never hurts to compare."

"No need. I have a good feeling about this one."

"Okay, then!" Jemima replied with a vibrant smile. "Let's go down to my office and get the paperwork started."

Two

Three weeks later, Marche received the keys to the house on Victor Street.

On Wednesday, she'd hired Moss Mover's, Inc. to transport her belongings from the locker at Sunshine Storage to her new address, and last night she'd packed their suitcases. This morning, all that remained for her to do was to load them into the car. After showering, she dressed in "moving" clothes and then dropped Stella off at daycare. It was nine o'clock when she arrived at her new home.

The movers were scheduled to arrive within the hour. Marche walked into the house and headed straight for the thermostat. "This won't do," she murmured when she saw that it had been set to eighty. Money wasn't a luxury she could afford to throw around. But she couldn't afford to suffer from heatstroke while moving heavy boxes, either. She promptly turned the notch down four degrees, then returned to the car for the first of the suitcases.

On her second trip outside, she spotted the moving truck turning onto the street. Marche waved to the driver. Resting her arm on the back door of the car, she watched as the truck stopped just past the driveway. The front wheels rotated to the left. Then the truck reversed into the drive. The motor went silent and two men jumped onto the pavement.

"Mornin'," the driver, a burly man with curly red hair, said.

"Hello," Marche replied.

The second mover, taller and thin as a scarecrow, unlocked the back of the truck and rolled up the door without a word.

"You just point and we'll do the work."

As the men unloaded the bed frames, Marche ran up the stairs to figure out who should get each room. She'd been so busy crunching numbers on paper that she hadn't given any thought to their actual living arrangement. Where should Stella sleep?

"The smaller one can go there," she said, pointing to the bedroom that faced the street. Then she moved to stand inside the doorway to the master bedroom. "And you can put the larger one in here."

Next came the mattresses, followed by two dressers and three night tables. The empty house echoed with heavy breathing and intermittent grunts.

"To the left, Marty," the burly man said. "No. The *left*. Shit!" A pause followed. "...Jammed my finger."

As the indecipherable muttering floated downstairs, Marche stepped out the front door. She inspected the contents of the truck. After the bedroom furniture, all that remained was the kitchen table with its chairs, the sofa and recliner, the coffee table, four sets of bookshelves, a mishmash of seats, lamps, and the TV. She'd sold the nicer pieces, like the curio and china hutch, to consignment shops before leaving the East Coast.

So this is what starting over looks like—like I've never lived at all.

The men spent another half an hour unloading the furniture. Then came the boxes, about thirty in total.

"You can put all of those in here," Marche said, indicating the den. She stood at the foot of the stairs, feeling awkward and useless as they carried the boxes in one and two at a time. There was nothing to do but watch, and she found herself staring at an indentation at the top of the front entrance door frame.

She suffered another awkward moment when the quiet man shut the back of the truck and the other handed her the receipt to sign. She gave him a ten-dollar tip and tried to avoid eye contact, embarrassed that she couldn't offer more. Then the movers were gone.

Marche heaved a sigh as she re-entered the house, grateful to finally be alone. She surveyed the mountain of cardboard boxes, thrilled at the prospect of keeping busy for several days—weeks, perhaps. When she worked, she felt safe. When she sat still—when she had time to think—she became vulnerable. She wholeheartedly embraced any opportunity to prevent the unpleasant intrusion of her thoughts.

"Time to get started."

There were boxes labeled "kitchen," "bathroom," and "books," while others had been identified as "kid stuff," "miscellaneous," and "Marche."

"Kitchen first," she said, after she'd separated them into sections.

She took a swig from her bottled soda and bounced on her toes like a boxer preparing for a round in the ring. She even put on gardening gloves—though they really weren't necessary for the work at hand.

"Okay, let's do this!"

Skipping, she transported the towels, rags, and smaller wares into the kitchen. The dishes slowed her down to a clumsy swagger. The cast iron cookware left her huffing and puffing.

Chugging on her warm beverage, her gaze lit upon Stella's boxes.

"You're next," she said, pointing a finger.

Half of Stella's boxes contained toys; the other half contained mostly clothes. One by one, she hoisted them up the stairs. By the third trip, she began to wonder why she had chosen a house with two floors.

When she had deposited the last of Stella's boxes into her new bedroom, Marche wandered over to the spare room across the hall.

She frowned. What would she do with this space?

When Stella was an infant, Marche had dreamed of owning a four-bedroom home with a pool. Now she had a place with three bedrooms and more square footage than she knew what to do with.

"Plenty of time to figure it out later," Marche declared, returning to the den.

She found a box marked "miscellaneous" and carried it to the second floor. For now, she would use the extra room for storage. Up and down. Up and down. Marche spent the next several minutes absorbed in the mind-numbing activity of ascending the stairs and dropping boxes in their newly assigned locations. The muscles in her legs ached from the exercise. Her heart pounded in her chest, leaving her short of breath. The cool air had started to warm and sweat began to gather at her hairline. She yanked the gloves off her moist hands, wetted her dry throat with more tepid soda. She had to resist turning the thermostat down further.

Only a few boxes now remained in the den.

Marche lifted one that was labeled "bathroom," her eyes glued to the floor as she crossed the short distance to the stairs. The white vinyl was too bland, she thought. It could use a rug. Maybe something abstract, with greens and blues?

A scuff mark near the foot of the stairs caught her attention. Setting the toiletry items aside, she began to scrub the floor with her rubber sole.

As she busied herself with rubbing the fat gray lines into oblivion, a foul scent drifted to her nose.

"Eww. Gross."

Marche lifted an index finger to her nostrils, but it was no match against the offensive odor. A peculiar mixture of onions, mold, and rotten eggs mingled in the stagnant air with cardboard, dust, and perspiration. She fought the urge to gag as she dug her sneaker into the floor and kicked at the stubborn streak. The sickening smell faded as she wiped away the last vestiges of gray.

Marche lowered her hand and sucked in a deep breath.

She gave the vinyl one more enthusiastic swipe of her foot and was ready to move on when her ears detected a soft rustling sound—like leaves brushing across pavement in an autumn breeze.

Her limbs froze, her head jerked upwards.

Did that come from the second floor?

Before she could properly process the information or concoct a rational argument to explain the unexpected noise, she saw it. The train of a dress—black and glossy like silk—dragging along the floor. Something that shouldn't have been there *was* there. Then it disappeared, like a slithering snake, past the banister and down the hall.

Though Marche didn't spook easily, the skin on the back of her neck tingled with a sudden inexplicable chill. She laid one hand on her abdomen—as she used to do when she was pregnant with Stella—and flexed the other hand at her side. She licked her lips and then rubbed them together. The fingers on her abdomen twitched.

"Hello?"

She waited but neither saw nor heard anything else.

"Is someone there?"

Seconds of silence passed. Marche lowered her hand and ascended the first step. *I did not imagine that. I've never hallucinated in my life. Not when Mom and Dad died. Not when I had heatstroke. Not even when Dom—* She gripped the railing and lifted her foot onto the next step.

"You can get into a lot of trouble for being in here," she shouted. "I haven't invited you. You're trespassing."

No reply. Suddenly overcome with anger, Marche tramped up the remaining steps. Who had the gall to enter her house without knocking? Who had the nerve to look through her rooms!

She marched forward, a fearless queen on a mission to defend her kingdom, ready to yell bloody hell and phone the police. She could handle a confrontation; she almost craved one.

"Where are you?" she called as she reached the second floor.

She stormed into Stella's room first. A quick peek inside the closet confirmed it was empty. She looked in the master bedroom next. It, too, was vacant. She headed toward the spare room, her heart drumming blood into her ears.

"I know you're in there," she said. "There's nowhere else to hide."

She crossed the threshold and the deluge of words she had prepared to speak died in the back of her throat.

"Hello?"

Unpacked boxes littered the room; her work gloves lay on top of one of them. The open bottle of Pepsi sat forgotten on one of the windowsills. The closet contained nothing but a pull chain.

Marche shifted on her feet, wrinkled her brow.

She *had* heard faint scuffling; she had *definitely* seen that dress. But where was the evidence?

Marche maneuvered through the labyrinth of boxes, accidentally knocking one of the gloves onto the floor as she stepped up to the window that faced Washington. What did she expect to see? A quick downward glance confirmed that there weren't any cat burglars scaling the walls of the house. She moved to the other window and looked out. The backyard was empty except for a couple of mourning doves pecking at the grass.

Marche turned from the window, confused. Halfway to the door, she retrieved the fallen glove and returned it to its partner.

Then, as her right foot crossed the threshold, she felt a tap on the shoulder.

Marche's breath caught in her throat. Though her arms and legs were caked with sweat, her body suddenly went cold all over. She wanted to flee the room—to run down the stairs and out the front door. But she suppressed the childlike urge.

Common sense declared that she had misidentified the chilly, metallic touch on her skin. It wasn't someone's finger poking her, but a blast of frigid air from the vent above her head.

There's no one behind me.

I'm alone in this room.

I'm alone in this house.

Slowly, she turned.

Marche's eyelids fluttered open. She blinked several times as her vision swam in and out of focus. When it finally cleared, she realized she'd been staring at one of the walls in the spare room.

But why was she lying on the floor? What the hell had happened?

"Ugh."

Marche groaned with discomfort as she rolled into a sitting position. A dull pain lanced through her head. She placed a hand at the back of her skull and gingerly explored her scalp. Her fingertips encountered a tender bump. Had she fainted and hit her head on the doorknob?

"Some homecoming party," she mumbled.

As she dragged her hand away from her head, she noted the hands on her watch and jumped up.

She was ten minutes late getting Stella from daycare.

Three

Bridget had insisted on celebrating "moving day" with a home-cooked meal. So at six o'clock, Marche pushed the doorbell at 713 Carmichael Drive. A lofty chime resonated through the space beyond.

"You don't need to ring the bell!" Bridget said, swinging the door open. "Just come in."

"Auntie Bee!" Stella shrieked.

"Hey there, Sweet Cakes." Bridget lifted her niece onto her hip, a smile brightening her features. "Did you have fun at Melody's today?"

"Uh huh. I drawed apple and nanna trees."

"That sounds yummy. I'd like to see them. Will you show me later?"

Stella nodded enthusiastically. Marche shut the front door as Bridget carried Stella into the living room.

"Where's Trey?" Marche asked.

"In the shower. He'll be out in a minute." Bridget lowered Stella to the floor and grabbed a doll from a nearby shelf. Placing it in Stella's hands, she said, "Would you like to keep Bianca out of trouble while Mommy and I get the food ready?"

"Uh-kay." Dropping to her knees on the thick carpet, Stella cradled the doll in her lap. "Watch out for *who*? What do you *mean*? Who's *that*?"

What a weird conversation to have with a doll, Marche thought as she followed her sister into the kitchen.

As usual, Bridget had prepared a meal so generous that a small team of lumberjacks would walk away satiated. "The corn pudding should be ready any second," Bridget announced. "Can you carry the chicken out to the table while I finish tossing the salad?"

"Sure."

The table, large enough to seat eight people with elbow room to spare, had already been set. Marche placed the chicken next to a basket of rolls. Then, because she couldn't seem to help herself, she swapped one of the knives with a fork.

"Where's my fork?" Trey asked once they sat down to eat.

"Um." Bridget's gaze darted about the table. "Oops. Sorry, hon. My mind must've been elsewhere," she said as they traded silverware.

Marche smiled.

"This looks delicious." Trey leaned over to kiss Bridget on the mouth, and Marche's expression faltered.

"Yeah," Marche added. "You really outdid yourself."

Bridget dipped her head slightly. A faint blush spread across her pale features, darkening the freckles on her nose. "Help yourselves to the food, everyone. Trey, would you do us the honors with the main course?"

Trey carved the chicken and passed around slabs of the white meat while Marche scooped small portions of green bean casserole and corn pudding onto Stella's plate.

"Did you get everything moved into the house okay?" Trey asked.

"Yeah," Marche replied, helping herself to some salad. "Nothing seems lost or broken."

"You may want to consider doing an inventory, if you haven't already," Trey said. "A buddy of mine from the chemical engineering department discovered that one of his boxes had gone 'missing' after he moved. Expensive stuff too. Sports gear, I think. Since he'd documented everything, he was able to get reimbursed for about three hundred dollars."

"I'm not really concerned about it." Marche stabbed a tomato sliver from the salad and mixed it with the corn pudding. "There's nothing worth stealing, anyway."

"I'm going to miss having you and Stella around," Bridget said. She rested her chin on her hand and gazed at her niece, a thoughtful expression on her face. "I love having a kid in the house."

"I would think you'd get your fill of them at work," Marche replied. "A room full of first graders for six hours a day? You should count yourself lucky you get to come home to peace and quiet."

"Not Bridge," Trey said with a chuckle. "If she hadn't become a teacher, I do believe she'd have gone into pediatrics."

Marche tried to focus on the meal. Everything tasted good. Too good. The chicken was moist, the corn sweet. Was there anything that her little sister couldn't do well?

"Eat your food, Stella." Marche tore a dinner roll in half and handed the smaller piece to her daughter.

Stella shoved the entire bit into her mouth, her cheeks puffing out like a hamster's; she picked at a green bean with her fingers.

Late afternoon sunlight speared through the dining-room windows. The chandelier above their heads refracted some of the light on the walls, the table, and the blue lead crystal vase which Bridget had filled with yellow roses.

"When do you start your job?" Trey asked.

Marche rested one of her palms on the tabletop. Without being conscious of it, she caressed the smooth mahogany surface with the pad of her thumb. "On Monday."

"You excited to be doing something new?"

"I'm used to working with books," Marche replied.

"Ah. Right. I guess there must be a lot of similarities between managing a bookstore and helping people in a library—"

"It's business," Marche interjected. "People want facts. Or they want to be entertained. Or they want both. The only difference is that one charges for its services while the other provides its goods for free."

"Have you ever worked in a library before?" Trey asked, reaching for his glass of Perrier.

Marche noticed her restless thumb and quickly withdrew her hand. "Once," she replied, "for about a year when I was in college."

"It must've made a strong impression on you since you're dipping your toes back in the water."

"I really enjoyed it," Marche said. "At the time, I thought I'd become a librarian."

"Oh? What happened?"

Marche's stomach muscles contracted; her appetite soured. "Shit happened," she replied, her voice flat.

Bridget winced.

Marche wondered at her sister's reaction. Was it the fact that she'd cursed in front of Stella? Or was it the inadvertent reminder of their shared tragic history?

"I'm sorry to hear that," Trey said.

Marche focused on the chandelier; the light dancing off its crystalline surface made a pretty contrast to the ugliness in her head. Trey was too polite to prod into her life. But she was going to tell him about it, even if he didn't ask.

"You've probably heard the story before. It was April and our parents were celebrating their twenty-fifth wedding anniversary. Mom and Dad decided to mark the occasion with a European vacation. Bridget was only sixteen at the time, so I agreed to come home for a couple of weeks to keep an eye on her. They landed in France without a hitch. But they never made it home. Their plane crashed somewhere over the Atlantic."

No one spoke for several seconds. Marche's fork scraped the plate where she pushed around a leaf of lettuce. Beside her, Stella chomped noisily on a piece of chicken larger than her mouth.

"So Jake and Sally got a new dog," Bridget said. "They rescued it from the shelter. She's absolutely adorable. I think—"

Marche only half-listened as her sister chattered on about the benefits of owning a mutt over a purebred. Then the conversation turned toward cat ownership versus dog ownership, and why they (she and Trey) might prefer to adopt a cat rather than a dog. Marche was on the verge of yawning from boredom by the time her sister finally announced dessert.

Marche stacked Stella's plate on top of her own and handed them to her sister, who had begun to collect the dishes.

"Be right back," Bridget said in a singsong voice.

Once she was out of earshot, Trey looked at Marche. "I didn't mean to dredge up painful memories. That was thoughtless of me—I'm sorry."

Marche grabbed her glass and sipped the water, wishing desperately that the Perrier was vodka instead. "Don't worry about it," she replied. "I'm fine." She noticed, however, that her hand trembled slightly as she set the water back on the table. She rubbed her fingers up and down the glass for distraction, watching and feeling the condensation roll down in small strings of limpid droplets.

"Who wants brownies?" Bridget said, bustling through the doorway with a dessert plate. The china made a soft *clink* when she placed it on the tabletop.

Stella's eyes sparkled with eagerness as Bridget set two pre-cut squares before her on a clean plate. "Mmm!" she squealed.

"I thought you avoided chocolate like the plague?" Marche helped herself to a brownie. It was rich and gooey and stuck to the roof of her mouth like peanut butter.

Bridget grinned. She reached for a piece of the dessert, weighed it in her hand as though it was a precious gem.

"I'm through with dieting. No more stepping on the scale. No more measuring body fat. There are more important things in life, right?" She took a generous bite. "Like enjoying good food."

Suddenly irritated, Marche turned to Stella, who wiggled like a worm in her chair.

"Let me see those hands." Marche grabbed a napkin and roughly wiped down Stella's fingers. "What a filthy little girl."

"Ow," Stella said, wiggling more.

"Well, if you wouldn't dig into your food like some kind of barn animal, I wouldn't have to work so hard to clean your little paws, now would I?"

"How's the unpacking coming along?" Trey asked.

"I haven't really had a chance to get any of that done yet." Marche paused to wipe a brown smudge from Stella's cheek. "I spent some time this morning moving boxes around." *And then I fainted.* "Then I spent an hour this afternoon trying to figure out how to get the damn TV hooked up for Stella."

"I know how that is," Trey replied. "If you're not a pro, electronic equipment can be a real pain in the a—"

Bridget cleared her throat. Trey smiled sheepishly at her and mouthed the word "sorry."

"Is there anything that I can do?" Bridget asked. "I could stop by tomorrow and help you sort through some things. I really wouldn't mind."

"No, that's all right," Marche said. "There's really not much to unpack. I just need to hang up the clothes and put away the dishes."

"But you said you hadn't even started yet."

Marche tossed the used napkin on the table and took another drink of the Perrier. "There is a spare bedroom that I'm not quite sure what to do with. I was thinking that I might turn it into a playroom. Maybe when everything else is settled, you can help me come up with some decorating ideas."

"Okay," Bridget said, clapping her hands. "Just say the magic word and I'm on it."

Stella bounced up and down as though she had springs in her pants. "Poof!"

Trey chuckled and bent forward to ruffle his niece's hair.

After dessert, Bridget brought out a pack of cards. "Who's up for a game of Old Maid?"

"Me-me-me! I love Ol' Maid!"

Bridget looked inquisitively at Marche.

"Count me out," she said. "I always end up with the Old Maid."

Four

Marche stood in front of the queen-sized bed and surveyed the items before her.

Three suitcases lay open on the mattress. Shirts, jeans, and shorts spilled out of two of them. The third one held socks, stockings, blouses, and dress pants. The shoes she'd stored in boxes.

Gathering up the socks, she stuffed them in the bureau drawer, above the bras and beneath the underwear. She collected the stockings next and had just dropped the assortment of nude and black hosiery in with the socks when Stella called her name.

"Mommy!"

"What is it?" Marche shouted as she walked back to the bed.

As expected, the blouses were a wrinkled mess. Marche lifted the first one out of the suitcase and frowned. It was shell pink with ruffles at the neckline. She laid the garment on the comforter and rubbed her palm down the front, but the stubborn creases remained.

Sighing, she grabbed a felt clothes hanger off the bed and worked it through the neck of the blouse. She hung it in the six-foot wide closet and picked up a cream-colored blouse next. The long-sleeved top was as wrinkled as the one before it. Marche grunted in frustration and skipped the futile hand pat. As she placed the second blouse in the closet, Stella shouted for her again.

"Mommy! Mommy! Come 'ere!"

"What do you want, Stella?" Marche yelled over her shoulder. She pushed the shirts to the end of the closet nearest the window and returned to the bed. "Damn. I wish she'd just come up here when she's got something to say," Marche muttered as she picked up a third blouse.

"Come 'ere, Mommy!"

Marche glanced over the rumpled garment and dropped it on the suitcase. "Okay, okay," she mumbled. "I'm coming!"

She found Stella sitting on the living room floor in front of the sofa, her legs splayed out under the coffee table. She gripped a yellow marker in one hand and used the palm of her other hand to hold a sheet of white construction paper in place.

"Did you want to show me your picture?" Marche asked as she looked in from the doorway with her hand on her hip.

Stella scribbled at a ferocious pace. Her little fingers were white at the tips where she squeezed the marker too hard. She didn't ease up when Marche spoke to her.

"Stella!"

"Huh?" The child looked up briefly, saw Marche, and went back to her coloring.

Marche walked over to the couch and sat down. Leaning over Stella's shoulder, she glanced at the picture in progress. A mess of red and yellow covered the paper. The subject matter remained elusive, even to Marche's astute eye.

"What did you want, Stella?"

The child set down the yellow marker and uncapped a brown one. "Nuffin'," she chirped, scribbling brown lines through one of the yellow blobs she had drawn.

"Then why did you call me?"

"I didn't."

Marche crossed her arms and stared at her daughter, who continued to doodle at a fervent pace. "Don't play games with me," she said in a stern voice. "I heard you call out for me. Clear as day."

"I didn't, Mommy."

"Do you want me to take your markers away?"

Stella stopped coloring. She looked at Marche and shook her head vehemently. "Un-uh."

"What did you call me for?"

"I didn't!" Stella's eyes widened; tears glittered in the corners.

"Fine," Marche said, trying to quell her growing irritation. She had too many chores on her list for the day to engage in an argument with a five-year-old. Placing her hands on her knees, she stood up.

"If you need anything," she said from the doorway, "then come upstairs and ask. Don't squawk through the house like a parrot."

Stella nodded, her light brown curls bobbing softly around her head. Marche felt a twinge of guilt for yelling at her. Stella was usually a very well-behaved child.

Marche was halfway up the stairs when a knock sounded at the front door. Turning, she slowly retraced her steps. Could it be Bridget? Peering through the peephole, she discovered it wasn't her sister, but an older woman whom she didn't recognize.

"Can I help you?" she asked when she had opened the door.

"Hi there!" the woman said. Dressed in a peasant shirt, mauve capris, pink sandals, and a matching headband, she reminded Marche of a flamingo—albeit a somewhat short and plump one. "I'm Shelley Franklin, your next-door neighbor."

"Marche Baker," Marche replied, extending a hand. "Nice to meet you."

Shelley grasped her fingers warmly, firmly. "I wanted to welcome you to the neighborhood. Saw the moving van yesterday. I'm so happy that someone finally bought the place. Brought you some cookies. Do you like chocolate chip?"

"Do I ever," Marche replied with a smile. "Would you like to come in?"

"I sure would! Where would you like these?" She motioned to the plate in her hand.

Marche rubbed a hand on her jeans and stepped aside. She closed the door as Shelley crossed the landing.

"How about the kitchen? It's a bit of a mess at the moment. I hope you don't mind," she said, leading Shelley down the hallway.

"Oh my, you weren't kidding!" Shelley set the cookies on the kitchen table and surveyed the room with impressively wide eyes. "Is there anything I can help you with? I don't mind getting my hands dirty."

Marche pulled a drinking glass from the box she'd placed on the counter. With quick precision, she unpeeled the newspaper wrapping and dropped the crumpled business section on the countertop. "That's kind of you. But I've got a handle on everything. Thanks."

Shelley nodded, her enthusiasm undimmed. "I hope you don't mind my prying," she said after a moment, "but I just have to ask. Weren't you a little spooked about moving into the place?"

"Why would I be?" Marche asked as she wiped down the glass with a dry cloth.

"Well...because of what happened here."

Marche's hand stilled. "What happened?"

Shelley brought her fingers to her mouth, her eyebrows raised to a comical degree. "You mean you don't *know*? Jiminy Cricket, how could they not *tell* you?"

"Tell me what?"

"The man who lived here before—Charles Louis—died in this house. Nothing abnormal, mind you. It was a heart attack, according to the obit."

A cold shiver ran down Marche's spine. Absently, she reached for another glass. This time, her fingers stumbled over the packing so that it took her twice as long to unwrap it.

"The horrible thing about it was that no one knew he had died. He was a hermit. And I guess he didn't have any relatives that he kept in touch with. If it hadn't been for the envelopes piling up in the mailbox, Lord knows how much longer it would have gone unnoticed."

"Guess that explains why no one wanted to buy the house," Marche said. An unbidden image of an elderly man stooped over in the living room chair entered her thoughts. She quickly changed the subject, but not before her imagination had conjured up maggots squirming through a pair of decaying eyeballs.

"How long have you lived here?" she asked.

Shelley stepped up to the counter and leaned against it, looking casually around the room. She tapped one open-toed shoe on the floor. Marche felt sure that the woman was studying every crack and crevice. If Marche had overlooked a single cobweb—and there had been many spider webs in the cabinets and on the windowsills to eradicate—her new neighbor would undoubtedly light upon it.

"Let me see... We moved here in 1999 when The Pearla Company offered Hank a job he couldn't refuse. So it's been about eighteen years now. Time sure flies, doesn't it?"

"Sometimes." Marche pulled another dusty glass from the slightly dented cardboard box. "I'd offer you a drink, but I haven't gone shopping yet. I do have running water and clean glasses if you'd like something to sip on."

"Don't worry about me, dear. I'm fine." Shelley gave a theatrical sigh and studied the room some more. "Is your husband around? He doesn't work on Saturdays, does he?"

Marche opened one of the cabinet doors and wiped down the interior with a damp dishrag. "My husband is dead."

"Oh, me and my mouth." Shelley's chipper expression softened. "I am *so* sorry."

Marche thrust her head inside the cabinet to inspect a suspicious dark spot. Determining that it was a natural stain in the wood and not dirt, she withdrew. She wiped the area with one last broad stroke and then tossed the rag into the sink.

"You said that your husband works for The Pearla Company?" Marche said.

"Yes, ma'am. Plans to stay there 'til he retires December of next year."

"What does he do?"

"Works with computers. Don't really know the details. Hank talks about it sometimes, but I haven't got a head for technical jargon."

Marche began setting the glasses in the cabinet. "I have a brother-in-law who works there."

"Really? What's his name? Maybe I know him."

"Trey Klein."

Marche pushed the glasses into place and began to clean the rest of the dishes in the box. She didn't have much to say this morning, but most mornings during the past six months she'd felt that way. Shelley was a nice distraction, like listening to radio commercials. When she spoke, Marche felt that it was all right if she stopped thinking for a while.

"Hmm… Name doesn't ring a bell. It's a large company, though. Wouldn't be surprised if we brushed shoulders at some party or other without knowing it."

They lapsed into silence. But it wasn't the kind of silence that left Marche fidgeting with restlessness. Shelley had a calming presence about her that made the air seem lighter.

"You've got a nice view of our lawn from here," Shelley said, peering out the kitchen window. "I don't know if you've noticed the flowerbeds, but Hank loves to spend his free time with his hands in the soil. We've also got a vegetable garden 'round the other side."

"I bet you make a killer vegetable soup."

Marche finished the glassware and opened the box holding the plates. There was a good chance that she might spend the rest of her life in this house, and it appeared as though Shelley Franklin was not about to uproot anytime soon—not with such a lovely lawn and garden. The thought pleased her.

"I'm not a bragging woman; I let the cooking speak for itself. Speaking of which, you absolutely must come over for dinner sometime. We love to entertain."

Marche turned on the sink and held a plate under the spigot. "That'd be nice."

Just then, Stella filled the kitchen doorway. Like a sprite, shoeless and in a frilly lavender summer dress, she darted past Shelley and hid behind Marche's pants.

"Hello, little one!"

Stella peeked around Marche's legs, peering shyly at the neighbor. Marche placed a hand on her smooth crown and smiled at Shelley. "Stella, this nice lady is our new next-door neighbor. Say hello?"

"Hi," Stella said in a high-pitched, muffled voice.

"I'm Shelley," Shelley said, leaning forward to get a better look at Stella.

Stella remained plastered to Marche's side like an insect glued to flypaper. "I'm sorry," March said to Shelley, "she's at that stage where she gets shy around everyone."

"Doesn't bother me a bit," Shelley replied. "I've got two grandbabies close to her age. I'm used to their quirks."

Stella inched away from Marche so that she could tilt her head upward to gaze at her. One little hand reached up and tugged at her waistline.

"What is it, honey?" Marche asked, looking down.

"Can I have somethin' to eat?" Stella whispered.

Marche bent down to whisper in return. "In a little while. I'm going to do some more work in the kitchen and then I'll make you a grilled cheese sandwich. Afterwards, you can try one of Shelley's yummy cookies. Sound good?"

Stella jerked her head up and down and then scurried out of the room like a cat after a mouse.

"What a gorgeous child," Shelley said, grinning from ear to ear. "You must be so proud."

Marche thanked her, absently thinking as she spoke that Stella looked too much like her father. She smiled to hide the sadness that suddenly burst like a popped balloon, causing a sharp pain in her chest.

"My oldest granddaughter, Coral, is three. I imagine that she'll get along swimmingly with your girl."

"We'll have to set up a playdate."

Marche grabbed another cardboard box and opened it. Forks, knives, and spoons lay in bundles. She grabbed one of the large restaurant quality napkins, unscrewed the twisty tie, and spilled the kitchen utensils onto the counter. They clattered onto the surface, sounding like nails dancing on a pan of aluminum.

"That's my hubby," Shelley announced, pointing out the window.

Marche peeked out the window as she dampened a washcloth. Across the way, she spotted a shirtless man wearing brightly colored shorts with a rolled-up bandana wrapped around his pink head, pushing a lawnmower through the grass.

"He's like clockwork with that machine," Shelley said. "That's his routine during the summer. Every Saturday, trim the lawn. Only thing that'll keep him indoors is the weather."

Marche nodded. She rinsed the knives and then unrolled a pack of spoons. She moved slowly, inspecting each piece of silverware for specks of dirt before depositing them in the dish rack.

Shelley heaved off the counter and dipped her hands in her pockets. "Well, I think I'd better leave you to your work. I've intruded long enough already."

Marche accompanied Shelley to the front stoop. "I'm really glad that we met. Thanks for stopping by."

"My pleasure," Shelley said. "I look forward to having you and Stella over for dinner soon."

"Definitely. I appreciate the invite."

Marche watched Shelley plod across the yard to her house. As the older woman reached the driveway, she turned to blow a kiss to her husband. *What a lovey-dovey couple*, Marche thought when he returned the kiss. She chuckled. But then she remembered Dom, and the incurable ache that she'd experienced in the days after his death returned.

She felt around the inside of her pocket for the pack of cigarettes she'd bought at the convenience store the night before.

"I know what you'd say," she said in her bitterest of tones. "But you're not here to say it, are you?"

She pulled out the fresh pack of cigarettes. A second later, she frowned, wondering where she'd left her lighter. She patted her other pocket and sighed heavily when she discovered it there.

Lighting the cigarette, she looked at the street. The strip of pavement was quiet except for a teenage boy on a bicycle. He stood in the gutter a few houses down, straddling the black aluminum frame, staring at her. Even when their eyes met, his gaze remained unwavering. *Strange kid.* Marche flicked the cigarette onto the driveway after a lengthy puff, reentered the house, and locked the door.

When she peeked out the living room window, he was still there. Immobile. Watching.

Marche backed away from the window and rubbed her arms, suddenly cold. Returning to the kitchen, she finished cleaning up the silverware. The next time she looked out at the street, the boy with the bike had gone.

Five

Marche began her first day of work that Monday. In the morning, she drove to City Hall, where she went over paperwork with Florence, the director of human resources. An hour later, she pulled into the library parking lot.

The Egret Bay Public Library had first opened its doors to the public in 1948. Since that time, the organization had quintupled its number of circulation materials and relocated twice. It presently occupied a stretch of land along Pine Avenue near protected woodlands. One of Egret Bay's post offices sat directly across the street, sandwiched between a video game store and a pizza parlor.

This was Marche's first time seeing the library; she'd interviewed for the job over the telephone while she was still in Haven Shores. Even though Egret Bay had one of the smallest libraries in the county, it still featured an impressive two-story design, replete with a clerestory above the entrance. Marche walked past the drive through—where patrons could drop passengers at the front door—and met up with Florence inside the lobby.

"The circulation department is just inside these doors, to the left," Florence said.

Marche followed her to the counter, where a woman with bright orange hair stood waiting for them.

"Phyllis, may I introduce you to our newest employee? This is Marche Baker." Turning to Marche, she said, "Phyllis is the circulation supervisor and your direct supervisor."

"How do you do?" Marche said.

"We're so glad you're finally here," Phyllis gushed, oblivious to Marche's extended hand. "Thomas left four months ago, and we've been short-staffed ever since. Everyone does what they can to help pull their weight, but it's never enough. With you here, things should start to run a lot more smoothly."

"Well, it's been a pleasure meeting you," Florence said to Marche. "Welcome to Egret Bay."

"Thank you, Florence."

"Enjoy the rest of your day," Phyllis said to Florence with a dismissive flick of the wrist. "Come, Marche. I'll show you the circulation workroom first."

Phyllis led Marche behind the circulation counter and to the backroom, her pace swift and sure. Marche nearly broke into a jog as she tried to keep up with the woman's long stride.

"Here we are," Phyllis said, pushing through a set of double doors. "This is the supply room on your right. And this"—she took two more steps and pointed a red-nailed finger down an illuminated hallway—"is the Friends' workroom. They keep their backlog of items stored here. That door at the end opens into the Friends Shoppe."

They moved further into the room, stopping in front of a table littered with books, magazines, and random items, such as a box of greeting cards and a used board game.

"This is the donation table. Don't worry about the mess. Genie takes care of organizing it all. She's the only circulation clerk who's authorized to make decisions regarding the items placed here."

"What do you do with donations?" Marche asked.

"The librarians in charge of collection development examine the hardcovers that are in nice condition. But most of the materials—VHS tapes, paperbacks, decorations—go into the Friends Shoppe for sale. Genie also sets items aside for the Salvation Army—items that are in good condition, but really aren't sellable or pertinent for the collection."

"So everything finds a home."

"For the most part. You'd be surprised by what some people donate, though. We keep a box of latex gloves up here," Phyllis said, pointing to a shelf behind the table. "I would love to hang up a banner outside that reads: YOUR TRASH IS NOT OUR TREASURE—"

Marche laughed.

"You think I'm kidding, but wait until someone hands you a book with rat droppings caked into the pages. Unfortunately, the director is a bootlicker—keep that to yourself—who's afraid of offending any of our well-meaning patrons. Hence, the gloves."

Phyllis showed her the lockers next. "Let me know which number you choose, and I'll print a label for you."

The staff refrigerator, with its outdated almond-colored panels, hummed noisily alongside the mailboxes. "Feel free to put whatever you want in the refrigerator. Our policy is simple. The cleaning crew empties the shelves every Friday evening. You leave it, you lose it."

"Fair enough."

"Back here," Phyllis said, leading her toward the opposite side of the room, "is the drop box." She opened a door to a closet-sized area. Inside, Marche saw two metal chutes with bins wheeled beneath them. "On days when the aides aren't here, you need to check the drop every couple of hours or so. The bins can fill up pretty fast, especially after a holiday."

Marche nodded. She almost wished she'd brought a tape recorder with her. The circulation supervisor barely breathed between sentences, making it difficult for her to digest everything. After just ten minutes of descriptions and explanations, her brain felt like an overloaded computer program, ready to crash and burn.

"I feel like I should be taking notes," Marche said, half-jokingly.

"Don't worry too much," Phyllis replied. "I don't expect you to remember everything—or anything, really. Right now, I just want you to get a feel for the place. This is going to be your home away from home, so I want you to be comfortable."

"Got it," Marche murmured, her neck and shoulders relaxing.

"You've worked in a library before, haven't you?"

"Several years ago."

"Then you'll be fine. Circulation work is just like riding a bike. Once you learn it, you never really forget it. At least not the basics, anyhow."

Phyllis closed the door to the book drop and then motioned Marche toward a collection of empty book trucks.

"The most important thing for you to remember is that you label your cart—there are signs for sorting, shelving, sensitizing, and check-in. We don't want to have someone wasting their time checking in materials if you've already scanned them," she explained.

Marche nodded.

The workroom tour concluded a few minutes later at the sorting shelves, seven-foot tall steel ranges that stretched for twenty feet.

"We keep the children's and young adult books on this side. The parent-teacher collection also goes here. All of the adult fiction and non-fiction books are sorted on the other side.

"We only sort the twenty-eight-day materials back here," Phyllis continued as they headed back to the double doors. "The new books and A/V materials are sorted at the circulation desk before they're re-shelved."

Back in the circulation department, they stood at the checkout stations and waited quietly—much to the relief of Marche's vibrating eardrums—for several minutes, until the line of patrons at the counter dwindled and there was a brief moment of inactivity.

"How's it going up here, guys?" Phyllis asked. "Any issues today?"

"Only the usual," a woman with wavy black hair said. "There was a patron in here about ten minutes ago disputing a fine, so I told him to take a card."

Phyllis then listened as the other three clerks provided a brief summary of the morning's events: the printer jammed twice, a patron complained about someone looking at pornography on one of the computers, the security guard had to kick out an ornery patron who brought food into the library, etc. Phyllis nodded; apparently, these were commonplace incidents.

Once everyone had spoken, Phyllis conducted the introductions.

"Hello," four voices uttered in unison.

"Hello," Marche echoed.

"We could certainly use your help up here," the woman with a curly white bob remarked.

"This is Genie," Phyllis said. "You've been here... How long is it now?"

"Twelve years come October," Genie replied.

"In addition to working the front desk twenty hours a week, she also runs the Friends Shoppe."

Marche's eyes widened with admiration; the woman must be old enough to be someone's great-grandmother!

"Work keeps me fit," Genie replied with a scratchy laugh, as though she could read Marche's thoughts.

"This young gentleman here is Felix," Phyllis continued, motioning to the only man at the desk. "He's great with the ladies. Aren't you, Felix?"

"The grannies love me," Felix agreed, his expression serious. Just how "young" he was, Marche couldn't tell. But she suspected that he was at least forty-five. Faint lines creased his olive complexion and streaks of gray dulled his jet-black hair.

"Ebony is our queen of the romance collection," Phyllis said, placing her hand on the woman's bony shoulder. "She knows everything there is to know about Debbie Macomber, Linda Lael Miller, and Lisa Kleypas. Among others."

Ebony held up her hands, the diamond on her finger sparkling under the fluorescent lights. "Guilty as charged," she replied.

"And this is Sarah," Phyllis said, motioning to the young woman who sat at the last station. "We've been extremely lucky to have her on our team. Sarah's only part-time, but she picks up a lot of extra shifts to help out."

"I look forward to working with all of you," Marche said. She extended a hand to everyone in the small group.

"Keep up the good work, guys!" Phyllis said as a patron approached the counter, balancing a pile of paperbacks.

Marche spent the next forty minutes on a walking tour of the library. The first floor housed the children's department which, Marche soon discovered, was her favorite area in the building.

Vibrant three-dimensional prints on the walls displayed various folkloric images: a mermaid cradling a harp and sitting on a sandbar; long-haired fairies swimming among sea kelp; a wizard pointing his wand at a glowing wave. A castle tower in the far corner, which served as a puppet theater, completed the fairytale setting.

The only slightly unwelcoming element in the children's department appeared in the form of the children's librarian. With snow-white hair drawn into a tight bun and a formal suit without a wrinkle in place, Roberta looked better suited to a correctional facility than a place of learning. *At least put her in cataloging or acquisitions, where the public doesn't have to see her*, Marche thought, forcing a smile she didn't feel.

"I like your hat," Marche said.

"As high as a bat," quipped Orlando, the children's youth services clerk.

"Did you steal it from a cat?"

"Whatever makes you think like that?"

"Do you talk like that with the kids?" Marche asked as Orlando straightened his red-and-white striped hat.

"Heaven forbid," Roberta muttered.

Orlando leaned across the work desk and spoke to Marche in a conspiratorial whisper. "Do you think she realized she just played the game?"

Marche glanced at the stern-faced woman, whose nose was dipped in a literature journal. "I think if she did, she'd redden with shame."

"Ha ha. I like your sense of humor."

"He won't last long," Phyllis said as they rode the elevator to the second floor. "That woman is an ice cube. She freezes the life out of everyone who works in that department."

"I see," Marche replied, offering no other comment.

On the second floor, she met one of the reference librarians on duty, the administrative services director, and the library director. For the final part of the tour, Phyllis took her into the technical services workroom behind the magazine stacks and introduced her to the lone full-time cataloger.

For the rest of the day, and all of the next, Marche worked behind-the-scenes. Phyllis wanted her to get comfortable using the operating system. "Once you have a firm grasp on the circulation module, we'll move you out front." So she retrieved items from the book drop, checked in materials, and sorted. She also spent a few hours upstairs shelving nonfiction books to become better reacquainted with the Dewey Decimal System.

On Wednesday, she moved to the front desk with the other circulation clerks. She shadowed Ebony, who began her training session by explaining circulation policies: how many items patrons could check out at a time, how long items could be checked out for, what happened when a patron reached their maximum limit in fines, etc. Then she lectured her on the Florida statute regarding the privacy of library accounts.

Marche was familiar with the law—she'd enforced a similar policy at the bookstore she managed. To avoid appearing pretentious, she merely nodded along as though the information was news to her.

"Only someone with proper identification or a corresponding library card can request information on an account," Ebony said. "No exceptions. Ever. Trust me on this. You don't want to be charged with a criminal offense because you told Joe Schmo that his teenage son is checking out books on how to cope with homosexuality."

Sarah, who'd just finished checking out DVDs to a patron, joined in the conversation.

"The intentions are good," she said. "But man! Some people develop horns when you tell them you can't check a book out to them because it's being held under someone else's account."

"Parents are the worst," Ebony added. "Like, 'What do you mean I can't get my daughter's book? She needs it for her homework assignment! You guys are unbelievable. Who's in charge? I want to file a complaint.'"

"Yeah." Sarah nodded. "Count yourself lucky if you only get one of those in a week."

Six

Marche pulled into the driveway and killed the engine. Though it was already a quarter after six, the springtime sun still shone brightly in the blue sky. She smiled to herself as she stepped out of the car. Monday was Memorial Day, which meant that the library would be closed. That also meant that she had a full three-day weekend ahead of her.

A vacation from life, she thought.

Marche turned to open the back driver-side door. As she did so, her gaze fell upon a house across the street, three plots down. The structure itself was not really noteworthy. It featured a plain white facade and a gray-shingled roof; like most other houses on the street, it also had a single-car garage. No, it wasn't the house that had grabbed her attention, but the person camped out on the front porch, engrossed in a book.

Although she'd moved into the neighborhood more than six weeks ago, Marche still hadn't introduced herself to any of the neighbors. And no one, except Shelley Franklin, had knocked on her front door.

Now, as she unlatched Stella's seatbelt, her buoyant mood inspired her to make a spontaneous social visit. "Let's go for a walk," Marche said as Stella scooted off the seat.

"Uh-kay!" Stella squealed.

They crossed the street hand in hand. When they reached the other side, Marche let Stella run in front of her. Stella squatted at the second yard, where she found a small patch of buttercups. Scooping up a handful of the yellow flowers, she sniffed them and then crushed them against her face. Marche chuckled when Stella had finished; smudges of pollen dotted her cheeks and chin.

"Stop right there, Stella!" Marche called out a few seconds later as her daughter reached the third driveway. Looking toward the front porch, she waved. "Do you mind if we come up?"

"Suit yourself," the man replied.

Marche motioned for Stella to follow her up the driveway. As she neared the house, dogs barked excitedly through the closed front windows.

"Hi," she said.

"Howdy, Miss Baker."

Marche blinked. "How did you know my name?"

The man nodded toward the corner of the street, where her house stood. "I've seen you coming and going. When an old man doesn't have much to do, there's not too many a thing escapes his notice." He set the novel he was reading across his knees, the pages facing downward.

"Oh. Well, no need for formalities. Just Marche is fine."

"So noted. Name's Rory Vale," the old man said, shaking her hand. His palm, roughened with calluses, scratched her skin. "Who's the little 'n'?"

Stella, who had stopped following Marche, was squatting in the middle of the driveway beside Vale's royal blue El Camino. She poked at something on the ground—probably a snail or a black beetle.

"Stella," Marche called out. "Come on up here." The child continued with her play, looking up only when Marche repeated herself, her voice an octave higher. "Really, she's so absent-minded," Marche said, by way of apology.

Stella skipped up the drive, the pink frills on her shirt dancing with her energetic movement.

"This is Rory," Marche said to Stella.

"Roar-roar?" Stella's eyebrows scrunched together, her nose flared, as she tried again to pronounce his name. "Roar-roar-ruh?"

"What about Vale?" the old man prompted. "Can you say that?"

"Vale!" Stella shrieked. Then she grabbed Marche's slacks and peered around her hips. "Giant," she said, pointing at Vale. "Giant! Giant!"

"Oh!" Marche said, turning to her neighbor. "The other day, when she was looking out the front window, Stella told me she saw a giant. I thought she was making up stories."

Vale gripped the arms of his lawn chair and belted a hearty laugh. "I tend to have that effect on children," he said when he had caught his breath.

Even if he wasn't the giant Stella proclaimed he was, Marche thought, he certainly sounded like one. Vale's voice boomed. His words carried the all-encompassing, yet charismatic tone that public speakers needed to draw in crowds, or that pastors needed to practice if they aimed to strike the fear of God and Satan, Heaven and Hell, into the hearts of their churchgoers. If he was a character in a cartoon, a single word from his lips would likely rattle the windows in their frames and cause the door to fall from its hinges. Despite his intimidating tone, his blue eyes—bright as a robin's egg—twinkled with kindness.

"Have you lived in the area a long time?" Marche asked.

Vale closed his book, gripped it by the spine, and set it on the chair as he stood. On his feet, he reached well over six feet tall. "More years than I can count," he replied, looking down the road. "How do you like the house?"

"We're settling in all right."

"Nothing going bump in the night?"

"Just the usual creaks and groans," Marche replied. "Can I invite you over for a drink?"

"Why, yes. I think you may."

Marche gripped Stella's hand once more as they crossed the street. At the house, she unlocked the front door and waited inside the foyer so that she could shut the door behind her guest. Vale hesitated. He touched the doorframe, looked up for a moment, then ducked as he crossed the threshold.

The house was tidier now, and the kitchen well-stocked with food. Stella sped up the stairs and into her bedroom. Marche set her purse and keys on the small table by the door and ushered Vale into the kitchen.

"Lemonade okay?" Marche asked, grabbing two glasses from the cupboard.

"What color?"

"Um..." Marche opened the refrigerator and reached for the plastic pitcher. "Yellow."

"Sounds good."

"I'm afraid I still don't really know anyone around here," Marche said as she poured the drinks. "Only Shelley Franklin. So I'm glad we got to meet today."

Vale thanked her for the glass of lemonade and gave a knowing nod. "Nice lady," he said as he sipped the sweet refreshment. "I've met her a time or two."

Marche pulled out a chair at the kitchen table and invited Vale to do the same. "I lucked out. Neighbors can really make-or-break a place, you know?"

"That I do," Vale agreed.

"I was surprised when she told me about the house, though. I didn't realize it had a macabre history."

Vale grunted; Marched assumed that was his version of a chuckle. Some of the lemonade splashed out of his glass, unnoticed. "Can't say I'm surprised she brought it up. I've seen that little lady tiptoe around the windows before, trying to peep in."

Marche expected him to say something else but he seemed to forget about her. He looked at the ceiling, the walls, and the floor as though he were trying to recapture something lost long ago and still out of reach.

"I understand that the previous owner died here, but...is that so unusual?" Marche asked.

Vale clucked his tongue.

"I suspect it wasn't the way he died so much as the way he lived that might've made some people curious." Vale leaned back in the chair and rolled the half empty glass between his large, arthritic hands. The motion attracted her eyes like a magnet, and she found herself staring. Thin, cross-crossing scars covered the backs, and his knuckles were white and knotted. When Vale grasped the glass firmly in one fist, his thumb overlapped his middle finger.

A thought suddenly occurred to her.

"Did you know the person who used to live here?"

Vale lifted the glass and nodded. "I knew him." As he drank the lemonade, his shirtsleeve slipped down a few inches, revealing a rope-like scar that twisted around his wrist. He lowered his arm, and the ugly mark disappeared under the flannel.

"I was good friends with Chuck. He was a fine, fine man." Vale tilted his head backward as though to stop a sudden onslaught of tears.

"His death must have been hard on you."

Marche bit her lip as soon as the words hit the ceiling. How could she say something so base, so shallow? She looked out the kitchen window, embarrassed by her trite response.

"It *was* hard, but you learn to expect that sort of thing," Vale said. "You expect it, and you deal with it, and you get on with your life."

"Let me get you some more lemonade," Marche said, reaching for his empty glass.

"No, thank you. I've had enough."

Marche stood in the center of the kitchen, unsure of what to say or do. Why had she been so careless as to bring up the subject of death? Why? When it would only lead her to relive her own losses.

The carefree mood that had carried her through the afternoon vanished. Life lost its color once again; everything became gray. Did she care about making friends with the neighbors? Did she care about anything at all? Just then, she wanted nothing more than to curl into a ball and weep.

"You make a dazzling cup of lemonade."

Vale's words jolted her back to reality. "Thank you," March said, forcing a smile. "It's instant."

"Tsk-tsk. A good chef never reveals her secrets."

Marche set the empty glass in the sink. She tried to think of something interesting to say, but nothing came to mind.

"Have you spent a lot of time in this house?" she finally asked.

"Well," Vale said, "let's just say that I have some memories here. Hundreds, in fact. Some good, some not so good. But that's life, isn't it? You can't have fluff all the time."

Vale folded his hands on the table. Marche tried to ignore the mountain of knots and scars; she focused on the man's pleasant face instead.

"Chuck and I were boyhood pals. The house I live in now was my parents'. They willed it to me when they died, and the missus and I sold our own place to move back here. That was thirty-some-odd years ago."

Marche drained the rest of her lemonade and added the glass to the other dirty dishes.

"Did you know that this is one of the oldest properties in Egret Bay?" Vale asked when her back was turned. "Not the house, mind you; it was knocked down and rebuilt in the early '30s, but the plot itself. The Louis family goes way back."

Marche set the plug in the sink and turned on the faucet. "Wouldn't they have had more land? This is a pretty average-size plot."

"Fred Louis sold off everything but the house after the missus died. By the sixties, this area had turned into a proper neighborhood."

Marche turned off the water faucet and sat down again. Silence filled the room. Glancing at her hands, she noticed dirt lodged underneath one of her fingernails. She curled her fingers so the nails wouldn't show.

"Where's that fairy of yours?"

"In her bedroom," Marche said. "I imagine she's playing with her toys."

"She's a cute one."

"She takes after her father," Marche replied.

"Ah."

"He's dead."

"Ah."

Marche could no longer endure Vale's piercing gaze; she stared at his shirt collar instead.

"Got any other family around here 'sides your fairy?" Vale asked, his bushy brows lifting into matching pyramids.

"My sister lives over on Carmichael," Marche replied. "And that's it." She folded her arms over her chest, imagining her limbs were a shield that prevented her visitor from seeing what emotions lay hidden beneath. "What about yourself?"

Vale held up his left hand. "A widower like you." He gazed at the plain gold band on his third finger for a moment before he lowered his hand to the table.

Marche relaxed. Taking the focus off of herself felt good. She wanted to ask Vale more questions so she could forget about her own slices of sadness.

"What was your wife's name?"

“Marlene.” Vale smiled, but he didn’t get that same faraway look in his eyes as when he stared at the house’s sparsely decorated walls.

“What was she like?”

“She was the most wonderful dame I ever knew.”

Vale stood, the wooden legs scraping loudly on the red and white vinyl as he pushed in his chair. He leaned forward, hands braced on the back of it. Whether he grasped the inanimate object for support or for distraction, Marche was unsure.

“She was a fantastic wife and a terrific mother, and it was damn tragic when she passed away,” Vale said in a slow, steady voice. “Damn tragic.” He let go of the chair, shook his head, squared his shoulders. “But that’s the way of life, isn’t it?”

Marche jumped to her feet. Heading toward the cabinet opposite the refrigerator, she opened it. She felt feverish inside her bones. Thoughts of Dom did that to her sometimes. When she remembered that she was alone, the heat overcame her until she almost suffocated from its intensity. Hardly anything helped when she got to feeling that way. She reached blindly toward the back of the cabinet and pulled out a bottle.

“Would you like a real drink?”

God. Even her voice sounded hot. She needed to cool down fast. Before the heat built up in her throat and face. Before flames spewed out of her mouth.

Vale eyed her curiously and cocked his head to one side. “That’s kindly of you, but...”

Marche loosened her tight grip on the bottle and glanced down at the vodka. “Right,” she murmured. “It’s too early in the day.”

Although she hated to, and every nerve in her body screamed against it, she returned the liquor to its hiding place. When she closed the cabinet door, she noticed her neighbor eyeing the walls again. Marche wrung her hands to keep from fidgeting.

“Would you like to walk through the house?” she asked.

Vale removed his baseball cap and held it between his large hands. “It’d be a pleasure.”

Marche guided him through the first floor, remaining respectfully quiet as he sorted through his memories in the refurbished rooms.

"Used to be a storage room," he said about the downstairs half bath. "Betty insisted they install a toilet on the first floor for visitors."

They continued up the stairs.

"This is original," he said, patting the rail of the gallery balustrade.

"I don't follow?"

"When they tore down the first house, they recycled bits and pieces to use in this one."

"Why did they do that?" Marche wondered.

"Pride, I gather," Vale said with a shrug. "Keeps the original place alive, so to speak. The Louis men had a strange way about them when it came to property. Chuck, too. Come hell or high water, he kept his home in pristine condition. Even after..."

"After what?"

"Oh... Never mind that."

Marche showed Vale the bathroom and both of the bedrooms. "This room is still in limbo," Marche said about the third room. "I'm thinking of converting it into a playroom. But I haven't yet decided how I want to decorate it."

Though she'd unpacked all the necessities within the first week, most of the boxes containing miscellaneous items remained untouched. She feared casting her eyes upon certain things—namely, mementos of her dead husband. She wasn't ready yet. She wasn't sure she ever would be.

Vale walked toward the window overlooking Washington. His foot snagged on one of the boxes, but he caught his balance easily and leaned on the windowsill to peer outside.

"If I were you," he said, "I'd hang up a lot of pretty pictures and leave out any mirrors."

Marche gazed at the plain, cream-colored walls. "Are you a superstitious man, Vale?"

Another grunt.

"Seen too much in this lifetime to bother with hocus-pocus, mumbo jumbo. Whatever you call it. I speak from experience. Mirrors...you don't want 'em here."

Marche opened her mouth to speak, but then snapped it shut. She felt the hotness boiling inside of her again. She wrung her hands. Her feet itched and she felt like jumping up and down or running through the house and screaming at the top of her lungs. She could think of nothing but relieving the torment. Closing her eyes for a moment, she imagined the glass bottle once more in her hand.

"Well, I better get going," Vale said, turning from the window. "Dogs are prob'ly getting antsy to go outside."

"Thanks for visiting," Marche said at the front door.

"Well then," Vale said as he stepped onto the stoop and shoved his cap back onto his head. "Now that we know one another, don't be a stranger, hear?"

Marche nodded.

Though he was at least eighty, Vale gave the impression of being a man twenty years younger. He had a slow, bow-legged stride which made him look as though he'd spent the last two weeks riding bareback on a stallion. There was a liveliness in his gait like Dom always had, and he walked with his shoulders pulled straight back.

Marche sighed. The fire in her gut had finally begun to peter out. Shutting the door, she returned to the kitchen.

"Time for dinner," she muttered.

Her gaze shifted to the cabinet several times as she steamed the vegetables and baked the tuna casserole. But she kept herself in check. The telephone rang just as she was straining the spinach.

"Hello?"

"Hey, how are you?" Bridget asked, her voice overflowing with good cheer.

"Busy. Dinner's almost ready."

"Oh, okay. I won't keep you then," Bridget said. "I just thought I'd see if you wanted to shop around for ideas this weekend. You know, for that room you were talking about. Does tomorrow work for you?"

"Tomorrow's fine," Marche replied.

"Great! I'll pick you up around eleven?"

"Sure."

"All right. See you soon. And give Stella a hug and kiss for me."

Seven

Marche exited The Domino Effect with Stella by her side. Re-entering the mall, she bumped into a man talking into a Bluetooth.

"Dude, that's what I'm saying. Tell Raquel—"

"Oops," Marche mumbled. The man narrowed his eyes in irritation and walked on, continuing his conversation without missing a beat.

"Ow," Stella squealed.

"Sorry," Marche said, loosening her hold on Stella's fingers.

She stepped out of the main current of traffic while she waited for Bridget. Her sister shuffled along, writing notes in a polka dot spiral notebook. After a few more seconds, she stuffed the pen and paper into her purse and caught up with them.

"I think that's our place," Bridget declared.

"I'm hungry."

Marche looked down at her daughter, whose upturned face sparkled where Bridget had spread fruit-scented gloss on her cheeks.

"I was getting tired of window shopping anyway," Marche said.

"And what does the Berry Princess want?" Bridget asked in her sweet-toned voice.

"Twisty bread!" Stella piped.

"There's a pretzel shop at the food court," Bridget said to Marche.

They maneuvered through the crowd of shoppers and past kiosks where clerks sold items such as incense, massages, or two-for-one sunglasses. The mall was as busy on Memorial Day weekend as it would be come the winter shopping season.

"Not interested," Marche said to a salesperson trying to peddle a "new and improved" hair straightener. "No thanks," she replied when someone else shoved a remote-controlled toy helicopter in her face. Finally, they reached the food court. Marche heaved a sigh of relief, grateful to be free of the commercial war zone.

Stella fidgeted with impatience while they stood in line at Paolo's Pretzels. The food vendors were swamped, and they had to wait for the staff to pull a fresh batch of pretzels out of the oven. Eight customers—and several long minutes later—their turn came. Marche ordered a cinnamon twist pretzel for Stella and a hot tea for herself.

"I'll have a cinnamon twist as well," Bridget added.

They scanned the food court for a vacant spot and located a table near the center. Crumpled pieces of foil with remnants of chili cheese fries littered the mesh surface. Bridget picked up the trash with pinched fingers and wiped the tabletop with a paper napkin. Marche pulled out a chair for Stella; the metal legs of her own chair wobbled when she sat down beside her.

"I really liked that storage unit with the cubed sections," Bridget said, biting into her food. "What do you think?"

"Maybe." Marche grabbed a stir stick and added a packet of sugar to her tea.

"What are the dimensions of the room again?" Bridget asked.

"Eleven by fourteen, I think."

"Hmm. Well, I think it's an economical solution. You could use the bottom row for Stella's toys and put other things, like books and whatnot, on the higher shelves."

"I guess."

The high ceiling—which featured clear panels to admit the sunlight—turned the food court into an echo chamber. All around them, the monotonous drone of chatter swirled in the open air like a blanket of invisible fog. A few yards away, a teenage girl tossed a coin into a fountain. The aquatic theme—appropriate since the mall was about five minutes from the beaches—featured two leaping dolphins, a manatee, and a sea turtle. Water spouted from a branch of brown coral.

"You don't sound too crazy about the idea," Bridget observed as she wiped her thumb on a crumpled napkin. "Should we research more options?"

"It's not that," Marche replied. "I'm dragging my feet today, I—"

"I wanna ride the escator."

Stella's shrill voice rang in Marche's ears, rattling her frazzled nerves. "Small bites, Stella. You don't want to choke on it."

Stella looked mutely at her. Grimacing, Marche yanked on the pretzel that jutted between her daughter's lips. She ignored the fact that it was wet with saliva and tore it into several small pieces. Unfolding a clean napkin, she dropped the gooey chunks onto it.

"There. Now you can eat properly. Hmm?"

Stella looked down at the mutilated segments and studied them carefully. She played the eeny-meeny-miny-moe game, then snatched up the bit that her finger landed on last. She tossed the food in her mouth and chomped noisily.

"Escator, Mommy."

"When you're done eating, okay? And please don't talk while you chew. It's disgusting."

Stella whined, a clear indicator that a tantrum was on the horizon.

Marche tested her tea and tore open another packet of sugar. A dull throbbing began to press at her temples.

"Are you doing all right?" Bridget asked. She leaned forward on her elbows, her eyes trained on Marche's face.

"It's nothing really," she said. "Just..."

"Dom?"

Marche blew on her steaming cup, breaking eye contact with her sister. That single word, spoken with such earnestness, struck hard. One of her eyes twitched, and she quickly rubbed it with the back of her hand.

"I didn't sleep well last night. That's all," she said. "Look, maybe you should tackle this project by yourself. You have a knack for design. It's your natural bent. I couldn't even match my clothes when I was a kid. And look at Stella—she's a mess of clashing colors."

Bridget laughed. "Well, Marche, what do you expect when you let a five-year-old choose her own outfits?"

She motioned to Stella, who wore rainbow-colored plastic bracelets on her wrists, a pair of orange overalls, and a lime green shirt with Care Bears on the sleeves. She was the epitome of cuteness, except for the fact that she was stuffing her mouth with a misshapen hunk of pretzel too large for her to chew.

Marche shrugged and sipped her tea.

"Excuse me."

A grandmotherly voice, soft as a dove's coo, drifted over Marche's shoulder. Marche turned in her chair to see who had spoken; she didn't recognize either of the two white-haired women seated at the table behind them.

"Yes?" Marche asked.

"Pardon me for prying," one of the women said. Dressed in a violet jacket and canary yellow dress, she resembled a walking Easter egg. "I couldn't help but overhear that your name is Marche."

"Yes," Marche repeated.

"That's such an unusual name," the woman said. "In fact, I've only heard it used once before. I was wondering if, by any chance, you might be the same person who bought the house on Victor Street?"

Marche's eyebrows shot up in surprise. "That's right. But how..."

"Humph!" The woman elbowed her friend, whose neutral-colored outfit looked drab in comparison. "I'm Agatha Marshall," she said as her acquaintance rubbed her injured arm, scowling.

Marche looked at her uncomprehendingly. "Do I...?"

The woman smiled, revealing a set of milky yellow teeth. "Formerly Agatha Louis."

"Oh," Marche replied. "I see."

Beside her, Stella had stopped eating. She played with her food, imagining that each chunk of pretzel represented a different species of dinosaur. "Grr," she growled. "Grr-grr."

"I didn't attend the closing," Agatha said. "Business of that nature bores me to tears."

Marche nodded, reached for the cooling cup, and sipped her tea while the woman prattled on.

"I was Chucky's twin sister. I was named executor of the estate when he passed on, dear soul." She kissed the tips of her fingers and glanced upward. "How are you getting on there?"

"We're comfortable," Marche replied.

"I said they should have knocked that house down with a wrecking ball after Chucky died, but the real estate agent seemed to think it was worth something. So I let him do his thing. It's not that I have anything against the house, but it just got *too old*. Even when I was a little girl, I felt like it was going to collapse in on me at any moment."

"Is there something wrong with it?" Bridget asked, craning around Marche to be seen.

Agatha glanced at Bridget as if noticing her for the first time. "Wrong with the house?" She paused, sucking on her bottom lip. "My mother died when I was just a tot, and I liked to think sometimes when I was growing up that she might show up in the doorway to my bedroom one night. But it never did happen."

Marche frowned.

"You were hoping the house was haunted?" Bridget asked. She rummaged through her purse and pulled out a hand mirror.

"Pshaw!" Agatha looked again at Marche; her voice quivered with excitement. "Have you heard the bells?"

"What?" Marche asked, perplexed.

"Have you heard the bells?"

Uncertain, Marche looked from Agatha to the woman beside her. "The neighbor's wind chimes," she replied slowly, "are the closest I've come to hearing any bells."

Agatha shook her head. "I promise you, it's no wind chime. I used to hear those bells when I was a young girl."

"I heared a bell," Stella announced.

Marche choked on her tea. She set the paper cup on the table and rubbed her neck. The chair teetered precariously as she re-crossed her legs.

Bridget, who had been checking her teeth in the mirror, suddenly snapped it shut. "What did you say?"

"I heared it," the child repeated.

"Did you now?" Agatha replied, smiling once again. Stretching her arm past Marche, she patted Stella on the hand. "Oopsies. Got a speck of crumbs on my fingers."

Stella giggled as Agatha rubbed her brittle, wrinkled fingers together.

"And where did you hear the bell?" Agatha asked.

"In the empty room," Stella whispered.

"Let's get you cleaned up," Bridget said, grabbing a fresh napkin off the table and wiping pretzel bits from Stella's mouth.

"Which room is that?" Agatha asked.

Marche hesitated, but she couldn't think of a tactful way to avoid answering the woman's question. Besides, what harm could it do? "It's the room on the second floor that overlooks the backyard."

"That's the one!" Agatha proclaimed, snapping her fingers. "Never be afraid if you hear those bells, little girl."

Stella looked at Agatha with wide, bright eyes. "It's pretty."

"Yes, they are. They're very pretty."

Marche quickly gulped down the remainder of her tea and stuffed the dirty napkins into it.

"Glad to have met you, Mrs. Marshall. We have to get going—we have an appointment at the escalators."

The old woman curled her fingers into the mesh tabletop, bobbed her head as though she'd reached an important decision. A look of wonderment filled her dark eyes.

"I should stop by sometime—pay my respects to the place. I can show you where all the secret niches are. I bet you would like that, wouldn't you, little girl?"

"I'm afraid we aren't ready for visitors," Marche lied. *And didn't you just say you wanted it razed to the ground? Where's the respect in that?* "The house is still a wreck. Moving boxes everywhere... You know how it is."

"Little things like that don't bother me, dear."

Bridget fished some change out of her purse as they stood up to leave. "What do you say we throw these into the fountain?" she asked Stella. "Goodbye, Mrs. Marshall."

"Bye-bye, dears."

"You never told me about those noises in the house," Marche heard the older woman say as they walked away.

"You never asked," Agatha quipped.

"What a whack job," Marche said under her breath.

"Maybe so," Bridget replied, "but she seems nice enough."

At the fountain, Bridget explained to Stella that throwing money into the water helped make wishes come true.

"I wanna pony!" the child squealed as she threw a penny into the water. "And ice cream!"

Bridget laughed. "You're supposed to keep your wishes a secret," she said, bending down to Stella's level. "Try putting this one in the water without saying anything."

Stella hurled a nickel into the fountain. It made a small *plup* sound as it submerged.

"There you go. Very good."

Bridget handed Stella a few more coins and then gave a quarter to Marche. Marche contemplated the coin in her palm and then tossed it in the water. It landed on a penny, heads up.

"Did you make a wish?" Bridget asked.

Marche scanned all the coins in the water. They shimmered copper and silver under the afternoon sunlight.

"What's left to wish for?" she said, unable to keep the bitterness out of her voice. "Escalators, Stella?"

The child clapped her hands, forgetting to toss the last coin into the water. "Yay! Yay! Yay!"

Eight

Marche attended a barbeque at her sister's house at noon. About two dozen people came to the Memorial Day get-together, including three friends from Bridget's college, co-workers from both The Pearla Company and Plumdale Elementary, and neighbors. Marche passed the time reclined in a chair by the pool, paperback in hand. The weather held up nicely. Fluffy white clouds hovered over the house, and the sun shone in the sky like a light bulb without a lampshade.

At two o'clock, she returned home with Stella.

They sat in the driveway, the engine idle, while Marche dialed the neighbor's number. "We're outside waiting," she said when Shelley answered the phone.

"Lovely! We'll be out in a jiff."

Marche reached for the air conditioner knob and blasted the cold air. Though it was technically still spring, Egret Bay felt like a furnace.

"I hope there's a lot of shade at the park," she muttered.

She drummed her fingers on the steering wheel. In the rearview mirror, she could see Stella playing with her Matchbox cars. She waved them around like magic flying carpets and made *zoom-zoom* noises.

The Franklins' front door opened a short while later. A young child in a pink striped skirt and matching pink shirt bounded out. Shelley lumbered across the lawn behind her, toting a car seat in her arms.

"Wait by the car!" Shelley said. She waved to Marche before opening the back door. "Jiminy cricket, it's hot out here."

"Still up for playtime? We can always reschedule."

"We're not marshmallows. We won't melt, right?" Shelley said as sweat beaded along her hairline. She bent over to strap in the car seat. "Besides, Coral's been looking forward to the park all morning. It'll break her little heart if we don't go now."

The seatbelt *clicked*.

"Stella, sweetheart, this is my granddaughter, Coral," Shelley said as she placed the honey-blonde toddler in the backseat beside her.

"Hi-ya!" Coral screeched.

"Hi," Stella replied in a timid voice. She dropped the toy cars and stared at Coral as though she was an exotic animal at the zoo.

"There!" Shelley said. "All set."

"This is your oldest?" Marche said.

Shelley closed the door and readjusted the seatbelt to fit her larger frame. "She's a lively one, isn't she? Gets it from her father, I suppose. Adam was always a rowdy child."

"Which way is it to the park?" Marche asked. Putting the Neon in reverse, she backed out of the driveway.

"Turn right at the stop sign," Shelley said.

They drove for half a mile on Washington before turning left on Castlewyn. The residential road curved like an S-shaped ribbon. The first half featured ranch-style homes; the second half had an upscale apartment complex, accompanied by a golf course. At the end of the green, they crossed a short concrete bridge, followed by the sign for Castlewyn Park. The iron gate stood wide open, the hours of operation indicating that the park closed at sunset.

"Looks like just about everyone in Egret Bay had the same idea," Marche said.

"There's another playground further in," Shelley said. "Let's try that one."

They motored past the first playground, a baseball diamond, a soccer field, and a boat ramp. Marche steered the car around a bend and over another concrete bridge, this one crossing Castlewyn Lake. Trees—pine, oak, beech—cast elongated, fingerlike shadows on the pavement. The second playground rolled into view. Their plan to avoid the crowd had failed. It was just as busy here as elsewhere.

"I guess this is as good as it gets," Marche said as she parked the car between two SUVs.

Shelley turned around in the seat, spreading one arm across the backrest.

"Are you going to take Coral under your wing and show her how to play on the playground equipment?"

Stella nodded vigorously.

Marche tucked her purse under the seat, pocketed her keys, and got out of the car. The scent of burning charcoal permeated the air. At one of the nearby picnic shelters, a large party of people filled all the tables; smoke rose from the grill in thick puffs. "Aghh! Aghh! Aghh!" Youngsters ran around the pavilion, screaming and shooting each other with water guns.

Stella wriggled as Marche unfastened her seatbelt. "Ducks!" she said, pointing at a group of mallards waddling through the grass.

Shelley opened the other back door and lifted Coral out of the car seat. "Are you girls ready to have fun?"

Stella hopped onto the pavement, circled the car, and reached for Shelley's free hand.

"Can I pet a duck?" she asked.

"You could try darlin', but they might bite you. That is, if they don't fly away first."

"They fly?" Coral chirped.

"That's right," Shelley replied. "Just like mockingbirds or crows."

"Ducks are fat," Stella said with a giggle.

Marche settled on top of a weathered picnic table, the surface spotted with bird dung. Propping her feet on the bench, she cupped her hands around her elbows. Shelley lectured the girls at the jungle gym. "Climb slowly. And make sure you hold on to the rails. Can you do that for Grandma Shell?"

"Uh huh!"

"Okay!"

"We'll be right here watching you," Shelley said, pointing to the table as she approached Marche. But the girls had already begun to spin a set of plastic tic-tac-toe blocks and weren't paying attention.

"You ought to get a good night's sleep tonight," Shelley remarked. She plopped onto the bench and stretched her legs, wiggled her pink-painted toenails.

A woodpecker hammered on one of the tall trees. At another picnic table, a young woman rocked a baby in a bouncer. On the lake, a small motorboat roared to life.

"Stella's usually a heavy sleeper," Marche replied. "She has had a few nightmares recently, though."

"Oh dear. Well, maybe if she's worn out enough, she'll be too tired to dream."

"Maybe." Marche glanced upward. The cornflower blue sky now appeared a shade closer to denim. The clouds, though still white, had thickened.

"I used to come here every weekend when the kids were little," Shelley said. She leaned her elbows on the table and fanned herself. "Back in the day, it was one of the city's best-kept secrets. Now it's impossible to go on the walking trails without bumping shoulders with someone."

From where they sat, Marche had a clear view of the lake. Under the changing sky, the water looked gray. A seagull landed on a *No Swimming* sign at the lake's edge and cawed madly at an unseen foe. Beyond it, a fish jumped into the air and landed with a splash. Out of nowhere, an anhinga flew past the sign and swooped into the watery depths.

Marche reclined, her hand narrowly missing bird poop where she gripped the edge of the table.

"Makes me feel young again to see the tykelets horsing around like that," Shelley said.

Marche nodded. And then suddenly she felt envious of their youth, of their ability to play on a sunny afternoon and not have to worry about weighty topics like finances or loneliness. *Wish I could be that carefree.*

The girls were preparing to slide down the yellow kiddie slide together. Coral sat first and Stella wrapped her arms around her like a protective big sister. "Hold on," Stella said. She scooted forward and they sped down the plastic tube, landing hard on the recycled rubber mulch.

"Uh-oh," Shelley murmured.

Coral began to cry, her features twisting into a bright red mess. Shelley stood. But before she'd taken two steps, Stella quieted the wailing by patting Coral on the head.

"She's a natural, isn't she?" Shelley remarked. "Maybe you'll be the mother of a doctor someday?"

The girls climbed up the four steps, ready to go through the process all over again. They screeched with laughter. No tears this time.

"That would—"

Marche's train of thought crashed and burned; her smile froze.

As the girls kicked up rubber, the airborne pieces hovered in space. They melded, forming a haunting black silhouette against the trees. *The dress!* Then the illusion shattered, the pieces scattering on the ground.

Marche closed her eyes.

She was no longer at the park, but in the house. It was moving day—the day she'd fainted. Once again, she stepped into the spare room. Found nothing but boxes. Felt the inexplicable tap on her shoulder.

Marche tried to open her eyes, but they felt sealed shut. As if someone had blown frost across the lids. *Don't turn, don't turn, don't turn!* But she couldn't change what had already happened. The memory, now that it had surfaced, refused reburial. And so she remained in the room, forced to relive each nightmarish sensation.

The muscles in her throat constricted when she saw the figure; her breath stopped. Her chest pounded at a reduced rate until everything around her fell in sync with its rhythm. In the background, a blue jay flying by the window hovered for two full seconds instead of one.

That's not real! It can't be real!

Yet the figure remained.

Its gown was ivory. The style was simple—no lace, sequins, or fancy cuts. The fabric, nearly transparent, covered the arms from the shoulders to the wrists. The neckline was high and rounded. The plain skirt flowed down to the knees. It was an unremarkable piece of clothing that might have hailed from any decade of the past century.

But the face...

Marche touched her own cheeks and chin for reassurance. The skin was there as it should be, plump and elastic over her bones. When she applied pressure, she felt the outline of her teeth. Of course! A person couldn't function without a face;

it just wasn't physiologically possible. No amount of rationalization, however, could change the fact that this figure *did not have a face.*

Stringy brown hair hung from the scalp in wet clumps, covering the ears and clinging to the pasty forehead. But that's where the resemblance to a living entity ended. A black hole claimed the space where the nose, mouth, and eyes should have been..

Marche clenched her fists at her side. She felt light-headed but unable to draw a breath. She trembled at the knees.

I'm going to faint.

She swayed slightly, her gaze slipping downward.

The ivory gown was no longer ivory. Where the abdomen should have been, a splattering of blood soaked the material. The figure's hands (beautiful, alabaster, manicured hands) clasped something in front of the bright red mess.

Those hands—beautiful even when caked in blood—resembled a doll's hands. As if they had been crafted out of porcelain by a genius of the art. The fingers, short but slim, pressed against the bodice of the dress. What were they holding? Something suspiciously organic protruded between the fingers.

Marche swayed again as bile threatened to rise in her throat.

Intestines!

Then finally, mercifully, her eyes fluttered shut.

Air *whooshed* out of Marche's lungs; her eyes popped open. She sat up straight on the bench, rested her fingers at the base of her throat, and felt her pulse pounding rapidly beneath the skin. She swallowed thickly.

"Looks like the weather's taking a turn," Shelley observed. She slipped off her sunglasses and tucked them into her fluffy crown.

"Yeah, I think you're right," Marche said, taking a deep, steadying breath. She snuck a glance at Shelley, but the other woman didn't appear to have noticed that anything was wrong; she watched the girls, a contented smile on her face.

"Good thing we got here when we did," Shelley continued. "Might only have another twenty minutes before the angels decide to pour their buckets."

A quarter of an hour later, the sun dipped behind the clouds. The clouds, now slate gray, darkened.

"Did you feel that?" Shelley said. "It's spitting."

The girls were clambering up the slide in reverse. Coral grabbed Stella's sock when she lost her footing. Then Stella slipped and they both went sliding down on their tummies. As they shrieked with laughter, thunder sounded in the distance.

"I'll start the car," Marche said.

"Come on, sugarplums," Shelley called out as she walked toward the slide. "Time to go. You don't want to get struck by lightning."

A fat drop of water landed on Marche's nose as she unlocked the car door. By the time they'd buckled the girls in their seats, the rain had graduated to a downpour.

Driving home took twice as long. Even with the wipers on full speed, Marche still struggled to see through the windshield. The rain—shooting like bullets from the sky—cloaked the earth in a thick woolen blanket. By the time they reached Victor Street, Marche had decelerated to ten miles per hour.

Hank appeared on the Franklins' front porch as soon as Marche parked the car. Hoisting a bright green umbrella over his head, he rushed across the yard.

"My knight in shining armor," Shelley cooed as he held open the door for her. Hank towered over her, shielding her from the rain while she extracted Coral from the car seat. Arms full, she turned to Marche. "Keep dry!" In another second, they were gone.

Marche reached under the passenger seat, but the umbrella that she usually kept there was gone. "Wish we could have had an escort too," she murmured. Reaching over the backseat, she unfastened Stella's harness and gave her a Cheshire cat grin. "Ready to run?"

Despite the short distance, they were drenched to the skin by the time Marche ushered Stella into the house.

"How would you like some hot chocolate?" Marche asked, turning on the hall light. Stella shook her head like a dog fresh from a bath. "I'll take that as a yes.

Let's get you changed first, though."

Marche pulled a shirt from the pile of clean clothes she'd yet to fold, and laid Stella's wet clothes on the wooden linen rack.

"Why don't you go turn on one of your favorite toons?" she said as she towel-dried Stella's hair. "The hot chocolate will be ready in a minute."

"I wanna see Bugs!"

"Okay. Bugs it is."

While the water heated in the microwave, Marche selected two hot chocolate packets and mismatched mugs. From the living room came snippets of noise and dialogue as Stella flipped through the channels.

"If I can hear it, it's too loud," she murmured as rain pelted against the windowpane. *Why does Dom insist on letting her turn up the volume like that?*

Then she remembered, and she bit her lip to keep from crying out.

I'm a widow.

Dom is dead.

Lightning flashed, thunder boomed, and the electricity flickered out.

Nine

THE SLOW, BOILING HEAT blossomed into a blistering blaze in the days that followed. By the first of June, the outdoor thermometer verified that summer had indeed made its entrance three weeks early. The temperature in Egret Bay hovered between ninety-five and one-hundred-ten degrees every day.

While Marche sat behind the circulation desk cool as a cucumber, people paraded through the library doors with reddened cheeks, circles of dampness at their shirt collars and armpits, and (thankfully, not too often) flaunting their body's natural odors. When Marche accepted items from sweaty palms, she was especially glad she worked in a controlled environment of seventy-two degrees.

"It feels nice in here during the summer," Sarah said as a patron wearing a bicycle helmet walked away, "but in the winter it's like a storage freezer."

"I suppose I should invest in a good pair of gloves, then," Marche replied. She pushed out of her chair to look for the hand sanitizer. "I tore my last pair hanging up Christmas lights in the front yard a couple of years ago." *While we were still a family*, she silently added.

"Shop much?"

Marche located the bottle of Purell next to the cash register. "Not when I can avoid it," she said, squirting a quarter-sized drop of the solution onto her palm. She scrubbed vigorously and then shook her hands in the air to dry them. "Is it usually this busy during the summer?"

"Murphy's Law," Sarah replied. "Traffic always increases when we're short staffed."

Ebony was on vacation, Felix was out sick with the stomach flu, and Genie was in the workroom sorting through donations. By Marche's estimation, they would probably be without help for at least another hour.

A woman with bleached hair approached the desk just as Marche returned to her chair. "Can someone help me?"

"What's the problem?" Sarah asked, her tone polite.

"I'm working on my resume, and there's too many spaces on the page."

"Did you—"

"Can't you just show me? I'm in a hurry." The woman turned and walked away without waiting for an answer.

"Good luck," Marche whispered, giving Sarah a thumbs-up.

Sarah exited the circulation area and approached a group of computers that had been placed—much to the circulation staff's displeasure—a few feet away from the checkout counter.

As Sarah bent down to assist the woman, Marche continued to scan the materials that she'd collected from the inside book drop.

"Were you able to figure it out?" she asked when Sarah returned.

Sarah leaned over so that the computer monitor obscured her face from the public's view. "It wasn't a spacing issue," she softly said. "She'd hit the enter key too many times between paragraphs."

Marche chuckled. "Not surprised. She asked me for help twice yesterday. She really needs to go upstairs where Reference can help her. She doesn't have a *clue* about what she's doing."

"Right on, sister," Sarah replied. Grabbing a DVD off the cart, she scanned the barcode on the back cover. "I have a feeling it's going to be one of those days."

Five minutes later, a woman dressed in a button-down blouse and diamond earrings approached the desk.

"I need to pick up a book for my husband. Here's my ID," she announced, thrusting her driver's license in front of Marche's nose.

"Is the book on your account?"

"No. It's on my husband's. It's *his* book."

"All right," Marche replied. "Then I'll need to see his library card in order to check it out."

"I don't have his library card," the woman said, "or I would have given it to you. You can use my ID to look up his account. We have the same last name, same address. Everything is the same."

"I'm sorry," Marche said, trying to sound sympathetic. "But unfortunately, I'm not allowed to access the account without his library card."

The woman snatched her driver's license out of Marche's hand, her brown eyes gleaming with annoyance. "I have been married to the same man for twenty-two years, and you're giving me bullshit about a goddamn library book?" The clipped words cut through the air like a razor blade. "Who's in charge here?"

"The supervisor isn't in right now," Sarah said as the patron she'd been assisting walked away. "But she would tell you the same thing. It's Florida law."

"Would you like her business card?" Marche asked.

"Unbelievable!" the woman barked, storming off. Her high heels clomped loudly as she stepped through the lobby doors.

"What a piece of work," Marche said.

"Sometimes I think the heat brings out the worst in people," Sarah replied, twisting her silver necklace between her fingers.

"You're too generous. I'm sure that woman is like that regardless of the weather." Marche sighed. "Do we have any stress balls around here?"

Sarah thought for a moment. "Next time you get a patron like that, just imagine a large wrecking ball suddenly crashing through the ceiling and flattening them."

"Outwardly non-violent, yet still effective." Marche grinned. "I like your style."

"If I break into spontaneous laughter, you'll know why."

At three o'clock, the Cozy Mystery Madness Club disbanded and foot traffic doubled at the circulation counter. It was like rush hour on the highway, but with canes and walkers instead of cars and buses. As soon as one patron left the desk, another promptly appeared.

The club, hands-down the most popular program at the library, met for an hour every Thursday afternoon. Moderated by a volunteer, participants discussed everything mystery—from novels to short stories, plays, films, etc. Crowding around the circulation desk, they checked out books written by Agatha Christie,

P. D. James, and M. C. Beaton. Some of them supplemented their reading material with popular TV shows like *Murder, She Wrote* and classic films like *Rear Window* and *Dial M for Murder*.

In between checking out materials, Marche helped two different patrons with the printers. "They're cash and coin only," she explained to the second person. "No cards." The phone rang unanswered at least five times. A crotchety middle-aged man complained about the noise coming from the children's department. And a teenager reported a stolen bike; since the library only employed security officers three days a week, Marche had to contact the police department .Sarah sighed dramatically when the last patron stepped away from the desk. "Do you think it's safe to breathe?"

Marche rubbed her temples in response. When a man in Bermuda shorts and flip-flops approached the counter, she greeted him with an exaggerated smile.

"How are you today?" he asked, pushing forward a stack of books covering economic trends and history.

Marche patted her head. "Well, we've pulled out all our hair and now we're wearing wigs."

The Jimmy Buffett lookalike spun his car keys on a suntanned finger and laughed. "I thought the library was supposed to be a quiet place where you could go to get away from it all."

Marche scanned the man's library card, which lay barcode-up on the books. "Not in the real world."

"It's the third biggest myth," Sarah exclaimed.

"After what?" Marche asked, unable to resist.

"The existence of Bigfoot, of course."

"Of course," the patron echoed.

"And George Washington chopping down a cherry tree."

"You mean that's not true?" the man said, feigning surprise. He winked at both of them as he collected his books and walked away.

"You are classic," Marche said.

Sarah leaned back in her chair and stretched. "I'm not sure how I should take that."

"I just mean that I find you very unique."

"Again—ambiguous."

Marche laughed. She enjoyed working with Sarah, probably because she saw a younger version of herself in the woman. Sarah represented the person she might have become...under different circumstances.

"How is school?" she asked after a while.

"Oh, you know... Lots of busy work."

"What I would give to have that kind of busy work," Marche replied, unable to keep the wistfulness from her voice.

"You could always go back," Sarah said. "I'm sure you'd qualify for some sort of financial assistance, being a single parent and all. Why'd you quit school, anyway?"

"My parents died in a plane crash when I was nineteen," Marche replied. "My sister was too young to take care of herself, and none of our relatives stepped up to the plate. After I got a full-time job at the bookstore, my grades started to suffer. Got a few too many Cs on my transcript, lost my scholarships, and that was the end of it."

"Ouch. That's way harsh."

Marche grabbed a stack of scrap paper and a pair of scissors from the drawer. "Now I'm a single parent, hardly getting by. I just don't see a college degree in my future."

"Jeez. That really sucks."

Marche shrugged. Shortly after she and Dom had married, she'd entertained thoughts of returning to college. Then she'd gotten pregnant and had a baby.

"How far into the program are you?" Marche asked. During their first shift together, Sarah had explained that she was pursuing her Master's of Library and Information Science. Puffing with pride, she said that she dreamed of becoming an archivist.

Now the young woman bolted upright in her chair, bug-eyed with excitement. "This is my third semester. One of the courses that I'm taking covers informational resources for the humanities. For this one project, I have to create a mini-grant for an art museum."

"Sounds fun."

"Ugh. It's like pulling teeth." Sarah collected her hair and tossed the thick mass over her shoulder. "I sit down to write, and I have no idea what to say because I have *no* idea about what I'm doing."

"Have you asked the professor for help?"

"I would, but that's useless. Other students have already posted questions in the discussion board—"

"Discussion board?"

"Yeah. It's an online class," Sarah said, as if that explained everything. "Anyway, there are already questions posted, but Dr. Reynolds is no help at all. He just gives vague, ambiguous responses. The worst of it is, I think he thinks that what he says actually makes sense."

"I'm sure that you'll figure it out. You're a smart girl—I bet you'll ace the assignment."

"Maybe. If I don't develop an ulcer in the meantime."

Marche set aside the cut pieces of scrap paper. The remaining stack was still about a quarter of an inch thick.

"I almost wish I would have gone into history like Evan. But I have *no* desire to teach."

"What's your boyfriend's focus?"

"American history," Sarah replied. "He's particularly interested in the nineteenth century, and he's totally passionate about local history."

"Have you been together a long time?"

"Two years."

The phone rang, interrupting their conversation. Sarah reached for the receiver. "Egret Bay Library, this is Sarah speaking. How may I help you?"

While Sarah helped the patron on the telephone, Marche checked the indoor book drop. As she collected a handful of items from the bin, she noticed a petite elderly woman approaching the counter. Setting the books aside, she returned to her station.

"Hello. Can I help you?"

"You don't remember me, do you?" the woman replied, baring her teeth. She wore an outrageous ensemble of orange and plaid, with bright green barrettes glittering in her thin white hair.

Marche stared at the woman, her mind blank. "Um..." When the patron leaned forward and gave a conspiratorial wink, recognition finally set in.

"Mrs. Marshall," Marche said slowly, "how good to see you."

"I didn't know that you worked here," Agatha said. Placing a reusable bag on the counter, she pulled out some paperbacks. "I just love the library. Don't you?"

"Do you come here often?" Marche asked, silently hoping that the woman would say no.

"At least once a month." Agatha rummaged through her oversized purse. "I like attending the mystery club. I'm always on the lookout for new whodunits. Good ones, I mean. With all the garbage out there nowadays, it's hard to find a decent plotted murder. Hmm." She dumped the purse on the counter and sorted through the contents with both hands like a dog digging for a bone. "Blast it! But I can't seem to find that card. How bizarre. Ah!" she exclaimed. "Here it is."

Clutching it between her fingers (topped with outrageously long, sparkling green nails), she presented the card to Marche.

"Thank you," Marche murmured, averting her gaze as Agatha scooped all of her belongings back into the purse.

"I'm so sorry I haven't had a chance to visit you yet. I've been busy all week. Hair appointments. Nail appointments. You understand what that's like. Don't you, dear?"

Marche forced a smile as she slipped a due date card into each book pocket. "No worries, Mrs. Marshall."

"Oh, but I hate not keeping my word," Agatha replied, dropping the library card back into her purse. "A person's word means so much."

"It's okay, really."

"How is the little one doing?" Agatha asked.

"She's just fine. Thank you for asking." Marche pushed the books forward. "These are due back in a month. Have a nice day."

Agatha shouldered her purse, her dark eyes focused on Marche. "Have you heard the bells yet?"

"No, I haven't heard any bells. Just the neighbor's wind chimes."

"No matter. You'll hear them soon enough, I reckon."

Agatha packed the books into her reusable bag. She turned to leave, took a half-step, and then changed her mind. Planting one of her hands on the counter, she leaned forward, her face close enough that Marche could smell pickles and yogurt on her breath.

"I started hearing the bells when I was fifteen."

"Is that right?"

Agatha nodded. "When you hear the bells, it means that something good is going to happen."

Sarah coughed. Out of the corner of her eye, Marche could see that she had lowered her head and covered her mouth with both hands.

Marche tilted her head to the side, curious despite herself. "What makes you say that?"

Agatha brightened. "Because the first time I heard the bells, I was fifteen. By the time I was sixteen, all of my dreams had come true." She lowered her voice as though she were speaking of a confidential matter. "And *that* is how I know what I've told you."

"I see..."

"You *will* see," Agatha said, straightening. "Too-da-loo."

"Happy reading," Sarah called out.

Agatha waved and stepped through the doors.

As soon as the woman disappeared from sight, Sarah burst into a guttural laugh. "What a funny bunny," she said when she finally caught her breath.

"You laugh now," Marche replied, "but you might not think it so hilarious if she knew where *you* lived."

"Point taken." Sarah wiped a tear from her eye.

"You do realize that she's completely serious, don't you?"

Sarah succumbed to a fresh fit of giggles, her face crimson. "I could see that," she said between gasps of air. "She's like...a jigsaw puzzle where some of the pieces are missing. But, like, permanently."

Marche nodded; she couldn't have come up with a better analogy herself.

“So she knows where you live, huh?” Sarah said. “Where are you located again?”

“On the corner of Victor and Washington.”

“Victor and Washington,” Sarah mumbled. “Now why does that sound familiar?”

“Excuse me.” A man with a banana yellow bandana hanging from his neck approached the desk. “You might want to tell someone that there’s a mess in the men’s room. Someone stuffed paper towels in the last stall and it’s overflowing.”

“This day just keeps getting better and better,” Marche murmured as she reached for the walkie talkie.

Ten

By the time Friday night rolled around, Marche was delirious with exhaustion. All the same, she couldn't resist the temptation to stay up late with a book.

"Sleep tight," Marche said after tucking Stella into bed at eight o'clock.

"Don't let the bedbugs bite," Stella finished.

Marche flipped the light switch and headed into the kitchen for a glass of lemonade. In the living room, she traced her finger along the spines of the books on the shelves. It had been so long since she'd had the luxury to lose herself in a story. After a moment of indecision, she selected her favorite Austen work.

Crawling into bed, she propped herself against the pillows. She slowly read through the first few chapters of *Persuasion*, savoring each well-crafted line. She had just paused to sip her drink when a loud cry sounded from Stella's room.

"Ahh!"

Startled, Marche glanced upward. A moment later, another scream sounded. Marche dropped the book, threw off the covers, and hopped onto the floor.

Bounding through the doorway, she quickly crossed the few steps leading to Stella's bedroom. Pushing the door open, she felt along the wall for the light switch.

Stella sat upright in bed, clutching the sheets to her chin. She shrieked when the light came on, her hazel eyes round with fright.

"What's wrong, Stella?!"

Marche rushed to the bed, stepping on a Lego block along the way. "Shit," she hissed, as pain shot through her foot. But she had no time to nurse the injury. The moment she sat down, Stella leapt into her arms.

"Scary, Mommy! Scary!"

Marche caressed Stella's hair; it was damp with sweat.

"Shh. Shh. What was scary?"

Stella tucked her head under Marche's chin and continued to cry. As the seconds ticked by, her loud wailing de-escalated into muffled sobs. Marche felt her small body trembling beneath her, and she hugged Stella with more intensity than usual.

"What was scary, Stella?" Marche repeated after a few minutes had elapsed.

When the child finally spoke, her voice was so soft that Marche had to strain to hear her. "The lady."

Stella was sniffling now. Both of her hands, clenched into fists, rested on Marche's arm. She slowly relaxed as Marche held her close.

"What lady, Stella?"

Marche scanned the room, but saw nothing to indicate that this was a nightmare-inducing space for a small child. A few Barbie dolls lay scattered in one corner of the room. Some half-dressed and others completely nude; most exhibited funky hairstyles courtesy of a rainy afternoon, an encouraging aunt, and a pair of scissors. In another corner, she spied the familiar pile of stuffed animals. None of these appeared the least bit threatening. A pink elephant that Dom had won at a county fair three years back was the largest of the bunch, but it looked friendly even in the shadows. The closet was doorless. Dresses, shirts, and animal print shorts hung from the hangers. A collection of flip-flops and sandals littered the otherwise clean floor. All in all, the room looked like a comfortable little girl's room—even in the dark.

"I dunno."

Marche felt Stella's nose wetting her shirtsleeve. She grimaced involuntarily and tried to ignore it.

"What did she look like?"

"Um..." Stella sniffled and then coughed. "Black."

"What else? Did she say anything? Do anything?"

Marche rubbed Stella's back. The nightmares mystified her. Before they'd moved to Egret Bay, Stella had always slept soundly. So why now? Was this a delayed reaction to losing her father? Marche thought over the past few weeks. She counted three—no, four—other instances when Stella had woken up screaming. Though Marche asked for details, Stella never seemed to remember anything except a woman dressed in black. The following morning, she never had any recollection of having a nightmare.

"She said..." Stella sniffled again, hiccupped.

Marche's brows furrowed. Pulling slightly back, she gazed into Stella's wet eyes. "She said something to you?"

Stella unfolded her hands, gripped Marche's arms with unnatural strength. She nodded fervently.

"What did she say?"

"She said..."

Fresh tears pooled in Stella's eyes and Marche had to encourage her with more back rubbing to complete the sentence.

"...she was gonna hurt me."

"Oh, Stella," Marche said, hugging her tight. "No one is going to hurt you. I promise. Dreams aren't real, you know."

"She...scared...me."

"I know, I know. But it's all right now. You're safe. Whatever you see when you're asleep stays there. When you wake up, whatever you're afraid of...is just gone. Sleep time and wake time are two separate worlds. They don't ever mix. Not ever."

"Can I sleep with you, Mommy?"

Stella was talking into her chest now. Marche thought about her night of relaxation and sighed.

"All right, but just for tonight. Okay? You're too big to be sharing a bed with me."

Standing took some effort—she felt like she was carrying an eight-pound child in her uterus again. As Marche steadied on her feet, unable to favor her smarting foot, she scanned the room one last time. Still, she saw nothing that could explain what might be prompting Stella's night terrors. With a sigh, she crossed the room and turned off the light.

Marche laid Stella on the side of the bed that Dom once used and pulled the blankets up to her shoulders.

"I miss Bianca."

"I'll ask Aunt Bridget to bring Bianca with her when she comes over tomorrow. Will that help you feel better?" Marche grabbed a tissue from the box on the dresser and gently wiped Stella's damp face.

"Uh-huh," Stella replied through a yawn.

"Think you can sleep now?"

"Uh-huh."

"And what are we going to dream about this time?" Marche asked.

"Umm..."

"How about lollipops and unicorns?" Marche suggested.

"And talking dolphins," Stella added, her eyelids fluttering shut.

"And puppies that can fly."

"And giraffes that hop on their heads," Stella murmured.

When Marche leaned over to turn off the bedside lamp, Stella was already drifting into slumber, her head tucked deeply into the pillow.

"And little girls who have picnics with their mommies," Marche whispered, kissing Stella softly on the cheek.

Eleven

Bridget arrived the next morning, just as Marche was setting the breakfast dishes in the sink.

"I heard someone placed an order for Miss Bianca?" Bridget said, waving the doll in the air.

Stella shrieked with delight and clutched the doll to her chest.

"Thanks," Marche said. "She's got so many toys. I don't know why she's attached to that doll."

"It's fine. That's what I kept it for, anyway." Bridget held up the plastic shopping bag she'd carried with her into the kitchen. "Ready to get started?"

Stella skipped her way to the living room where a Sesame Street marathon was currently playing on the television. "Big Bird and Cookie Monster are funny," she said to the doll, giggling.

"Don't change the volume," Marche warned. "It's loud enough." Then she followed Bridget up the stairs and into the spare room. "What kind of goodies did you bring?"

Bridget turned the bag upside down, spilling the contents onto the floor. There was a roll of painter's tape, a roll of plastic tarp, a handful of paintbrushes, plastic trays, and a slew of color samples.

"First order of business," Bridget said, "is to pick a color."

"Christ, Bridget," Marche said, eyeing the rainbow of paper squares on the floor. "There must be a hundred choices here."

She picked up two blue samples, held them under the sunlight, squinted; they looked identical.

"If you're not happy with the color, you won't want to spend time in the room. Right? I focused on shades that I thought you'd find relaxing. What do you think? See anything you like?"

"I don't know," Marche said, feeling overwhelmed before they'd even started. "All I see is a pool of green, gray, and blue. They all look the same to me."

Bridget brought her thumb to her mouth, caught the nail between her teeth. "Okay," she said after a moment's thought. "We'll start simple." She organized the samples into three stacks. "Which color family do you prefer?"

Marche considered the options. The grays made her think of stormy weather. When she looked at the blues she felt, well, blue.

"Green is nice," she finally said.

"Yeah," Bridget replied. "There's a meadow-like vibe, isn't there? We could get stencils and paint ladybugs and flowers on one of the walls. Make the room look like an indoor park. I bet Stella would love that."

Marche shrugged.

Bridget gathered the green squares and spread them on the floor, solitaire-style. "Okay, pick four."

Marche pointed to four of the lightest shades. Tucking the selections into her pocket, Bridget left to purchase the samples at the home improvement store three miles down the road. While she was gone, Marche transferred the leftover moving boxes from the spare room into her bedroom. Perhaps if she had to look at them every day, she might actually feel motivated to tear open the flaps, peer inside, and sort through the various pieces of her life.

Marche decided that they'd paint the samples on the wall facing the backyard. She was in the process of taping the plastic sheet to the floor when Bridget returned with four pint-sized cans.

Prying off the lids with a flathead, Bridget stirred each color with a flat stick. Then she set out four trays and poured a color into each one.

"Here," she said, handing Marche a couple of paintbrushes. "You take two and I'll take two."

Marche felt a twinge of annoyance at Bridget's assertive tone, but said nothing. Bridget looked up at the wall as she plucked a stray bristle from one of the brushes.

"Let's paint a patch near the baseboard, one in the middle, and another close to the ceiling."

"Is that really necessary?"

"The colors might look different depending on the angle of light. This way, you'll know for sure which shade you like best."

"We'll need a ladder for the top one," Marche said after they'd completed painting the other squares. "I can't reach that high and you're shorter than me."

"Need help?"

"Nah. I got it."

Marche returned from the shed a few minutes later, her arm hooked through a six-foot ladder. When they'd finished the topmost sections, they joined Stella in the living room. There, they drank cold Pepsi and watched Sesame Street while they waited for the paint to dry.

"That's Big Bird," Stella said, pointing at the screen.

"He's pretty tall, huh?" Bridget replied, ruffling Stella's hair.

"Like a giant!"

"She calls lots of things giants," Marche said, thinking of the neighbor who lived across the street.

Bridget leaned against the couch cushions, sipped from the soda bottle. "Everything seems big when you're a kid. Remember that woman who owned the birds? The one who gave me the doll?"

Marche thought back to their childhood home. The yards on their street were spacious and clean—except for one. Numerous trees populated Mrs. Miller's yard; their branches stretched and tangled with each other, creating a thick canopy over everything. Wheelbarrows sat at the bases of the trees, weeds and cacti sprouting from them. Feeders hung every few yards, their seeds attracting all species of birds. From within the house, canary song could be heard at all hours of the day.

"I remember," Marche said. "She let us climb on the trees."

"Well, I could have *sworn* she was as tall as a giraffe. I saw her by chance a few months ago. She's hardly five feet tall!"

Marche nodded. She glanced at the doll, propped up beside Stella on the floor. She'd never liked it. Maybe because it was too cute, with its pale face and rosy cheeks and soft platinum blonde hair. Or maybe it was the fact that Mrs. Miller had given it to Bridget as a birthday present—when she'd never once remembered Marche's. And now Stella had formed an attachment to it.

I hate that doll.

Stella laughed when Big Bird jumped over the Cookie Monster.

"Why'd you decide to call it Bianca?" Marche asked.

"Hmm?" Bridget turned from the television screen. "Oh, I didn't. I always called her Tori. Stella's the one who insisted on changing the name."

"I wonder where she got the idea from?" Marche leaned forward so that she was speaking into Stella's ear. "Do you know someone named Bianca?"

Stella responded by picking up the doll and showing it to her. "Bianca."

"Right," Marche replied. "That's Bianca."

"Which one's the winner?" Bridget asked.

They stood in the spare room, studying the patches of paint. Marche's gaze flitted back and forth between the colors. Even dry, the colors looked identical. She pointed to the color on the far right. "That one, I guess."

"Okay, so it's..." Bridget consulted her tiny spiral. "Cucumber Mint."

"I'll buy the paint tomorrow. Should two cans be enough?"

"Should be." As Bridget studied the topmost square of Cucumber Mint, her gaze shot to the ceiling. "What's that?" she asked, jerking her chin upward.

"I believe it's called an attic. Most houses have them."

"And your sarcasm is duly noted," Bridget replied, not sounding the least bit offended. "Have you checked it out yet?"

"I wasn't going to."

"Why on earth not?"

"Why on earth should I?" Marche returned. "Attics are creepy. They give me the heebie-jeebies."

"What if the former owner didn't clean it out? There might be some cool knick-knacks up there. Maybe something artsy for the walls?"

Bridget's eyes sparkled with excitement; Marche decided not to mention that the previous tenant had died.

"Let's check it out," Bridget continued, practically bouncing on her toes.

"You seriously think there's something worthwhile up there?"

Marche studied the square in the ceiling more carefully. Three feet long by two feet wide, it would be easy to fit through. Whether or not the attic contained anything at all—or of any value—was another matter.

"Where's your sense of adventure? It'll only take a few minutes. And it's not like you've got anything to lose."

Marche sighed. "I'll look for a flashlight. It's probably dark as sin up there."

Grinning, Bridget positioned the ladder beneath the attic door. "Good idea."

Marche went into the bedroom and, scanning the boxes, located the one labeled "tools." Tearing off the duct tape, she fished through the contents. She found a heavy-duty flashlight underneath the tape measure and level. Picking it up, she paused.

She hadn't had the courage to tell Bridget about what she'd seen in that room. She couldn't bear the look of skepticism that she knew she'd discover on her sister's face. Not that she could blame her. After all, who would believe a story like that? Marche sucked in a deep breath. *I don't believe it—and I'm the one who* saw *it.*

Even so, she still experienced a moment of wariness every time she crossed the threshold. As if she expected something to materialize from thin air and jump out at her. And now Bridget wanted to explore the attic.

Marche squeezed the flashlight in her sweaty palm. It was true that she found attics creepy. But the real reason she'd wanted to avoid it was not something that she could talk about.

"Time to put on your big girl pants," Marche muttered. She re-entered the room to find Bridget pushing against the attic door. "Is it stuck?"

"There's some resistance, but not much. I think I've almost got it."

A muffled splintering sounded as Bridget pushed firmly on the surface. Slowly, the panel gave way.

"I think...I... There!"

Bridget's hand disappeared briefly as the panel shifted upward. A thick cloud of dust flew into her face.

"I'd say...he...definitely did not...clean out this room...before...he moved," she said between coughs.

"I bet it's crawling with bugs."

"Flashlight?" Bridget said, wiggling her fingers as she extended her hand. She clicked the power button and cautiously popped her head through the hole.

"Do you see anything?"

Bridget held onto the ladder as she flashed the light around the attic. "It's beyond dirty, but I don't see any dead rats." She climbed through the hole. "You coming?" she called through the opening.

Marche placed her foot on the bottom step, hesitated, and then quickly hoisted herself up the remaining rungs. When her head cleared the opening, she paused again.

The attic was smaller than she'd anticipated. It was long but narrow—maybe one-third the width of the bedroom—and seemed to span the length of the house. More a hiding place than a proper attic, as though the builder had included it as an afterthought.

"Is it safe?" Marche asked as she launched into the room.

"Feels sturdy," Bridget replied.

The low ceiling added to the attic's gloominess; Marche could only move about on her hands and knees, and even then, she was cramped for space.

The room smelled of dry wood and mothballs. With each of their movements, a fresh puff of dust danced in the flashlight's beam. Marche coughed, sneezed, then coughed again.

"Well, what do you think?" Marche asked. She pulled her collar over her nose, a makeshift mask to forestall the next gagging fit.

Bridget rolled onto her buttocks and scanned the floor yet again. "It's emptier than I imagined," she lamented.

"That's an understatement. There's nothing here."

Bridget pulled her knees up to her chest as she waved the flashlight around.

The light fell upon an object in the far corner.

"What's that?" Marche said, her interest suddenly piqued.

"A box?"

Marche crawled forward, her hands and knees sweeping dust all the way. The air tickled her nose; she stopped to sneeze, her eyes watering.

"Ugh. I can't handle much more of this," she said, her voice thickened with phlegm. "Let's grab whatever it is and get out of here."

"Fair enough," Bridget replied. "Is that a trunk?"

"Looks like it." Marche felt for the back, locked her fingers at the corners, and pulled. "It's a little heavy, but I can manage. Keep an eye out for me, huh? Make sure I don't fall through the door."

Marche swiped her finger across the top of the trunk. Beneath the streak, the cherry wood gleamed a rich brown. Its overall size was about eighteen inches by twenty-four—the kind of chest where one might store their grandparent's foreign coin collection and tintypes. The exterior of the box was plain. One side featured a small indentation, as though someone had kicked it with a steel-toed boot. The craftsman had attached a lock, now broken, which dangled uselessly by one side.

Maybe Bridget had been right? Maybe there *were* treasures to be found?

"I feel like a Goonie," Bridget said. "Come on. Let's see what's inside."

Marche curled her fingers around the lid and lifted. Though the hinges creaked slightly, it opened without protest.

"That's it?" Bridget blew through her lips and fell back.

Marche sorted through the documents, careful not to tear any of them. "That's it," she confirmed. "Just a bunch of old papers."

Twelve

"Time for a break," Marche said with a sigh, rubbing her temples.

It was half-past one. Her stomach was grumbling. And she'd just finished assisting a Deaf person whose mile-a-minute gesticulations had sent her head spinning. It hadn't helped that she couldn't read sign language and the young man refused to write.

"Run while you can," Ebony said.

"Can you check the drop while you're back there?" Genie asked.

"Sure. No problem."

Marche exited the circulation module and pushed out of her chair. She rounded the holds shelf just as a new line of patrons formed at the counter. *Whew.* Escaping the desk was no joke. If she'd been a second slower, she'd have had to postpone her break at least another ten minutes.

Pushing through the workroom doors, she was grateful for the sudden silence that greeted her. The aide was out on the floor shelving books, and the only volunteer she'd seen at the library today had checked out before noon.

Marche grabbed her lunch from the fridge, brewed a cup of chamomile tea, and seated herself at the counter overlooking the woodlands. Today was as hot as yesterday. But there was a slight breeze and seeing the pine trees quiver and the butterflies flutter was almost as relaxing as listening to a lullaby. She looked out the window, content to think of nothing as she chewed her food.

"Is that you, Marche?" Phyllis called through her office door. The woman's voice, naturally loud, carried like a siren across the short distance.

Marche crumpled up her sandwich wrapper and tossed it in the bin. "Yes, it's me."

"Are you busy? I need to talk to you about something."

Marche glanced at the clock as she approached her supervisor's office. "I have time. I was just finishing my break."

Phyllis glanced up from her newspaper and waved Marche into one of the office chairs across from her desk.

"What word describes both a type of dog and an athlete?" She tapped the black and white squares of the crossword puzzle with her pencil eraser. "Five letters."

"Um..." Marche stared at the cross decals populating the lower half of the office window while she thought of an answer. Some were silver and gold, others silver, and others gold. They were all ornate, like the stickers you'd find in the scrapbook section of a craft store. Their placement on the glass created the illusion that she was looking out at an opulent graveyard among the reed-like tree trunks. "Boxer?"

Phyllis's fingers stilled, her lips puckered. "Yes! That's it." She scribbled in the answer before setting the paper aside. When she looked up, the sunlight pouring in through the windowpane lit up her hair like a flame.

"How are things going? Settling into the department all right?"

"Absolutely. Everyone's helpful." She started to ask a registration question about seasonal library cards, but Phyllis interrupted her.

"You never met Jeff, did you?"

"No. I've heard his name mentioned once or twice, though." *But not in a complimentary way,* she silently added. Earlier in the week, a man in blue spandex shorts had asked Genie for Jeff's phone number. After she'd refused to give him the information, and he'd hobbled away, she'd snorted like an irritated bull. *"One fly attracts another,"* she'd said. And Ebony, seated at the station next to her, had nodded.

"He was my former assistant. Great guy. Even left work early one day to help out my step-granddaughter when she didn't know how to drive the stick shift she'd bought. Very dependable. It was such a shame to see him go."

"Ah." While Marche considered the probability that her boss might be the only person on staff who actually felt that way, a loud monkey's cry issued from the computer speakers.

"Must be an email," Phyllis said. "Just a minute." She clicked on the task bar and opened an icon, her eyes speeding across the screen. "Pain in the ass. Listen to this." She traced a fingernail across the monitor and proceeded to read a complaint that one of the library patrons had lodged against Ebony. "And I quote—'That mousy woman with the purple glasses should be fired. Never, in all my years, have I ever been so abominably treated by an employee.' End quote."

"How much was the fine?" Marche asked.

"Fifty cents."

Marche whistled. "That's a whopper."

"I've seen people throw tantrums over a dime. Nothing surprises me in this business." Phyllis heaved a sigh. "Guess I'll waive the late fee. Less of a headache that way. *And* I'll apologize profusely on Ebony's behalf. Though I'm sure this lady's just being a bitch. There's no way Ebony would have done that."

Phyllis started to type, her fingers clacking noisily on the keyboard. Marche crossed her legs and swung her foot. "Oops," she murmured when she accidentally kicked the desk. She was thinking about the book drop. Even from across the workroom, she could hear the metal clanging as someone threw items down one of the chutes.

"That should take care of it," Phyllis said, turning from the monitor. "I've been meaning to have a chat with you since last week. But things like this"—she hitched a thumb at the computer,"—keep popping up. Sometimes I feel more like a politician than a library employee."

Marche nodded and stifled a yawn. On a personal level, Phyllis bored her to tears. Marche had never had much tolerance for shallowness. And her boss was about as deep as a wading pool. Learning that Phyllis had called an employee out of work for non-work-related matters knocked her down yet another notch in Marche's book.

"So, we were talking about Jeff."

"Yes," Marche agreed.

"He left the library in December, and I've been without an assistant since. With budget cuts and all, I wasn't sure if we'd get to hire another one."

Marche sat up a little straighter, folded her hands on her knees. Finally, Phyllis had something interesting to say!

"I've been hounding our director about it for months. I really can't function to the best of my ability without an assistant."

Marche nodded. At the same time, she found herself unintentionally glancing at the crossword puzzle lying on top of the desk calendar.

"So, here's the news. We *finally* got the go-ahead to advertise the vacancy. It'll be posted on the city website next week. What do you think?"

"That's wonderful," Marche said. "I'm sure everyone will be relieved to have the extra help."

"About the *job*, Marche. What do you think? The assistant functions as the head of the department when I'm off the clock. You've managed a bookstore, haven't you?"

"Oh!" Marche exclaimed, playing dumb. "You mean—"

"That's right. You have the credentials and you already work here, so I'd say your chances of getting the promotion are strongly in your favor." *Ring! Ring!* Phyllis glanced at the phone display and reached for the receiver. "The opportunity's there, if you're interested. You'd have more responsibility. But the pay would reflect that."

"Of course."

"Phyllis speaking," the supervisor said, placing the receiver to her ear.

Marche walked away from her boss' office, smiling from ear-to-ear. She hummed as she emptied the book drop. Not even touching a book soaked in a suspicious yellow liquid which dripped onto her shoe, could quell her good cheer. When her shift was over, she called the human resources department and spoke to Florence.

"No need to fill out an application," the woman said. "Just shoot me an email stating that you're interested in the position. I'll contact you when it's time to schedule an interview."

At last, Marche thought, things were looking up!

Thirteen

THE WATER FELT JUST right—not too hot, not too cold. Marche plugged the drain and let the faucet run full blast as she helped Stella undress.

"Lift up your arms."

Marche tugged on the shirt as it caught around Stella's head and then worked on her pants. When the child was fully unclothed, she jumped into the bathtub, splashing water onto Marche.

"Hey, watch it. You got me wet," Marche said with a laugh.

Stella stretched out on her stomach and kicked at the water.

"Do you want some bubbles?"

"Yeah!"

Marche pulled the bottle of bubble bath out from beneath the bathroom sink and squirted a teaspoon's worth under the faucet. Bubbles formed instantly. Giggling, Stella blew holes in the expanding white froth.

Marche picked up the beach bucket she kept next to the tub and dumped Stella's toys into the water. A plastic Miss Piggy bobbled erratically on the surface. A red plastic boat fell sideways onto the water and gradually sank. A Matchbox car took a treacherous nosedive into the deep unknown. Several other toys floated up and down in a soft rhythm.

Marche turned the nozzle off when the water was about six inches deep. Stella grabbed a miniature Styrofoam animal and set Miss Piggy on its scaly green back.

"Zoom. Zoom. Zoom-zoom-zoom."

"What's Miss Piggy doing?" Marche asked.

Perched on the toilet seat, she watched Stella play. Bath time was as fun for Marche as it was for her daughter. If ever she could forget who she was and what a wretched mess her life had become, it was when Miss Piggy jumped into the mountain of soapsuds.

"She's being boat-chased!" Stella recovered the sunken red boat and placed an army figurine in it.

Marche planted her elbows on her knees, cupped her chin in her hand. "Who's chasing her?"

"The bad guy in the boat." Stella pushed the red boat and the motor noises intensified. She turned as the army toy chased the Muppet figure to the other side of the bathtub.

"Why does he want to catch her?" Marche asked.

"Cuz Froggy is mad at her."

"I see."

Miss Piggy's reptilian ride suddenly jumped into the air and fell down, creating a Niagara-sized splash. The red boat rocked perilously on the waves.

"Why is Kermit mad at her?"

"I dunno."

Marche sighed. Staring at the bubbles, she felt at ease. Tranquil. She watched Stella play for a few more minutes and then stood.

"Mommy's going into the other room. Call me if you need anything. Okay?"

"Uh-huh," Stella replied, flipping the boat upside down.

Leaving the bathroom door open, Marche headed toward the spare room at the end of the hall. She hesitated in the doorway before entering. The faltering step, the hitch in her breath—it was almost as if she expected to see something. Marche swallowed and stepped forward. The dimming light speared through the bare windows, illuminating the trunk. She flicked on the light switch.

She hadn't thought of the letters until this afternoon when a patron, who was interested in genealogy, asked her opinion on the interpretation of an old document. "I think that's Mary," she'd said. "And that's Paul...or is it Pearl?"

As she studied the old scrawl, faded and distorted by Xerox, she recalled the rush of excitement she'd experienced when she was twelve and had discovered her parents' old correspondence. She'd spent an entire rainy afternoon sprawled on the living room carpet, poring over each paper. As she read the letters—from friends, relatives, classmates—she felt like she'd met a version of her mother and father she hadn't known existed. When they died, she organized the letters according to date and placed them in a scrapbook. On days when she missed them the most, she flipped through the pages. Perusing their writings was more therapeutic than looking at their photographs. For the briefest of moments, the words on the paper brought them back to life.

Now she looked at the box, still in the center of the floor where she'd left it five days ago, and felt a sudden curiosity to explore its contents.

Folding her legs beneath her, she leaned forward and lifted the lid. Before, paint fumes and dust from the attic had dulled her sense of smell. She'd observed nothing but what her eyes had registered—papers discolored and creased with the passing of years. This time, however, her nostrils flared with recognition. Tucked under the scent of wood and musty papers: the faintest trace of perfume.

Could it be...love letters?

Marche sifted through the top layer of papers but found little of interest. Some were single-page typed documents of a technical nature, others handwritten. They had been carelessly handled, covered in telltale brown-ringed stains, the edges curled. There was a secretarial certificate, a marriage certificate for Charles Randolph Louis and Elizabeth Jane Langford, recipes recorded on index cards. On a half-sheet, folded twice, she found a poem about cowboys and horses. Accompanying it, on heavier stock, was a poorly rendered sketch of a brown stallion.

Carefully, one by one, she placed the papers in a pile on the floor.

When she reached the bottom of the trunk, she saw the treasure she'd been seeking. Note cards. Four inches square. Gray-striped. Tied together with a single yellow ribbon, the stack was about two inches thick.

Thrusting her hand into the box, she eagerly withdrew the mysterious bulk. She held it to her nose and inhaled. Her eyelids fluttered shut. *Lavender? Vanilla? Whatever it is, it smells sweet. Like a bouquet of dried flowers.* Someone had cherished these cards; she'd no doubt about it.

"I wonder if these were Elizabeth's?" Marche mumbled, thinking of the marriage certificate.

Cradling the letters in her lap, she tugged on one end of the bow. Pulling the ribbon free, she draped it over the side of the box. Then she thumbed through the cards. She counted twenty-three in all.

Picking up the topmost card, she unfolded it.

The handwriting caught her attention first. It was slanted, broad, and nearly indecipherable. And it didn't match the style in which the date was written. Placed at the top right-hand corner, the month and year (September, 1952) had been recorded in a darker, blacker shade of ink. The letters were smaller, the lines cleaner.

Marche read the contents slowly. A few words she was unable to identify with certainty, but she understood the gist of it.

It was a poem. Well, a juvenile attempt at one. The writer ("Butch," according to the signature) was certainly no Shakespeare. His prose was flowery but unoriginal as he compared his beloved's beauty to the sky at sunset.

"Faster, Piggy, faster!" Stella squealed down the hall.

Had Elizabeth Langford kept letters from a former lover? Butch seemed an unlikely nickname for someone named Charles. But then...

Marche glanced at the top of the letter. It had been addressed to "Angel," so maybe Elizabeth wasn't the recipient after all? She'd assumed it was an endearment. But what if Angel was the girl's actual name?

"Then who...?"

Marche checked the other letters. All had been dated in that same neat hand. Marche made sure they were in chronological order and then picked up the second letter.

The notes started out simple, straightforward yet sweet. Butch reminded her of adolescent boys she'd known in high school—eager to please, but also just as eager to appease his raging hormones. He lavished Angel with compliments and begged her to meet him at various secret rendezvous spots. When he sensed a potential rival, he threatened to retaliate by going to an upcoming barn dance with a girl named Wilma.

"High school, indeed," Marche murmured.

By the seventh letter, it became obvious that their relationship had progressed beyond innocent flirtation. Marche felt herself blushing. The content was intimate, almost obscene, as Butch made observations about Angel's body that only a lover would know.

Marche paused in her reading to check her watch; Stella hadn't made a sound in nearly ten minutes. "How're you doing in there, Stella?"

"Good!" came the high-pitched reply, followed by a fresh round of splashing.

In the letters that followed, the relationship between Butch and Angel seesawed from a gentle state of calm, lapping waves to one characterized by tumultuous sea swells. Beginning with the twelfth letter—which revealed that Butch had followed through with his promise to take Wilma to the dance—all feelings of tenderness steadily disintegrated. Gone was the fumbling yearning to please. Gone was the adoration. The letters—short and terse—simply started and ended. No recipient.

Seriously? Marche thought. *You took the girl's virginity. She's not some stray dog you can just shoo out of your yard when you no longer want to play.*

"Jump Froggy! She's getting away!" Stella exclaimed. The resounding splash sounded like a messy one.

"Keep the water in the tub!" Marche yelled, temporarily distracted by the unpleasant thought of having to mop the bathroom floor.

As she set down the twentieth letter, she wondered if she should continue. The flutter of anticipation she'd felt when she unearthed the letters had dwindled. In its place she felt deflated and sorry that she'd ever opened them. But then she *did* continue. Because there were only three letters left.

In the next note, which consisted of a single paragraph, Butch spoke of "nonsense" and "very bad tidings." For the first time, he also revealed Angel's identity.

Marche quickly sucked in her breath. "Agatha Marshall?" she whispered, unbelieving. Then, as if to answer her question, the letter continued: *The bell you're hearing doesn't exist. It's all in your head.*

Marche shook her own head. The annoyance she felt toward the old woman softened ever so slightly; Butch was obviously a cad.

The last letter was, by far, the worst of the lot. Marche cringed as she perused the contents. The words, pressed so hard into the paper that she could feel their outline on the other side, were weighted with hate and anger. She could almost hear a man's voice shouting the words into her ears.

GET RID OF IT.

She reread this line—wondering if it could possibly refer to anything other than an abortion, which she doubted—and then moved on. *Chuck said you might go live with your cousins upstate. It's a good idea. Leave and don't ever come back.* As she closed the letter, she wondered why Agatha had kept it. Why torture herself by holding onto painful memories? Why not rip it to shreds? Or burn it?

Marche felt slightly sick, her mouth dry. She re-tied the letters and returned them to the box. Then she hastily gathered up the other papers and tossed them on top. She'd assumed the contents had belonged to someone long dead and buried. Not someone very much alive and with whom she'd actually engaged in a face-to-face conversation. Twice. *I'm no better than a busybody. A no-good busybody.* She wondered how she would keep a straight face the next time Agatha approached her. For there was no doubt in her mind that she *would* see the old woman again. *Damn me and my no-good curiosity.*

Shutting the lid, she stood up and turned off the light.

"Time for bed," Marche yelled. "You've been in there almost an hour." She expected to hear a whine of protest as she stepped into the hall. No matter how long Stella spent playing in the water, she always seemed to want just a little more time.

"Stella?"

All seemed unnaturally quiet in the bathroom. She couldn't hear any "wee wee Froggy got Piggy" exclamations or the kicking up of water. If she hadn't filled it herself, Marche would think that the bathtub was empty and that Stella was fast asleep in bed. *Something's wrong.* Running the last few steps, she rushed into the bathroom.

Her heart dropped.

Where was Stella? She saw the bath toys floating on the bath water, but nothing else. It couldn't be—

"Oh my God—!"

She ran to the bathtub, her heart constricting painfully in her chest. The bubbles had long since dissolved. She peered into the clear water hoping, praying, that the unthinkable hadn't happened. Instead, she encountered her worst fear.

"Nooo!"

Stella lay on her back, still and completely submerged. Only the tip of her nose broke the surface. She looked asleep, her eyes shut and her features relaxed. Her brown hair floated like a halo about her head.

"Nonononono..."

Marche thrust her arms into the cool water and slid them under Stella's back. Water sloshed out of the bathtub; Miss Piggy bobbed furiously up and down in the waves.

"Wake up, baby, wake up!" Marche shouted.

She laid Stella on the floor and caressed her pale cheeks, unsure what to do. Panic and fear made her stupid.

What do I do?

She moaned.

She'd taken a course in CPR, but that was nearly twenty years ago. Was she supposed to breathe into Stella's mouth eight times or four? Was she supposed to do twelve chest compressions or just eight? Was she even thinking of the right numbers at all? *I can't remember!*

Marche cried in frustration. Somewhere in the back of her mind, she heard Dom speaking to her, compelling her to action. His voice was calm but firm. Soft yet hard. He was the lighthouse guiding her to safe harbor during a storm. *Seconds are minutes; minutes are hours. You have no time to waste. Move it, Marche. Move it, now!*

In one swift motion, Marche turned Stella onto her side and slapped her back. When the child didn't respond, she balled her hand into a fist. She pounded once, twice, three times between her shoulder blades.

"Come on, Stella! Come on!"

Fresh tears welled in Marche's eyes, mingled with the bathwater as they streaked down her cheeks.

"Open your eyes." She groaned. "Make her open her eyes, Dom. I don't care if you're dead, you selfish son of a bitch. Just *fix* this! Our daughter is...Our daughter is..."

She lifted her fist again and...Stella coughed.

Marche felt something come loose inside of her. As if she'd been wearing a corset around her organs and the laces suddenly broke.

"That's a good girl! Come on, Stella! Wake up!"

Marche opened her hand and patted Stella roughly on the back. The child coughed a second time and water gushed out of her mouth in a clear stream. Marche kept her on her side until it seemed that she had coughed up everything in her system. Then Marche grabbed the towel from the counter and wrapped Stella in it. Picking her up, she cradled the child in her arms.

"How do you feel, baby?" Marche asked.

Stella's fingers were white and pruned, but color was slowly creeping back into her face. She looked at Marche with half-closed eyes and mumbled something incomprehensible.

"You're okay," Marche said, hugging her tighter. "You're okay, Stella. And Mommy won't let anything bad happen to you ever again. I promise."

Marche stood in the kitchen two hours later, the bottle of vodka in her hand. The emergency room doctor who'd examined Stella was rough in his manners but thorough. "Her lungs are clear and her heartbeat's fine," he declared. "Lethargy is normal—expect her to sleep heavily for the next several hours. If she contracts a fever, starts coughing, or seems disoriented, bring her to the hospital immediately."

Marche took Stella home and tucked her into bed. Though she should have been exhausted—from the traumatic experience, from the late hour—she was wide awake.

Now she unscrewed the cap on the vodka. Lifted it to her lips. Paused. She recalled the expression on Vale's face when she'd offered him a drink during his visit. It wasn't the hour of the day that had prompted that reaction from him.

It was the way she'd held the bottle; the desperation in her voice that she hadn't been able to mask. The memory of it embarrassed her. But, more importantly, it knocked sense into her brain.

Before she could taste its contents, she recapped the bottle and stuffed it back into the cabinet.

Crossing the kitchen, she reached for the cigarettes that she'd left on top of the refrigerator. She stepped onto the front porch. Closed the door quietly behind her. At the foot of the driveway, she stopped.

She tipped the pack upside down and extracted a cigarette. She was trembling now, so violently that she dropped the lighter in the process. She squatted to pick it up. The pavement scraped her knuckles. Instinctively, she hissed. But she didn't mind the pain from the slight abrasion. In fact, she welcomed it. She *deserved* it.

Lighting the cigarette proved troublesome; it was like trying to shoot a swinging target with blurred vision. When the tip finally caught the flame, burned orange, she struggled to bring it to her lips.

The first drag, long and deep, stung her lungs. The second drag, just as drawn out, stung a little less.

And so she stood there—shaking in the hot night air and saturated in her own self-imposed cocoon of smoke—until there was only one cigarette left in the pack.

Fourteen

"Natty showed me how to make a cat with a cradle with string."

Marche rested her fingers on the keys, which dangled from the ignition. "Which one is Natty?"

"'Member, Mommy?" Stella had awakened Thursday morning without any lingering side effects from her near-drowning experience. Today she was as energetic as ever, practically bouncing in the back seat. "'Member the brownie spot on her face?"

Marche thought for a moment and realized that she did remember. Stella liked to dig up roly-polies with Natalie in the playground.

"Is she your best friend?"

"Uh-huh. I like Mayjane and Jack too-oo," Stella said, the last word drawn out like a train on the track whistling its approach.

As Marche shut the driver's door, Stella's muffled words pattered against the closed windows. She smiled. From the moment she'd picked Stella up at Melody's Ensemble, she hadn't stopped chatting about her eventful day.

"—and we holded the flag," Stella continued as Marche opened the back passenger side door.

"That sounds super neat."

"Uh-huh."

Marche unbuckled the seatbelt and Stella scooted off the seat, the backs of her legs rubbing noisily against the vinyl.

"So you have lots of best friends, then? What a lucky girl."

Marche walked down the driveway to check the mailbox. Opening the lid, she discovered a pizza flyer and a handful of envelopes.

“Bane is fun too,” Stella declared, hopping among the weeds.

Marche sifted through the mail. Most of it was junk she could toss straight into the garbage. Behind the electric bill, however, she found an envelope addressed to Malcolm Greene.

“He likes to play hopscotch with me and Mayjane and he is goo-ood.”

“He sounds like a fun boy to play with.”

“But when he has to jump over the square he’s not s’posed to, he falls over. It’s so funny.” Stella covered her mouth with both hands and giggled.

“I bet it is,” Marche agreed. “But you know, it isn’t nice to laugh at other people. What if you hurt Blaine’s feelings?”

“His feelings?” Stella seemed to think about it as she kicked the grass with her yellow jellies.

Marche’s purse slid down her shoulder; she tried not to drop the mail as her elbow dipped with its weight. Stepping onto the stoop, she sorted through the keys and unlocked the front door.

“Are you hungry?”

Stella stood inside the foyer, jumping up and down like her feet were on fire. “Un-huh.” Strands of hair whipped her cheeks as she shook her head.

“What I’d give to have just an ounce of your energy,” Marche said, suddenly feeling drained.

Stella flew up the stairs on her tiptoes. A few seconds later Marche heard the unmistakable *clang-rustle-clang* of Stella sorting through toys.

Marche dropped the purse and mail onto the small table by the front door and headed into the living room. Plopping onto the sofa, she closed her eyes. The house was quiet except for the occasional clattering noise drifting down the stairs.

“Chicken noodle soup,” she muttered. “And cornbread.” Yes, that mouth-watering combination would suffice for tonight’s five-star dinner.

Marche sat up and rubbed the lines that seemed permanently etched into her forehead. As she stood and stretched, she considered the mail on the table. Which house was it again? She retrieved the envelope and read the address a second time: 712 Victor Street. Climbing onto the couch, she anchored her knees in the cushions and lifted the corner of the white lace curtains. Gazing to the left, she wondered how far down the street Malcolm Greene lived. She leaned forward and craned her neck. From this angle, she couldn't see beyond the fourth house on the opposite side. Large block lettering posted above the garage identified it as 848.

Just as she was about to drop the curtain, Marche noticed a figure out of the corner of her eye. Whipping her head to the right, she saw a boy on a bicycle. The same boy she'd seen before. *What is he doing?* He'd parked in the middle of the residential street, one foot hitched on a pedal, and was looking directly at her.

Marche pressed her face close to the windowpane. She lifted her hand and waved, shooing him away as though he were an egret perched on the hood of her car. The boy responded by flicking her a double birdie and extending his tongue in a snakish salute. Then he twisted the handlebars, kicked the bike in motion, and sped down Washington.

"What the hell is up with that punk?" Marche wondered.

And why was he staring? She couldn't recall ever seeing him before she'd moved into the house. Did he live nearby? Was it possible that she'd had a close run-in with him while she was driving, hadn't realized it, and he'd followed her home? Moving away from the window, she shook her head. *He's probably just some weirdo neighbor who likes to get under people's skin.*

Marche headed up the stairs. Inside Stella's bedroom, she discovered a makeshift tent constructed from a pillowcase and two boxes. Stella held a Barbie doll in each of her hands; she talked at a fervent pace, gleefully bossing the timid doll around with the belligerent one.

"Hey, bug."

"Shh," Stella said to the blonde-haired doll. "Mommy's talking."

"We need to put a pair of shoes on those feet," Marche declared while walking toward the closet. "We're going on a field trip."

Sorting through the messy closet floor, she managed to locate a pair of matching pink, strawberry patterned flip-flops. Stella made a whining sound as Marche slid them onto feet.

"Do I hafto?"

"Yes, Stella. You aren't old enough to stay home by yourself. Now stand up."

After a third *stand up*, uttered in the stern tone of a mother about to lose her temper, Stella reluctantly obeyed. She curled her fingers into a small fist, however, and pounded her thigh in objection.

"Behave yourself," Marche warned. "Or there won't be any dessert for you tonight."

Upon reaching the foyer, Marche grabbed the envelope addressed to Malcolm Greene and opened the front door. One foot over the threshold, she recalled Bicycle Boy. She returned inside for the house keys and, for safe measure, turned the deadbolt.

"Where we goin'?" Stella asked.

"Just down the street."

"Are we gonna see Natty?"

"No, baby. Natalie doesn't live on our street."

"Where *does* she live?"

"Don't know, bug. You'll have to ask her if you want to know."

Unhappy with that reply, Stella pouted and quit speaking. *Crankyville on the horizon,* Marche thought with a sigh. She placed a hand firmly on one of Stella's small shoulders as they crossed the road.

Marche soon wished that she'd changed out of her work clothes before leaving the house. Her long-sleeved blouse and matching black slacks soaked up the sunlight like a water-starved dog lapping at a puddle. The cloudless sky and still air didn't help matters.

Vale, lounging in a chair on his front porch, looked up from his book to wave at them as they neared his yard.

"Howdy," he called out. "Fine weather we're having today, isn't it?" Incredibly enough, he seemed to mean it. Why else would he be wearing denim jeans and a shirt with sleeves that covered his arms to the wrists?

"Maybe if you're a reptile," Marche replied, returning the salute. "I'm sweating pools here."

Vale guffawed, refitted his baseball cap, and returned to his reading.

The address Marche sought was located three plots down from Vale's. The numbers 7-1-2 had been painted at a vertical slant on a novelty mailbox in the shape of a friendly gray porpoise. The mail slot appeared between the mammal's extended flippers, under its cartoonish grin. Marche slapped the envelope across her palm. As she contemplated leaving it to the dolphin's care, she noticed the black Toyota Sequoia parked in the open garage.

"Time to meet the neighbors? Come on, Stella," she said, giving her daughter a slight nudge forward.

Unlike all of the other plots on Victor, this one didn't have a single tree on it. The grass was thick and green and free of weeds. Alongside the house, hibiscus bloomed in a rich rainbow of reds and pinks. Trimmed hedges lined the front porch. As they got closer, Marche noticed bronze dolphin statues, with diamond accented blowholes, jutting through the plants at regular intervals. An ocean-themed mat welcomed visitors at the front door. Beside it stood a hand painted ceramic flowerpot showcasing stylized starfish and seahorses. Sunflowers sprouted from the center.

Opening the screen door, she knocked lightly.

As the seconds ticked on, Marche began to wonder if anyone was actually home. Stella crept over to the hedges and squatted. Reaching out, she tentatively petted one of the dolphins. "Oooh," she cooed. Then she began to talk to the decoration like she did with her toys, telling it what a pretty animal it was.

Marche lifted her hand. Maybe no one had heard her? She knocked a second time—hard enough to redden her knuckles. Another solid minute ticked by. Finally, when she was about to call it quits and go home, the doorknob turned. A man wearing a Hawaiian shirt, half-tucked into a pair of cargo shorts, opened the door. He was of average height and build, a slim gold chain hanging around his neck.

"Mr. Greene?" Marche asked.

"Yes?"

"Hi, I'm Marche Baker. Your new neighbor. I bought the house on the corner."

The man's welcoming smile cracked. The change was subtle—so subtle that Marche almost didn't catch it. "Yes?" he repeated, his dark eyes expressionless.

Puzzled by his reaction, she quickly explained the mishap. "I received a piece of your mail by mistake."

She held out the envelope.

Malcolm stared at her hand, unmoving. A moment of silence stretched between them. Marche cleared her throat and stretched her arm a few inches further. She felt like a trapper offering a can of tuna to a feral cat. Uncertainty rolled off him in waves, as palpable as the air conditioning that wafted through the open door. She flapped the envelope. At last, he took it. But he touched the paper reluctantly, pinching the corner with the tips of fingers, holding it before him as though it possessed an infectious disease.

"Thank you," Malcolm said. "Please, feel free to pop it in the box if it happens again."

"Okay, I——"

The door closed in her face.

Marche stood there, open-mouthed. "Well, I never..." She ran her hand through her hair and turned from the house.

"I like the sea, too. Daddy used to..."

"Say goodbye to the dolphin," Marche barked. "We're leaving." Without waiting, she paraded Stella down the driveway.

What just happened? Had she said something offensive? That couldn't be the problem. All she'd done was introduce herself. Was it her body language? But she'd smiled and kept her voice polite. So what *was* it, then? She scowled—offended and confounded in equal parts.

As she stepped onto the road, a lime green Dodge Charger nearly flattened her toes.

"Hey! Jackass!" Marche yelled. "Watch where you're going!"

The tires squealed as the driver quickly braked and swerved into a driveway near the dead-end side of the street.

"Assholes," Marche murmured as two young men hopped out of the car and swaggered toward the house. Bending down, she wrapped her arms around Stella and hoisted the child onto her hip. By the time she reached Vale's, she was huffing and puffing under the weight.

Vale met her at the end of the drive. "Heard the commotion," he said. "Everything all right?"

"Just dandy."

Marche paused and took a deep breath. Lowering Stella to the ground, she took another deep breath.

"Truth be told, I'm irritated as hell. First the punk"—she gestured toward Washington"—then the grump." And she jerked her chin in the opposite direction. "Then...did you see the way that brat was driving?"

"Aye."

"I mean, this is a neighborhood. Not a highway. What if Stella had run into the road?"

Marche bit her lip; her throat ached with emotion. *Don't think about car accidents.* Frustrated, she jerkily unbuttoned her shirt sleeves and rolled them to her elbows. "Do you know Malcolm Greene?"

"I do," Vale said, rocking on his heels.

"Is he the neighborhood Grinch or something?"

"I'm not sure I get your meaning," Vale replied.

Stella ran into Vale's yard and began to kick every mushroom in sight. One of her flip-flops flew into the air. Oblivious, she continued to zigzag through the grass.

"Watch out for ants, Stella!" Marche turned to Vale. "I was just at his house. All I did was introduce myself, and he slammed the door in my face."

"Is that so?" Vale plucked a toothpick from his front pocket and stuck it between his teeth. Directing his bright blue gaze toward the Greene residence, he folded his arms in a thinker's pose.

"I wish it weren't," Marche replied.

After a moment of silence, Vale shifted his gaze in the opposite direction. Focusing on the street corner, he said, "I wouldn't take it personal."

"Kind of hard not to when the man almost clipped my nose."

"It ain't his fault. Not really."

Marche shook her head, confused. "Is he ill?"

Lifting a weathered hand, Vale began to twist the toothpick in his mouth. "It's the house."

"Excuse me?" Marche shielded her eyes with a hand, as though seeing her companion more clearly would clarify her hearing.

Vale looked down at her, his eyes seeming to shimmer in the sunlight. “I’ll tell you all about it if you like, but you’ll need to come inside. This calls for a drink.”

Fifteen

THE CHORUS OF BARKING—AUDIBLE from the street—magnified tenfold as they neared the porch. Vale opened the screen door. Marche trailed two steps behind, with Stella close enough to bump into her backside if she suddenly stopped. Inside the house, two large canines of mixed heritage greeted them with wagging tails. Stella squealed with glee; Marche fell back a step.

"Down, girls!" Vale ordered.

The dogs quieted instantly. Trotting off, they settled underneath the dining room table, their heads on their paws.

"I thought you had a zoo in here," Marche said.

"Nah. Just the two of 'em. Loud as lions, but harmless as bunnies." Vale removed his White Sox cap and hung it on the mail and key holder nailed to the wall just inside the front door. "What'll it be?"

"Tap water's fine. Thanks." Marche followed her host into the kitchen, which was less like a room and more like a hallway that stretched behind the den.

Vale fumbled through a mess of items above the refrigerator and withdrew a bottle of whiskey. Reaching for two square-shaped tumblers from the dish rack, he turned on the spigot and filled one glass with water. "Ice?" Marche declined. Tipping the whiskey bottle, which was two-thirds full, he carelessly poured several ounces into the second glass. Honey-colored droplets splashed down the sides and left a rim on the countertop.

"Thanks," Marche said when he handed her the water.

Vale picked up the whiskey-filled glass and headed into the den. "Make yourself cozy," he said, with a grand sweep of his gnarled fingers.

Marche briefly considered where to sit. Her options were limited to a beige sofa placed in front of the window, a red faux leather recliner beside it, or a wooden rocker in the opposite corner. She chose the sofa.

As Marche lowered her weight onto it, a collection of dog hairs floated up from the plaid throw tucked into the cushions. She rubbed her nose to stave off a sneeze. Stella crouched beside her, elbows planted on the sofa, her bottom sticking out. Marche offered her some water and she sipped absentmindedly, making small slurping noises as she stared across the room at the dogs.

Vale, meanwhile, put on a comical show. Though the rocking chair bordered on tiny, he seemed determined to fit himself into it. First he bent forward, standing with his torso almost parallel to the floor. Then he bent his knees—a delicate maneuver which required several seconds of intense concentration. At last he made contact with the seat. A satisfactory grunt passed through his lips. The wood, surprisingly, remained mum.

"Sturdier than it looks," Vale said.

"Must be," Marche agreed.

"Marlene's father built it when she was expecting. Spent her whole life rocking away in this chair. Knitting, sewing, reading. You name it." He patted the armrest. "I feel a little bit closer to her when I sit here."

"Has she been gone long?"

"Four years," Vale said, his chest rising on a sigh. "Natural causes."

There wasn't a coffee table in the room, just a few end tables. Marche set her glass on the Mission-style piece beside the sofa, between a TV guide and the remote control. *Natural causes.* She turned the phrase over in her mind. Why did it sound odd? Perhaps it was because those closest to her had most certainly *not* died from natural causes.

"They don't bite," Vale said to Stella. "Calamity and James are good dogs. Why don't you try petting 'em? They like little girls."

"Are they used to kids?" Marche asked, suddenly apprehensive.

"Aye. The dogs usually hitchhike in the Camino's bed when I drive to Jessie's on Sundays. She cooks a fine stuffed turkey," he added.

"Is that your daughter?"

"Granddaughter," Vale replied. "Her twins are little monsters and get into everything. The dogs help to keep 'em occupied."

Stella narrowed her eyes in concentration, focusing intently on the large beasts as Vale spoke. After a moment's hesitation, she stood upright and puffed out her tiny stomach. She laid a hand on Marche's knee as she stepped forward. "Umm," she said. Taking another step forward, she paused. The dogs, sensing that they might get a new playmate, thumped their tails encouragingly on the floor.

Vale watched Stella pussyfoot toward the dining room. He waited until she'd squatted under the table before he spoke.

"About Malcolm..."

Marche leaned forward and draped her hands between her knees.

"I've known him for a very long time," Vale said. "He and Vance—that's my son—went to school together."

"Are they friends?"

The old man balanced the untouched whiskey upon his knee. "That's right. Vance lives in Chicago. He flies down for a visit every six months or so. After all these years, the two of 'em still find time to chum around together."

Marche felt a moment's regret that she'd never formed a long-lasting friendship with anyone. Jane from grade school became Stacey from junior high, who then became Monica from senior high. She'd made a few friends at the university before she'd dropped out, but they'd gradually faded out of the picture. The only one she still kept in touch with was Vanessa. But they rarely communicated beyond brief emails wishing each other "Happy Birthdays" and "Merry Christmases." The closest she'd come to an extended, meaningful relationship was Dom—and their time together had been cruelly cut short.

"The point is, Malcolm was a good kid. And that hasn't changed. He's not the sort of man who takes to telling stories."

"What do you mean?" Marche asked.

Lifting the whiskey halfway to his mouth, Vale paused. He lowered the glass and tapped his fingers on the rim. For the first time since she'd met him, he stared at his feet while he spoke.

"Malcolm believes that your house is haunted."

Marche's heart fluttered with surprise. "Come again?" she asked, shifting uncomfortably on the sofa.

Vale looked up, his face somber. "I tell you this only because I'd hate for you to hold a grudge against the man. Whatever you might think, he's a decent soul."

Plucking a dog hair from her pant leg, Marche tried to keep her voice neutral. "Why does he think that the house is haunted?"

"One night—oh, about ten years back, I'd say—there was an accident on Washington. It was a pretty serious bang-up job. Kid without a license—and drunk to boot—smashed into one of the utility poles. Knocked out the electricity for half a block."

Vale stretched his legs before him.

"People get curious, you know? They want to know what's going on. Me? I saw all I needed to see from the front porch. But Malcolm—he decided to join the crowd of onlookers."

"Woof! Woof!" In the dining room, Stella was hopping around on her hands and knees. The dogs, still lying on the floor, threw their front paws happily in response. A soft *ruff* followed suit.

"About eleven o'clock, someone starts knocking on the front door. Not your casual *rat-a-tat-tat*." Vale cocked his head as if he could still hear the sound. Hear it and analyze it. "No. There was something hurried, something desperate about it.

"So I slip on my robe. Open the door. And there's Malcolm. Standing there. Chest heaving. Eyes a-bulging. If ever you could apply the phrase 'white as a sheet' to a Black man, it was then."

Lifting the glass to his lips, he swallowed a mouthful of whiskey.

"I invite him inside and he stumbles over to the couch—right where you're sitting. He's shaking, so I offer him a drink. I wait for him to calm down. And he tells me—"

Marche inhaled a dog hair and sneezed. Vale looked toward the table wedged between the rocker and television set. He shuffled around some magazines, lifted paperbacks.

"No tissues, I'm afraid. Can I get you a towel?"

"I'm all right," Marche said, touching her finger to her nostrils. "What did Malcolm tell you?"

Vale resettled against the chair back, rested the glass on his knee.

"He tells me that he's walking past that house—your house—when he happens to look up at it. Everyone on the street is out of power. But there's a window on the second floor that's glowing—candlelight probably. And in that light, he sees the outline of a person. It's a woman, he thinks, with long dark hair. Now, it's a moonless night. And this person is in silhouette. There's also the distance to take into consideration. But..." Vale swished the contents of his glass. "Malcolm's convinced the woman is staring at him. Gives him the willies."

"I don't get it," Marche said.

Vale paused for effect. "There was no woman in that house. Chuck was a widow. Had been for many years."

"Maybe he had a visitor."

"No," Vale said with a firm shake of the head. "Not Chuck. He'd started his hermiting ways by then."

Marche leaned back—and instantly regretted the decision. Another mass of dog hairs lifted into the air. She sneezed again.

"I don't mean to sound rude," Marche said, her eyes wetting. "But how does a woman standing in a window suddenly make a house haunted?"

"Well, that's just the first part of the story," Vale replied in a matter-of-fact tone. Swallowing a generous portion of the golden-brown liquor, he coughed and continued.

"Malcolm gets to Washington, and he's watching the goings-on along with everybody else. He's distracted by the paramedics, the stretchers, the police officers roping off the scene with tape. He forgets all about the woman he's seen in the window. Then he decides to head home."

"Woof, woof!" Still on her hands and knees, Stella hopped towards Marche and then hopped back to the dining room table. "Woof, woof!"

"What happened?" Marche asked, trying to tune out Stella's noisy antics.

"Malcolm turns to leave," Vale continued, tapping his foot on the floor. "He's walking past the house when he stops. He turns around. No particular reason.

Just feels like catching one last glimpse of the red and blue lights. Then he turns back and...there's a woman standing on the road before him. And he's *certain* that she's the same person from the window."

"Is that it?" Marche asked when her host said nothing else.

"That's all that he told me," Vale replied. "Don't mean there's not more to the story, though."

Marche pulled her shirt sleeves down and re-buttoned them at the wrists. "Malcolm must be one of the sensitive types. That doesn't sound very frightening to me." She stopped. What had she seen in that upstairs room? She shook her head to banish the unpleasant thought and gazed into the dining room.

Stella was playing with one of the dog's ears—the dog with the brown and white patches saturating its coat. She folded back the furry triangles and draped them across the dog's head like a hat. Vale had underrated his dogs' demeanor; they had the patience of saints.

"Mr. Vale..." Marche sucked in her breath and squeezed her hands. "You don't really believe in ghosts and haunted houses, do you?"

"I'll tell you what I *know*," Vale replied. "I have never seen a grown man so frightened out of his wits as Malcolm was on that night when he tottered through that front door and consumed two full glasses of whiskey in under five minutes."

"But a haunted house? Really?"

Vale shrugged.

Despite the sun beating on her back, Marche felt a chill between her shoulder blades; she loosened her fingers and clasped her elbows. "I don't believe in ghosts." But who was she trying to convince? Vale or herself? "Only tortured psyches. That woman must have meant something to him. Our memories, our guilt—they can trick our eyes into seeing things that aren't there."

Again, Vale shrugged.

"Besides," Marche said, in an attempt to put the matter to rest, "who could possibly be haunting the house?"

"I have my suspicions." Vale's hand shook as he lifted the glass and emptied its contents; some of the whiskey missed its mark and dribbled down the side of his mouth.

As he set the empty glass aside, Vale suddenly looked ten years older. His large blue eyes narrowed into slits. When he exhaled, he sounded feeble and tired.

"Betty Langford," he said at last, wiping the whiskey from his chin with a shirtsleeve.

"Who—"

"Chuck's wife."

The second dog, which resembled a shepherd mix with its bushy gray tail and pointed snout, trotted into the living room and sat by her master's side. Tilting her black nose upward, she nudged at the gnarled fingers dangling over the armrest.

Vale patted the dog's head and continued.

"Chuck fell in love with Betty when he was still in high school, but he enlisted in the army after graduation. Wanted to see the world, I guess. Came home—oh, I think it was about a decade later—and romanced her all over again." Vale sighed. "Chuck was the happiest I'd ever seen him when he and Betty tied the knot. If poor Betty hadn't died so young...I imagine they'd have lived happily together for a very long time."

Except for the sound of the dog's panting, the room was silent. Marche glanced toward the dining room and saw Stella lying on her stomach, petting the canine's coat in a slow caress. By the looks of things, she'd probably be asleep within five minutes.

"What happened?" Marche asked, turning back.

"It was horrible—in the end."

Vale gave the dog a final pat on the rump and then stretched his legs again. The dog whined once before curling up on the floor in front of the television.

"Chuck and Betty married in 1967. Two years later, Betty got pregnant. That's when the, uh...the problems started."

"Problems?"

Vale tipped his head forward and closed his eyes. "She became forgetful at first. She'd set something aside—a pot, for instance—and then not remember where she'd put it. Then she'd find it days later in some obscure part of the house. This was early on in the pregnancy, before she was even showing."

He opened his eyes.

"Chuck didn't know what to make of it. He came to me, you know, but I wasn't of much use. Marlene never experienced anything of the kind when she was carrying Vance. The only difficulties she'd suffered were swollen feet and an insatiable craving for jalapeno peppers."

"I used to crave chips and ice cream in the middle of the night," Marche said.

Vale shook his head, lost in thought.

"As Betty got further into the pregnancy, Chuck caught her talking to herself. Sometimes she mumbled under her breath, other times, she ranted. A few times he came home to find her shouting into a corner, as though there was someone there. All of this was fairly harmless, but then...Betty started keeping a knife under her pillow. Chuck didn't know about it until he woke up bloody one night with a deep gash in his arm."

"Oh, no!" Marche softly exclaimed.

"Then, a few weeks before her due date, Betty took a knife with her into the tub." Vale rubbed his eyes with the pads of his thumbs. "I won't go into details, but...it was ugly. Worse than your worst nightmare."

Marche covered her mouth with both hands. Vale didn't need to give her a description of the scene for her to see it.

"By the time Chuck found her, there wasn't anything anybody could do. Except to clean up the mess and bury the poor lass."

Vale coughed.

"I can't imagine any rest in the afterlife for an end as violent as that," Vale said. "If anyone were to haunt that house, it would be Betty."

Vale's final words settled on the air like a noxious odor. Marche picked up the glass, sipped the warm water. But she couldn't wash down the metallic taste that had settled at the back of her throat.

Sixteen

Marche waited until after she'd tucked Stella into bed to prepare for her shower. The rational part of her brain declared that she'd put it off for this long because she didn't want to have to worry about Stella getting into trouble while she was in the bathroom. The primal part of her brain—the part that she tried to suppress—argued that she was hesitating because she didn't want to spend time in the room where a woman had suffered a grisly death.

Standing at the bureau, Marche considered the various colors of underwear at her disposal. Red, blue, ivory, black. Most of them were cotton. A few were silky with a lace trim waistband. All of them were practical—she'd never cared for the sexy styles on display at high-end lingerie stores. Comfort before fashion, she always declared.

You're stalling, one voice said.

I'm not, replied the other.

Next, she sorted through the gowns. The fabrics felt too heavy, too warm for summer. She opted for the tee shirt drawer.

You're afraid, the first voice said.

I'm uncomfortable, replied the second. *There's a difference.*

She grabbed the first garment her fingers touched and slammed the drawer shut. In the hallway, she held the nightclothes against her chest like a shield.

The light in the bathroom was still on from when Stella had brushed her teeth. For once, the child had seemed uninterested in bath time. And Marche, for once, hadn't felt inclined to press the issue.

Now she stood in the doorway to the room, a knight ready for battle. Examining the space with fresh eyes, she found nothing extraordinary about it—nothing that would indicate a bloody history.

The bathroom featured a not-so-charming fusion of antique and modern. The end result made sense, Marche thought, considering that Agatha—responsible for selling the house—had stood at the helm. The renovations included: vinyl flooring the color of sand; an oval sink with an attached oak cabinet beneath it, just large enough to store soaps and cleaners; and a towel rack drilled into the wall beside it consisting of three brushed nickel bars to match the overhead light fixture.

And then Marche had added her own touches of newness: a bamboo hamper placed under the towel rack, the fuzzy blue coverlet for the toilet seat, and lime green frog toothbrush and hand soap accessories that she placed on either side of the faucet. She'd also hung a medium-sized print of Haven Shores' coastline on the wall beside the door. When she washed her hands or flossed, she could see the clear blue waters reflected in the bathroom mirror.

The mirror, on the other hand, had *not* been updated. Flush against the wall, it was rectangular with the silver warping along the edges. The aquamarine wall tiles looked decades old; cracks threaded through some of the squares adjacent to the floor and bathtub. Then, of course, there was the tub itself. The mauve ceramic surface had chipped in a couple of places and a light brown stain ringed the edge.

Marche released a pent-up breath. The mismatching ensemble made sense to her now. Charles and Betty probably chose blue when they updated the bathroom. Then, when Betty... Marche shook her head. Charles must have replaced the bathtub with whatever was in vogue or on sale. She could empathize with how he must have felt when the salesperson asked him which model he wanted. In the aftermath of death, who cared about something as trivial as color coordination?

"I'm sure that's it," Marche said. "There's no way he would have kept the same tub."

Feeling only marginally better, she set her clean clothes on the toilet seat and disrobed, tossing her dirty laundry in the hamper. Taking another deep breath, she stepped into the tub. Goosebumps broke out on her flesh as her bare feet touched the cool surface. She reached for the shower curtain—teal with olive green lily pads, emerald frogs, and glittery yellow-orange goldfish. As she pulled it shut, a soft *thump* sounded down the hall. Marche paused. Tilted her head. Listened.

Maybe one of the boxes in her bedroom had fallen over?

She turned the shower nozzle, involuntarily jumping as the icy water splashed down on her. "Sss. Cold-cold-cold." She reached for the washcloth, scrubbed her face and arms. The muscles in her shoulders relaxed as the temperature gradually increased and the heat soaked into her flesh.

Reaching for the shampoo bottle, she lathered the sweet-smelling gel into a foaming heap upon her head. She let it sit. For a moment, she basked in the steam and the pineapple fragrance. She pretended that she was someone else. Somewhere else. Then she ducked under the spray and squeezed her eyes shut.

As the water massaged her head and the suds circled the drain, Marche found her thoughts inevitably drifting toward happier times. She recalled the first few years that she and Dom had spent together, the fun adventures they'd shared before Stella was born.

"Ouch!"

The engagement ring caught in her hair, stinging her scalp where she'd tugged too hard. Blindly, she untangled the strands; the band slipped off in the process. "Jesus Christ." Eyes still shut, she squatted and patted the bottom of the tub for her ring. Her searching hands finally located it on the metal drain. Slipping it back onto her third finger, she stood.

Marche tilted her head so that the water blasted her face. Holding her breath, she let the water pelt her skin for so long that she couldn't feel it anymore. Her cheeks went numb. The water roared in her ears, drowning out every other sound in the world.

She waited until the water began to cool before turning off the faucet. The bathtub felt like a sauna. Within its close quarters, she had washed away her worries and regained a sense of equilibrium.

Yanking the curtain open, she stepped onto the bath rug and squished the fabric between her toes. She bent over the tub, wrung her hair until a small stream of droplets plopped into the basin. Then she grabbed the bath towel. As she patted her neck and shoulders, another *thump*—louder than before—sounded down the hall.

Marche stilled.

When nothing else happened, she continued to wipe her arms and back. She dragged the towel across her stomach and down her legs.

Hanging the towel on the rack, she reached for her fresh clothes. She was pulling the cotton underwear over her hips when the thumping noise repeated. Had Stella gotten out of bed and decided to play with her toys?

"Stella?"

Marche stood by the bathroom sink in nothing but underwear and listened intently as the steam from the shower clung to her clean body. The only sound she heard was her own breathing.

Grabbing the tee shirt, she slid her arms through the sleeves. The garment—an Aerosmith concert souvenir from the nineties—had been Dom's. Though the artwork had faded, the threads remained intact. Now, as she pulled the shirt over her head, the hem falling past her hips, she felt as though she was draped in a protective blanket.

The *thump* sounded again, this time followed by a series of footsteps, clunky-sounding and inexplicably swift.

Marche's heart skipped a beat; a series of chills raced down her spine. She pressed her palm to her chest and clamped her teeth together. Slowly turning the door handle, she stepped out of the bathroom.

She peered into Stella's bedroom first. Everything—toys, clothes, furniture—remained in their former positions. Stella, curled up under the sheet, breathed softly in her sleep.

The spare room?

Marche swallowed her hesitation and twisted the knob. The door swung silently on its hinges. The light from the hallway slanted through the opening, illuminating the two paint cans and other paraphernalia she'd prepared for tomorrow's project, the box of letters, and nothing else. Shutting the door, she turned to the only room remaining on the second floor.

Marche licked her lips and tucked a clump of damp hair behind her ear.

Rubbing her arms, she crossed the floor. As she neared the doorway, a draft chilled her skin. She glanced upward. The vent above her head blew a constant stream of cold air. She wrote a mental note to check the thermostat when she went downstairs. Then, her bare feet touched the threshold to her bedroom.

Upright boxes and an unmade bed greeted her. What else had she expected? Jacob Marley? Still, Marche frowned. She would have preferred a mess on the floor to nothing. Where could the sound have come from? The attic? Marche shook off the thought. She and Bridget had removed the only item that was up there.

Had she imagined it? Marche bent her right leg at the knee and scratched her other leg with her big toe. Was there any other explanation?

"Damn it."

Marche stomped back to the bathroom and dumped the hamper's contents into a smaller basket that she could easily carry downstairs.

She hummed an Aerosmith song while she tossed blouses and slacks and socks into the washer. The laundry equipment, like the bathtub, screamed ancient. The knobs jiggled when she turned them, the buttons stuck, and rust lined the edges of the lid. As she measured out the detergent, she mouthed a silent prayer that the machine would give her at least a year's worth of loads before conking out.

With the washer rumbling noisily in its slow and steady rhythm, she headed into the kitchen. She decided to wipe down the countertops and sweep the floor after she had filled the dishwasher. That appliance, at least, was on the newer end of the age-spectrum. She emptied the dish rack last.

As she put away the remaining silverware, she noticed that the laundry room had gone silent. *Perfect timing.* She lifted the lid and reached inside. The everyday clothes she tossed into the dryer. The work clothes she hung on a metal pole that reached from one length of the room to the other.

Only when she had finished, and she could dredge up no other chores to postpone the inevitable, did she decide to call it a night. Though it wasn't quite ten-thirty, she felt physically and emotionally drained.

Marche mounted the staircase slowly. As she climbed, she surveyed the numerous nicks and scratches carved into the railing. She traced some of these markings with her fingers. Perhaps Bridget might have some tips on touching up the wood?

Dom's extra-large tee shirt swished about her thighs as she made her way upward. On the second floor, she studied the banister. Vale had told her it was part of the original structure, hadn't he? The wood was a shade darker, the random grooves deeper. Marche paused, her fingers hugging the rich wood.

She looked at the first floor—with only the front door, part of the hallway, and a glimpse of the living room sofa visible—and wondered how everything would have looked when Charles and Betty were newlyweds. Would the floors have been hardwood? The wall alongside the staircase covered with wedding photos? What about before then? When the house was first built?

Glancing upward, Marche noticed a patchwork job on the ceiling. She squinted in thought. Had a chandelier once hung there, suspended above the foyer? It would certainly make sense. But then, why remove it?

Shrugging, Marche killed the hall light and entered the master bedroom.

She covered her mouth as she yawned. She surveyed the messy bed, took a step toward it, and then froze. She jerked her head in the direction of the closet. For the briefest moment, she thought she'd seen something out of the corner of her eye—something dark and shadowlike.

"What the hell is wrong with me tonight?" Marche exclaimed, irritation overriding her unease.

Steaming, she navigated through the boxes and looked inside the closet. Pushing the clothes hangers aside, she checked the back wall. All clear. The shoes on the floor were undisturbed. Winter blankets and unused candlesticks remained in their respective locations on the shelf above the clothing pole. Absolutely nothing had been usurped or rearranged.

Marche stepped back, hands on her hips, vexation mounting. *You're a grown woman. Quit acting like a spooked cat!*

As she remained fixed to the spot, running over the night's events in her mind, something warm and wet and gooey touched the side of her foot. Startled, Marche sprang backward and pressed a hand to her chest. Jerking her head to the right, she searched for the source of her agitation.

"Ugh." Sickness swirled in Marche's gut and rose in her throat like mercury in a thermometer. "Oh, God," she uttered with a soured breath. "Ugh." Grasping her thighs until her knuckles turned white, she bent forward and retched.

Seventeen

"Aren't you a little early?" Marche asked. She ran a hand through her knotted hair as Bridget walked past her and into the foyer.

"You said eleven, didn't you?" Bridget replied over her shoulder.

"Yes, but—"

Marche looked at the living room clock; the hands pointed to the eleven and two, respectively.

"Mornin', sweetie pie," Bridget said, joining Stella in the den. The child sat cross-legged on the floor before the television set, Bianca perched on her lap. Bridget bent down and planted a kiss on Stella's head.

"Auntie Bee!"

Bridget appeared almost childlike with her light brown hair combed back into a ponytail; her cheeks glowed with good cheer. Some of her gaiety briefly faded, however, when she gazed fully at Marche.

"Is something wrong?"

"No. Not at all," Marche said, covering her mouth with the back of her hand as she yawned. "Just didn't get enough sleep."

The previous evening lingered vividly at the forefront of her mind. After overcoming the initial shock of her discovery, she had jackknifed and dry retched several times. Once she'd gotten the heaving under control, she ran down the stairs and curled into a ball on the easy chair. She remained like that for hours, frozen with fear—not with the fear of what she had seen, but with the fear that she hadn't actually seen anything at all.

When the living room clock ticked one, Marche had rolled out of her fetal position and gone back upstairs. She passed through the doorway and looked at the spot on the floor. The gruesome image had disappeared, just as she predicted it would. *Guilt. Hallucinations. One feeds into the other.* Isn't that what she'd said to Vale?

Marche blinked.

The closed curtains couldn't block out the glaring morning light; it seared through the white lace like the flame of a candle burning its way through a piece of paper. She was glad of it. The daylight kept her warm when her memory of the night's events would have her trembling with cold.

There had never been a doubt in her mind as to what it was she had beheld by the dull lamplight. Blood caressed her skin with sticky warmth—blood mixed with the amniotic fluid of a placental sac. Marche followed the trail of red watery goop to its source. Several inches away, she discovered what looked like a fetus lying on the floor amidst tissue and blood.

The sight had made her retch.

Then the fetus pulsated in a steady rhythm as though it were still alive. It thrived on the sounds of her sickness, throbbing harder when her stomach muscles contracted. It seemed to quiver with eagerness when she felt her insides screaming with pain. Between each heave, she stared at the thing by her feet. Then an immobilizing cramp—similar to labor pains—seized her. By the time she had recovered, the horrific phantasm had vanished.

"Hello? Earth to Marche."

Marche tore her gaze away from the television screen and looked dumbly at Bridget, who now stood in the doorway.

"I'm sorry?"

"Are you ready to get started?"

"Yeah," Marche replied. "Just give me a minute to change."

"What's wrong with what you've got on?"

Marche glanced down at the Aerosmith shirt. "It was Dom's."

"But it's so *old*. It's probably been through the wash a thousand times." In a softer voice, she added, "I don't think that he would mind."

"I don't..."

Marche was glad that Bridget followed behind her as they climbed the stairs.

For a few seconds, she feared that she might actually cry. And Bridget seeing that would only make it worse.

Would she ever fully recover from Dom's death? For two weeks after his burial, she could hardly get out of bed to care for Stella. When it came to attending to her own person, she spurned even the barest of necessities. Sleep had been all she wanted. She'd had no appetite. The simple act of breathing had hurt her chest.

Those endless days of seeing and feeling nothing had been tantamount to a living death. She had scaled mountains since then. In the morning, she could slip out of bed without wishing for nightfall. She could even laugh with Stella while watching *Shaun the Sheep*. But how much time had to pass until she could speak of her husband without feeling that arrow of absolute loss piercing through her entire being?

Sorting through the shirts in her dresser, she pulled out a loose-fitting V-neck.

"The paint is ready," Bridget yelled through the closed door.

"Okay."

Marche slipped out of the shirt. She pressed it to her nose and inhaled, imagining that she could detect Dom's scent trapped in the threads. Then she folded it neatly and tucked it into the far corner of her sock drawer.

She joined Bridget in the spare room as soon as she finished dressing. They worked quietly for nearly an hour, the silence punctuated only by the rustling of clothes and the swishing of wet bristles against drywall.

Normally, Marche enjoyed quiet activity. Today, however, she found the hushed atmosphere a trial to weather. Last night's hallucination tampered with her thoughts, floating before her eyes like a cat toy on a string. It dangled there, taunting her, and she swatted at it with her disgust. It disappeared in a flicker, only to return. She repeated the process until her head ached with the effort. What could make it go away? With each passing minute, her freshly sowed guilt intensified.

"I loved Dom, you know," she said, breaking the silence as she dipped her brush into the tray of paint. The ugly image undulated and then faded. Oh, yes, she felt better already.

Bridget was on the other side of the room, squatting as she slathered green paint on the corner of the wall between the closet and the window overlooking the backyard. Her hair had fallen out of the ponytail in multiple places. She shoved some of the stray strands into her hairband and looked over her shoulder at Marche.

"Of course you did. He was a really good guy." Her voice softened. "We miss him, too."

Marche balanced on the ladder, stretching her arm upward as she painted the uppermost section of the wall. "I mean that I *really* loved him," she said without looking down.

"I know."

Marche continued to flick her wrist back and forth in a continuous motion as she dragged the brush across the wall. She remained silent for a long time. The guilt hadn't been there before last night. Now that it had flowered, she was eager to pull it out by the roots. "Let me ask you a question."

"Okay."

"If Trey wanted something, and wanted it badly, would you help him try to get it?"

"That's pretty vague," Bridget replied. "Is this 'something' legal?"

"Sure. Whatever." Marche's headache began to recede. She had never doubted that she'd done the right thing. Not once. "But even though this is something that will make him happy...it might also ruin your relationship."

Marche scanned her work; she'd missed a spot.

"What do you do?" she continued.

She covered the white blotch, leaving her immediate work area completely green. After quickly surveying the wall, she stepped onto the floor. She moved the ladder a couple of feet to the right, careful not to spill the tray of paint that she'd left sitting precariously on top of it. Climbing the steps, she grabbed the brush. She wiped the bristles against the side of the tray and quickly started a new field of green.

"Would you help him get what he wants?"

"I don't know," Bridget said after a lengthy pause. "In the end, I guess I'd have to consider what would make him happiest."

Marche frowned and laid the brush along the incline of the plastic tray. Descending the ladder, she positioned herself in front of the window overlooking Washington. She looked at the narrow expanse of lawn below. A rarely used sidewalk bisected the fertile green grass. Then her gaze drifted toward the road.

Washington was a two-lane thoroughfare that intersected the busier streets of Egret Bay. It featured a slow-but-steady stream of traffic from sunrise to sunset. Cleaning crews regularly swept the gutters. Palm trees and oaks vied for dominance along the sidewalks. In many ways, Washington was a portrait of the city itself: quaint and clean with a touch of chaos.

Bridget joined her at the window. Her small face reflected in the glass beside Marche's. "What's on your mind?"

"Always the sacrificial lamb," Marche murmured.

"Huh?"

"Nothing," Marche said. The hallucination suddenly reappeared before her eyes; she curled both hands into fists. Quickly, before she could change her mind, she spat out the words. Just as quickly, the pulsating fetus crawled back into the shadows. "Dom wanted another baby. Can you believe it?"

The reflection in the window tilted its head in a contemplative gesture. "The way Dom doted on Stella, I'm not really surprised."

Marche laid her hands on the windowsill and closed her eyes briefly. She smelled paint and sweat and Bridget's peppermint gum. Opening her eyes, she looked up at the sun.

"Well, I was. I was really surprised," she said. "Of course, I was shocked the first time—when he told me that he wanted Stella. I guess I figured that since he'd grown up without parents and had always lived such a carefree life, he wouldn't want a child to hinder his freedom."

Plump white clouds floated loftily in the sky. Marche watched their shapeless forms without seeing them.

"It turned out that he was really a domestic man after all. Who would've guessed with the mountain biking and the climbing, the surfing, the traveling, that he would have ever wanted kids?"

Marche sighed. She tried to conjure her husband's face as she spoke but succeeded only in picturing Stella.

"A few months before he died, he told me that he wanted another child. I argued with him about it. I said that Stella was enough."

She traced the windowsill with her finger as she gazed up at the empyreal blue and white quilt that covered Egret Bay.

"So now you're upset because you and Dom didn't get to have another child?" Bridget suggested, her voice soft with sympathy.

Marche felt her cheeks redden. She slapped the windowsill, and a pricking sensation burned at the base of her palm. Had a sliver of wood broken the skin?

"Don't try to be a fucking psychologist!" She took a deep, calming breath. "I'm not asking for your input. I just want to talk."

Bridget took a step back. Her eyes rounded with hurt and shock; she bit her bottom lip.

"I'm sorry," Marche said, crossing her arms over her chest. "It's just that this is hard for me to...um, say out loud."

Bridget nodded—a tentative movement that disclosed her uncertainty.

Marche stared at the floor. She focused on a section of plastic that had torn free from the painter's tape.

"I was pregnant all along." A bitter laugh rumbled through her chest. "Looking back, it seems that he must have sensed it on some subconscious level. Of course, I didn't realize it until afterwards."

"Oh!" Bridget exclaimed.

Kneeling down, Marche secured the stray plastic with a fresh piece of tape. "I had an abortion as soon as I found out," she continued. "I did it for us—for me and Dom. Another child just wouldn't have been any good. I knew it, even if Dom didn't."

Anger flared up, hot and fresh.

"And now he's dead."

"Bianca broke!" Stella held up the doll, pouting.

“Oh, no.” Bridget rushed into the living room and squatted beside Stella. “What happened?”

“I dunno.” Stella shook her head, her lips trembling with emotion.

“Can I see?” Bridget asked, holding out her hand. “Where did she break?” She examined the doll with care, touching its limbs and turning it over.

“There.” Stella pointed to the doll’s skirt; the red velvet had ripped at the hem.

Marche gave Stella a reassuring pat on the head. “It’s okay, bug. I’m sure Aunt Bridget can fix it for you. Isn’t that right?”

Bridget nodded. She was fingering the three-inch tear, her gaze thoughtful. “Of course I can.”

“Yay!”

“I’ve got a needle and some thread at home. She’ll be right as rain in no time.”

Stella smiled. But then her face suddenly became serious, her eyebrows knitting together so that she almost looked like an adult trapped in a child’s body.

“What’s wrong?” Marche asked, rubbing Stella’s back.

“I dunno.”

“Bianca’s clothes are really old,” Bridget added. “It’s not your fault, sweetie. I’m surprised they’ve lasted this long.”

Secretly, Marche was glad for an excuse to get rid of the doll. *Good riddance,* she thought as Bridget carried it through the front door.

She wished it would break for real.

Eighteen

First, the alarm sounded late.

Marche scurried back and forth through the house like a madwoman as she prepared breakfast for Stella and searched for the pants she'd laid out on the couch the night before. To her dismay, the milk was clumpy and her slacks were nowhere to be seen.

"Pop-Tarts sound good?"

"Uh-kay!" Stella squealed.

The box felt suspiciously light in Marche's hands. Peeling back the flaps, she discovered that it was empty. "Guess it's eggs instead," she grumbled. After dedicating more time than she could afford at the stove, she then lost another precious few minutes sorting through clothes in the hamper.

"Oh, this is useless," Marche said with a groan.

The washing machine had not granted her the year's worth of labor she'd asked for. Instead, as if to mock her, it completed just two more wash cycles. On the third round, it made an ominous rattling noise followed by a loud, mysterious *clunk,* and then died. That had happened on Tuesday. It was now Friday, and she still hadn't found time to get to the cleaners.

Grimacing, Marche withdrew a pair of black slacks from the pile. They smelled slightly musty when she pressed them to her nose. But at least the creases wouldn't be too noticeable. She pulled them on, telling herself with a forced optimism that the day would surely get better.

She wolfed down breakfast at the kitchen counter, carelessly scooping the lukewarm eggs into her mouth. Too carelessly. With the second forkful, she stabbed her bottom gums with the tines. "Ouch!" she hissed, nursing the wounded spot with her tongue. As if that wasn't bad enough, she also over-tipped her glass of orange juice, splashing the contents down her shirtfront.

"Arghhh!"

Marche abandoned the plate of food in order to hunt down a new blouse. She thundered up the stairs, darted into the bedroom, and tore off her soiled top. Blindly, she plucked a navy blue sweater off one of the hangers. The ascot neckline hugged her throat in an irritating way. She tied the attached scarf with trembling fingers, wondering why she'd kept the blasted thing.

They left the house fifteen minutes behind schedule.

The trip to Melody's Ensemble usually took less than ten minutes. Today though, the scenic route along Bilmswheel Avenue was backed up for a mile and a half. Stop and go. Stop and go. During the extended commute, Marche's gaze periodically darted toward the glove box where a crumpled box of cigarettes lay in waiting.

God, what I'd give for one right now.

Marche hadn't smoked since Stella's incident, a little more than two weeks ago. She'd first picked up the habit when she was juggling two jobs and the care of her younger sister. She'd gathered the willpower to quit after she met Dom. It was easier then. He had watered the wilted roses of her life until they bloomed again. When he died...she'd been weak. And bitter. And smoking felt perversely satisfying. She hated Dom for abandoning her. And he'd hated that she tarred up her lungs and breathed dragon's breath. With each inhalation, she felt like she were issuing him a challenge. *You want me to stop? Then show yourself, coward.* She knew that her pattern of thinking didn't make sense. But when was grief ever rational?

Finally, the daycare center loomed into view. Tires squealed softly as Marche swerved into the small parking lot off Harden Street. In her haste, she forgot to use the turn signal, and a horn sounded belligerently behind her.

"Up yours," she murmured.

The lot was empty except for a few staff-owned vehicles parked along the left side of the building. Marche turned into the parking space closest to the front door and jerked the Neon to a stop.

Rounding the car in a dash, she scooped Stella out of the child restraints and sprinted toward the building.

Melody's Ensemble, a single-story concrete block structure, featured murals of children on its three outward facing walls. They donned overalls, pattu langa, raincoats, or sundresses. They jumped in puddles, skipped rope, sat with building blocks, and played patty cake. One of the side walls emphasized music, with each smiling child holding some type of instrument—a tambourine, xylophone mallet, maraca, or drumstick. Staffless quarter notes hovered in the space above their heads. The artwork, bright and cheerful, made the preschool look like an inspiring playground for learning and cultural experiences.

Marche couldn't deny that she'd been influenced by the exterior when she'd selected her daughter's daycare. At the moment, however, she hardly noticed it as she pulled open the front door and set Stella on the floor.

Jessica, the facility's youngest staff member, was arranging the students' belongings in the cubbyholes across from the reception desk. Her carrot-colored braids bobbed on her shoulders when she looked up.

"Good morning!" Smiling, she took Stella's princess-themed backpack from Marche's outstretched hand.

"Hi, Jessica." Marche placed a palm on Stella's back and nudged her forward. "Be a good girl, Stella!"

Flicking a quick wave to the assistant, she ran out the door and hopped into the car. She glanced at the time on the car radio as she steered out of the parking lot. *Damn. Already two minutes late.*

During this leg of the drive, she avoided traffic jams and sailed through the lights. Tugging at the scarf around her throat, she estimated that she'd reach the library in record time.

Shortly after she turned onto Felicity Lane, however, a black and white tomcat peered between two garbage cans and darted across the pavement. *Christ!* Without thinking, she veered sharply to the left. Though she managed to avoid hitting the animal (which disappeared over a privacy fence without a single backward glance), she lost control of the car.

Marche slammed on the brakes as the Neon snaked across the opposite lane.

Luckily, there wasn't any oncoming traffic. But there *was* a speed limit sign that stubbornly refused to move out of the way. She closed her eyes in apprehension, wincing as the car struck the steel pole.

Crunch! Marche flopped forward and banged her chin on the steering wheel. Pain erupted in her mouth. She fell backward, momentarily stunned. Then she worked her jaw up and down, traced her fingers along the gum line. She sighed. Nothing broken. No teeth missing.

In the next moment, her relief turned to anger. "Oh, come on!" she shouted, punching the seat. Would nothing go right today?

Snorting like a bull about to charge, she stepped out of the car and walked around the front to assess the damage. Though the street sign now swayed a little to the right, most of the damage appeared to have occurred at the cost of the Neon. The grille bowed in at the center, and the left turn signal lamp had popped out; it now dangled precariously by a few wires.

Marche crossed her fingers that the damage was purely external. "God damn it! This *cannot* be happening to me!"

She slapped the hood of the car, ran a hand through her hair, pulled at it so that the brown mass looked messier than before, and hopped behind the wheel.

Reaching for her purse, she withdrew her cell phone and dialed the extension to Phyllis' office. The line transferred to voicemail after five rings. Cursing, she dialed the circulation desk next. No one answered there either.

She tossed the phone aside and checked the rearview mirror. The lane was clear in both directions. Patting the dashboard for luck, she reversed.

She encountered yet another obstacle on Pine Avenue: she'd forgotten about the scheduled roadwork. Bob's Barricades blocked off the entrance to the library's main parking lot. In the space beyond, workers dressed in reflective orange vests diligently paved over the old asphalt.

Marche sped past the building and turned right onto Maple View Drive, a cobblestone street which led toward a gated community called Great Pine Estates. A quarter of a mile inward, she spotted the opening to the library's secondary parking lot.

The overflow lot was half the size of the main parking area. Patrons and staff rarely parked here since the walking distance to the building was also twice as far.

Marche eased off the gas and killed the engine. Seven cars already occupied some of the narrow spaces, most of them belonging to her co-workers. She immediately recognized Ebony's white Escalade (which monopolized two slots) and Phyllis' rusting Buick LeSabre parked alongside it.

Despite all of the morning's mishaps, Marche was only ten minutes late. She heaved a sigh of relief as she got out of the car. Hugging her purse to her side, she hustled across the parking lot.

Two steps from the handicap ramp, she slipped into a pothole.

"Oh!"

Her right foot sank ankle-deep in rainwater. She withdrew the sopping appendage, appalled at the sight of dirty water dripping from her shoe.

"Ugh."

Marche tried to resume her swift pace, but a dull pain wrapped around her ankle, forcing her to hobble the rest of the way. By the time she rang the bell on the staff door, it was a quarter past nine.

"We were starting to worry about you," Phyllis said, not sounding the least bit worried. She held the door open for Marche to pass through.

"I'm so sorry, Phyllis. I tried to call."

"Rough morning?" The circulation supervisor eyed Marche's soiled shoe with critical eyes.

"Couldn't get much worse." Marche limped to the lockers and stowed her purse inside number four. "I wrecked the front end of my car on the way here."

"Lord have mercy! What happened? Are you okay?"

"A cat ran out in the road," Marche replied, thinking, as she spoke, that her supervisor was less interested in her welfare and more interested in having something to gossip about. The woman was closer to a parrot than a dove. "I'm a touch sore, but I think everything's okay." She made her way to the staff restroom, flicked on the lights, and grabbed a fistful of paper towels. "Pothole outside jumped up out of nowhere," she explained. As she turned to face her supervisor, she noted the thin trail of gray-tinged water she'd left in her wake. It shimmered like slug-slime on the white linoleum.

"That lot's in a rotten state. They're supposed to repave it when the front lot re-opens on Monday. Well," Phyllis said as Marche rubbed the muck off her shoe, "I'm glad that you're all right." She grimaced at the wet floor before disappearing into her office.

Marche finished brushing down the sides of her shoe, hastily wiped the linoleum clean, and then joined her co-workers at the front desk.

"You look like you got run over by a truck," Ebony said as Marche wobbled to her station.

"I feel like it, too." Marche adjusted the height on the chair. She guessed, from the fact that her knees bumped the desk, that Sarah had probably sat there the night before. "This has been one hell of a crazy morning."

She opened the circulation module and typed in her password. "How's it going here?"

"I'm just about done stamping the due date cards. And that's all that's left of the drop," Ebony said, pointing to the small pile of items on the cart between Felix and Genie.

"At least we get to start the day caught up."

As things turned out, they didn't really need a head start. Aside from a few early birds, hardly anyone stepped through the doors. By eleven-thirty, Marche was twiddling her thumbs in boredom.

She spun in her chair until she faced Felix, who sat at the station on her right. "Felix."

Her co-worker had his hands folded on the desk and was gazing out of the windows to the woods beyond. At the sound of her voice, he blinked and turned to look at her. "Yes?"

"What's new in your life?"

The question seemed to confuse him. Felix wasn't a man of many words, and he often avoided small talk. "Nothing's new," he replied after a moment.

"Have you gotten over that stomach virus?" Genie asked.

"I believe it was food poisoning."

Ebony, who'd plucked a nail file from one of the desk drawers, paused to survey her progress. "Do you know what caused it?" she asked without looking up.

"I'm fairly certain it was the spinach and ricotta dish I had at Antonio's."

"You have to be careful with spinach," Genie remarked. "A close friend of mine contracted salmonella from it."

"Yes," Felix said.

"Food poisoning is the pits." Ebony smoothed the curve of her pinky nail with a flourish and tossed the file back into the drawer.

"I can handle diarrhea and vomiting," Felix replied. "The intolerable part is having to deal with all the women."

Marche cocked an eyebrow. This was the most she'd heard Felix talk at any given time; she suspected that they'd hit on just the right nerve. "What women?"

A muscle flexed in Felix's jaw as if the recollection caused him distress. "My sister stopped by the house the morning after I became ill," he said. "She insisted on keeping me company and cleaning the house."

"I wish my husband would take care of things when I get sick," Ebony lamented. "I'm lucky enough if I get a mug of hot tea."

"I prefer solitude," Felix replied. "After Vickie left, all the women on the block started knocking on my door."

"You should be glad people care about you," Genie said in her pragmatic, no-nonsense tone that people sometimes mistook for grumpiness.

Felix slouched in the chair. He worked in an environment where women outnumbered men four to one. Marche smiled inwardly at the irony.

"This girl who I didn't even recognize stopped by on the second day to see if I needed anything. Then Mrs. Graham delivered homemade chicken noodle soup to my door. Bethany and Stephanie—the twins who live across the street—asked me what I wanted for Sunday breakfast. Even Dorothy, who can barely make it down the street with her walker, offered to do my grocery shopping. I finally just shut off all the lights and climbed into bed." Felix paused. "I had to stay at my son's house on Sunday just to get away from all the nagging."

"You should find yourself a new lady friend," Genie said. "Get married, then those women won't so much as set foot on your doorstep."

"No, thank you," Felix replied. "One time around the block was enough for me. I prefer the simple life of a single man."

Marche shared a humorous glance with Ebony. The conversation seemed to tire Felix, and he immediately sank back into silence. Genie went on her lunch break a few minutes later.

At ten past noon, patrons suddenly began to trickle through the main doors in swift succession.

Marche and the other assistants gradually shifted from having very little to do to not having any free time at all. Almost every patron who stepped up to the counter required extra attention. One needed to pay for a lost video, which meant Marche had to consult with Phyllis for a replacement cost. Another wanted to place holds on several books. As luck would have it, the elderly man didn't know any of the authors, and half of the titles he'd written down were misspelled. Marche spent fifteen minutes searching through the online database as she attempted to track down the correct items. Before she could complete the requests, the telephone rang.

At the other end of the line, a hearing-impaired man barked out an inquiry. Marche spoke at the top of her voice until she was almost hoarse, having to repeat each statement a second or third time. When she tried to explain that she'd have to transfer the call to the reference librarian, he became irate.

"I'm sorry," Marche replied. "All I know is what's printed on the flyer." The peach-colored paper described the free musical entertainment that the library hosted one Friday a month. "There isn't a description of the band here. You'll need to speak with the staff member who does the booking."

A flash of black and white crossed her vision. Marche glanced up from the flyer to see Agatha Marshall, dressed in a zebra-print jumpsuit, smiling at her with tangerine painted lips.

"Please hold for a moment," Marche said to the man as she transferred the phone call. Dropping the receiver in its cradle, she breathed deeply. "Can I help you?"

"Well, hello there!" The overhead lights highlighted the yellowness of Agatha's bared teeth, giving Marche the surreal, fleeting impression that her face was a cardboard cutout and her mouth was an animated citrus fruit. "You're looking well."

"I'm just a happy, busy bee."

"Sounds like job security."

"I suppose so," Marche replied. She recalled her upcoming interview for the Circulation Clerk III position and her spirits lifted. "What can I do for you today?"

Agatha set her oversized bag on the counter and draped her wrinkled hands across the straps. "My grandson has a book on hold, but he can't make it into the library. I was hoping that I could pick it up for him."

"Do you have his library card?"

"No," Agatha replied. "Do you need it?"

"I'm afraid so," Marche said. "We're not allowed to access someone else's account without a library card." She braced herself for the negative reaction that she encountered seventy-five percent of the time, but Agatha seemed unperturbed.

"I figured as much," she replied. "That's all right, dearie. I'll just tell Luke that he's got to come get it himself."

Agatha leaned forward. A pair of pewter bracelets encircled her thin wrist. One of the bands featured a lotus flower, the other showed two plump goldfish touching lips. They clanged against one another as she extracted a piece of paper from her bag. "I was watching a program on TV the other day, and I heard about a book that sounds interesting. Can you tell me where to look for it?"

"I'll be happy to. What's the title?"

Marche tracked down the call number for the book and directed Agatha upstairs. The woman looked especially old and frail as she shuffled past the circulation desk toward the elevator. For the first time, Marche pitied her.

A brief lull in activity stole over the department. Ebony went on break even though Genie hadn't yet returned from lunch. Marche rested her elbows on the countertop, chin in hand.

Felix was scanning in materials when Agatha stepped out of the elevator. "May I offer you some assistance?" he asked, looking up.

Agatha gave a dismissive wave and continued walking.

"I'm curious," Marche said when Agatha placed her books on the counter.

"How do you resist Felix's charms?"

"Who?" A puzzled expression crossed over the woman's face as she sorted through her plastic cards.

"Felix," Marche repeated, nodding toward her co-worker.

Agatha cast a careless glance in his direction and then swiftly resumed the hunt for her library card. The lines around her mouth crinkled as she pursed her lips. "There has only ever been one man in my life," she said, her tone heated. Finding the correct card, she thrust it forward.

"What's your husband's name?" Marche asked as she scanned the barcode.

"Luther," Agatha said after a pause. She stuffed the card back into her wallet.

"He must be a very special man." Marche placed due date cards in the three books and pushed the pile toward Agatha. "Actually, I just remembered something."

"Hmm?"

"I found a trunk in the attic. I suppose it must have belonged to your brother."

"Is that right?" Agatha replied. "I'm surprised he kept it after all this time."

"Would you like to have it?" Marche asked.

"Yes." Agatha nodded. "I think I would."

"I can bring it with me to the library. If you'd like to—"

"There's no need for you to go to all that trouble, dear. I'll be more than happy to pick it up at the house."

"Are you sure?" Marche asked.

"Absolutely," Agatha replied. "After all, I still owe you a housewarming call."

Nineteen

An electrical storm brewed in Egret Bay.

A bolt of lightning sprang from the earth a mile away, and a pillar of the purest white light flickered through the bare windowpane. The flash illuminated Marche, who lay unconscious on the bed, sheet and blanket discarded. Crackling thunder quickly followed. Marche stirred. Whimpering like a small child, she turned from the window.

Beneath closed lids, her eyes moved rapidly in all directions.

Blackness enveloped her. Thick and impenetrable, it wrapped around her like a coarse woolen blanket.

She whimpered again. Where was she? In a closed room, or an open space? Without a sliver of light, it was impossible to tell. And was she standing upright, or on her head? Was she reclining, with her nose facing the ground? Or perhaps she lay on her back, eyes directed toward the starless canopy above? Disorientation swelled within her. Unable to focus on anything concrete, her mind began to spin.

Become.

Gradually, she adjusted to the nothingness. A loose string pulled taut. She closed her eyes, drew a steadying breath. She decided to examine her surroundings. Maybe she could detect a crack in the solid wall of darkness? When she opened her eyes and tried to turn, however, she discovered that she was unable to move. Complete paralysis plagued her body. She couldn't even bend her wrists or wiggle her toes.

Hot air passed through her parted lips in soft puffs. She attempted to speak, but could utter no sound.

Confusion settled over her senses like a fine autumn mist.

She could see nothing, hear nothing, feel nothing. She tried to wade through the events of the recent past...and crashed into a brick wall. She was able to think, "My name is Marche Baker." Yet she had no idea what that meant. Was she tall or short? Pretty or plain? Did she have friends? Family? What were her hobbies? Surely she excelled at something. But what? She was a blank slate—a baby born fresh into the world.

The air suddenly changed. It thickened, became heavier. She labored to breathe. Even the deepest inhalation left her starved for oxygen. She began to feel lightheaded.

As she struggled to adjust to the atmospheric change, she became aware of a physical presence standing behind her. An abstract thought blossomed. She sensed the familiar.

M-D-O.

The letters flew at her in a rush. She imagined them circling one another in a frenzy—like members of a marching band scurrying to assume their proper places in line. The name formed, caressing her naked skin like perfume, tickling the hair follicles in her nose. Did she really smell peaches and honey? Or was this simply a vivid recollection?

She was looking at a jigsaw puzzle, where each of the pieces had been placed in the wrong order. Slowly, the pieces began to disengage and rearrange themselves. The border cohered first—the four edges hinting cryptically to the nature of its inner parts. Then the middle pieces shifted: sideways, upwards, downwards. The process was slow and arduous, as if a thousand pieces composed a single image. Then everything locked in place.

Dom.

This was her husband. He loved peaches and honey, his favorite breakfast dish.

Happiness spread through her limbs like warm sunshine. She forgot about the oppressive darkness and her uncooperative muscles. She forgot everything except that she was married to an adoring and supportive husband. Inwardly, she smiled. She would prepare peaches and honey for him as soon as the world righted itself again.

She yearned to look over her shoulder. Wasn't he standing there, just a few feet away? She could feel him studying her with quiet intensity, dissecting her person inch by inch. Could he see all of her merits and her faults? Was he proud of her? Surely he wasn't disappointed?

Doubt dampened her spirits. *Please.* She wanted to look at him, to say with her eyes what she could not say with her voice: she would be good to him and he would be pleased.

Her breathing became more labored. If only she could see him, hear him, smell him, *touch* him! Just knowing that he was there was not enough. She was insatiable; she needed more.

I have to say something. I have to let him hear my voice!

She exhaled, imagining the tightening of her pharynx as the air passed through it at a measured rate. The veins in her forehead pulsed with effort. She made three attempts, then a fourth. No matter how hard she concentrated, she couldn't produce even a whisper of a sound.

Tears of frustration threatened to fill her eyes. But she soon realized that it was an empty threat. Because she had no tears to cry. She'd completely dried up. Why was she here? What was the point? She couldn't move. She couldn't speak. She couldn't even cry. She was a mannequin in a store window, completely lifeless.

Was there anything worse than knowing that she couldn't communicate with Dom, even when he stood within an arm's reach of her?

Yes.

The blood drained from her face; even her earlobes felt cooler. Shock, like a bolt of lightning, shot through her body.

She had been wrong.

Terribly, horribly wrong.

Dom wasn't standing behind her. Something else hid in the darkness, crouching in expectation. Twitching with glee. It watched her in the pitch black, some *thing* that fed on her paralysis. Whatever it was, she should never have mistaken it for her beloved husband.

Tremors started in her ankles and spiraled upward, gaining momentum like an avalanche. Beneath her frozen skin, her nerves sparked with fire. Caught between two extremes, she felt certain that she'd either crack or disintegrate.

Thud.

The sound, like a ten-pound weight dropping onto a hardwood floor, echoed in the darkness behind her.

Thud.

Louder. Closer.

Thud. THUD.

Her breath hitched in her throat.

THUD-THUD.

Closer. Faster.

THUD-THUDTHUD!

Her heart hammered painfully against her ribcage. Goosebumps that she couldn't see broke out on her arms. Her breath passed through her lips in shallow spurts. She could hear the blood rushing through her veins.

Silence filled the space.

She held her breath. The thing was still there; she felt its presence more tangibly than ever. This was a waiting game, she realized. She couldn't escape. She could only float there, like a worm dangling on a hook while a hungry fish circled round it, analyzing it with its round, unblinking eyes.

I won't let it win. I won't be a victim.

She closed her eyes to the blackness and tried to draw Dom's face in her mind. Miraculously, it worked. His blue eyes twinkled; he smiled. She imagined smiling back. Then he reached out to touch her.

He began to stroke her neck with cold, cold fingers.

The sensation was like a punch to the stomach. The air rushed out of her lungs; brilliant red and yellow stars flashed behind her eyes.

Dom's face disappeared in the darkness.

Her eyelids flicked open. Staring into the dark void, she wondered if she'd finally met her end. When she tried to breathe, the grip on her throat tightened.

Oh my God, it really wants to kill me. But…I'm not ready to die. Not yet!

Her eyes bulged with the pressure. Her tongue seemed to thicken and fill up the back of her throat. Her thoughts dissolved into a muddled mess. An all-consuming emptiness draped over her senses.

The fingers gripping her neck were bones without flesh. They never tired. Their merciless, unrelenting strength seemed superhuman.

Another bony hand touched her lower back, the skeletal finger pressing into her flesh. It traced a circle about the size of a quarter. With each rotation, the pressure intensified. By the fourth, a hole began to form in her skin.

One by one, the organs in her body started to shut down.

"AHHH-AHHH-AHHH!"

The pressure around her throat disappeared; the pain in her back ceased. Marche opened her eyes and saw the ceiling in her bedroom. She tested her arms and legs; all four were completely mobile.

Inhaling deeply (she really was short of breath), she dragged a hand down her face. Her skin was cold and damp.

"AHHH!"

The sharp scream pierced through Marche's thoughts. Jumping out of bed, she ran to Stella's bedroom.

Stella sat in the far corner of the bed, precariously close to the edge. The sheets covered her entire body, leaving nothing visible below the chin. Her widened eyes looked too large for her small face.

"Mommy!"

"What's wrong, Stella?" Approaching the bed, she folded Stella into her arms. Sobs rocked her body.

"The dark lady... She tried...to hurt...me."

A bolt of lightning flashed, lighting up the room. Crackling thunder followed. The sound startled Stella, whose crying transformed into an ear-piercing howl. Marche winced.

"It was just a bad dream, honey. That's all. You're awake now and everything's fine. See?" Marche tipped Stella's chin upward and pointed around the room. "There's nobody else here. It's just you and me—like always."

Stella's watery eyes surveyed the area. Slowly, her wailing dwindled into a series of sniffles.

"Do you want to sleep with me tonight?" Marche asked as she cradled Stella to her chest.

"Uh...huh."

"All right," Marche said. "Let's do that."

As she lifted Stella off the mattress, the child wrapped her limbs about Marche's neck and torso like a young chimpanzee clinging to its mother. She squeezed tightly as if she feared Marche would drop her.

"Let go a little?" Marche prompted. Stella did the opposite instead, digging her heels into Marche's back. And then she felt it—a dull, burning ache at the base of her spinal column.

In the bedroom, she pried Stella from her body and placed her on the mattress. Then she picked up the comforter, which had fallen into a heap on the floor, and tucked it around her shoulders.

Marche sat beside Stella. She brushed the hair off her forehead, waited until her eyes finally fluttered shut. Then she lay down on the other side of the bed. Sliding a hand beneath her nightshirt, she tentatively touched the bothersome spot on her back. She hissed with surprise and pain.

Her exploring fingers touched what felt like a fresh cigarette burn.

Twenty

"Be careful you don't lose your toy."

"Uh-kay, Mommy," Stella replied, in a careless manner that suggested she wasn't really listening.

"I mean it. We're not going to come back if you forget it."

Stella crouched before the row of red plastic seats, her bare knees touching the dirty floor. "Uh-huh." The earless Mr. Potato Head that she'd brought to play with executed numerous somersaults between the seats.

Marche considered sitting down, but then changed her mind. The armless chairs were scooped in the center and screwed to the wall. She wasn't sure they'd hold her weight; they looked like they should have been replaced a decade ago. Most of them showed some degree of vandalism—messages carved into the surface, doodles traced in permanent marker, jagged cracks along the backs.

When she'd stepped into Harrison's Laundromat an hour ago, there'd been three other customers. Two twenty-something women doused in cheap perfume swapped stories by the dryers. The third person, a large older woman dressed in various shades of brown, folded clothes on a narrow plastic table. She hummed loudly, Spanish lyrics bursting from her lips at odd intervals.

The songster left first, her basket close to overflowing with earth-toned fabrics. The chatterboxes soon followed. Since then, no other shadow had darkened the doorway. Except for the tumble of clothes, the place was quiet.

Marche checked the machine; eight minutes remained on the wash cycle. She leaned against the whirring apparatus, her face to the parking lot.

Spending a Saturday night at the laundromat was not her idea of fun. She'd rather binge watch one of her favorite television shows or read a novel. But the clothes needed washing and the magic fairies hadn't once lifted their wands and offered to help.

The summer sun lowered over the horizon, leaving the sky a psychedelic canvas of carnation pink and lavender. The pigments swirled around each other like paint mixing in water before swimming off in different directions. Minutes ticked by. Somber shades of gray and blue slowly displaced the light colors. As she contemplated the celestial show, a dark figure darted across her vision.

Marche moved over to the entrance, pulled open the door, and peeked around the corner. Then she jerked her head inward and took an instinctive step backward.

Stella remained preoccupied with Mr. Potato Head. With unabashed glee, she plucked off appendages and re-stuck them in all the wrong places. The lips took root in the head; the twinned eyes became the feet. And where, oh where, might the hands end up?

Marche licked her lips and stepped out the door, confident that Stella wouldn't notice her absence.

The boy stood five or six yards away, straddling his black ten-speed in front of Bo & Belt's Gaming Corner. He seemed oblivious to Marche's presence as he peered through the windows.

Marche walked slowly toward him. From his profile, she could see that he leaned toward the pale side. His hair was black as coal, smooth and sleek—and surprisingly, it looked clean. The hand dangling at his side had fingers long and thin, the nails clipped and dirt-free. He might pass for a preppie, except for his clothes. Despite the heat, he wore a trench coat over his slim shoulders. Olive green cargo pants bunched around the tops of his Dr. Martens.

"Excuse me," Marche said when she was just a few steps away. The words came out weak—barely above a whisper. Embarrassed by her timidity, she tapped the boy on the shoulder.

He stiffened at her touch. As he straightened, his body shifting under the bulky clothing, his height increased by several inches.

"Excuse me," she repeated, louder.

He turned. The arcade lights bounced off the silver gauges lining his left ear.

Marche squinted. Then she looked the boy square in the face and her breath caught in her throat.

She'd been mistaken. Though he was definitely the same person she'd seen on Victor Street, she'd miscalculated his age. From a distance, she'd thought he was a teenager. It was the bicycle, she realized. She'd just assumed...

The young man stared, his expression blank.

Marche wavered. For a moment, she considered retreating. Then she uttered a string of mute curses. What difference did it make if he was thirteen or twenty? She'd approached him for a reason, hadn't she? She swallowed her discomfort.

"Who are you?" she asked.

The man said nothing, his lips pressed firmly shut.

"I've seen you on the street. And I've seen you watching my house. What do you want?" As the silence stretched between them, Marche's irritation magnified. What the hell was wrong with this guy? Why wouldn't he answer her?

She balled her hands at her sides and squeezed. She needed to keep her voice calm. *Be the adult*, she told herself.

"What's your game?" she asked, struggling to keep her tone level. "What are you playing at?"

The man's almost-black eyes narrowed into slits. Without warning, he lifted one foot and thrust it out behind him. The hard heel hit Marche on the shin, just below her kneecap.

She cried out in pain and bent forward to massage the wounded area. "Dumb shit!" she shouted as the man pedaled off into the darkness. "Don't show your face again, or I'll call the police!"

With a groan, she straightened and limped back to Harrison's. *My poor right leg,* she thought, remembering yesterday's parking lot mishap. Stella stood in the doorway. She held Mr. Potato Head—who presently wore a mustache for a hand—to her chest.

"Mommy?"

"Go back inside," Marche said.

"What happened, Mommy?" Stella asked, sounding as though she was on the verge of tears.

"Nothing, bug." Marche pressed her hand between Stella's shoulder blades and guided her to the chairs. "Just play with your toy and don't worry about it. We'll be going home soon."

Stella quietly reassembled Mr. Potato Head's body parts while Marche tossed their wet clothes into the laundry basket.

"Time to go," she said after she retrieved the last stray sock from the washer.

They walked to the car in silence. Marche strapped Stella into the seat and set the clothes on the floor next to her feet.

"Was he bad?" Stella asked when Marche turned on the headlights.

Marche checked the side mirrors before backing out of the parking space. "Yes, Stella. He was a little bad."

"Why?"

"I suppose..." Marche tried to form an intelligent answer, but she struggled to find the right words while she navigated through traffic. "I guess I was a little bad too."

Half a minute passed. Then Stella's small voice rose from the backseat once more. "What did you do?"

The upcoming traffic light turned red. "I spoke to someone I didn't know." Marche glanced over her shoulder at Stella, who was watching her with wide eyes. "You should never talk to strangers. Never."

"It's bad?"

"Yes, Stella. It's very bad. And it can get you into a lot of trouble."

Twenty-One

The resurfaced pavement looked wet under the late afternoon sun. It smelled funny too, the odor rising from the ground like steam after a rain. Marche wrinkled her nose. The rubber-like scent reminded her of the shredded tire pieces used for mulch at the park.

Marche waited outside the staff door for Ebony, whose shift had ended at the same time.

"Whew," Ebony exclaimed, joining her outside. "Am I ever ready to call it a day!" Slinging the strap of her Coach purse over one shoulder, she stepped off the curb.

"Tired?" Marche asked, keeping in step.

"Sore's more like it. Did I tell you I started a kickboxing class last week?" Marche nodded, but Ebony was too wrapped up in her thoughts to notice. "We had our second session last night. It was *brutal*. I'm hurting all over today. All I've been able to think about since I rolled out of bed this morning is climbing into the Jacuzzi with a bottle of Merlot and a book."

"Sounds heavenly," Marche replied. Sunlight reflected off the windshield of a Dodge Charger, the glare momentarily staining her vision with fuzzy, dancing black orbs. "I've been dreaming about taking a nap all day."

"Mmm. Wouldn't it be nice if employers rolled out mats at noon and let everyone rest for an hour?"

"Who *wouldn't* like that idea?" Marche stuffed her hand into her purse. After a quick search, she located the sunglasses tucked underneath her wallet. "You should put that in the suggestion box," she said as she slipped the tinted lenses over her eyes.

"Ha! Well if nothing else, I suppose it'd give the 'bootlicker' a laugh."

"Ugh. Seriously," Marche remarked. "How can Robin think Phyllis is so great when she's always bashing him behind his back?"

Ebony shrugged as she stepped up to the Escalade. "Ignorance is easier to deal with? See you tomorrow," she said, sliding into the driver's seat.

"Drink a glass of wine for me."

"Consider it done," Ebony replied, chuckling and pulling the car door shut.

Marche plodded across the pavement, enjoying the mild summer weather; for once, the thermometer hadn't exceeded eighty-two degrees. Squirrels chattered in the trees lining the two sides of the parking lot. A male cardinal flitted toward a pick-up truck, shaded from the sun by a collection of red maples and slash pines. Settling onto the passenger-side mirror, the bird chirruped and fluffed at its reflection.

Marche reached for her keys, unable to suppress a yawn.

Sleep had proven elusive during the past few days. The first phone call came at ten-thirty on Saturday night while she was watching Ron Pearlman woo Linda Hamilton in an episode of *Beauty and the Beast*. She'd paused the show and reached for the cordless. Who else could it be but Bridget? Though they'd originally agreed to work on the spare room that day, Trey's parents had derailed their plans with an unexpected visit.

When Marche spoke into the receiver, however, no one replied.

"Hello?" she said three times.

The silence continued and, shrugging, she hung up the phone.

The second call came forty-five minutes later when Marche was in the bathroom brushing her teeth. The ringing cut through the silent house like a hot knife parting butter. She scrubbed faster. Spit out the toothpaste. Wiped her mouth with the hand towel. Halfway through the sixth ring, the voicemail cut it off.

She was crossing the bedroom when the phone suddenly resumed its shrill song. She sat on the mattress, tucking one leg underneath her, and drew the receiver to her ear. Again, no one answered. She stared at the phone with knitted brows. Perhaps the reception was bad? Or maybe someone had accidentally dialed the wrong number?

She crawled under the sheets, turned off the light, and closed her eyes. Exhausted from her broken sleep the night before, she quickly drifted into unconsciousness.

The invasive sound of the telephone, jangling on its base, ripped her out of her slumber. Marche rubbed the sleep from her eyes and felt blindly for the phone. “Hello?” she rasped. When silence issued from the caller’s end, she muttered an oath and dropped the cordless on the mattress—too tired to care about anything but getting more sleep.

It rang again.

Marche shot into a sitting position. Glancing at her watch, the glowing hands visible in the darkness, she saw that it was just past three o’clock. Snatching up the receiver, she punched the “talk” button.

“Okay, bozo,” she said, her voice calm and clear. “I’ve had enough of this juvenile behavior. If you’ve got something to say, you best say it now.” After a pause, she added, “Yeah. That’s what I thought. Don’t call back.”

This time, she got up and disconnected the phone.

When she lay down, however, she couldn’t fall back to sleep. She tossed and turned and kicked her legs. She listened to the occasional car passing by on Washington, her eyes following the trail of the head beams on the walls. She traced the outlines of the boxes scattered about the floor and thought of the objects they contained. She remembered the nightmare—the thing that wasn’t Dom and the mysterious injury she’d discovered on her back.

She finally gave up on sleep when Stella’s voice floated through the open doorway at nine o’clock.

Rolling onto her back, she rubbed her bleary eyes. Her muscles protested when she sat upright. The joints in her feet cracked when she stood. She reached for the telephone cord hanging loosely from the nightstand and plugged it into the wall. She checked her voice messages, but the mailbox was empty. The caller ID identified the offending number as “private.”

Bridget called Sunday afternoon to reschedule their work on the spare room for next Saturday. “I’ll bring Bianca, too. I’m sorry I haven’t been able to get it back to Stella sooner.”

"Don't worry about it," Marche replied. "Why don't you just keep the doll at your house? Then she'll have something to play with when she visits."

"Are you sure that's okay?"

"Yes, it's fine."

Marche tucked Stella into bed at nine o'clock. Though she hardly ever turned off the lights before eleven, Marche quickly followed suit. Giddy from sleep-deprivation, she fell asleep as soon as her head hit the pillow.

The phone rang.

Her eyelids fluttered open. She stared at the foot of the bed, her limbs heavy with sleep.

Riiiiiiing. Riiiiiiing. Riiiiiiing.

She lay there, caught in a state of semi-consciousness. Unable at first to identify the sound, she ignored it. Slowly the cobwebs of confusion melted away.

Riii—

She closed her eyes as the voicemail clicked on. Whoever had called would leave a message if it was important.

RIIIIIING!!!

"For god's sake," she mumbled.

She reached for the phone, but sleepiness left her clumsy and weak. The receiver slipped through her fingers and clattered to the floor.

"Just leave a voicemail," she grumbled.

But the persistent caller refused to give up. Struggling into a sitting position, she looked for the cordless. It had fallen between the table and wall. Lowering herself to the floor, she reached into the narrow space. The tips of her fingers grazed the antenna. She stretched further, and her fingers curled around it. Success! As she withdrew the phone from its hiding place, she bumped her head on the table.

"Owww."

Marche rubbed her scalp; waves of invisible fire gathered in the center of her skull and radiated outward.

When she finally answered the phone, she was very awake and very cross.

"Hello?"

The phone clicked; the dial tone droned in her ear.

"What the hell?"

She buried the receiver under the extra pillow, lay back down, and tried to ignore the dull pain in her head.

Twenty minutes later, the phone trilled again. This time she unplugged the cord without checking the caller ID.

When Monday morning dawned, she felt as sluggish as a sloth, and not at all in the mood to interact with society. The day presented one annoyance after another. Driving to and from work, she managed to get stuck behind every single snowbird left in the state. (A challenging feat, given the time of year.) At the circulation desk, every other patron who approached her seemed to need an attitude adjustment. The frozen pizza she served for dinner gave her an upset stomach. And then Stella begged for a story at bedtime.

"Please, Mommy," Stella cried. "I wanna hear a story. Please, Mommy. Pleeease."

Marche opened one of Stella's Dr. Seuss books, resigned to fulfill her daughter's request. The letters swam on the page. When she tried to wrangle them into focus, the strain hurt her eyes. Setting the book aside, she made up a story—not an easy task, given her lack of creative endowments. It took her nearly thirty minutes to compose a beginning, middle, and end that satisfied Stella's expectations.

"Night."

"Night-night, Mommy."

The phone rang at midnight. Exasperated, Marche nearly ripped the cord from the wall. Hours passed before she drifted into a fitful slumber.

Now, as she reached the Neon and unlocked the door, she resolved that she would unplug the phone *before* she went to bed.

Ring!

Marche shifted the car from reverse to park and withdrew the cell phone from her purse. She half-expected to see an unknown number and was surprised to see that it was her brother-in-law.

"Hello?"

"Hi, Marche. How are you?"

"I'm okay." After a pause, she added, "Is something wrong?"

Trey drew a long, shaky breath. “It’s Bridget,” he finally managed to say. “She’s in the hospital.”

Twenty-Two

Apprehension clutched at Marche's heart and squeezed.

"I'll get there as soon as I can."

She wouldn't ask for details—not on the phone. Instead, she focused on practicalities. Where was the hospital located? Which was the best route to take? She scribbled the directions on the back of a receipt that she fished out of the change box. The pen danced in her fingers; if she hadn't written the words herself, she wouldn't have been able to decipher the messy scrawl.

She called Shelley during the commute to Melody's Ensemble to ask if she'd babysit Stella.

"Of course I'll watch her for you," her neighbor said, her voice soft with sympathy. "Whatever you need, just ask."

Marche pinned the paper between her fingers and the steering wheel. As she neared the address, she examined the street signs with unwavering intensity, vaguely aware that she was driving several miles over the speed limit. *Focus. Focus. Focus.* If she considered what awaited her in the hospital room, she might fall to pieces. After everything that she'd been through—first her parents and then Dom—she couldn't help but imagine a worst-case scenario. And how would that help the situation? It was better to think of nothing at all.

Granton Memorial Hospital resembled a small college campus with its numerous outpatient facilities bordering the hospital grounds. Turning onto the side road Trey had indicated, she passed a two-story radiology building, a women's center, and a small retention pond teeming with bird life. She braked at a four-way intersection before making a right. The hospital, located on her left, towered over the other buildings in the area. Its name stretched across the gray facade like a blue ribbon on a gift box.

Driving by the emergency entrance, she followed a sign directing inpatient care visitors toward the back. The lot behind the building was packed. Rather than shop around for a convenient space, she parked in the first vacant spot she came to near the last row.

Marche turned off the engine. *Focus. Focus. Focus.* She stared at the steering wheel, at her hand gripping it so tightly that her fingers ached. She exhaled.

Slowly, she gazed upward. She focused on the dashboard, dusty from neglect, and then the windshield. Specks of pollen littered the glassy surface. Then she gazed through the glass to the building beyond.

Marche's adrenaline rush took a sudden nose-dive. She remembered her exhaustion; she felt weak, vulnerable. She considered the gearshift. Did she have to go inside? Of course not. She could curl up on the seat and bawl her eyes out if she wanted.

But I won't do that.

Gritting her teeth, she shoved out of the car and trekked up the slight incline, bisecting row after row of cars. The hospital's main entrance, made conspicuous by a navy blue awning, was on the right side of the building. A wide handicap ramp led straight to the doors, a set of cement steps flanking either side.

Marche climbed the steps and walked through the automatic double doors. Cold air splashed over her perspiring skin, making her shiver. She consulted the paper, crumpled and moist from her sweaty grip, and discovered that she hadn't written down Bridget's room number. Or maybe Trey had forgotten to mention it?

"Could you tell me which room Bridget Klein is in?" she asked the man at the information desk. She fidgeted while he clicked the mouse, his fingers flying across the keyboard. Then he stared at her, blinking, and she realized that he'd already spoken.

"Anything else I can help you with?"

"Would you mind writing that down for me?"

"Sure, I can do that." He handed her a Post-it note, the numbers so large they spanned the entire paper.

Marche nodded her thanks and went in search of the elevators. The lobby was next to a waiting area populated with hard-backed chairs and potted plants. She pressed the glossy black service button; it was sticky with a jelly-like substance. She looked around for something that she could wipe her fingers on and spotted a container of sanitizer wipes on the wall beside one of the snack machines.

A loud *ding* sounded. Marche snatched a wipe and jogged back to the lobby. The doors to the middle elevator opened. She stepped back, scrubbing her hand, as an orderly exited with an empty wheelchair. When the entryway was clear, she hopped inside and used the dirtied cloth to press the button for the fourth floor.

The cables spurred into motion. There was a subtle jolt, and then the brief sense of weightlessness as the car began its ascent. Marche gripped the hard plastic railing that lined all three walls and closed her eyes.

God, how she loathed hospitals. She hated the cold, sterile environment. And she hated that odor. It was always there, clinging to the air. *Surgical gloves dipped in cough syrup.*

She recalled her admittance to Adler-Whittington Medical Center when she'd gone into labor with Stella.

The birthing experience had been difficult. First, the baby hadn't turned properly—she'd settled sideways in Marche's uterus. The doctor pressed her hands on Marche's stomach, kneading her until Marche was sore from the pressure. Thankfully the tactic had worked. With the baby's head in the correct position, she hadn't needed a Caesarian. But then the labor stalled at six centimeters. No progress for eight hours.

Marche's blood pressure had risen; the obstetrician recommended cutting her open and pulling the baby out. The thought of a scalpel frightened Marche to tears. She dug her nails into Dom's arm, begged him not to let them wheel her into the operating room. She recalled how he'd given her a forced smile of encouragement and then looked away, unwilling to speak the words she needed to hear.

She knew that she'd cornered him. But she didn't care. "This is *your* fault!" she'd screamed. "I hate you for doing this to me!"

Dom nodded, his voice thick with unshed tears. "I know, sweetheart. I know. I'm so sorry."

Another hour passed. By some miracle, she dilated to ten centimeters, avoiding the need for surgery.

"Okay, Mrs. Baker, it's time to push," the doctor said.

Marche pushed until she thought her intestines would fall out. A faraway voice declared that the baby was crowning. What did that mean? Wave after wave of pain sliced through her. She screamed and pushed and screamed again, sweat stinging her eyes. She felt a gush. The pain and pressure evaporated. It was over.

In the end, she was too fatigued to care about the wailing thing that the nurses took away to clean and weigh. When a cherry-cheeked woman carried the baby to the bed, Marche waved her away and closed her eyes. All she wanted to do was sleep.

Days passed before she could walk without discomfort. For weeks she had nightmares involving knives and blood.

The elevator doors opened.

A nurse dressed in peach scrubs glanced dismissively at Marche as he walked by, clipboard in hand.

Marche entered the floor and threw the used wipe into the first trash can she saw. Experiencing a moment of lightheadedness, she slapped both cheeks hard enough to make the skin sting.

She stepped toward the information desk where a woman with a severe white bob sat, telephone in hand. The lighthearted red-and-green peppermint smock draped over her frame contrasted acutely with her pinched features and sharp tone.

"I'm sorry, sir, but—no, sir. That's what I'm trying to tell you. Sir, we have no record of that person—"

Marche grew impatient as the conversation lingered on. She scanned the area for directions. Blue signs affixed to the walls showed white letters, numbers, and arrows. The information looked like gibberish to her tired eyes. She peered down the corridor to her left.

A young man with short, curly black hair fiddled with supplies on a cart. He held a clipboard in one hand and scribbled notes between counting items. The lettering on his bright pink shirt identified him as a volunteer.

"Excuse me," Marche said, approaching him.

"You need help with somethin'?" he asked, looking up.

"I'm looking for room 418. Can you tell me where it is?"

"Yeah, I'll show you."

Dropping the paper and pen on a stack of hand towels, the volunteer continued straight. He swaggered down the hallway before her, casting a snooping glance into all of the open doorways they passed.

Marche sighed with relief, grateful to have someone leading the way. Each corridor looked identical with its blue signs and brown doors; in her exhausted state, she quickly became disoriented.

"What ward is this?"

The volunteer squinted at her, and Marche suddenly felt as though she'd asked an odd question. "Recovery," he replied.

A woman in a wheelchair, whose left leg was dressed in a cast from the toes to the knee, raced down the hall as though she was late for an appointment. A few doors down, they passed two doctors conferring quietly over a set of notes.

The volunteer turned down another corridor. There was a white-haired man in a hospital gown, dragging an IV pole alongside him. A man and woman approached an open doorway, the latter holding a bouquet of roses and baby's breath; they smiled, waved, and quickly disappeared inside the room. Across the hall, a heavily freckled boy sat in a chair playing with a handheld game system. A trio of women chatted warmly at the nurses' station, their words tumbling over each other.

"Ralph said he's taking me—"

"I heard that place is fabulous—"

"Are you going to wear that strapless—"

"Make sure you try the glazed chicken with—"

The conversation faded as Marche followed the volunteer down yet another corridor, this one lined with windows. From this height, she could see the tops of palm trees, the sloped parking lot, and the Gulf of Mexico shimmering in the distance.

The volunteer stopped and pointed. "Right up there."

"Thanks," Marche murmured.

"Uh-huh." The volunteer jogged ahead, flagging down another person in pink who was rounding the corner at the end of the hall. "Yo, Jerome," he called out. "I been lookin' for you everywhere, man. What you been up to?"

Marche held her purse to her chest like a teddy bear. Now that she'd made it this far, she paused. Should she have stayed home? Swallowing her uncertainty, she shuffled down the hallway. Anxiously, her eyes registered the numbered plates beside the doors: 415, 416, CLEANING 4-C, 417...

The door to 418 was shut.

Marche licked her lips. Raising her knuckles to the wood, she knocked. She waited. Listened. Maybe Bridget was asleep? Taking a deep breath, she grabbed the lever and pushed open the door.

Trey sat next to the bed, hunched over, his elbows on his knees. He was looking at Bridget who was staring at the television. Neither noticed her entrance.

"Hi," Marche said softly, tentatively.

Trey shifted in the chair. "Hi, Marche. I'm sorry, I didn't hear you."

"It's all right," Marche replied. She smiled to hide her surprise. She'd never seen her brother-in-law so disheveled. His hair, usually styled back with gel, stuck up in various places. His eyes were red-rimmed—whether from tears or exhaustion, she couldn't tell. The shadow of a mustache darkened his upper lip.

Trey leaned over the bed to kiss Bridget on the cheek before standing up. "I need to stretch my legs," he said. "I'll be back in a few minutes."

Marche nodded.

The door clicked shut behind Trey. Marche stepped toward the bed, her fingers nervously tracing the length of her purse strap. "How are you feeling?"

"I told Trey not to bother you," Bridget replied, her gaze still fixed on the television.

The small room had a closet-sized bathroom to the right of the door. A dresser with three drawers sat under the television set, an empty coat rack beside it. A monitor standing on the other side of the bed tracked Bridget's vitals.

An IV inserted into the back of her right hand led to a bag filled with clear fluid. Dark shadows lined her eyes; her lips were cracked and swollen as though she'd chewed them. Her fine hair was matted to her forehead and the sides of her face. She looked pitiful. A prize poodle changed into a scrappy mutt.

Marche sat in the chair, still warm with Trey's body heat. "It's no bother," she replied. "He was right to call." She placed her purse on the bedside table next to a cup filled with half-melted ice chips.

Bridget refused to look at her. She huddled into herself as though she were cold. Without thinking, Marche placed a hand on her shoulder. Bridget cringed.

"Sorry," she said, withdrawing.

"Please go away," Bridget whispered.

Marche leaned back in the chair, unsure what to do. She folded her hands in her lap and looked at the television. Though it had been muted, she could tell from the actors' mannerisms and animated expressions that it was the Spanish channel. It looked like a dance competition. Three people sat at an elongated table while colorfully dressed men and women spun around a brightly lit floor. She waited until a commercial break before speaking again.

"Are you all right?"

Bridget inched her way into a sitting position and leaned against the wall. "Leave me alone," she said, her voice a touch louder. "I don't want you here."

"Please talk to me," Marche said. A lump formed in her throat. "You're in a hospital bed. I'm concerned."

Bridget snorted.

"Are you sick?" Marche hesitated, afraid to hear the answer to the question she needed to ask. "Do you have cancer?"

Bridget laughed—a harsh, bitter sound that seemed alien coming from her lips. "You really are clueless, aren't you?" She clutched at the thin hospital sheet bunched around her waist.

"Trey didn't say. I..."

"Fine," Bridget said after an extended silence. "If you really want to know, I'll tell you." She twisted the sheet between her hands. "I was pregnant. And now I'm not."

A whoosh of air rushed out of Marche's lungs. She slumped forward, flooded with relief. "Oh, thank God," she said. "I was so worried. I thought that maybe—"

"Stop it."

Marche shot upright, startled by the venomous tone in her sister's voice. When she looked at Bridget, she briefly wondered if she was hallucinating. Bridget was sneering at her. Why?

"What?" she asked, baffled.

"Don't you *dare*," Bridget spat. "I won't have it. You hear me? Don't *pretend* to care when you don't."

"But I do care."

"Shove it, Marche. You're nothing but a selfish bitch."

Marche gripped the sides of the chair. The room tilted sideways—like a boat on choppy waters. Her lightheadedness returned. Was it true? Was her sweet-natured sister actually hurling daggers of ice at her? How could that be?

"What are you saying?" she asked, a slight tremor in her voice.

The woman wearing her sister's skin pounded a fist on the mattress. "You've resented me ever since Mom and Dad died. But you know what? No one asked you to sacrifice your dreams in order to take care of me. You gave up everything because you *wanted* to. Because you were too afraid that you would fail. You made me your excuse and then you hated me for it."

"That's not true."

Marche closed her eyes. Why wouldn't the room stop moving? She tried to make sense of the words that the woman with her sister's voice had spoken. Were they true? She shook her head in denial; her throat ached. When she opened her eyes, she found that the world had righted itself. Bridget also looked like Bridget again, though her features remained contorted with emotion.

"It's true and you know it," Bridget said.

"Why would you say that?"

"Because you never let it go!" Bridget's voice, unused to shouting, cracked.

"All these years I've tried to...to...but you've never been anything but jealous. And you've always despised my accomplishments."

Marche tried to respond, but no words came out.

"How could you think that I wouldn't notice when it's always been so obvious?" Bridget continued, her voice hardened with bitterness. "You've hated every happiness I ever felt because it wasn't yours. You were jealous when I went to college because you never graduated. You were jealous when I started teaching because you weren't satisfied with your own career. And you couldn't stand it when I married Trey because he had a better job than Dom. So what are you doing here, Marche? Did you come here for your own amusement? Does it make you happy to see that I've failed at something? Huh?"

Marche shook her head again. "We're sisters. You're my only family, I—"

"What are you doing here? What are you doing here? WHAT ARE YOU DOING HERE?"

Tears of frustration gathered at the corners of Marche's eyes. She blinked them back. "I'm not happy that this happened to you."

"Bullshit." Bridget sagged against the wall. Releasing her death-grip on the sheet, she made a show of patting down the wrinkles. "You care so much, huh?"

"Yes, I do."

Bridget folded her hands in her lap and looked coolly at Marche. "Did you notice that I was anorexic?"

Fragments of memories collided and separated. What had those first few years with Bridget been like? All Marche could remember were sleepless nights, cartons of cigarettes on the kitchen table, microwaveable dinners piled high in the freezer, crappy jobs with crabby customers.

Everything between the lines remained hazy. Back then, her life had felt like it was smothered in a fog. One day blended seamlessly into the next. Even the holidays passed unnoticed. How could she remember Bridget's problems now if she'd been too rundown and depressed to notice them in the first place?

"All I ever wanted was to have babies with Trey, babies that I could smother with love. Now I can't even have that. I have a uterus that won't work. Because even though you were there, you were never really there."

"I'm sorry you feel that way," Marche replied, on the verge of tears.

"You've always been so absorbed in your own little world," Bridget continued as Marche grabbed her purse and headed for the door. "Everything that happens outside of it is insignificant to you."

As Marche rushed through the hospital corridors, desperate to reach the outdoors, a whispering voice at the back of her mind reluctantly acknowledged that not everything Bridget had said was untrue.

Twenty-Three

"Stop dragging your feet," Marche said.

She walked through the aisles of Appleton Supermarket with a slight bounce in her step. She'd slept soundly the past two nights. Disconnecting the landline before bedtime had ensured her the peace and quiet she'd needed to recharge. When she awoke this morning, she felt like a newly changed butterfly emerging from its cocoon.

"Stop dragging your feet," Marche repeated to Stella, who was hitching a ride on the shopping cart.

Stella pouted. Reluctantly she lifted her jellies off the floor and planted them on the chrome bar.

"Attention stockroom associates," a male voice said over the intercom. "Clean up behind aisle two. Attention, clean up behind aisle two."

Marche tilted her head backward to consult the red and yellow sign dangling from the ceiling overhead. They were in fruits and vegetables—aisle nine.

"I want gummy bears."

"Maybe if you're good," Marche said. She reached for a can of sliced pears and placed it in the cart.

"Puhleeease..."

"I said *maybe.*"

Marche grabbed three more fruit cans before browsing the vegetables. When she'd finished stocking up on canned peas and spinach, she scratched them off her list and turned the corner.

"I want puhghettios!" Stella chimed.

Marche skipped the next two aisles and then suddenly braked. "Maybe," she said, not really listening. Backing up the cart, she turned down aisle eleven.

Racks on the left side of the aisle featured magazines, paperbacks, word puzzles, and daily planners. Hair products—shampoos, gels, sprays, dyes—filled the shelves on the right. Marche ignored the items on display, her attention focused instead on the person thumbing through the latest edition of *Go Fishing*.

"Mr. Greene?" she said, parking the cart a few floor tiles from where he stood. "Hi, I don't know if you remember me? I'm Marche Baker, from down the street."

Malcolm stiffened, straightened, slapped the magazine shut. "I remember," he replied, returning the periodical to its assigned slot.

Marche's smile wavered. Avoiding her neighbor would have been easier, but she really wanted to break through his icy exterior. Why couldn't they be on friendly terms? "I can't believe how hot it's been lately!" she said with forced enthusiasm.

"Hmm."

"Does Egret Bay get like this every summer?"

"Not every summer."

Marche grabbed a magazine at random. She blushed when she read the title; she was twenty years too young to require any advice offered in *AARP*. "I guess you're probably too used to the weather here to notice, huh?"

Malcolm shrugged.

Opening the magazine, she scanned the table of contents. "Nope," she murmured in an attempt to cover her blunder. "This isn't the issue Shelley was talking about." As set the magazine aside, she noticed a girl in a print tee with tied sleeves leaning against the racks just a few feet away, a copy of *Seventeen* in hand. "Is this your daughter?"

"Granddaughter," he replied, his stony expression unchanged.

The girl glanced up, flashing a set of braces. "I'm Lissa."

"Hi, Lissa," Marche said. "I'm your grandpa's new neighbor. I moved into the house on the corner."

"Nice to meetcha."

"This is my daughter, Stella."

Stella was leaning over the cart so that the ends of her golden-brown hair grazed the groceries. In one courageous moment, she lifted her head to peek at Lissa. Then in a flash, she lowered it again, like a scared ostrich ducking its head in the ground.

"Cool," Lissa said, returning to the glossy pages of her magazine.

Marche shifted her attention back to Malcolm. He continued to avoid looking at her, his gaze flitting across the racks.

"Rory Vale told me that you and his son grew up together."

"That's right," Malcolm replied. "What of it?"

"I was thinking of hosting a barbeque the next time Vance is in town," Marche improvised. "You should join us. And bring the family too, of course," she added, motioning to Lissa. "I'd love to hear some of the local history—you and Vance must have tons of interesting stories to share about growing up in Egret Bay."

Malcolm's eyes narrowed as she spoke. "I don't think so." He turned to his granddaughter. "Lissa, why don't you go find Mee-Maw and see if she needs help with anything."

"Okay."

"Now, please."

"Just a minute, Paw-Paw. I'm reading about humiliating moments. This stuff is rich."

"Lissa! Put. It. Down."

"Aww, man." Lissa placed the magazine haphazardly on the rack and paraded past Marche, her shoulders drooped to an exaggerated degree.

"Excuse me—"

"Wait." Marche held out a hand; Malcolm eyed her exposed palm as though she'd dipped it in poison. "You seem like a nice person. And I'm a nice person," she said, pressing her hand to her chest for emphasis. "I don't understand why you won't speak to me."

Malcolm sighed.

"Have I done something wrong?" Marche continued. "Have I said something to offend you? At least tell me what it is so I can apologize."

Shaking his head like a man defeated, Malcolm finally met Marche's gaze. "Look," he said slowly, "we cannot associate with one another. That's just the way it is. Pushing the issue is…it's futile."

"But *why*?"

Malcolm took a deep breath. When he exhaled, a string of unintelligible words poured from his lips.

Though Marche strained to hear, "baby" was the only word she recognized. "Excuse me?"

Malcolm pressed his lips together in a grim line. He moved closer to Marche and leaned forward, keeping his back to Stella.

"She held…" Malcolm gulped, his Adam's apple bobbing. His eyes glistened—with what? Fear? "She was holding a mutilated baby in her arms!" he hissed. "I won't have anything to do with that house. Or with anyone who lives in it. Understand?"

He stormed down the aisle and disappeared, leaving Marche in a state of confusion.

"Mommy?"

Marche blinked, as if awakening from a trance. Had Malcolm really just said that? Was he mad? *Yes, he's mad. And I've given up trying to be neighborly.*

"Mommy?"

Marche relaxed her grip on the cart handle and pushed it forward. "What, Stella?"

"I want chips!"

"I thought you wanted gummy bears?" Marche replied. *The man is mad. I don't care what Vale said about him; he's completely bonkers.* She felt as though she'd slipped through a crack in reality and fallen headfirst into an episode of *The Twilight Zone*.

"Nuh-uh." Stella grabbed the sides of the cart and shook her head back and forth. "I want chee-does!"

"We'll see," Marche said.

She navigated the cart through the store with leaden feet. Though she tried to purge Malcolm's words from her mind, they stubbornly remained like an unwanted guest.

She didn't just hear the words—she saw and smelled them, too. They tumbled about behind her eyelids, composed of letters gleaming the bloodiest red. Their fluid lines, constantly dripping like melting ice cubes, revolted her; their metallic odor overwhelmed her nasal passages. Suddenly, she recalled the pulsating fetus she'd imagined on her bedroom floor.

Her stomach churned.

"How would you like to help make fudge for Shelley?" Marche said, forcing herself to think of other things. She wanted to thank her neighbor for babysitting Stella. Even though she wasn't very talented in the kitchen, she'd decided to make a homemade dessert.

"What's that?" Stella asked, tilting her head to one side.

"It's like fancy, super-sweet chocolate."

"Yummy!" Stella smacked her lips and jumped up and down on the chrome bar.

"Don't jump! You might fall and hurt yourself."

Turning down the baking aisle, Marche consulted her grocery list. Three of the ingredients she needed should be stocked here: cane sugar, unsweetened chocolate, and vanilla extract. She found the unsweetened chocolate first and dropped a box into the cart.

"Excuse me," a reedy voice said from behind.

"Certainly."

Marche wheeled the cart closer to one side so that an elderly man carrying a shopping basket could pass.

As she reached for the vanilla extract next, she thought of the old man—the windbreaker that he wore despite the suffocating heat, the pronounced stoop, the trembling in his step.

Will that be me in fifty years? The probability made her shiver. Dom had been her true life partner. They would have grown old together if not for the accident, she was sure of it. Even if she met someone with half of Dom's greatness, she doubted if she had any love left in her to give. She still had Stella, but that was hardly a consolation. Deep down, she feared that her daughter preferred her sister to her.

And Bridget hates my guts, apparently.

Marche hunted down the cane sugar, which she located toward the end of the aisle on a shelf near the bottom. "You excited about making fudge after dinner?" Marche asked. She leaned across the cart and stroked Stella playfully on the cheek with a forefinger.

"I want cookies!"

"This fudge is special," Marche said. "Grandpa taught me how to make it when I was a little girl."

Stella stomped her feet on the chrome bar, making the items in the cart rattle slightly. "I want cookies!"

"Don't you think it would be fun to make fudge?" Marche continued in her most cajoling voice. "Then you can give some to Shelley and tell her that you made it all by yourself. I bet Shelley would like that, don't you?"

"Umm..."

"What do you think?"

"I want cake!"

Twenty-Four

"I'm confident that with my experience in management..."

Marche belted out the words, certain that no one passing by would hear her as she pushed the mower across the front lawn. The interview for the Circulation Clerk III position was scheduled for Wednesday, and she was determined to wow the hiring committee.

Bridget hadn't been entirely wrong in her candid assessment of her in the hospital room. Marche wasn't happy with her career. Though she enjoyed her job at the library, she craved more. She was starving for a challenge. Before Dom's death, she'd considered returning to school. As a single mother, she could no longer afford that dream. But if she had a higher paying position...

She stopped to toss a stray tree branch onto the driveway. Wiping the sweat from her brow, she continued forward.

The heat remained oppressive, even at seven in the evening, so she'd opted for a bathing suit and shorts. In addition to its high temperatures, Egret Bay was also suffering from a drought. Rain hadn't fallen in more than a month—not since the day she and Shelley had taken the girls to the park. The grass, more brown than green, crackled under her feet.

Near the mailbox, she ran over an ant pile. "Ugh. Nasty little devils!" She tramped a path to the backyard and went inside the shed.

"Where did I put it?" she muttered.

A wealth of unopened boxes filled the small space. Though she'd had the foresight to label them "outdoor stuff," she hadn't taken the time to write anything more specific regarding their contents.

The first box she tore open contained extension cords. The second held a trowel, shears, a watering can, and other gardening tools. *Maybe I should give these to Shelley*, she thought, closing the flaps. The third and fourth boxes didn't have what she was looking for either. She finally found the ant poison in box number five, located just inside the door.

Returning to the mailbox, she poured a healthy dose of the powder over the mound. Unfortunately, she stood too close. When the ants scattered, a small army of them climbed onto her tennis shoes. She screeched and stomped her feet. Although she managed to brush them all off, a small red welt appeared on one of her ankles.

She finished with the yard a short while later and pushed the mower into the shed, where it fit snugly between the ladder and boxes. She felt soiled to the bone. Dirt lined her fingernails and caked the creases inside her elbows. When she licked her lips, she tasted salt. Her scalp itched; her bare toes felt slimy inside her shoes. Gathering up a pair of beach towels she'd left inside the front door, she trotted over to her neighbor's.

Shelley reclined in a lounge chair under the jacaranda. She watched over Stella and Coral, who were chasing each other around a turtle-shaped wading pool.

"Would you like a chair?" Shelley asked as Marche approached. "I can ask Hank to bring one out for you."

"I'll just use the towel, but thanks."

Marche cast a longing glance at the Franklins' in-ground swimming pool, surrounded by a forty-eight-inch white vinyl fence.

"Fancy a dip?" Shelley asked.

"Was I being that obvious?"

"The bathing suit," Shelley said with a chuckle. "Go ahead. Enjoy yourself."

Marche stripped down to her one-piece and unlatched the gate. The clear water looked cool and inviting in the fading sunlight. Holding her breath, she dove into the deep end and emerged near the steps. She kicked off the wall and swam several laps across the twenty-foot distance. When her muscles began to tire, she closed her eyes and floated. Cicadas serenaded her from the neighboring trees; the girls' squeals of delight as they played in the yard mingled with their song.

Marche thought of her sister. She'd sent Trey texts every day to see how Bridget was faring. Each time her brother-in-law responded with brief but reassuring messages. Today he'd informed her that Bridget would return to work on Monday. "I'm so happy to hear she's doing well," she replied. "Tell Bridget I'm thinking of her." As she pressed the "send" button, she recalled the ugliness of Bridget's curled lip when her sister accused her of heartlessness. Would Bridget reveal that same expression if they stood face-to-face now?

Marche flipped over and swam a few more laps before getting out of the pool. She padded back over to Shelley and the girls, grass debris clinging to her wet feet. The towel felt toasty on her bottom.

"Did you hear about that accident on the Courtney Campbell this morning?" Shelley reached for a fudge square; she'd set the dessert plate, along with a pitcher of fruit punch and four glasses, on a small plastic table beside the chair.

Marche leaned back on her elbows. "No, I didn't. What happened?"

"Man drove his wife and kids into the gulf."

"How horrible!" Marche sat up and grabbed a piece of dessert. "Do they know why?"

"Heaven knows," Shelley replied, licking chocolate from her fingers. "Reporters said he got laid off from his job months ago, but never told anyone. Pretended everything was peaches and cream. Guess he just snapped."

Marche recalled Stella's pale, unresponsive face in the bathwater and shuddered. "Those poor kids. And the wife, too."

"That's not the end of the story."

"How's that?"

"Guy didn't die. Had a change of heart at the last second."

Marche reached for a glass of punch to wash down the chocolate stuck in her throat. "Didn't I hear a story last month about a woman who left her car running in the garage?"

"I remember that. There was an infant in the backseat." Shelley slapped her shoulder; the mosquitoes were swarming out of the woodwork in droves. "It's this godforsaken heat. Sometimes I think it's enough to drive even the sanest person a little crazy. You know, the papers say this is the hottest Egret Bay's gotten in sixty years? The number of heatstroke cases has already quadrupled from last year."

"That's no joke," Marche said with a whistle.

The girls were crouching at the hedges alongside the Franklin house. Their cries of excitement intensified as they rushed back to the wading pool. Stella sat down on one of the seats (flat, round, and colored white and black to resemble a turtle's eye) and tossed a toad into the water.

"Make it swim!" Coral screeched. "He-re! He-re! Make it swim he-re!"

Marche slipped her shoes onto her feet and stood. "Time to go back inside, Stella. Put the toad back where you found it."

"Now, Mommy?"

"Yes, now. Go on. Put it right there—right under that bush beside the flowers. Good job. Here's a towel. Now let's get you dried off."

Marche spent the next three days absorbed in preparation for the interview.

As she swept the floors, she addressed various pieces of furniture as though they were members of the hiring committee. When she showered, she recited an impromptu speech to Stella's Miss Piggy, which she'd placed on the soap dish. Brushing her hair before the mirror, she practiced her facial expressions. Should she show her teeth? Widen her eyes? Tilt her head to the right? Or maybe the left side looked better?

After tucking Stella in for the night, she brainstormed on paper. She wrote down her strengths, considered the key points of the position, and determined how one complemented the other. Then she composed a monologue rich with strong verbs and compelling adjectives. Afterward, she lay in bed anxiously mulling over each line. She doubted herself. Should she re-write her introductory comments? Was her concluding statement strong enough? She felt like a schoolgirl preparing for an exam. Except that there was more at stake than red marks on a paper. This wasn't a classroom. This was "pass or fail" in the real world. And a weak performance would negatively impact her plans for the future.

Preparing breakfast on Tuesday, she recited her speech at a feverish pace. She stumbled on her way to the refrigerator, the words subsequently stumbling from her mouth. She started over again. Perfect. It had to be perfect. If she messed up a single phrase, the remaining lines collapsed like a house of cards.

"Speak slowly. Calmly. Articulate clearly. Make a statement. Make an *impact.*"

"Who are you talking to, Mommy?"

"Nobody. Just giving myself a pep talk for tomorrow's speech," Marche replied as she set a bowl of cereal before Stella.

"What's a speech?"

"It's, um..." Marche realized that she'd stuffed the milk in the cabinet and the cereal in the refrigerator. "It's something that you prepare in advance to say to somebody," she replied as she put the food items in their correct places.

"What's a advance?"

"It means beforehand."

"What's beforehand?"

And so Marche spent the remainder of breakfast engaged in a question-and-answer session with Stella.

Twenty-Five

"When are you taking your lunch break?" Sarah asked.

It was a quarter to noon. Though the hands on the clock ticked steadily by the second, time seemed to stagnate. Marche felt like a parched customer at a restaurant where the waiter's nowhere to be found. Anxious to get on with her interview, each second expanded to an unnatural length.

"About twelve-thirty, I guess," Marche said. "Why? What's up?"

"I've got something to show you."

"Can it wait until tomorrow?"

"I won't see you tomorrow."

"Oh. Right." Marche straightened the discarded due-date cards in her basket. As she organized first the red cards (for twenty-eight-day books) and then the blue (for fourteen) she said, "My interview's at two. I was hoping—"

"You're not worried about it, are you? The job's a shoo-in. I read the posting—you're a perfect fit, and everyone here knows it. The city'd be foolish to hire someone else."

A Post-it note fell off the counter and fluttered to the floor. Marche picked it up, saw that it was a name and contact number regarding a set of lost keys, and taped it to the counter. "That may be so, but I can't afford to be cocky."

Sarah took advantage of the brief lull at the circulation desk to touch-up her hair. "You've practiced, haven't you?" she said as she unclipped her tortoiseshell barrette. "You've thought about what to say?"

"Of course," Marche replied. "Non-stop for three days."

"Cripes, Marche! You're in worse shape than I thought." Running her fingers through her wavy mane, she worked out the kinks and repositioned the hair clip.

"If you don't relax a little before the main event, you're liable to blow a fuse. What do you say? Up for some show-and-tell?"

Marche thought about it. Maybe she *was* a little too wound up. What if someone on the interview panel asked her a question and her mind suddenly went blank? "All right," she said.

Sarah held up both thumbs. "Score!" she exclaimed, smiling broadly.

"Let's use the staff kitchen," Sarah said, retrieving a blue folder from her locker. "So we'll have privacy."

They grabbed their food from the refrigerator and rode the elevator to the second floor. The doors opened to silence.

Here, no one (except for the occasional belligerent patron) spoke above a whisper. An unwritten agreement between staff and library-goers honored the reference department as a sanctuary for the gathering of thoughts, the search for knowledge, and the formulation of new ideas. A book falling onto the floor was tantamount to a wrecking ball knocking a hole into the roof. The slightest disturbance produced a shock to the nerves, eliciting scowls from all within earshot.

Marche and Sarah passed the reference desk, where the librarian on duty was helping a girl find books about Abraham Lincoln. A man with curly red hair and a scraggly beard stood at the printing station nearby. Thumping his foot with impatience, he stared at the librarian as he waited for assistance.

The break room was located just past the short stacks of newspapers and periodicals. Marche never used the room when she was by herself—it was too isolated, too austere. Tucked into the back corner of the library, its windows overlooked the rear parking lot and the fringes of Great Pine Estates. Marche opened the door. The overhead lights automatically flickered on, illuminating the room's two tables, microwave, toaster oven, and stainless steel sink.

Sarah popped her frozen meal into the microwave. Pulling out a chair at the table closest to the windows, she opened a green Tupperware container. She picked up a celery stalk, put it back without taking a bite, and reached for the folder instead. With reverential fingers, she extracted its contents.

Marche sat down opposite her. Reaching inside her brown bag, she withdrew the lunch she'd prepared that morning: a ham and cheese on rye sandwich, yogurt, and a bottle of Pepsi. Peeling back the cellophane wrap on her main course, she cast a cursory glance at Sarah's mysterious collection of papers. "Are those newspaper articles?"

"Mm," Sarah replied, splaying her hands over the sheets. "Evan drove to the university library in Tampa to print them from microfiche."

"What's so interesting about them?" Picking up one of the triangular halves of her sandwich, she took a hearty bite.

Sarah drummed her fingers on the tabletop. "When you first told me where you lived, I thought the location sounded familiar: Victor and Washington. Something 'clicked' in my brain," she declared, pausing in her drumming to snap her fingers. "But I wasn't sure why."

Marche unscrewed the cap on her soda bottle and took a sip; the carbonation tickled her throat.

"Last night it hit me. It's the *Louis* house."

Marche took another bite of her sandwich. "That's right," she said, covering her mouth as she chewed. "The previous owner's name was Louis."

"You don't get it." Sarah's voice resonated with awe; her busy fingers stilled.

"I guess not."

"It's *the* Louis house," Sarah said. When Marche merely shrugged, she widened her eyes for emphasis. "The Louis family has *history*."

"Oh?" Marche tilted the soda bottle and drank deeply.

"It's all right here." Sarah waved a hand over the papers. "Evan collected everything he could find on them. The 'Louis Curse' is one of his favorite subjects."

Marche choked on her Pepsi. She set the bottle aside, uncapped. "What are you talking about?" she asked between coughs.

"All of the women—dating back to the 1800s—have died prematurely."

Sarah's response caught Marche off guard. She looked at the sandwich, hovering before her lips, and set it down. "Come again?"

"Well, that might not be entirely true," Sarah conceded. "Evan hasn't researched all of George Louis's descendants—just the direct line connecting to the people who lived in your house."

Marche leaned forward, overwhelmed by a budding curiosity. She hadn't been lying when she told Malcolm Greene that she was interested in learning the local history. "You've got my attention."

Sarah closed her eyes and remained silent for a moment. Then she nodded, opened her eyes, and stared at the bulletin board across the room, where the director of human resources had tacked up flyers regarding work safety, state laws, and local jobs.

"Okay," Sarah began, her voice robust with excitement. "So George Louis—he's the first generation American. He sails over from England in 1759 and settles in New York. He makes a name for himself in the shipping industry and marries Nora Coldwall, the daughter of some affluent family who's been around since the pilgrims."

Sarah shifted her attention to Marche. Eyes ablaze and body humming with energy, she resembled a ghost tour guide—minus the period costume. "They have a slew of kids. Like four boys and two girls, or something like that. Their oldest, John, he's an adventurer. He's also something of an egomaniac. George and Nora dote on him. Whatever John wants, John gets."

A childhood memory bubbled to the surface—her mother and father swinging Bridget by the arms, while Marche trailed behind with her sand pail. She blinked away the remembrance, forcing herself to focus on Sarah's words.

"In 1799, John decides he wants to explore the world. George is already dead, and Nora has more money than she knows what to do with, so she gives her son the funds he needs to secure a ship for his travels.

"John sets sail...and no one hears a peep from him for *eight* years. Then suddenly he docks at port—the ship full of exotic goods, a heavily pregnant woman on his arm. Who is she?" Sarah curled the corner of a paper absentmindedly. "John claims that they're married, but no one knows anything about her family background or even which country she's from. The locals describe Marietta as a tall woman with 'dark hair and darker eyes.' She hardly speaks, but when she does, her voice is so heavily accented that she's difficult to understand."

The microwave beeped. Sarah, absorbed in her storytelling, ignored it.

"So John and Marietta move in with Nora. But John's got plans. He's like a peacock—he wants to show off his feathers. So what does he do? He dismantles the *Hercules* and uses whatever parts aren't too sea-worn to enhance the new home that he's building for his wife and child. Before he can finish it, though, tragedy strikes. Marietta dies in childbirth. Then a year later, his mother also dies."

Sarah paused for breath. "So this is where the story starts to get weird." She ran the tip of her finger over the papers and selected an article on the periphery of the pile.

"John finally finishes construction on the house and moves into it with his son and Jenna—Marietta's midwife. Jenna nurses baby Andrew, and within a few years, she becomes the new Mrs. Louis. Then, in 1813, John finds his pregnant wife hanging from the upstairs railing."

Marche grimaced. The image of a faceless woman—round in the stomach, dangling from a rope with twitching feet—swam into her vision. She thought of the banister on the second floor of her home. Would that be sturdy enough to hold dead weight? The thought made her shudder. She swallowed what food she'd been chewing and set the remainder of her sandwich aside.

"Why did she kill herself?" Sarah continued.

Marche shook her head at the rhetorical question.

"Is it guilt? After her suicide, the locals start theorizing that John's first wife didn't die from childbirth complications. Maybe Jenna lusted after John? Maybe John found having a foreign wife too much to handle? At any rate, Jenna dies and John doesn't remarry."

Setting the article aside, Sarah studied the other clippings silently for a moment. "That's just the beginning," she said, grabbing another paper. "John and Marietta's only child grows up, gets married, and raises his family in the same house. You'd think that would be the end of the story. Happily ever after, right? *Wrong*. In 1847, Andrew decides that his young, sickly daughter needs to live in a warmer climate. So he uproots the family to Egret Bay. But before he does that, he dismantles parts of the house—floorboards, railings, doors—relics from his father's ship. Like his father before him, he uses these pieces in the construction of his home."

Sarah paused. "Is this relevant? Maybe, maybe not," she said with a slight shrug. "Two years later, Andrew's wife, Lucille, has an accident. One of her husband's workers is in the yard chopping wood. Lucille goes outside to hang up the wash. It's the flukiest thing. As she's walking past him, the man loses his grip mid-swing. The axe blade hits her near the collarbone, practically decapitating her."

The saliva in Marche's mouth seemed to dry up. She balled up the cellophane, careful not to spill any crumbs on the table, and tossed it into the garbage. "Was it—" She cleared her throat. "Was it really an accident?"

"That's the worst part of it," Sarah replied. "There's a witness—six-year-old Charles sees Mommy nearly losing her head."

Marche reflexively touched her throat. "Oh my god. I can't imagine how traumatizing that must have been."

"And not just that," Sarah added. "He discovers his sister's body twelve years later."

"No!" Marche opened her yogurt cup and stirred the contents.

"Yes." Sarah nodded. "Charles finds her at the foot of the stairs, her head twisted almost three hundred and sixty degrees."

The blueberry flavor tasted bland; Marche pushed it aside.

"There's more." Sarah shuffled the papers around before plucking another one from the pile. "Charles marries Carlotta..." She paused for a moment as she searched through the old type. "Excuse me. *Cassandra* Pierce. According to neighbors, they have the postcard life. Then, in 1883, their oldest son, Frederick, discovers her with her head in the cookstove."

"Did they use gas for stoves in 1883?"

Sarah gave her a pointed look. "She didn't die from carbon monoxide poisoning."

"Huh?"

"She'd been preparing the Thanksgiving roast. It was the *smell* that finally alerted everyone to what had happened."

Marche pushed away from the table, the chair's legs scraping noisily on the tile. She tossed away the yogurt cup. What little appetite she had at the beginning of their lunch break abruptly fled.

Sarah continued: "Eventually, Frederick inherits the house. In 1932, he rebuilds it—again, reusing some of the original pieces. And in 1942, his wife Paula puts a gun to her head. She spends eight days in the hospital before finally biting the bullet. The couple has a set of twins, Charles and—"

"Agatha," Marche said. She sipped the soda to ease her parched throat.

"That's right. Charles and Agatha." Sarah picked up another paper. "Like all of the Louis men before him, Charles stays in the family house. And in 1969, his pregnant wife kills herself in the bathtub."

Marche walked over to the sink to rinse the spoon. The water splashed warmly over her fingers.

"That's where it ends," Sarah said. "I'm assuming that Charles never remarried or had children."

Marche recalled her conversation with Vale. "No, he didn't." She rejoined Sarah at the table. With jerky movements, she shoved the spoon back into the lunch bag.

"Of course, all the deaths are easily explainable. Though I think the head in the oven is a bit sketchy. Maybe someone snuck up from behind and knocked her out? Who knows?" With her first two fingers, Sarah traced an invisible design on the tabletop. "You moved into the house belonging to, like, the most infamous family in the area. And you didn't even know it." She collected the papers into a neat pile and shoved them back into the folder.

"I'll have to give you a tour sometime," Marche said.

Sarah, misinterpreting the sarcasm in Marche's voice, beamed. "Evan would totally love that. I guess I'd better stop talking though and start eating if I'm going to have anything for lunch today." She retrieved her food from the microwave. As she stabbed the chicken with a fork, she turned a quizzical gaze upon Marche. "Would you like to look through these for yourself?"

She slid the folder across the table. It glided over the surface, stopping at a slant beside her bag. Hesitantly, Marche opened it.

It was a cheap paper folder—the type with pockets and prongs that sold for a dime at office supply stores at the start of the school season. Sarah had stuffed all of the papers into one pocket. Marche withdrew the entire stack.

At first, she examined them for their aesthetic value. She admired the layout of the type, the varying fonts, and the quality of the paper (hinted at through the transference process). The majority of the articles were short—not more than a paragraph. Most of them were obituaries.

For the next few minutes, she quietly perused the death notices while her co-worker munched on celery stalks and chicken Alfredo. Sarah had covered most of the information they contained. Marche was impressed. Evan had thoroughly researched the topic, collecting obituaries for all of the direct descendants, including those who had lived in her house.

In addition to these records, there was also an exposé on the first Charles Louis, who ran for a political seat in the county in 1886. The piece was dated three years after Cassandra's death. The concluding section read: *"Mr. Louis is a man whom one may rely upon through any hardship. He has experienced the type of loss that can immobilize the most stoic of men. Not only has he endured the death of his wife, but also that of his beloved mother and sister—all under the same roof. Yet he has risen above these personal tragedies to become the prosperous man who stands before you today. His own testament of triumph should leave no doubt in one's mind: Elect Mr. Louis, the man who will carry this community to greater success. Elect in your future."*

"Makes you wonder how much he really cared about his family," Marche murmured.

Sarah finished her celery stalks and closed the lid on the Tupperware container. "That's how Evan happened upon the 'Louis Curse,'" she said. "He was taking an ethics course and decided to write his research paper on local politicians of the nineteenth century. If this guy hadn't used his dead family as fodder for his campaign, Evan might never have discovered it. It's not exactly common knowledge, you know. From what Evan can tell, no one's ever written about the Louis deaths."

Marche skimmed through the rest of the papers, the last of which detailed the deaths of Betty and—several decades later—Charles Louis. In the process of slipping the articles back into the pocket, she discovered a sheet of paper that she'd initially missed.

"What's this?" she asked.

Sarah glanced across the table. Hastily, she swallowed the last bite of chicken. "Ignore that, it's just one of Evan's crazy theories."

"He has a *theory*?"

"Oh, you know." Sarah gave a slight shrug. "He plans on writing a book about Egret Bay someday, with a chapter devoted to the Louis family. So naturally, he likes to fill in the blanks, figure out what the journalists might have omitted." Creating rabbit ears, she said (in a deepened voice that Marche guessed was supposed to imitate her boyfriend): "'Echoes of the unspoken trapped between the lines.'"

Marche perused the scribble. At first, she didn't understand what it meant. The yellow paper, torn from a legal pad, listed a series of questions. She read and reread them.

Jealous midwife?

Natural death??

Why only the women?

House demolished; rebuilt.

Can a location be cursed?

Is Marietta the key?

"You know, what you said isn't exactly true," Marche commented.

"Huh? Which part?"

"You said *all* of the Louis women died prematurely."

"Mm-hmm," Sarah replied, swallowing another bite of chicken.

"But Agatha didn't die young. In fact, she's still alive and kicking."

Marche returned the papers to the folder. As she closed it, the enormity of what she'd just learned hit her like a shock of cold air. She almost laughed (except that it really wasn't funny) at the irony.

Her sole purpose for relocating to Egret Bay had been to escape the tragedy that had become her life. Instead, she had purchased a testament to human misfortune and misery.

Twenty-Six

Marche couldn't stop fidgeting. She smoothed down the front of her suit and picked imaginary lint from her sleeves. She rolled her head from side to side until the bones in her neck popped. Weaving her fingers together, she bent them outward so the joints cracked. She curled her toes inside her shoes. Then, leaning back in the chair, she pointed her toes upward until the muscles in her calves ached.

Marche was stifling a nervous yawn when Phyllis finally fetched her for the interview. "Ready?"

Marche quickly nodded, logged out of the circulation module, and stood.

"We're rooting for you, kiddo," Genie said with a wink.

Marche smiled nervously at Genie, Sarah, and Ebony before following the supervisor across the main floor.

"The interview's going to take place in one of the smaller conference rooms upstairs," Phyllis said, leading Marche to the elevator.

They rode the car to the second floor without speaking. When the doors opened, Phyllis turned left. They strode past study tables—even during the summer, there were kids bent over their books, preparing for exams—and then entered the stacks. The conference rooms were located along the wall on the other side.

"It's this room up here," Phyllis said as they passed the large print mysteries. Opening the door, she stepped inside.

Marche straightened her shoulders, took a deep breath, and followed.

The panel was smaller than she'd expected, with just two other people present. Both of them rose to their feet when she entered.

Florence, who stood closest to the door, extended her hand first. "Hi, Marche, how are you?"

"I'm doing fine, thanks. And you?" Marche said, returning the handshake.

The other person in the room was Robin Maxwell, the library director. Marche had conversed with him only once—during her phone interview for the circulation clerk position. (When Phyllis had given her the grand tour on her first day, he'd been too busy to do anything but say a quick hello.) Marche didn't take it personally. Since she first set foot in the library, she'd never seen him interact with anyone below supervisor status.

Robin was tall—nearly as tall as Vale—and his expression stern. His grip on her hand was cold and firm. "Mrs. Baker, we're glad to have you here today."

"Thank you, Mr. Maxwell. I'm excited for the opportunity to be here."

Marche walked around the oblong table. Though it was long enough to seat ten people, someone had removed the extra chairs, placing them in stacks along the wall. As she began to lower herself into the chair placed opposite the interview panel, she noticed Phyllis waiting expectantly, hand extended.

"Oh!" Marche shook her supervisor's hand from a half-squatting position, blushing at her faux pas.

The director, seated directly across from her, spoke first. "On behalf of Egret Bay, I would like to thank you for expressing interest in this position and for taking the time to meet with us today."

Marche dipped her chin in acknowledgment.

"Before we begin, I would like to explain to you how the hiring process works. This particular committee consists of three individuals: Phyllis Tuttle, the circulation supervisor, Florence Brodeur, the director of human resources, and myself, the library director.

"Once we have conducted all of the interviews, we will consider the merits of each candidate. In the case of a tie, we will use a ranking system. Once the candidate has been selected, the committee will make a recommendation to the city manager. The entire process may take anywhere from one to three weeks. If you have any concerns in the meantime, you may contact Florence." Robin folded his hands on the table. "Do you have any questions so far?"

"No," Marche replied.

"Normally we would provide you with a brief summary of city and library policies. Since you are already a city employee, however, we can dispense with that aspect."

Robin waded through the formalities, his voice as colorless as his demeanor. While he spoke, Marche sat with her back as straight as a yoga instructor. She pressed her knees together and planted her shoes flat on the floor. She pulled her abdominal muscles taut. She kept her shoulders high. *Be confident. Be in control.*

"Florence has put together an information packet, which you may peruse at your leisure," the director continued.

Marche glanced briefly at the papers fanned out on the tabletop before her.

"The first sheet covers policies and procedures. The second addresses the benefits, which are identical to what you already receive as a full-time employee. On the third, you will find a detailed description of the position. And the last one outlines the proposed schedule. If you would like to have a look at that now?"

"Certainly," Marche mumbled. Pulling out the schedule, she examined it.

"This is a full-time position requiring forty hours a week. Right now we're looking at Tuesday through Saturday. Eleven-thirty to eight during the week and eight-thirty to five on the weekend." Robin assessed her with steady gray eyes. "Are you available for these hours?"

"I am," Marche said without hesitation.

"Good," Maxwell replied in that same monotone manner. "The official title for this position is Circulation Clerk III. This position reports to the circulation supervisor who, in turn, reports to the director. Though this is not a supervisory position, per se, the job will require a moderate amount of supervision, overseeing the department in the supervisor's absence. Is that understood?"

Marche nodded.

"You'll notice on the third sheet that the proposed duties for the Circulation Clerk III have been outlined in detail."

That was a vast understatement. The third sheet was actually two pieces of paper stapled together with blocks of single-spaced type covering both sides. Marche gazed across the expanse of black and white but found herself unable to focus on any of the words.

"First and foremost, the Circulation Clerk III assumes responsibility for scheduling the staff in the circulation department."

Marche nodded, for perhaps the fifth time in as many minutes, and mentally scolded herself. Why was she behaving as though she had a neck made of rubber?

"The Circulation Clerk III will also assist with booking the program rooms and maintaining the information kiosk in the lobby. Other tasks include assisting with the ordering of office supplies, assigning prices for lost and damaged items, resolving patron conflicts, registering patrons for library cards, and checking out materials." The director paused. "We have drafted a schedule to accommodate these sundry tasks. Barring special circumstances, the workweek will consist of eighteen hours at the public service desk and twenty-two hours at a private station in the circulation workroom."

Robin paused, reordering the papers before him.

"I realize that this is a tremendous amount of information to digest all at once," he said. "Are there any details that you would like to have clarified? Or questions that you have regarding the job description?"

"Not at the moment," Marche replied.

"In that case, the committee has some questions that we would like to ask you. To keep the process fair among the candidates, we won't ask anything spontaneous."

Words and phrases that Marche had prepared for the interview filled her mind like helium inflating a balloon. From the moment she sat down, she'd been so preoccupied with not forgetting what she wanted to say that she only half-heard the director's ten-minute introduction. Eagerly, she waited to begin.

Robin picked up a fountain pen, uncapped it, and read the first question. "Why did you apply for this position?"

Marche took a preparatory breath...then felt the world jerk to a stop.

Everything that she'd practiced—every noun, verb, and adjective from her speech—suddenly slipped through her grasp like water through a sieve. Seconds ticked by. The blood rushed wildly in her veins; her heart thumped to a rhythm so maddening that it almost produced pain. Could they see her jugular dancing a merry jig?

The eyes of the panel studied her with acute interest. Marche's confidence thinned until she felt like a microbe squirming under a slide. What had she wanted to say? The silence became a palpable, fifth presence in the room. She opened her mouth to speak, unsure what words might tumble forth.

"I enjoy working here," she stated. "Also, I think that the experience I've acquired as a manager applies directly to this position."

Silently, Marche groaned. The response sounded so stilted, so lame to her own ears. Surely it must sound even worse to an audience—especially one with high expectations. She cleared her throat and smiled brightly.

Robin scribbled a few lines. Marche watched the pen glide over the page. The director's fingers were long and hairless with square tips. Transfixed by the baby-smooth skin and immaculate fingernails, she suddenly wondered if he received professional manicures. Along with that thought came an image of him wearing pink tights and a tutu.

A bubble of laughter collected in Marche's throat.

Oh, shit. Don't laugh. Don't laugh. Don't laugh.

Beneath the table, she clenched her hands until the nails carved half-moons into her flesh. She clamped her mouth shut and swallowed roughly.

"Where do you see yourself in five years?" Florence asked next.

Marche moistened her lips. "Ideally, I'll be working here as a Circulation Clerk III—perhaps with increased responsibilities."

All three heads bent forward as the panel put pen to paper.

"I also hope to have completed a bachelor's degree by that time," Marche continued, the threat of hysteria momentarily quelled. "After that, I intend to pursue an MLS. Ultimately, I'd like to transition from a paraprofessional position to one of professional status. If you choose me for this position, I guarantee that you'll be making a worthwhile investment for the organization."

A hint of a smile played about the corners of Florence's lips. Looking up from the paper, she put forth another question. "If you could have lunch with any three people, living or dead, who would you choose?"

Marche smiled, finally at ease. After a moment's thought, she rattled off the names of a few well-known literary figures, comfortable in the knowledge that her answer would impress the panel. Or maybe not? Phyllis didn't bat an eye—but she'd probably never read a novel from start to finish, let alone anything of classic literary status. Though Florence's features seemed to flicker with recognition when she mentioned writers from the Victorian era, the director remained impassive. *Maybe he doesn't even like books,* Marche thought.

"Is this me?" Phyllis asked, pointing to the paper.

"Yes, it is," Robin replied.

Marche looked to her supervisor and waited. Whatever had caused her mental hiccup at the start of the interview seemed to have vanished. Her performance was still salvageable. All she needed to do was maintain this momentum in order to blow the competition out of the water.

"What do you like most about working in the library?" Phyllis asked.

Marche made a pointed effort of making eye contact with each committee member as she spoke. "Obviously, I love being surrounded by books," she began. "But I also enjoy working with the public. I find interacting with patrons intellectually stimulating and emotionally rewarding. There's a kind of serendipitous learning that makes every day different and interesting. The library really is the best place to be, and I feel very fortunate to work here."

"Mm-hmm," Phyllis replied as she recorded notes on paper. "Very good."

Another pause ensued. The room was quiet, so quiet that Marche could hear the director breathing from across the table.

Phyllis waited until the others were ready to continue. Then she read the next question. "Given the job description, what qualities do you think are most important for someone in this position?"

Marche needed only a few seconds to comb through her memory files as a bookstore manager to compose an appropriate answer. "Strong customer service skills," she said. "The ability to solve problems efficiently..."

As she spoke, a scene unfolded in her mind. It played like a memory—vivid but fleeting. (Three seconds? Four?) Engaging her senses, she *heard* and she *smelled*. But it was not a recollection that belonged to her: she was an audience member observing actors on a stage.

A young woman steps onto a porch, screen door slamming shut behind her. She's young. Maybe twenty? Her blonde hair, collected into a braid, drapes over one shoulder. She wears an apron and carries a wicker basket filled with clothes. Though pale-skinned, her cheeks are ruddy with warmth.

She descends the stoop and rounds the house, her steps slowed by the weight of wet garments. She stops to slap a mosquito feasting on the back of her neck. Then she glances over her shoulder and smiles at a dark-haired boy gazing through a second-floor window. Securing her grip on the basket, she continues forward.

Behind the house, a man in dirty, sweat-stained clothes is chopping wood. His shirtsleeves, rolled up to his elbows, reveal forearms thick with rippling muscle. He places a block upright and splits it with a single, well-aimed blow.

"Good work, Henry," the woman says.

The man grunts. Without looking at her, he positions another block on the ground. He lifts the axe, prepares a heavy swing.

The woman walks near him, her attention focused on her destination—a clothesline several yards away.

Neither takes heed of the crow circling in the air above them, so neither notices when it suddenly swoops down like an anhinga hell-bent on spearing a fish.

The animal flies at Henry, its black wings flapping wildly in his face. Henry shakes his head, losing his balance mid-swing. Blindly he totters forward—a huge bulk of a man without an ounce of grace in his body. The axe cuts through the air without purpose—

The woman looks up, her eyes widening with surprise and dread. Before she can react, the metal connects with her body. There's a sickening thwack. The skin at the base of her throat splits open. Red gushes out. The air thickens with a nauseating blend of blood and wood pulp. Slowly, the woman's head falls backward—tissue and muscle and bone exposed. The basket falls, the knees buckle, and the body crumples into a heap on the grass.

From inside the house, a little boy screams. "Mommy! Mommy! Mommy!"

"...efficiently and effectively," Marche continued, stammering. "A compassionate attitude is important as well. A good manager can weigh the pros and cons of a situation simultaneously, while also considering how things appear from the customer's viewpoint."

Marche bit the inside of her cheek, hoping the pain would distract her from the nightmare she'd just imagined. *I can't afford to lose focus. Not now.*

"Are you ready for the next question?" Phyllis asked.

"Fire away." Marche chuckled, but the sound came out garbled, like she was choking on a piece of meat.

Phyllis consulted the paper.

The silence weighed heavily on Marche. What must they think of her performance? She curled her lips into an expression of ease that she didn't feel and blinked as though she hadn't a care in the world.

"Please describe how you work alone—"

Marche choked back a scream.

Partway through the question, a dime-sized red dot appeared at the center of Phyllis' throat. With lightning speed, it stretched outward in both directions—a thick ribbon of scarlet. Like a flower separated from its stem, the supervisor's head fell onto the tabletop. Rather than roll, it bounced like a basketball, a pool of bodily fluids stamping like a footprint where it made contact with polished wood.

"—versus—"

Bounce.

"—how you—"

Bounce.

"—work—"

Bounce.

"—in a group."

The flame-haired crown came to a stop on her paperwork, its gooey underside distorting the ink. Dull eyes blinked at her dumbly.

"Um..." Marche found herself unable to tear her gaze from the disembodied head. She spoke to it, dry-mouthed, her voice reduced to a croak. "I'm sorry. Could you repeat the question?"

Twenty-Seven

The following Saturday, Marche went back to work on the spare room. The painting was complete except for the one wall that Bridget suggested they pattern after a garden. Marche had wanted to include her sister in this phase of the project, but if she waited for Bridget to come around, they'd end up painting through cobwebs.

She will *come around.*

But when Marche recalled the atmosphere in the hospital room, she felt uneasy. Some of what Bridget said had been true. In the clear light of day, Marche recognized that. Now she wondered how she would face Bridget when they spoke again. How should she apologize? And what exactly should she apologize for?

At the craft store, Stella enthusiastically pointed to every other stencil on display. "Which do you like better—this one or this one?" By holding up the stencils two at a time, Marche managed to narrow the "Stella approved" selection down to six. Dropping the butterflies, songbirds, and dandelions into the basket, they moved on to the paint department.

"What color do you want the birds to be?" Marche asked.

"Blue!"

"Okay, bluebirds it is."

Marche purchased a large pad of paper and a set of small brushes so that Stella could create her own masterpieces while she painted the mural. *Because I want her to have fun,* her inner voice insisted. *It's not because I don't want to work in that room alone.*

Back at the house, she spread a sheet of plastic on the floor beneath one of the windows. Then she poured paint into four plastic dishes.

"When you're finished with a color, you clean the brush like this." Marche dipped the bristles into the jar of water. "And before you pick another color, you dry it like this." She pressed the bristles to the paper towel to demonstrate.

"I know how to paint, Mommy. I'm not stoopid."

Marche chuckled. "Of course you're not," she said, handing the brush to daughter. "You're the smartest cookie in the whole bakery."

As she turned to work on her own project, the old trunk of letters caught her attention. Briefly, she thought of the women she'd read about in Sarah's newspaper articles—the wives and daughters of the Louis men. What was the probability—statistically speaking—that every single one would suffer an unnatural death? Marche shivered. If she believed in the supernatural, she might agree with Sarah's boyfriend that the family was cursed.

But I don't believe.

With a firm shake of the head, she withdrew the stencils from the shopping bag and set about taping them to the wall.

She worked on the dandelions first, tracing dark green stems (one style curved, one straight) across the cucumber mint wall. Backtracking, she added the petals. As she filled in the yellow pigment, her thoughts drifted—as they had so frequently during the past several days—toward the interview. She cringed.

I might as well have worn a clown suit.

Phyllis' talking head had taunted her for the remainder of the meeting. With great effort, Marche had managed to gaze upward—only to find herself faced with her supervisor's pulpy stump. She couldn't remember how she'd responded to any of the questions after that point, but she was sure that her performance had underwhelmed the committee.

Coating the brush with fresh paint, she started a new set of petals.

Another work week started. The heat rose to stifling levels, doubling the door count at the library. Retirees abandoned their posts at the beach, stepping through the lobby doors with sand clinging to their calves like a second skin.

Camp counselors, who normally led their young charges on nature hikes, instead held educational lectures in the children's department. Distracted by the extra hustle and bustle at the circulation desk, Marche had little time to wonder about the job she may or may not have gotten.

Friday morning blossomed under an auspicious sky. Mockingbirds filled the air with their melodious song, and ibises lazily patrolled the dry grass for insects. A soft breeze played about the highest branches of the highest trees. Even the roadways felt calm—drivers steered with care, green lights stayed green, and every red light switched to green before Marche could apply pressure to the brakes.

"Today feels like a good day," she said as she turned into the library parking lot.

In the evening, she decided to splurge on fast food, ordering pizza from Big Cheese Express. The pepperoni slices were hot and greasy and tasted delicious. They were also impossible to eat without making a mess. "What a monkey." Marche grinned as she gently wiped marinara sauce from Stella's cheek and chin. "Ready for a bath?"

"Yeah-yeah-yeah!" Stella replied, jumping to her feet.

Afterwards, they sat down at the coffee table to play a few hands of Go Fish. "Was that a yawn, young lady?" Marche asked as she lost the third consecutive round. Gathering up the cards, she returned them to the box.

"Un-uh."

Stella shook her head so emphatically that Marche couldn't help but laugh. "Go brush your teeth," she said. "It's time for bed."

Marche reached for the cell phone, which she'd plugged into the wall beside the sofa. As usual, she'd let the battery drain until it was completely out of juice. She checked the status: full charge. Unplugging it, she held her finger down on the power button.

The first thing she noticed when the screen came to life was the bell icon indicating that she had a voice message. Her heart fluttered. Was it Bridget, finally ready to make amends? She checked the call history. It wasn't Bridget. But the number looked familiar.

Marche's breath caught in her throat. *City Hall.* Pulse racing, she pressed the voicemail button and lifted the phone to her ear.

Let it be good. Let it be good. Let it be good.

"Hello!" the voice said. "This is Florence Brodeur from City Hall. I'm trying to reach Marche Baker. I have news regarding the Circulation Clerk III position that you interviewed for on the fifth of July. I just wanted to let you know that the committee was very impressed with your qualifications. It was a close call, but the City has offered the position to another candidate. I'm *very* sorry. If you have any questions, feel free to give me a ring at—" the voice slowly articulated a string of digits. "Have a good weekend. Bye-bye!"

Marche stared at the phone in her hand. She hadn't gotten the job? Calmly, she leaned into the sofa. She really hadn't gotten the job? Despite the interview debacle, she'd believed in Sarah's confidence that they'd promote her. She had the skills, and she'd proven them over the past two-and-a-half months she'd worked at the library. Phyllis had even encouraged her to apply. Certainly she wouldn't have done that unless she'd wanted Marche to serve as her right-hand man. That could mean only one thing. "I blew it."

She set the phone on the table and stared at the wall, unseeing. *I didn't get the job.* But the thought hovered somewhere above her, like a balloon detached from its string. She felt nothing.

"It's okay," she said in a quiet voice. "It's not the end of the world." Yet suddenly her life felt like a horrible dead end. "It's okay. It's not the end of the world."

"Can you read me a story, Mommy?"

Stella's voice drifted to her from the doorway. Marche drew in a shaky breath and exhaled slowly.

"Mommy?"

"What would you like to hear?" Marche asked, standing.

"I dunno." Stella twisted the hem of her nightshirt. Then she untwisted it, rolled it upward to her bellybutton, unrolled it, and twisted it again. "A funny story," she declared, standing on her toes.

"Funny sounds like a good idea." As she mounted the stairs, Marche glanced down at her daughter's crown of glossy brown hair. "Have you thought of a book yet?"

"Un-uh," Stella replied, tapping each of the balusters as she hummed a made-up song.

Marche repeated the question when they reached the second floor. Stella hopped several times and nodded, her eyes shining brightly.

"*The Sneezes*!"

"Oka-ay!" Marche said with exaggerated enthusiasm, making a fist pump. "Let's go find those Sneetches!"

She turned into the smaller bedroom and patted the mattress. Once Stella climbed onto it, she lifted up the skirt and reached under the bed. She gripped the edge of the plastic tub that she kept beneath it for storing books and pulled it out.

"Now where is that silly Dr. Seuss?" Marche mused as she scanned the spines of the books.

"Who's Dr. Sooz?"

"He's the author, silly goose."

"What's an awthur?"

"Someone who thinks up a story and writes it down. Dr. Seuss wrote a lot of your favorite stories—like *Green Eggs & Ham*."

"I like *Green Eggs & Ham*," Stella said with a giggle.

"I know you do—ah, here it is."

Marche extracted the picture book and slid next to Stella on the bed. She read the first page aloud and then helped Stella sound out the words on page two. They continued this process until they finished the book twenty minutes later. Next, they became acquainted with Edith from *The Lonely Doll*. Stella—warding off sleep with the stubbornness of a mule—begged for yet another story when Edith's ended. Marche acquiesced and they quickly selected book number three. Only at the conclusion of *Wynken, Blynken, and Nod*, did Stella finally close her eyes.

Marche placed the books back into the container and pushed it under the bed. Moving quietly, she tucked the sheet around Stella's small shoulders and switched off the light.

Wrapping her fingers around the knob, she pulled the door forward until only a sliver of light from the hall seeped into the bedroom. Then she crossed the short distance to her own room.

The cloud of depression that she'd ignored while reading with Stella finally burst. Marche leaned against the doorframe, deflated, and peered inside. The hall light cast distorted shadows on the floor where several boxes remained unopened. Flicking on the bedroom light, she began the customary routine of sidestepping them.

At the foot of the bed, she paused.

Photos. The word, scrawled at a diagonal on one of the boxes, caught her attention. Impulsively, she knelt before it.

A moment ago she'd wanted to crawl into a dreamless sleep—to put the wretched world on hold. Now fire coursed through her veins. She yanked at the duct tape with fury. She grunted, disgruntled when the gray strips stuck to her skin. Peeling it off her fingertips, she crushed the tape into a misshapen ball and tossed it onto another box.

Rolling onto her heels, she lifted the cardboard flaps. Inside she found photo albums, plastic bags containing negatives, and picture frames—some with the sample photograph still showing behind the glass.

The first frame that she picked up contained a picture of a woman. Golden hair cascaded over her shoulders, terminating at the crook of her elbow. She sat cross-legged and looked downward at a toddler in her lap. There was laughter in her eyes and a smile on her face.

"Hi, Mom," Marche said softly. She studied the image for a moment, letting the warmth of her mother's features comfort her. Then the longing for her physical presence began to overwhelm her and she had to look away.

Setting the frame on the bed, she again reached inside the box. The second picture featured Stella dressed as a ballerina for her first Halloween. The one after that was of her paternal great-grandparents, whom she'd never met. The next was a professional family portrait taken when Marche was ten. She set this frame on the bed with all of the others and returned to the box.

The next photograph made her breath catch in her throat.

She hadn't looked at any images of Dom since the accident. Now here he was, staring pensively at the ocean. A man full of strength and vitality. A man who should have had decades of life ahead of him. What had he been thinking about when she pressed down on the shutter? Was he picturing himself on a surfboard, riding the waves? Or maybe he was remembering the time when he went treasure hunting with his buddies "just for laughs." Did he ever regret giving up his carefree lifestyle to marry Marche and start a family?

"Oh..."

Dom's dimpled cheek tugged on the string which bound her composure. And in the blink of an eye, it completely unraveled.

A groan ripped through her chest.

She'd made a mistake opening the box. She wasn't ready for this moment. The wound was still too fresh. In her mind, Dom died all over again. The loss hit her as intensely now as when the Florida Highway Patrol had spoken to her on the telephone all those months ago.

That dreaded emptiness returned. Suddenly she had no desire to go on because...there was nothing. The world lost its value. Existence seemed pointless. What did she have to live for? The love of her life was gone forever.

Marche closed her eyes, and the agony intensified. Her throat constricted. She sobbed until her chest ached, until her eyes puffed with redness. She coughed. Swiped at the tears and snot dripping from her nose. Pressing Dom's photo to her chest, she wandered down the stairs.

In the kitchen, she poured herself a cup of water. Her arm shook and water splashed from the glass onto the countertop. She set it aside after one sip. Water couldn't ease her suffering.

Still clutching the frame, she reached into the cabinet across from the refrigerator. There—behind a stack of unopened ice cube trays—she located the bottle of vodka. She wrapped her fingers about the neck, squeezed tight, and withdrew it. Hungrily, her eyes absorbed the fact that three quarters of its liquid contents remained.

She held the bottle to her stomach.

The glass felt cool and comforting against her skin.

Heading into the living room, she hugged the bottle closer and closer.

Twenty-Eight

STELLA WOKE AFTER MIDNIGHT.

Her eyelids fluttered open in the semi-lit room. The bedroom door was slightly ajar. A yellow glow from the hall filtered through, casting shadows everywhere.

Restless, she kicked off the sheet.

Except for the television playing downstairs, the house was quiet. *Mommy's awake.* Now what?

Stella didn't want to lie still—she wasn't the least bit tired. Focusing on her feet, she began to wiggle her toes. She moved the big ones first and then the second biggest. "This little piggy went to marrr-kit," she sang. "This little piggy stayed ho-ome." When the littlest piggy cried "wee-wee-wee" all the way back to its mommy, Stella heaved her shoulders and pouted. How bored she was!

I want to build a Lego castle.

But what if Mommy comes up here and sees me?

As much as she wanted to play, she didn't want to get into trouble for climbing out of bed in the middle of the night.

Frustration plagued her. What could she *do*?

And then she noticed the shadows on the walls.

In a matter of seconds, the everyday world slipped away and the trappings of enchantment took its place. Stella's ordinary self ceased to be. Now she was Stella, the student of a wizard! She pictured Bianca as a person, dressed in a sparkly blue dress and matching pointed cap. Miss Bianca had locked her in this underground laboratory with strict instructions. "You must study the ways of magic, my young wizard." Stella giggled. Why did Miss Bianca sound like Auntie Bee?

Stella grabbed the Barbie doll on her nightstand and held it like a wand.

Thus prepared, she began to examine the ink-like images.

Each shadow was unique. A massive blob in the corner opposite her bed looked like a circus tent. The tiny splash of black by the door reminded her of a rabbit. Above the closet, she noticed an oddly shaped impression that might have been a spider; after a thorough inspection, she decided that it was actually a ballerina with arms raised up and one knee drawn to a point.

Stella wiggled her toes again. With her right hand, she lifted the Barbie. She pursed her lips in concentration. Where should she begin? Then she pointed her mighty wand at the corner of the room.

A simple flick of her wrist and she turned the circus tent into a rocket. Then she blinked dramatically, flicked her wrist again, and changed the rocket into a horse-drawn carriage. She giggled some more. The possibilities were limitless!

Hmm...

Stella gazed about the room for other interesting shadows to play with.

The rotund shape next to the closet resembled a bear. Stella smiled when she saw it because it reminded her of Yogi. Frozen in mid-leap, a picnic table filled with goodies remained just beyond the reach of Yogi's outstretched paws. The shadow on the left side of her door looked like an airplane. Beside it sat a scrawny cat, grooming the fur on its chest.

A *clunk* sounded downstairs. Stella's gaze darted toward the sliver of light pouring in from the hall. She listened carefully; no other noises followed. *Mommy must be walking on her tiptoes!*

The glamour of her magical assignment quickly returned, and Stella forgot that she'd heard anything at all. She focused on the doorknob. From this point, she followed a straight line to the very top of the door. She paused when she reached the space of wall between the doorframe and the ceiling. There, she identified a dark shape that might have been an apple. It was plump and juicy, and its skin would have shone a deep, luscious red if shadows could have color. Yes, it was definitely an apple.

Stella had just pointed her wand at it when a new sound caught her attention. Immediately, she gazed downward and sideways to the expanse of darkness near the door. Her eyes locked on the black mass, and she waited.

It happened again.

The shadow-cat meowed.

Stella froze. If she had *imagined* such a thing happening, she would have found it entertaining. But Stella recognized the difference between fantasy and reality. In real life, shadows didn't move of their own volition. They altered only when something external to them changed position.

Lying there motionless, she stared at the shadow-cat...and waited to see what might happen next.

Stella held her breath, afraid to breathe. Dare she even blink? Every part of her body felt immobilized. Invisible chains anchored her hands and feet to the bed; a band of lead secured her forehead to the pillow. How much longer could she endure?

Then the shadowy animal stretched its legs, arched its back, and pounced on another shadow, smaller and leaf-shaped.

The air rushed back into Stella's lungs.

Something else moved. There! By the closet! The fat bear crashed onto the table, climbed over the doorway, thundered down the other side, and then lumbered after the cat, tearing it to pieces with its monstrous claws.

Stella shrieked.

The Barbie doll fell from her hand. She scrambled to the foot of the bed where the sheet had collected into a bunch. Snatching the material, she scurried back to the pillow and pulled it over her face.

The sheet was so thin that she could see the moving silhouettes through the fabric. She squeezed her eyes shut. She pressed both fists against her ears and tucked her knees into her chest. Fear made her hands and feet turn cold; she curled her toes inward.

When she felt as though she'd lain like that for an hour, she opened her eyes. From what she could see through the sheet, everything appeared still. The tightness in her hands lessened; she relaxed her toes. Centimeter by centimeter, she pulled the material from her face.

The shadows had returned to normal.

Stella released the sheet and straightened her legs. She bent over the side of the bed. Where had the doll gone? After a quick search, she found it—upside down and backwards between the bed skirt and the table. She scooted to the edge of the mattress and reached down. When she'd scooted and stretched until she was practically on the floor, she succeeded in wrapping her fingers around the plastic legs.

She pointed the Barbie's feet at the ceiling. But the fun had gone; the wizard's laboratory was no more. She dropped the doll. Fatigue descended upon her like a fine mist. Closing her eyes again, she slept.

She began to dream.

She was on a beach that she'd never seen before. Her father, who'd been away for so long, stood next to her. In front of her, the water stretched on forever. She saw nothing but sand in all other directions.

There weren't any other people around, and Stella felt happy knowing that she would have her father's undivided attention. She gazed up at him now with pure adoration. His arms and legs were the same dark brown that she remembered. His short, curly hair still shone that luxurious shade of chocolate. Though she hadn't seen him for so long, nothing about him had changed. As she studied his familiar features, he tilted his face downward. Bright blue eyes sparkled at her.

"Daddy," Stella said with a smile.

"Daughter."

Her father took two steps toward the water and squatted. Barefoot and shirtless, he looked like a man who had never spent a day indoors. His tangerine swimming shorts clashed brilliantly against the water.

Stella studied the sand. It was white, almost too bright to look at in the sunshine. She kicked at the soft granules with her feet. With her heel, she dug a small pit. Then she used her toes to shovel the sand back in.

Her father began to sort through bits of seashells that the waves had washed ashore. The first shell he grabbed was white with swirls. After a brief examination, he tossed it into the water. It landed with a soft *plunk* and immediately disappeared from view. The second shell was salmon pink with ridges. The third was purple and shaped like a butterfly's wings. As Stella watched, he tossed shell after shell into the ocean.

"I want a shark toof, Daddy."

The scavenging continued without pause. Had her father heard her? He concentrated so intently, his furrowed brows never relaxing. Then he picked up a clamshell. Pivoting on his heel, he shared his find with Stella.

"It's hot," he said. "Look, the sun has baked it clean."

Stella inched closer. She looked at her father and then at the shell. Undoubtedly, it was the most beautiful one she'd ever seen. Whiter than the sand, it shone more brightly than it, too. Did the clam feel as smooth as it looked? Suddenly, Stella wanted to know the answer to that question more than anything else in the world. She reached out to touch it.

"Ow!" She withdrew her hand. The fingertip burned where it made contact.

"I told you it was hot, didn't I?"

Her father laughed. The sound seemed to echo everywhere. Then he extended his arms and hugged her. Stella liked that at first because her father hadn't hugged her in such a long time. After a moment, though, she began to squirm. Her father was still holding the seashell. It pressed against her arm.

"It's hot, Daddy. Hot."

The laughter continued. It also intensified; at its highest pitch, it transformed into a shrill cry. He hugged her even tighter.

"It hurts, Daddy. Make it stop."

Finally, the screeching ended. Her father spoke again, but his voice had changed. He sounded like a woman now. "Sorry, child, but I can't do that."

Stella cried out as the shell blistered the soft flesh below her shoulder. Instinctively, she recoiled. Only...her body remained fixed in place.

She wiggled. Suddenly she felt as though she'd been bound in mummy wrappings. No matter what she tried, she couldn't escape the suffocating embrace. Nor could she escape the pain. In a panic, she twisted her head back and forth. She cried out for release.

"Let go! Let me go!"

The arms continued to contract.

Stella screamed. She screamed until she had no air left. She paused just long enough to draw in breath and then she screamed again. Then...the atmosphere changed. Stella stopped struggling. Instead, she listened. And she watched.

The noises disappeared first. What happened to the waves? The ocean had stilled. Its amber-colored surface now looked like a sheet of stained glass. Overhead, a flock of gulls formed an oddly shaped cluster frozen against the sky. And what was wrong with the sky? Stella squinted. It seemed fake, as though it was nothing more than paint slapped onto a piece of cardboard with uneven strokes. Parts of the sky were clumpy. In other sections, the blue stretched so thin that the canvas peeped through the coat.

As Stella struggled (and failed) to comprehend the goings on about her, the steely grip on her body lessened. She focused once more on the man who looked like her father.

The brilliant blue of his eyes had paled to the point of translucency. The crow's feet widened and deepened. His cheeks (normally plump with health) began to shrink. Soon the whole of his face deteriorated to nothing but bone, with only the thinnest layer of skin to cover it. Then the skin disintegrated, and the eyes sank into the sockets and rolled upward so that they seemed invisible against the whiteness of the bones. And what of the bones? They became porous. Needle-sized holes peppered the surface, enlarged and multiplied. In a matter of seconds, the skeletal face had vanished.

All at once, blackness enveloped her.

Stella opened her eyes. Disoriented, she wondered where the sea had gone. Then she understood. She hadn't gone to the beach; she hadn't stood on the shore while her father plucked shells from its sandy bed. What she had thought so real was nothing more than a dream.

But something was wrong.

The pain in her left limb had not gone away.

Stella looked down at her arm and jumped. A ball of fire the size of her fist danced on the mattress, barely an inch away from her body. Quickly, she scooted to the other side of the bed.

"Mommy! Mommy!"

Tears formed in her eyes. What could she do? If she ignored the fire, wouldn't it get bigger? Her gaze darted from the flickering orange ball to the doorway.

Where's Mommy?!

The flame leapt higher.

Stella sobbed violently. Extending her hands, she tried to put out the flames. The heat burned her palms. She worked through the pain, desperate to muffle the fire. Tears spilled from her lids and dripped down her chin.

"Mommy!" she screamed. "Mommy!"

After a while her throat began to hurt; her voice became weaker and weaker until all she could muster was a whisper. Her arms felt heavy and tired. When she thought that she might collapse from exhaustion, the flames suddenly died.

Stella backed up against the wall and stared at the mattress. The bedsheet was spotless where it should have been charred. She tried to clutch the sheet and pull it up to her chin, but her hands burned like they were on fire.

Twenty-Nine

THE COUCH CUSHIONS WERE smothering her. Marche coughed once and cracked an eyelid. Then she flipped onto her back and opened the other one. Everything looked blurry. She wiped the sleep from the corners of her eyes and blinked several times. When that didn't help, she rubbed vigorously with her forefingers. Gradually, her surroundings sharpened into focus. She coughed again. Cautiously, she rolled into a sitting position.

The room was suffused in a warm white glow. How late was it? Ten? Eleven? As Marche contemplated the hour, she noticed Stella sitting cross-legged in front of the television.

"Hey, Sunshine, what are you—"

An arrow of pain shot through her skull, jig-sawing from one hemisphere to the other.

Marche pressed the heel of her hand against her left temple. She groaned in discomfort; snare drums and tambourines struck up a merry tune between the wrinkles of her gray matter.

She hunched over her knees until the worst of it passed. When the pain eased to a dull ache, she straightened and rotated her shoulders. She glanced at the clock as she stretched the muscles in her calves and thighs. It was a few minutes past noon.

"Jeez Louise. Talk about sleeping the day away."

She tried to run a hand through her hair, but a stubborn knot halted her progress partway through. Annoyed, she withdrew her fingers. In vain she attempted to straighten out the rumples in her shirt.

"Oh, this is hopeless," she muttered.

She collapsed against the sofa. She'd slept heavily through the night and all of the morning. Even so, she felt depleted of energy. Her rib cage expanded with a yawn. On the television screen, Sylvester enthusiastically pursued Tweety through a verdant lawn and past a doghouse. How would the cunning little bird win this time? Before she could see the episode to its conclusion, however, the telephone rang.

Marche looked at the jangling receiver and frowned. The needling headache had not dissolved as she had thought—merely entertained a temporary retreat. Now it revived with a vengeance. The trilling sound reverberated in her brain like a top spinning against the sides of a jar. Marche kneaded her forehead with her knuckles and impatiently waited for the noise to die.

And die it did, but only for a minute. Just as the thudding in her skull began to fade, the receiver resumed its clamorous song. "Go away," Marche said with a groan, covering her face. When the jarring noise ended, she sighed with relief. She wasn't even ready to think yet, let alone hold a conversation with someone.

At last, she forced herself into motion. She rubbed her cheeks and nose with her hand. And all at once, she became rudely aware of her body's physical condition. The skin on her forehead felt slick with oil; her scalp itched with dryness. She pushed to her feet, patting Stella's head on the way out of the room.

"Mommy's going to take a shower. We'll have breakfast—um, lunch—soon. Okay?"

Marche entered the foyer and paused. Glancing back, she saw a commercial for bug spray flash across the television screen. Stella remained fixated on the "Bug-B-Gone" advertisement as though it were one of her favorite cartoons. Marche shrugged. With sluggish steps, she headed up the stairs.

She pulled items randomly from the dresser drawers and headed into the bathroom. As she peeled off her clothing, she thought the ugly old mauve bathtub had never looked so inviting. She climbed into the porcelain basin and twisted the nozzle. The water from the showerhead massaged her upturned face, abrading the grimy layer from her skin.

Reaching for the shampoo bottle, she washed the grease from her hair. She cleansed the soft spot behind her ears; she scrubbed between her toes. All the while, the warm water pummeled her neck and shoulders in wordless encouragement. By the time she turned off the shower and stepped onto the bath mat, she was ready to start the day.

She dried off with yesterday's used towel. Then, leaning on the counter, she studied the reflection staring at her from the perspiring glass. Whose face was this? Had those lines in her forehead been there a year ago? And what about the gray creeping through the brown at the hairline? The woman in the mirror looked worn and old.

As she stood there cataloging the outward traces of her vanishing youth, a knock sounded at the front door.

Grunting, she reached for her clothes. Who could it be? Shelley knocked with a grandmother's touch, usually making such limited contact with the wood that Marche barely heard the summons. This knock sounded assured: two loud double raps and then silence. Marche wormed her arms through the sleeves of her tee shirt and pulled a pair of jean shorts up over her hips. She dressed with unhurried movements. If it was someone selling home security or handing out religious literature, she hoped they'd lose patience and walk away.

Another round of knocking sounded as she reached the top of the stairs.

"Yeah, yeah, yeah," she mumbled.

Marche reached the first floor. The determined visitor beat another rhythmic tattoo upon the door. Peering through the peephole, she discovered that it wasn't a solicitor after all. "Oh!" She unlocked the deadbolt and rotated the doorknob.

"I hope this isn't a bad time?" Trey asked, eyeing her bare feet and damp hair.

"Not at all," Marche replied, stepping to the side. "Come on in."

"Thanks."

Marche focused on the back of her brother-in-law's head as she closed the door. "Is something the matter?" she asked, wondering what could have prompted this surprise visit.

"No. I just..." He paused and turned. "I didn't mean to barge in on you like this. I called earlier, but no one answered."

Marche gave a wave of dismissal. "Don't worry about it. You're not interrupting anything."

Trey nodded and pocketed the keys he'd been twirling in his hand. Then he peered into the living room. "Is there somewhere we can talk in private?"

"Sure."

Marche padded down the hall, past the half-bath and storage closet, and entered the kitchen.

"This is nice," Trey said. "And you have a separate dining room, too?"

"Across the hall," Marche replied. "I don't use it, though. We eat most of our meals in here. Or in the living room."

"Are you going to update the cabinets?" Trey asked, inspecting the woodwork above the stove. "I can give you the name of the business Bridge and I used. They did a first-rate job on the office."

"That's not really on the agenda," Marche replied. Silently, she added that she couldn't afford a ten-thousand-dollar renovation, even in her wildest dreams. How typical of Trey to forget that she was poor as dirt. "Mostly I'm just sweeping and dusting. The floor mat is new." She indicated the two-by-three mat on the floor by the sink.

"Nice."

Was that slanting of the mouth because he'd suddenly realized his mistake? Marche took pity on her brother-in-law and pretended not to notice his discomfort.

"It's bamboo," she said, keeping her tone light. Walking over to the table, she pulled out a chair. "Why don't you grab a seat and tell me what's on your mind?"

Trey cleared his throat and stepped off the mat. "It's about Bridget," he said, selecting the chair adjacent to Marche.

"I thought you said that there wasn't anything wrong?"

"There's not. I mean, she's doing okay—much better than she was two weeks ago." Trey traced a forefinger along the edge of the table. Now that they were getting to the heart of the matter, he seemed hesitant to look at her. "It's about the texting." The finger stilled. "You know, the fact that you two still aren't talking."

So that's what this is about. Marche took a slow, measured breath. "That's Bridget's choice."

The sunlight filtered through the kitchen window, highlighting the blond tufts of hair on the backs of Trey's hands. His wandering gaze dropped to the center of the table—one of the least visually interesting areas in the house. Marche didn't use a centerpiece, and she only brought out placemats during mealtimes. The only item adorning its surface at the moment was a generic set of salt and pepper shakers. Naturally, Trey's attention gravitated toward these. "About that. Bridget told me—about what she said to you at the hospital."

The color rushed to Marche's cheeks.

Trey reached for the pepper shaker, angled it, and began to play with the latch. Marche suddenly wondered why she hadn't chosen an attractive set of shakers. They didn't cost much, and it was a simple way to add a spark of character to an otherwise bland space.

"Maybe it isn't my place to say anything, but I hate to see her like this."

"You don't have to—"

Trey shook his head, determined to speak his piece. "When they admitted her… I've never seen her so—so wild, so outside of herself. For a while, I was afraid they might have to keep her under a twenty-four-hour watch." He covered the latch with the pad of his index finger and tapped the pepper shaker against the table. *Clink. Clink.* "The nurses had to sedate her when she couldn't calm down. By the time you arrived, she didn't know north from south, east from west."

She was lucid, Marche thought, *and she meant every word she said.* The heat in her face intensified. She wasn't going to cry again, was she? The thought was sobering. She straightened her spine until it was as stiff as one of the table legs.

"I understand," Marche said. "I understand that she's in a lot of pain right now. I also get that she's got some sort of grudge against me that she's been nursing for years. I'm not trying to point fingers or assign blame where it doesn't belong. But *she* pushed *me* away. She has to make the first move. Until she's ready to talk, there's no point."

Trey set the pepper shaker aside and sighed.

"It's honorable of you to try to help, Trey, but Bridget's an adult. There are some things she's got to do herself. And this—" she threw her hands up in the air, "—is one of them."

"Fair enough," Trey said, wearing an expression of someone who'd been caught with his hand in the cookie jar. He sighed again. "It's just that it's hard to sit still when someone you care about is having a hard time. You know?"

Marche felt a sudden urge to reach out and pat Trey on the head. The reaction surprised her. Was she softening? She felt like she was seeing the real him for the first time—not the privileged engineer who led a perfect lifestyle, but the vulnerable man who suffered from personal problems just like everyone else. He loved Bridget, and he was clearly devoted to her. If Marche hadn't been so absorbed in her own misery, perhaps she would have appreciated him sooner. *Who knows? Maybe with time, we might actually become friends?*

"Would you like something to drink?" she asked, keeping her hands in her lap. "Or maybe a cookie?"

Her brother-in-law declined. "I should probably go. I told Bridget that I was shopping for socks. I'm afraid I'm not a very good liar."

Marche shifted her legs. Her skin still radiated heat from the shower, and the backs of her thighs created a suctioning sound as they unstuck from the chair.

"Do you mind if I say hello to Stella on my way out?" Trey asked, standing.

"You're her favorite uncle," Marche replied. "I'm sure she'll be thrilled to see you." *Good job leavening the mood with a lame joke*, Marche thought when Trey failed to retort that he was Stella's *only* uncle.

"Hey, kiddo," Trey said, entering the living room.

Marche expected Stella to hop to her feet—to squeal with delight and wrap her arms about his waist in a vice-like grip, to call out his name, "Uncle Trey! Uncle Trey!" and then raise her arms, begging to be lifted into the air, the brown strands of her hair cascading down her back like honey.

But Stella continued to stare at the screen as though Trey hadn't spoken. Quietly she sat, with her hands draped over her feet.

Marche creased her brows. The vague feeling of disquiet—which she'd been too out of it to acknowledge when she'd first awakened—returned.

"This must be one of your favorite shows, huh?" Trey said, crouching beside the child. He glanced at the television. A smiling young woman was demonstrating the effectiveness of a popular paper towel brand. "Let me guess. Is it Garfield or Bugs?"

"Probably *The Powerpuff Girls*," Marche said, her eyes trained on Stella. Why didn't she move? Why didn't she speak?

"Ah. They're pretty cool, huh?" Trey shifted the hair away from her face so that it settled around her shoulder. "Stella?"

He leaned forward. With his back toward her, Marche couldn't see the expression on his face. But she heard his sharp intake of breath. "What's wrong?" she asked, stepping forward. "What is it?"

Trey repeated Stella's name. He snapped his fingers in front of her face. "Stella, can you hear me?"

Marche rounded her brother-in-law and squatted. "What..." Her stomach flip-flopped. She forced herself to pause, to draw in a breath. "Stella? Sweetie?"

She searched her daughter's eyes. Rather than follow the movement on the television screen, they seemed to fix upon an invisible object that hung somewhere in the air in front of it. Unblinking, their centers radiated an eerie vacantness.

With trembling fingers, Marche touched her daughter's shoulder. Lightly, she rubbed. The skin beneath the cotton material felt cool. How long had she sat in this position, motionless? Two hours? Three? Half of the night?

"Stella?" Marche swallowed, but didn't succeed in ironing out the tremble in her voice. "Stella, won't you look at Mommy?"

When her cajoling tone failed to elicit a response, Trey snapped his fingers again. Still, Stella gave no indication that she saw or heard anything. It was as though they were sitting before a mere replica of a child: perfectly lifelike on the outside but hollow within.

"I don't *understand*," Marche cried. "What's *wrong* with her?"

Trey shook his head. He reached for Stella's right hand but withdrew as though he'd been shocked. "What the *fuck*."

The whispered exclamation—so out of character—sent Marche's pulse racing. Startled, she broke her gaze from Stella's unseeing eyes. Her brother-in-law's composure had cracked; his lips trembled with emotion. "Trey?"

"Her hands."

Confused, Marche glanced downward. Stella's hands hung limply over her feet. The fingers, slightly splayed, rested about an inch above the floor. From wrist to fingertip, the skin was unblemished. Other than the fact that Stella hadn't moved or spoken, she looked healthy and normal. There were no abnormalities, no physical indicators to explain her sudden withdrawal.

Frustrated, Marche snapped. "What are you talking about? Her hands are fine."

"Look."

Trey reached for her right hand again. Gently, he touched the tips of Stella's fingers with one hand and encircled her wrist with the other. Then, slowly, he rotated the appendage until the underside became visible to scrutiny. Marche gasped. He repeated the process with the left hand.

Each of Stella's fingers—from the base to the tip—glowed a soft, healthy pink. But not her palms. Here, the tender skin had darkened to an ugly red. It was dry and cracked, like a hard-boiled egg crushed against a countertop. The skin had also puffed and stretched, but it lacked any evidence of blistering. Though Marche didn't know much about burns, she thought that was a good sign.

Marche rubbed her knees and tried to gather her thoughts. Now that they had pinpointed the source of the problem, the solution seemed obvious. "Okay, we can deal with this." She focused again on Stella's face, forcing herself to speak with a calmness she didn't feel. "It's all right, sweetie. I know your hands hurt, but there's nothing to be scared about. Okay? The burns aren't that bad." *Oh god, please let that be the truth.* "We'll go to the doctor, and they'll get you fixed right up. I promise."

She reached for her daughter once more. This time, she hesitated in touching the delicate frame, afraid that the slightest contact might suddenly cause her to fall apart like a sandcastle dissolved by a turbulent wave. With care, she caressed Stella's head.

As she spoke, she searched for signs of comprehension. Stella made no movement; she didn't even blink.

Trey rose to his feet and turned. "It must have been some party last night."

"What?" Marche replied, distracted. She glanced up only when she registered his tone, in equal parts angry and censorious.

Trey stood beside the sofa, the neck of the empty vodka bottle protruding from his hand like an accusatory finger. Marche had forgotten all about it. But the bottle had been there all along—perhaps half-rolled under the table or jutting out from under the recliner—waiting for a sharp eye to detect its presence.

"What is this, Marche?" Trey demanded, his lips pressed into a rigid line.

"Really?" Marche replied, exasperated. "You want to talk about this now?"

Trey glared at her for a moment. "No, I don't." Bending forward, he set the bottle on the coffee table. "I suppose we should save this discussion for later—*after* I've taken Stella to the hospital."

Marche's eyes widened. "Excuse me?" she said, her voice rising with her temper. "You can't just waltz in here and shout orders like you run the place. This is *my* house and Stella is *my* child. You have no right—"

"Pull your head out of your ass."

Marche recoiled as though he'd slapped her.

"You think I don't see what's happened here?" Trey stepped forward, his stride purposeful. "You got drunk, Marche. You neglected your daughter and she got hurt. That doesn't exactly make you Mother of the Year, now does it?"

Marche opened her mouth to reply, but no words formed.

"I would be remiss in my duties as an uncle if I *didn't* take charge of the situation. For all I know, you might still have alcohol swimming through your system."

What could she say? Marche's shoulders sagged; her eyelids drooped. Confusion, uncertainty, and guilt assaulted her simultaneously. Was Trey right? Was this really her fault? As she studied Stella's blank features, she forced herself to consider the veracity of his statement. How could this have happened? How could she have *let* it happen?

"What are you doing?" she asked warily.

Trey placed his hands under Stella's arms and hoisted her to his chest. Like a marionette, her legs swung freely at the knees.

"Exactly what it looks like I'm doing." Trey appraised her with condescending eyes and sneered. "And you need to sober up."

Marche scrambled to her feet.

"All right, you've made your point. Maybe I did drink a little more than I should have last night. But I'm not drunk, Trey. Please. Don't act like this," she said, her tone imploring. "We can go to the hospital together."

"I don't think so." Trey stomped from the living room. Before she could utter another protestation, he had yanked open the front door and stepped outside.

Marche followed close behind, her hands tightened into fists at her side. "You're not being reasonable!" As she stepped onto the driveway, the hot cement baked the bottoms of her feet. "Would you please stop and think about this?"

Withdrawing the key ring from his pocket, Trey unlocked the back passenger-side door.

Marche felt like crying and screaming all at once; she grunted instead. She couldn't afford to engage in a heated verbal tango in her driveway. What if the neighbors saw? What would they think? She wanted to make friends with the people on Victor Street, not alienate them.

Another, more disturbing, thought curbed her temper. What if Trey, in a fit of anger, threatened to contact Child Protective Services? And what if someone then pointed to Stella's near drowning and determined that she was indeed neglectful—an unfit parent who didn't deserve to raise a child? *It's better to let Trey have his way now. There's no reasoning with him until he's calmed down.*

And so she quietly, reluctantly observed as Trey set Stella in the back seat.

Casting a lingering glance at her daughter, who was now securely buckled in, she ran around the car to the driver's side. "Call me when you've seen the doctor," Marche said as Trey turned the key in the ignition. She banged her fist on the window when he ignored her. "*Please,* Trey."

None of her pleading seemed to reach him. Her brother-in-law backed out of the driveway without giving her a second glance.

Marche beat down the urge to run after them. She could only watch as the car shot toward the stop sign, paused just long enough to allow for a station wagon to pass, and then disappeared around the corner. For half a minute or more, she stared listlessly at the vacant space. Only when the burning of her feet became unbearable did she turn back to the house.

Head hung low, she stepped inside and heaved all of her weight against the front door. "She'll be fine," Marche said, pressing a fist to her heart. "I'm sure it's not as bad as it looks."

All the same, she couldn't help but worry.

And she hated being apart.

She peered into the living room. Nothing about it—not the couch pillow on the floor, the box of playing cards on the end table, nor the cartoon flashing on the television screen—indicated that it had been the scene of a showdown. Then she noticed the culprit of her unrest.

Storming into the room, she snatched the bottle off the coffee table.

No matter how down in the dumps she'd been last night, she never should have taken a drink. No matter how badly she craved it, she should have abstained. She was an adult; she was a *parent*. She knew better.

Stella's burned hands flashed before her eyes as she stomped into the kitchen. "This never should have happened."

She flexed her fingers. Anger and frustration surged to the surface like volatile liquids mixing in a beaker.

Lifting her arm, she hurled the bottle with all of her might.

Thirty

The bottle didn't break into solid chunks—it shattered.

Marche slipped on a pair of tennis shoes, then retrieved the broom and dustpan from the storage closet. A cursory glance confirmed the magnitude of her temper. Particles of glass layered the floor in a fine dust. Slightly larger pieces sparkled where the sunlight bathed the checkered vinyl.

Wrapping her fingers about the broom handle, she set to work. She swept beneath the cabinets and refrigerator first, gathering dust and debris from every crevice into the center of the room.

The physical motion of bending and reaching and flexing distracted her from thought. Each sweep of the broom soothed her nerves; the erratic palpitations in her chest slowed until she could breathe with ease. But then an image of Stella's hands inevitably flitted through her mind, obliterating that peace. Trey's censorious attitude hung over her like a dark cloud, and she imagined Bridget frowning at her with disapproval. *If Dom were still alive...* Marche clenched her teeth as she thrust the broom into the black space beneath the dishwasher.

Moving jerkily and hastily, she cleared away the remnants of the bottle in no time at all. But idleness increased her agitation.

Reaching for the cordless, she dialed Trey's number.

"Hey, what's up?"

"Hi." Marche hesitated. Why had a woman answered the phone?

"Hel-lo?"

"Um, hi," Marche repeated. "Is Trey there?"

"You've got the wrong number."

The dial tone sounded in Marche's ear part-way through her apology. Flustered, she opened the drawer beneath the microwave. She dug through its contents until she unearthed the address book. On the sixth page—scribbled in blue ink—she confirmed her brother-in-law's cell phone number.

"A five," she muttered, "not a six."

Inhaling deeply and exhaling slowly, she studiously punched the correct string of digits. Her frown deepened when the line switched to voicemail after the first ring. *Of course. There won't be reception inside the hospital.* She hung up without leaving a message.

"I wonder..."

From the menu, she searched the phone's call history. Though unplugging the landline before going to bed had become part of her standard routine over the past couple of weeks, last night she'd forgotten about it. Sure enough, it was there. Twelve calls at irregular intervals from an unknown number. And she'd slept through every single one. Was it any wonder that Stella's injury had also gone unnoticed?

A tidal wave of self-loathing threatened to wash over her. Unwilling to succumb to the crippling emotion, she diverted her energy toward solving the puzzle of *how* Stella had injured herself.

Pacing the kitchen, she rubbed her hands together until her skin burned from the friction. Suddenly, she stopped. Stepping toward the counter, she examined every inch of its surface, including whatever apparatus sat within a child's reach.

The stovetop was spotless, save for the frying pan she'd forgotten to put away when she cleaned out the dishwasher. The microwave was empty. The toaster oven, as with the other appliances, showed no sign of recent use. Marche crossed her arms and surveyed her surroundings again, perplexed. How on earth had Stella burned her hands?

She explored the rest of the first floor. The dining room hardly seemed suspect. How likely was it that a properly covered electrical outlet could scorch even the smallest of palms? The laundry room proved equally unavailing; it contained only a broken washer, dryer, shelving for the detergent, and a small table for folding clothes. Stella spent most of her waking hours (when not in her bedroom) in the den. Yet there weren't any bare light bulbs or exposed wires to be found here—nothing the least bit hazardous.

"Unless..."

Marche returned to the kitchen and peered inside the trashcan. Glass and dirt littered the top. Grabbing the edge of the receptacle, she shook it until the sparkling debris trickled down the sides. Another dead end. There weren't any charred pieces of paper or melted plastic. Stella hadn't been playing with fire.

"I doubt she even knows how to use a matchstick," Marche mumbled.

She tied the ends of the bag and dumped it in the outside bin. After replacing the bag and washing her hands, she inspected the upstairs.

She checked the bathroom first, followed by the spare room and then her own bedroom. None of these spaces offered the slightest clue.

Finally, she crossed the floor to Stella's room. The space was dim, so she opened the curtains. Sunlight poured through the windows, washing the floor and walls with bright yellow-white light. Inside the closet, she found a giraffe print shirt scrunched up among the shoes. She pinched it between her fingers and gave it a firm shake, pressed it to her nose before selecting a hanger to work through the sleeves. She gazed at the rest of the room—at the pile of stuffed animals in the corner, the small dresser, and the bedside table with the Care Bear lamp. How very normal everything looked.

"I don't get it," she said. "What the hell happened?"

The bed was a mess. But when was it not? She straightened the sheet. The comforter had fallen onto the floor at the foot of the bed. She spread it over the mattress and folded it back. Then she picked up the pillow and fluffed it out.

She went back to the kitchen and re-dialed Trey's number, tapped her foot. Again, the line transferred to voicemail. She set the phone down; it made a loud clattering sound as it nestled into the base. She paced to the table and back.

Grabbing the teakettle, she filled it with water and placed it on the burner. While the water heated, she wiped down the countertops with a soapy rag. She rubbed vigorously and thoroughly until the Formica was clean enough to lick. The kettle whistled. She wrung out the cloth and draped it over the sink divider. She prepared the tea, stared out the window as it steeped. When it was ready, she sipped it unsweetened, standing at the counter.

"Might as well finish what I started," she said, eyeing the vinyl. Taking one last sip of the hot drink, she reached for the mop and proceeded to scrub the floor.

In record time, she had cleaned the kitchen floor and graduated to the hallway. She was just mopping the threshold to the dining room when she heard it: a series of knocks at the front door.

Marche looked up with a sudden jolt. For a brief moment, she wondered if Trey had actually contacted child protective services. After all, how many surprise visitors should she expect in a single day?

Get a grip. Angry as he was, he wouldn't go that far.

Swallowing her disquietude, she gave one last swipe with the mop and leaned the handle against the wall. As she approached the foyer, a cheerful female voice sounded from the doorstep.

"Yoo-hoo!"

Marche wrinkled her nose. The slightly high-pitched greeting, punctuated with a trill, pricked at her memory. Who sounded like that? One by one, she conjured an image of her female co-workers and neighbors. None of the faces matched the voice.

"Yoo-hoo! Anyone home? Yoo..."

Swinging the door open, Marche encountered a beaming, white-haired woman. Draped in a variety of colors (a fuchsia feather tucked behind one ear, green pear-shaped earrings clipped to drooping lobes, an orange floral dress that belonged on a figure thirty years younger, flats the color of red peppers which accentuated the bulging veins around her ankles), she looked like an exotic bird plucked from the pages of *Audubon*.

"Hello!"

Marche stared blankly at her visitor for several seconds as she struggled to recollect her name. "Mrs. Marshall, how are you?"

"Just as dandy as a flower after a warm spring rain," Agatha said. "Thank you for asking."

Marche glanced over the woman's head to the street beyond. A canary yellow Corvette was parked at the curb. "So were you just in the neighborhood, or—"

"Well, I didn't want to be rude, you know," Agatha said. "I did promise that

I'd visit, and I don't like to break my word." She pushed her chin forward for emphasis. "A person's word means so much."

"I wouldn't think you rude for all the world, Mrs. Marshall."

"You're such a cupcake," Agatha said. "May I come in?"

Though she wasn't in the mood to entertain anyone—least of all Agatha—she stepped aside to admit her. "Yes... Of course. Where are my manners?"

"Many thanks, dear." Agatha scuttled past Marche, clutching a tiny black purse that couldn't hold much beyond a wallet and a set of car keys.

Marche closed the front door. Now that she'd allowed the woman into her house, she wasn't sure what to do. Agatha looked at her in silent expectation. "Would you like a cup of tea?"

"Hmm. Why not?"

Marche retraced her steps to the kitchen. Agatha's flats clonked loudly on the floor behind her.

"It hasn't changed much," the old woman muttered.

"Pardon?" Marche added more water to the kettle, which was still warm, placed it on the stove, and turned the burner on its highest setting. Then she opened a cabinet and extracted a mug, white with cherries on it.

"Chucky never cared much for alteration," Agatha said. "Once he got used to something... Well, let's just say that he knew what he liked and when it came down to trying anything different, good luck to the salesman. Stubborn as a mule—that was my brother."

"Really?" Marche recalled her initial tour of the house with Jemima Bright. The real estate agent had made it a point to highlight all of the updated features: vinyl flooring in the kitchen and bathrooms, a two-year-old air conditioner, hurricane-proof windows. The kitchen appliances—though unattractive—retained the functionality of their age, which was not beyond five years. Chuck Louis had taken care of his house.

She set the fruit-themed mug on the counter.

Wooden legs scraped against the floor as Agatha settled into a chair at the table. She laid the handbag on the tabletop beside her.

"There are some changes that I'd like to make," Marche said. "But it's a big job. It'll probably take ten years to get everything done." *Or longer, since I didn't get that promotion.* She opened another cabinet. "What kind of tea would you like? I have lemon, blueberry, or black."

"I'll take black. To match my temper."

Marche withdrew the box of black tea and dropped a bag in each cup. Reaching for the kettle, she poured the steaming water in equal portions.

A car door slammed as she set the timer on the microwave. Marche gazed out of the kitchen window. In the driveway next door, Shelley was gathering armfuls of grocery bags from the trunk of her Camry. She headed for the house, looking as though she might topple over at any moment from the excess weight. She disappeared inside the front door for a few seconds before reappearing, empty-handed.

"You've got something that belongs to me."

"What?" Marche replied absentmindedly.

Shelley hooked her arms through several more plastic bags. Then she shut the trunk, waddled up the drive, and closed the front door. The windchimes on her porch tinkled lightly in response.

"You've *got* something that belongs to me."

"Huh?" Marche turned from the window and blinked several times. She couldn't comprehend the situation; she thought she was hallucinating.

Agatha Marshall was holding a gun.

"There's no need to panic," Agatha said. The sound of her voice—calm and controlled—wormed into Marche's brain, cemented her feet in reality. She felt herself go white with shock. "I have no intention of using this on you."

Marche stared dumbly at the barrel of the gun. The timer beeped. Her ears seemed stuffed with cotton, though, and she heard only a muffled sound that she couldn't readily identify.

"The tea is ready," Agatha informed her, waving the weapon slightly. She sat with her back against the chair, shoulders high. The black handbag lay open on its side.

"I take honey." Agatha paused. "Do you have honey?"

Marche swallowed. The muscles in her throat tightened, making it difficult to speak. She couldn't help but notice how steadily her nemesis held the gun in her pale, wrinkled hand. "Uh..." She swallowed again. What was the answer? Wait... What was the question? In vain, she tried to think, but her mind had slipped into a blank state. "I'm not sure."

"Let's not bother about it then," Agatha said. "I'll take sugar instead." She looked like an aged madam defending her brothel from non-paying clients as she appraised Marche with critical eyes. "You *do* have sugar?"

Sugar? Do I have sugar? Yes—I bought it for Shelley's dessert! But oh-my-God, where did I put it? Think, brain. Think! Marche shook her head, but the movement was stiff and her bones seemed to creak.

"Well?" Agatha pointed at the mugs. Her metallic purple fingernails—wrapped firmly around the weapon's grip—glinted in the sunlight.

Marche obeyed the monosyllabic command with slow, painful precision. Lifting the spoon from the spoon rest, she strained the first tea bag. The watery contents dripped into the steaming liquid.

With each movement, her gut jiggled like Jell-O. Her forearm trembled as she dropped the flattened bag in the sink. "How much—" She cleared her throat and tried once more to speak. The effort produced a frog-like croak. "How much sugar would you like?"

"Four lumps."

She found the sugar right where she'd left it, between the empty fruit basket and the refrigerator. The lid to the sugar canister seemed cemented shut; she split a nail prying it open. Tears smarted in her eyes. She scooped out a heaping pile of sugar, followed by a second, and then a third.

"That's enough."

Marche froze, her hand suspended over the open container. Slowly, she lowered it, sealed the sugar container, and dipped the spoon into the tea.

When she felt like she'd stirred it for as long as she could without testing the woman's patience, she wrapped her fingers around the mug's handle and faced the kitchen table. She advanced with careful, measured steps—fearful that if she tripped or splashed even a drop of tea, the unexpected movement might startle

Agatha into pulling the trigger.

Too soon, she reached her destination. Marche bent forward and, with both hands, placed the mug before her captor.

"Thank you." Agatha brought the mug to her lips. "It's good," she said, taking a sip. "Very sweet. Like a lollipop."

As Marche stood anchored to the spot like a soldier at attention, her gaze dropped to the table. The pepper shaker. Stupidly, she realized that Trey had set it on the wrong side of the saltshaker. In its previous spot lay the carcass of a black ant, upside down, dry, and crinkled.

"Your tea is getting cold."

Marche followed an invisible line from the dead insect to Agatha's mug. An ugly tangerine blotch stained the inner rim. Steam danced in the air like smoke rising from a crackling fire.

"Please," Agatha said, her voice coated in nectar, "join me."

Marche walked stiffly to the counter and rested her palms on the Formica. *Be calm. Stay smart. She's just a crazy old woman with a shoddy memory. Do what she says and maybe...* But she couldn't complete the thought.

As she reached for her mug, outside movement caught her attention. The front door to the Franklins' house opened! Marche's pulse raced as Hank appeared on the porch.

If only he would look her way! But then what? Marche wondered. If she jumped up and down and waved her arms, Agatha would surely shoot her on the spot. Still, if he would just glance in her direction. Despite the distance between their houses, maybe he would see the distress in her face. Then he could call the police and help would arrive...

Marche grasped at the idea like a desperate climber clutching at crumbling rock. She fastened a sharp eye on her neighbor as he traced a path to Shelley's car. Opening the trunk, he extended both arms and lifted a rectangular box from the compartment. Balancing the object in one hand, he shut the trunk, and he headed back up the drive.

I'm right here, damn it! Come on, Hank. I need you to see what's happening. I need your help. Just look this way!

Marche held her breath. Hank paused near the top of the driveway, toed something on the pavement. Then he gazed at the sky.

Okay, Hank. You're halfway there! Just turn a little to the left...

Hank lowered his head and entered the house without once looking her way.

The weight of defeat crushed her.

"Are you all right, dear?"

"I thought I felt a sneeze coming on," March replied. A nerve twitched in her cheek. She struggled to keep the tears from her eyes as she carried the mug to the table.

A few steps from her destination, the landline rang. The unexpected sound stopped her in her tracks. She glanced at the phone. Was it Trey, calling to give her a report on Stella's condition? Or maybe it was Bridget, wanting to apologize for her husband's rash behavior? Would Agatha allow her to speak with the caller? Could this be the opportunity she needed to escape this nightmare?

"I don't think you'll be answering that," Agatha said, cutting through her thoughts like a mind reader.

Sweat streaked from Marche's armpit down her side. Another ribbon of sweat coursed from her temple to her jawline. She gripped the mug tightly, ignoring the impulse to swipe a hand across her cheek. *No sudden movements. Just do what she says.*

The jangling stopped.

"Have a seat. I don't like sitting here alone. It makes me feel like an unwanted visitor."

Marche discovered that she was sitting. She didn't recall pulling out the chair or bending her knees until the seat stopped her from lowering any further. She only knew that she had been standing, and now she was not.

The barrel of the gun was closer now. Before, it had pointed at her abdomen. Now it was aimed at her chest. Marche imagined that she could actually smell the metal. She struggled to keep her wits about her.

"Where's your little one?" Agatha asked. "Is she here in the house?"

Marche wrapped her fingers around the mug. The heat seeped through the porcelain, warming her chilled skin. "No."

"Where is she?"

"With my sister."

"When do you expect her back?"

Stella's blistered palms flashed before Marche's eyes. "Tomorrow," she lied.

"You'll have to speak up. I'm just an old woman, you know. My hearing isn't what it used to be."

Marche repeated the word, a decibel louder.

Agatha nodded. The answer seemed to please her; she smiled. "Does this make you nervous?" Without warning, she tapped the table with the butt of the weapon.

Marche jumped. Hot liquid splashed from the mug and onto her fingers. Slowly, she withdrew her hands and rested them in her lap.

Agatha clucked her tongue. "You ninny," she said, a flabbergasted expression painted on her clownish features. "Didn't I tell you already? I have no intention of shooting you."

At the moment, all five of Agatha's fingers rested on the grip. But that did nothing to ease Marche's nerves. How quickly could Agatha touch the trigger? A single reflex meant the difference between life and death.

"It's only for security—in case you decide to give me any trouble." Agatha slurped the tea. A thin film shimmered above her top lip. "This is really very good," she said, shaking a digit at the mug. "What brand is it?"

"Lipton."

"Oh? I always buy Pink Rose. It sounds so distinguished, doesn't it? *Pink Rose.* But I do like this. Maybe I'll buy it next time."

Agatha narrowed her eyes. "Now let's get down to business, shall we? You know what I want."

Marche tried to swallow, but her mouth was dry as cotton. What could she say? She hadn't the faintest clue what Agatha wanted.

Agatha's irises shimmered with watery madness. "Stop playing stupid," she said when Marche remained mute.

"I'm not," Marche sputtered. "I don't—I mean—"

"The *letters.*"

Marche squeezed her hands tightly together; her knuckles were slick with tea. A few sheets of old paper—that's what this was about? "I don't understand… I never meant to keep them from you."

Agatha pursed her mouth. "Did you read them?"

Marche dug her toes into the floor. "No," she croaked.

"Are you sure about that?" Agatha studied her intensely while she caressed the handle of the gun with her thumb.

"I'm sure."

Thirty seconds or more elapsed in taut silence. Then Agatha smiled broadly; her tangerine lips stretched thin until they were nearly non-existent. "Good girl."

A bluejay squawked at the kitchen windowsill. Its jubilant, jarring voice penetrated the glass, spreading through the room like awkward background laughter.

"Where have you got them?" Agatha snapped.

"Upstairs."

"Where upstairs?"

Marche pointed at the ceiling, her hand angled in the direction of the dining room.

Agatha's smile softened. "How fitting. That used to be my room, you know," she said, readjusting the pink feather behind her ear. "Let's get them, shall we?" She got steadily to her feet, the gun firm in her grasp.

Marche's stomach muscles clenched.

"Up—get up."

Marche rose from the chair, her knees wobbling. She listed to the right and then to the left like a ship on choppy waters. She grabbed the edge of the table for support.

"You first," Agatha directed in a harsh, impatient voice. "Lead the way."

Marche clamped her teeth until her jaw ached. As she exited the kitchen, she heard Agatha shuffling behind her, sensed the barrel of the gun pointed at her spine.

The hallway seemed to stretch forever. Had it always taken this long to cross twenty-five feet? Her gaze latched onto the front door. With every inch she gained, she imagined how easy it would be to escape. Just a turn of the knob and she could be free.

She gave up on the idea as she stepped into the foyer. Agatha might appear frail, but she seemed to have no difficulty manipulating a weapon.

Just play her game, Marche reminded herself. *Do what she says and maybe she won't...*

Reaching the stairs, she placed a hand on the railing to steady herself. She climbed the first step. She felt as if someone had poured cement over each foot.

Halfway up the staircase, Marche celebrated the fact that she was still alive. When she reached its summit, she felt like a death row inmate who'd walked to her place of execution, only to receive a pardon at the very last instant.

"Keep moving."

Agatha poked Marche in the lower back with the gun. The abrupt contact shocked her, producing an uncomfortable hot trickle between her legs.

Slowly, she walked down the hall. The spare room was on the right, its door wide open. At the entrance, she paused.

"What are you waiting for? Get in there."

Reluctantly, Marche crossed the threshold. The room was bare except for the trunk; it sat in the center of the floor, where she and Bridget had placed it after dragging it down from the attic. She stopped when she had reached it.

"Bring it to me."

Marche flexed her stiffened fingers and followed the steely command. She began to pull the wooden box across the floor. The trunk was heavier than she remembered. Twice she lost her grip and fell backward. As she neared Agatha—who remained just inside the doorway—she switched from pulling to pushing. She continued to push until the edge of the box reached the tips of those ugly red shoes.

"And here it is," Agatha said.

Marche remained on her knees. When she lifted her gaze, she discovered the weapon was aimed at that critical spot directly between her eyes.

"Open it."

Marche laid her hands on the lid, caught in a standstill. Her heart felt ready to pound right through her rib cage, splintering her bones like an axe through wood.

When she lifted the top and revealed the disarray, Agatha would realize that she had lied. What would happen? Would she shoot her then and there?

Each second Marche stalled was an extra second of life. In her lowest moments after Dom's death, she had yearned for release from the physical realm. Now the realization that death was a simple reflex away numbed her. She wasn't ready to die. There were too many words left unspoken, too many wrongs not yet righted. She longed to see her daughter, to hug her and kiss her, and to share stories with her about Dom—and about her childhood with Bridget, and to tell her about the fondest memories she had of her own parents.

The wood felt cool and dry under her fingers.

It felt like a coffin.

"Open it," Agatha repeated in her calm, unwavering voice.

Thirty-One

"Agatha?"

The partially opened lid slipped through Marche's fingers. Cracking sounded as a corner of the chest splintered.

Agatha blinked in surprise and glanced over her shoulder. Vale stood in the doorway, wisps of hair sticking out on one side of his head as though he'd recently awakened from an afternoon siesta.

"What are you doing here?" Agatha demanded, a slight tremor of annoyance in her voice. She backed up against the wall. Shifting her glance from Marche to Vale and back to Marche again, Agatha refocused the gun.

Vale went wide-eyed when the weapon flashed before him. He swayed slightly, like a sapling in a soft breeze. One arm reached out for the doorframe.

Oh no! Marche thought, her heart squeezing in her chest. *Please, dear God. Oh, please don't faint. You're my only hope, Rory Vale!*

Vale lifted his gaze, his face suddenly expressionless. "Agatha, now I want you to listen to me very carefully," he said, his voice calm and collected—like an ice cream server asking a customer if she wanted an extra cherry on her banana split. "Put. Down. The. Gun."

Agatha sneered. "I can't do that."

"Why not?"

"I have to have my letters first."

Marche chewed her bottom lip. Her gaze flitted nervously between Agatha and Vale. The chest's wooden surface abraded her fingers where she clutched it tightly.

"Why do you need them so badly?"

"Because," Agatha spat, "she can't know what's written in them. No one can."

Vale dropped his chin and took a deep breath. "Those letters can't hurt you, Agatha. They mean nothing."

Agatha stomped her foot and growled. "Fiddlesticks! Of course they *mean* something. Why else would I have kept them hidden?"

"I don't mean to suggest that they aren't important to you," Vale said. Releasing his grip on the doorframe, he held both hands palm upwards in supplication. "What I'm trying to say is that nobody cares about a little girl's sentiments from fifty years ago. Don't you see? There isn't anything to worry about. You're building a mountain out of a molehill."

"Pooh!" Agatha shot a quick glance at Marche. "She found my papers—my *personal* correspondence—and she didn't return them to me. They don't belong to her. They belong to *me*."

Vale lowered his arms until they hung limply at his sides. "What do you think is going to happen when the police find out that you've threatened Mrs. Baker with a gun?"

Agatha blinked. For a split second, she seemed to waiver. Then her features hardened. "That's apples."

"You're holding a *gun*, Agatha. A deadly weapon. That's not to be taken lightly."

Agatha fiddled with one of her clip-on earrings. As she withdrew her hand, it fell to the floor unnoticed. "Be realistic, won't you?"

"Ag—"

"I'm not going to shoot her," Agatha barked. "I'm just going to take the letters and leave. If she told the whole town that I had a gun, who do you think they'd believe? Me—or her?"

While Vale tried to reason with the unreasonable, Marche stared at the barrel of the gun. As much as she wanted to, she couldn't divert her gaze from it—like driving down the road and spying a car accident on the shoulder. Though she dreaded seeing the aftermath, part of her mind craved to see the gore, to detect any hint of death.

Vale nodded. "You're right," he said in a conciliatory tone. "Of course everyone would believe you. You're Fred Louis's little princess, after all." Then he paused. Raising his eyebrows, he looked imploringly at Agatha. "But what about Mrs. Baker? You're not being the sweet girl I know, Aggie. You're scaring this poor woman. Is that what you really want? Are you going to be the mean bully? Is that who you really are?"

Vale took a tentative step forward.

Agatha remained still. It was as though his words had opened a doorway and she had stepped through it—straight into the past. The moment seemed transformative. Her aged exterior appeared to melt away, with a youthful version blossoming in its place.

"How do I look in this dress?" Agatha asked. Lifting the hem of her skirt, she rotated her hips so that the fabric fanned about her legs. The half-forgotten weapon dangled in her hand.

"You always look beautiful in your dresses," he said. "The belle of the ball."

Agatha giggled like a schoolgirl. Vale extended his hand and she stepped forward. Their fingers touched, then entwined.

"Oh, Butch."

As those two whispered words floated across the room, Marche recollected the content of the letters she'd read all those weeks ago. The careless, messy scrawl. The simple, unchanging signature. It had never occurred to her that Butch might be a pet name. And her neighbor had been childhood friends with Charles Louis. "Of course he's Butch," she breathed. Only after the words reached her ears did she realize that she'd uttered the thought out loud.

The spell broke.

The innocent enthusiasm vanished from Agatha's face. The wrinkles on her cheeks became more pronounced; the lines around her mouth deepened. Raising her arm, she stepped away from Vale. "Liar!" she screamed. All of her attention focused on Marche now. Her features twisted and contorted until she bore the grotesqueness of a ventriloquist's doll.

Marche blanched.

Agatha aimed the weapon, her thin arm shaking violently with rage. "You read them!"

At last Marche broke free of her paralysis. She began to crawl backward, her eyes bulging painfully in their sockets.

"Aggie," Vale said softly, soothingly.

But just as she had forgotten Marche a moment earlier, Agatha now seemed oblivious to her former lover. "You're a liar!"

Marche continued to back up. If she'd been able to, she would have climbed out of the window—preferring the possibility of broken bones to a perforated heart. Alas, the opportunity didn't arise. Too soon, the soles of her feet bumped into the farthest corner of the room. She was trapped.

"Liar! Liar!"

"Wait a minute," Vale pleaded. "Let's talk about this. Mrs. Baker is a good lady. I'm sure she hasn't touched your letters."

Agatha waved the gun up and down. "And I suppose that you're after him too, huh?" she screeched at Marche.

"Not true," Marche whispered, shaking her head. "He's just... We're just neighbors." The floor bruised her kneecaps; her wrists ached under her body's weight. Any ounce of dignity she possessed had fled. Unable to withstand the torment, she whimpered.

Vale tried to touch Agatha's shoulder, but she squirmed out of his reach.

"That's not the way it is," Vale exclaimed. "I would never do that to you. You're the only girl in my life. You know that's true. Now, what can I do to prove it to you?"

Vale's pleading proved fruitless. Nothing could penetrate Agatha's veil of madness. She approached Marche, her brown eyes narrowed into slits.

"You can't have him!" she shrieked. "You can't! I won't allow it! He's my man! Mine! You hear?"

Agatha unclenched her left fist and jammed her fingers into her hair. She clawed at the strands like a rabid animal tearing at meat. Then she drew her hand downward, a clump of curly white hair sprouting like plucked weeds between her fingers, her nails digging grooves into the side of her face.

The scent of worms and rotted earth invaded Marche's nostrils. It was a pungent combination, almost choking in its intensity. As she struggled to draw in fresh air, she realized that the odor wasn't coming from any external source; it originated from within herself. *I can smell death.* And then she stood above herself. As a separate entity, she watched in helpless horror as Agatha raised her other hand to steady her grip on the gun.

"Darling," Vale crooned.

Agatha's aim wavered.

"Sweet Aggie." Deep and throaty, his was the voice of an unscrupulous knight who wished to seduce the fairest maiden in the glen. It was a provocative voice, full of sweetness and a promise: the sun will bring gold and the moon, diamonds.

The poison in Agatha's eyes lost its potency. Her snarling mouth flattened into an expression of neutrality. "What, Butch?" she asked demurely, a thin red line dribbling down her scratched cheek.

Vale pressed a palm to Agatha's shoulder. This time, she accepted his touch. "You taught Wilma a really good lesson. I'm so proud of you."

"You are?" she said softly.

"Of course I am, my love." Vale leaned over Agatha's shoulder and spoke into her ear. "Now I can be certain that you are the only one for me," he continued huskily. "You've proved yourself, and now it's just the two of us. We can spend the rest of our lives together. Happy. Free. No one will ever be able to keep us apart."

Agatha smiled. Dropping her arms, she looked up at Vale.

"Are you happy now, dearest?"

"Oh, yes, Butch."

Vale touched Agatha's elbow. His fingers caressed her arm to the wrist, where they paused.

The gun dangled carelessly by Agatha's side. As Vale gazed into Agatha's eyes, his fingers grazed the weapon. It was at that moment—when the gun would have switched hands—that Agatha suddenly jumped back.

Vale's mouth formed a silent 'o' of surprise. At the same time, Marche's out-of-body experience ended. Slamming back into herself, she inhaled so quickly and so deeply that she nearly fainted from lightheadedness.

Agatha giggled. Lifting her heels, she began to dance. The bottoms of her shoes clapped the floor, producing a sound like mock bullets. Red suffused her cheeks as she tilted her head from side to side—a marionette loosed from its strings. She held up the hem of her dress and twirled. One circle. Two circles. Then she took to tapping the floor again. First the toes, then the heels, and back to the toes once more. She spun a third time. And the momentum carried her across the room until she was standing underneath the attic door.

As suddenly as the fit of hilarity began, it stopped.

"Do you hear it?" Agatha asked, slowly lowering her left foot. "Do you?"

The awe in her voice seemed to strike a chord in Vale; his chin dropped and his eyes teared up. "No, Agatha. I don't hear anything except for your lovely, lovely voice."

A brilliant smile lit Agatha's face and she squealed with glee. "Oh, it's so beautiful! Don't you hear them? Aren't they lovely?!" She laughed. "I never heard them chime so loudly before. They're beautiful—like wedding bells!"

Agatha was a ballerina dancing. She lifted her arms as though to have her fingertips meet at a point above her head—an elegant pose that never materialized. With her free hand, she reached toward the ceiling. With the other, she pointed the gun to her temple. Vale lunged forward but was too late. A deafening blast echoed through the house. Blood, bone shards, and gray matter splattered onto the wall.

Agatha's body crumpled to the floor in a vibrant heap.

Marche collapsed onto her side and vomited. Only when she'd emptied her stomach of all its contents did she lift her head. And then she immediately regretted it. More bile rose in her throat as the dead eyes stared at her and the blood flowed from the cadaver and collected in a puddle at her feet.

Thirty-Two

Sirens sounded shortly after Vale called the police. "Cops are on the way," he announced, returning to the room.

The mournful wailing grew louder. Then loud banging sounded on the front door—but neither Marche nor Vale moved. Voices called through the foyer and carried to the second floor. Footsteps rushed up the stairs.

A pair of legs appeared in the doorway. Words without meaning rang harshly in Marche's ears. She squinted as if in pain. More legs materialized. They walked toward her, and she found herself wondering how legs without a body could navigate across a room. Only when the legs bent at the knees and a pair of pale gray eyes looked into her own did she begin to swim out of her disorientation.

"Ma'am? Are you all right?" the paramedic asked.

"What?"

"Have you been injured? Are you hurt?"

Marche stared dumbly at the medical attendant as her brain slowly digested the questions. "No," she said. "I'm okay."

In the living room, she sat on the sofa while a female police officer questioned her. "No… I have no idea." She shook her head. "I didn't really know her. I only met her a few times. I'm sorry. I'm having a hard time thinking straight."

Throughout the entire exchange, Marche felt trapped inside a mental fog. At one point, she looked at the officer's head, bent forward as she scratched out notes on a small pad. The woman's red hair was pulled back into a tight bun; the dark roots were almost black. Oddly mesmerized, Marche puzzled over the fact that a person in law enforcement would choose to dye their hair the shade of ripe cranberries. The color just seemed wrong, somehow.

Random images flashed through her mind: red marks on a test paper, stop signs and traffic lights, blood spurting from severed arteries. She nearly gagged as she recalled the gruesome spatter on the freshly painted wall. Amidst the dandelions and bluebirds, Agatha's own personal contribution—three dimensional grubs (squirming and arcing) and misshapen ladybugs.

When the interview was over, Marche headed upstairs toward her bedroom. *Don't look. Don't look. Don't look.* Fixing her gaze on the floor, she managed to avoid peering into the spare room as she turned into her own. Closing the door, she stripped out of her soiled garments and left them where they landed on the floor. Pulling open the bureau drawers, she blindly selected clean clothes to wear. The yellow cotton shirt shook in her hand. As she worked her second leg through her jeans, she lost her balance and banged her hip on the dresser. She endured the pain silently, still too numb to cry.

Descending the stairs, she found Vale waiting at the front door.

A handful of emergency vehicles, their lights off, swarmed the front lawn. People whom Marche didn't recognize had formed clusters on both of the street corners. There were at least thirty of them; the youngest couldn't be more than twenty, the eldest was probably eighty. They were dressed like spectators at a ballgame, with sandals on their feet and baseball caps on their heads to block out the sun. And was she the spectacle they had come to observe? Marche had the distinct impression that she was no different to these onlookers than an oddity on display at a roadside freak show.

Vale caught her by the elbow when she tripped over her feet on the driveway. "Steady now."

"Thank you," she muttered, her teeth chattering.

As she and Vale stepped onto the street, Marche registered a variety of sounds: a door clicking forcefully into place, beads clacking against beads, sandals scuffling over pavement. And suddenly Shelley appeared at her side.

The bracelets on her left wrist jangled violently as she gesticulated. "Marche, Mr. Vale—are you two all right? What's going on? What on earth happened?"

Marche met her neighbor's gaze but found that she was unable to speak. *I can't talk about it. Not yet.* Putting the events into words would be like taking a jackhammer to a dam. One tiny crack in the surface and her self-composure would crumble completely.

"What was that terrible sound?" Shelley continued. "Hank said that he thought it was a gunshot. But I didn't think you even owned a gun, Marche. Did something explode in your kitchen?" She patted her chest as she gulped for air.

Marche shook her head.

"Now isn't a good time," Vale said.

"Hmm?" Shelley looked at Vale. The old man had spoken in a diplomatic yet firm voice that didn't leave room for argument. "Ohh, o-okay." Turning back to Marche, she said, "Call me later if you need to talk, hon. Don't worry about the hour. I'm here for you anytime." Hesitantly, she turned away, gazing at them over her shoulder as she retreated to her front door.

"Thank you," Marche repeated, not knowing what else to say to the man who had probably saved her life.

They concluded the brief trek in silence. Marche felt an invisible weight lift off her shoulders when they finally reached Vale's house and stepped inside. The dogs barked and jumped with excitement. Vale shushed them and led Marche to the back porch. The outdoor space consisted of two rocking chairs, a small table, and a plastic bucket filled with dog toys.

"I'm so thirsty," Marche blurted, dropping into one of the chairs.

The back door slammed shut as Vale reentered the house. The kitchen echoed with the sound of cabinets opening and closing.

A moment later, Marche received a glass of iced tap water and a striped dish towel. She slurped noisily and greedily and soon required a refill. When she'd quaffed two-thirds of the second glass, she leaned back and closed her eyes. Vale lit a cigarette.

"How did you know?" Marche asked after she'd rested for several minutes.

Vale sighed heavily. "I *didn't* know," he said. "I went outside to check the mail and I saw Agatha's car parked at your house. I got curious. Called your number, but no one answered. Then I got concerned. Decided to check things out firsthand. When I reached your stoop, I got a funny feeling in my gut. Just thank your lucky stars the bolt wasn't locked. Don't know if I'd have been bold enough to knock down the door." He paused. "Well, that's what happened. Something told me to get inside real fast and quiet-like." He stretched out his legs and crossed his ankles. "I didn't know she'd have a gun."

Marche looked out at the yard. The grass was brown in spots and unevenly mowed. The plot was bare except for a single citrus tree. Several of its fruits littered the ground, the rinds split open with gnats buzzing about the exposed meat. One of the dogs reclined in the shade of the tree's branches, her back legs stretched outward in a straight line. The other dog was in the midst of running back and forth from one length of fence to the other. Her paws kicked up clumps of grass; she panted loudly.

Vale suddenly hit the arm of the chair with his fist, creating a loud thump.

"I should have known that she was still sick. God damn it! I might as well have been the one holding the gun to her head." He brushed his thumb and forefinger brusquely across his mouth and looked away.

Marche thought of the previous times that she'd interacted with Agatha. Though she'd always considered the old woman peculiar, almost infantile in her behavior, she'd never once entertained the possibility that she posed a threat—to herself or to anyone else.

"No," she said quietly. "I don't think anyone could have anticipated what happened today."

Vale shook his head. "You can say that because you don't know the whole story."

The sound of regret underlying his words piqued Marche's interest, compelling her to ask the question she might not have asked otherwise. When she glanced at her neighbor and saw the severe expression on his face, her curiosity intensified. "What story?"

Vale cleared his throat. "I've never spoken to anyone about this, except for Chuck and his old man—and they were part of it. So that don't really count as far as I'm concerned. But after what you've been through, you deserve to know. You're part of it, too, now."

Vale stood. Grabbing one of the toys from the bucket, he opened the screen door and tossed it onto the grass. The dog that had been running stopped to retrieve it. She plopped onto the ground, chomping happily on the green rubber alligator until it squeaked. Vale shut the door and returned to his seat. He tilted his head to one side, grunted, then began.

"Agatha was mad-crazy about me." Soft creaking sounded as he rocked the wooden chair back and forth. "I was just a typical young buck. And I guess that was the problem. I teased Agatha just to get under her skin. I thought that the madder I got her, the hotter she'd be in bed."

Marche gazed at the cloudless sky. She tried to picture Agatha as a young girl, but it was impossible. The only image she could conjure featured a cadaver with a tangerine colored grin. She shuddered.

"The truth of the matter was that I used Wilma to bait Agatha. I told her that if she didn't stop dragging me along like a dog on a leash, I'd go out with the other girl."

As he spoke, the sedentary canine suddenly sprang to her feet and barked at a squirrel. Running the length of the fence with the ease of a tightrope walker, the gray creature stopped briefly to study the large beast, its dark nose twitching. Then it crossed into the next yard and disappeared. The dog worked out her frustration by pulling furiously at a patch of weeds with her teeth.

"The plan worked like a charm," Vale continued. "Agatha quit playing hard to get, and we had a good ol' time rolling around in the sheets. We had fun. Lots and lots of fun."

Marche studied Vale's features and wondered if today's events would age him greatly, devouring what youth remained in him. Would the spots of gray in his hair disappear and leave an entirely white mop upon his head? Would the lively shade of blue in his eyes dampen to a less vibrant hue? Would his tall stature slump forward, turning him into a hunchback?

"But then there was Wilma," Vale said. "After all that playing around, it turned out that she was the girl for me, after all. Funny how things sometimes work out, isn't it? Agatha was head over heels in love with me, but I didn't give two hoots about it. Day after day, all I could think about was Wilma's beautiful face and her sweet-natured personality. At night, I fell asleep imagining how it would be to hold hands with her. To hug her close and smell her hair. After a couple of weeks, I couldn't take it anymore. I asked Wilma if she'd be my girl. It was one of the happiest moments of my life when she said yes... Then I went and dropped Agatha like a ton of bricks."

Vale tilted his chair backward and stared at the roof.

"I've never forgotten that look on Agatha's face when I told her it was over. Her eyes completely changed. They didn't go round with dismay or anything—they just went blank. How do I explain it?" He paused. "I guess it'd be like if you were speaking to someone in English and suddenly you switched to Japanese. Yeah, it was kind of like that. When I told her I was breaking up with her, it was like she didn't understand what I was saying. She just laughed. That same old merry laugh of hers. She thought it was a joke, you know? So I set her straight. I told her that I was going to be with Wilma. That *she* meant nothing to me."

One of the dogs trotted over to the door and let out a soft *woof*.

"That'a girl," Vale said as he held the door open for the animal to walk through. He whistled to the second dog and waited until she'd joined her companion by the metal water bowls before he sat down again.

"I said the meanest thing that I could think of—I didn't love her. It's not that I had *stopped* loving her, it's just that I had never cared for her in the first place," Vale said, raking his fingers through his messy hair.

"I thought that'd be the end of it. Boys break up with girls every day and it's not the end of the world. Why should this be any different? Then I heard from Chuck that Agatha had locked herself in her room for two days and refused to eat."

Slowly, he resumed rocking.

"I had no sympathy," he admitted. "No empathy. Nothing. From my way of thinking, she was just trying to put on a show. And I could see right through it. She was like a shiny piece of bait on a hook, trying to lure in the choicest fish. Humph. Looking back, I can't believe what a cocky bastard I was."

Marche silently agreed.

Vale *had* been a bastard. There was no sugarcoating it. No excusing it, either. *But it's not his fault that Agatha spiraled into madness. She was born that way, wasn't she? It was in her genes.* Sarah's newspaper articles intruded upon her thoughts. *The Louis Curse. All of the women died prematurely. History repeats itself.*

Yesterday she hadn't believed in the curse; today she wasn't so sure.

"I saw her a month later at the bowling alley," Vale continued. "Wilma and I were lacing up our shoes when Agatha noticed the two of us sitting there together. I was worried that there might be a confrontation. But Agatha didn't leave her group, and the rest of the evening she acted as if she didn't know we existed. Damn, was I relieved. I thought she'd finally moved on... I was wrong, of course."

The dogs finished lapping from their bowls. The smaller of the two curled up on the floor beside Vale's chair. The other stretched out at the back door and promptly rolled onto her back, putting a tummyful of plush brown fur on display.

"A few weeks later, she came to the garage where I worked. Mason's, it was called. I'd started out there as a runt and stayed on 'til management changed in the mid-fifties. The day was a scorcher, but Agatha looked radiant—like she'd swallowed a cup of sunshine. Truth be told, I was afraid she was going to tell me that I'd knocked her up." After a pause, he added, "That would have been better."

A soft breeze disturbed the stillness, and Marche caught a whiff of charcoal. Somewhere nearby, people were enjoying a late afternoon barbeque.

"That's when Agatha first mentioned the bells. They chimed in her ears from the attic, she said. It was 'angel's music.' She knew that she was better for me than Wilma, and the bells had proved it. She said that pretty soon I'd know she was right."

Vale's tone hardened.

"Of course, I didn't take her seriously. I laughed at her and told her to go home. But she was so damn persistent. The day after that, she cornered me at Publix when I was buying smokes. 'What do you want?' I says. 'There's nothing left to talk about. We're over. Get it through your silly head. I'm with someone else now.' Whatever I said, it went right in one ear and out the other. I'd barely finished telling her off when she started babbling about those damn bells again."

Vale grunted.

"Some guys might get a kick out of having a skirt slobber all over them. Not me," he declared. "It made me sick. I wanted to slap her—knock some sense into her dumb skull. But all I did was pay for my smokes and leave.

"A couple nights after that, Chuck and I, and a few other fellas, were drinking beers and wiling away the hours at stud. That's when I told Chuck about the things Agatha had been saying. And that's when he started to worry that something might be wrong." Vale paused to crack his knuckles. "You see, Chuck's father never told him about the circumstances surrounding his mama's death. But Egret Bay was a much smaller place back then—and it's hard to keep things secret when everyone is always sticking their nose in everyone else's business. For years, Chuck had known that his mama had lost her marbles before she died."

Vale stopped rocking, rested his arms on the chair, and popped the joints in his neck.

"For a little while, nothing else happened. Agatha kept to herself, and everything was roses between Wilma and me. Turned out it was the calm before the storm. Just as I was beginning to think the situation with Agatha had completely blown over, she showed up at my parents' back door. The night was god-awful hot. So hot you could've fried an egg without turning on the stove. I'd have stripped down to the skin if I'd had the house to myself. And there she was, dressed to the hilt—fancy dress, her hair all done up, and her face lacquered in make-up. She even curtsied when she saw me. The situation was so ridiculous that I didn't know how to respond."

The dog lying by the door suddenly stretched, rolled over, and stood. She padded across the floor, stopping when she reached Vale's chair. She sat on her haunches and nudged her master's knee. Vale automatically dropped a hand and scratched the dog behind the ears.

"I asked Agatha what she was about, and she said that she had something she wanted to show me. Needless to say, I'd long run out of patience with her by then. I couldn't have cared less about anything she might say or do. But my parents were starting to get curious, and I didn't want Agatha to cause a scene in front of them. 'Make it quick,' I says to her, 'I'm busy.'"

Vale cleared his throat.

"She took me to her house. It was past nine o'clock, and the place was lit up like a Christmas tree. But as soon as we stepped into the front hall, I could tell that we were alone. There was this old grandfather clock that the family kept in the parlor. I remember I could hear the pendulum echoing through the rooms. It was the first time I'd ever noticed it—the ticking sound, that is."

Vale's voice softened and his speech slowed. The dog turned her head, licked Vale's hand, and then returned to her spot by the door.

"Agatha led me up the stairs and into her bedroom. And that's when I got the idea that she was going to try to seduce me. Well, I wasn't going to stand for that nonsense. I had promised myself to Wilma, and I'd meant it."

He held up a knotted finger for emphasis.

"I was just about to put Agatha in her place when I noticed the smell. It was faint—just a hint in the air. I couldn't tell what it was or where it was coming from."

Vale paused. He tilted his head to the side and squinted as though he was envisioning the room as he'd seen it all those years ago.

"There wasn't anything out of the ordinary that I could see. The vanity was cluttered with powders and perfumes. The bed was made up all nice with the sheet tucked in. The floor was clean. A red-checkered area rug covered half the floorboards. There wasn't a crease in it—not a wrinkle—so I knew straightaway there wasn't anything under it. I just couldn't figure it out. And all the while, Agatha was watching me with this gleam in her eyes. She stood so full of pride, like she'd just won first place in a pie-baking contest. Well, I was so confused that I thought my head might start spinning. 'What's going on here, girl?' I says. 'What are you up to?' But Agatha didn't say anything. Instead, she pointed to the attic and started to giggle."

Vale coughed. It was a violent affair that lasted several seconds and caused his shoulders to cave in. Then he cleared his throat and said that he needed a cigarette. When he reached for the pack on the table, however, he found it empty. "Christ," he muttered.

He disappeared into the house and returned a minute later with another pack of cigarettes clutched in one hand. He held the box in Marche's direction; she declined with a shake of her head. Vale secured a cigarette for himself and lit the end of it with unsteady fingers. He inhaled twice before he continued.

"I've always considered myself a manly man. Ain't many things in this life that have struck fear into my heart. The dark don't bother me, and in my younger days, I'd be the first to climb the highest branch of the highest tree. But I'll tell you something. When I put the ladder up to that attic door, I hesitated. I didn't know what the hell I'd find waiting for me up there."

Again, he puffed on the cigarette. Smoke rings rose into the air and dissipated.

"I didn't see anything at first except vague shapes. Then my eyes adjusted to the dark and I saw it. Right in front of me, right there on the floor. I didn't understand what it was. I saw the pieces, but not the whole. Then I got it like a punch in the face."

Vale's voice broke and he finished his cigarette in silence. The chair creaked as he rocked to and fro.

"Flour sacks pushed together—filled with hay," he said, lighting another smoke. "There were extensions on the second sack and protrusions from the bottom one—branches that she must have gathered from the woods. It was obvious to me that they were supposed to be arms and legs. Agatha had taken lipstick and rouge and painted a face on the topmost sack. She'd even glued tresses of hair to the top and sides."

"Whose hair?" Marche asked.

"Her own," Vale replied. "She'd twisted her hair into one of those fancy knots though, so at the time I didn't know that she'd cut any of it off. Gave me the willies, all right."

Marche realized suddenly that she was tapping her foot. She glanced at the shoe. Thorny stickers had accumulated on the laces. She bent forward. One by one, she plucked them off and tossed them onto the concrete.

"Nearly broke my neck scurrying down those steps," Vale said. "I hit the floor and bumped into Agatha. She fell down—fell so hard that I heard her teeth click. But she didn't even flinch. She just kept smiling and told me that we were free to be together again."

The cigarette butt glowed in the late afternoon light. Vale took a final puff and then crushed it in the ashtray.

"Did she think she'd kidnapped Wilma?" Marche asked. "Was she really that delusional?"

"Delusional? Yeah, that sounds like the right word for it," Vale replied with a nod. "I had a long talk with Chuck and his old man that night. Told 'em everything, every sordid little detail. That's when they made the decision to send Agatha up north to live with some relatives."

Vale withdrew another cigarette, smoking half of it before he continued.

"That was the last I heard of Agatha for a long time. When she finally returned to Egret Bay, she was married to Marshall. For all intents and purposes, she led a picture-perfect life. She had a husband who made her the center of his world. She didn't want for anything. Like a good little wife, she kept house and took care of her two girls. And she was a great hostess, too. You know how important it is to hobnob with all the right people. Especially when your husband's running for sheriff," he added. "Well, Agatha pulled off her duties like a pro. In no time at all, she'd worked her way into the knitting circles of all the prominent wives in the county."

Vale sighed.

"I guess you could say she pulled off 'normal' like a pro, too. After all these years... I let Chuck handle it on his own because Agatha was *his* sister, *his* business. But now I see that I was only taking the easy way out. I should have made sure that she got the treatment she needed back then. For that, I'm truly sorry to you, Ms. Baker."

Marche turned away, unsure how to respond. Was Vale seeking absolution for his past behavior? If so, she couldn't give him the peace of mind that he wanted.

"Why do you think she was so obsessed with those letters?" she asked.

"Search me," Vale replied with a dismissive flick of the wrist. "I should have realized that cracks like that never really mend."

Marche folded the dish towel and set it on the plastic table beside the glass of water. Though she still felt a little wobbly, her senses seemed to have returned to normal. Cautiously, she rose to her feet.

"I should go back," she said. "It's been a few hours. They might have cleared out of the house by now."

She shivered. For a while, Vale's talking had distracted her from thoughts of the house. Now she imagined herself there in such vivid detail that it felt almost real. She could see herself standing inside the foyer, staring at the staircase. She shivered again. Every time she walked up those steps she would relive today's death march.

"Can I walk you home?"

Marche held out a hand to stop Vale, who was about to stand. "That's okay. I can see myself out."

As she grabbed the door handle to leave, however, she cast one final glance at her neighbor. "Your wife's name was Marlene, wasn't it?"

"That's right."

"So what happened to Wilma?"

Vale over-tipped the cigarette box, and the few remaining filters spilled onto the table. "Well," he drawled, picking one up. "Turned out we just weren't meant to be."

Thirty-Three

Marche sat idly for a few minutes while the car's air vents blew cool air onto her cheeks. What should she say? So much had happened since Trey had stormed off with Stella this afternoon that she didn't even know how to feel about it anymore. Reaching for the cell phone, she dialed the number to her sister's house.

"Hello?"

"Bridget? It's Marche."

"I know," her sister replied with a sigh.

"I'm on my way over. I need to talk to you."

"Okay."

"See you in a few minutes," Marche said, hanging up.

She arrived at 713 Carmichael Drive a quarter of an hour later. As she parked the Neon and turned off the engine, she noticed Bridget sitting on the porch swing. Their eyes met briefly through the windshield. Marche looked away first, heart thumping uncomfortably. *Please let this go smoothly. I don't know how much more drama I can handle today.* Stepping out of the car, she plodded up the driveway—looking everywhere but straight ahead. Nicely trimmed flowers lined the front porch and wrapped around the side of the house. The pink, purple, and yellow perennials seemed preternaturally bright against the dimming daylight. Above, crows cawed from their resting places on the phone lines. The lamppost flickered on as she passed it.

Walking stiffly up the two porch steps, she joined Bridget on the swing. The slabs of wood creaked slightly under her weight.

"You're here for Stella."

"How is she?" Marche quietly asked.

Bridget cleared her throat. "She'll be okay. The burns weren't as bad as they looked."

"Thank heavens," Marche exclaimed.

"The doctor said to rub aloe on her hands a few times a day until the skin heals." Kicking at the ground, Bridget catapulted the swing into motion. Marche clutched at the armrest to keep her balance. "I'm sorry about what happened. I don't even know what to say. Trey was way out of line."

"Maybe so...but that's not what I came here to talk about."

Bridget turned to face her. Marche, swallowing her own discomfort, met her gaze. Her sister's expression was flat. *She's tense*, Marche realized. *I've never seen her this nervous before.*

"If this isn't about Trey taking Stella, then—"

"I'm selling the house," Marche declared. "I'll take whatever offer I can get. The sooner I can get it off my hands, the better."

Bridget scratched her elbow. As the seconds ticked by, her mouth softened and her eyes narrowed with confusion. "I don't understand," she finally said, the swing slowing to a stop.

Marche folded her arms across her chest and drew a deep breath. After everything that had occurred today, she wanted nothing more than to see Stella, take a hot shower, and surrender to sleep. But she had to explain the situation first. Bridget deserved to know what was going on. With as much restraint as she could muster, she detailed the afternoon's events.

As the words tumbled from her mouth, the navy sky turned black. Cricket song intensified. A frog bellowed from the hedges. Marche's arms itched with fresh mosquito bites. But she also felt soothed. The awkwardness between her and Bridget had dwindled. Morbid though the topic was, they were actually talking to each other.

"She was completely out of touch with reality. I just..." Her voice cracked as she relived the moment. "I don't know what might have happened if the neighbor hadn't shown up."

"I can't believe it," Bridget breathed when Marche had finished. "She seemed so harmless. I never would have dreamt..." She hugged herself. "Are you okay?"

"I'm fine," Marche said, holding out her arms. "See? Not even a scratch."

"No—I mean—I can see that you aren't hurt. But are you *okay* okay? Like, emotionally. Psychologically."

Marche took a deep, contemplative breath. "Who knows?" Would she have nightmares about Agatha when she closed her eyes at night? Would the sound of a car backfiring make her jump? Only time would reveal the extent of her trauma. "But I *do* know that I can't stay in that house another day."

"That's understandable," Bridget said. "I wouldn't want to stay there, either, after what you've been through."

Marche slapped at a mosquito that was feasting on her wrist, grabbed a tissue from her purse, and wiped the guts off her skin. "I brought some clothes for Stella. Can you keep her for a few days while I work things out?"

Bridget stared at her silently for a moment. Then she brushed her hair off her shoulders and cupped her chin in her hand like a model in an advertisement. "No," she finally said. "I won't watch her for you."

"What?" Marche replied, stunned. "Why not? You're always so eager to spend time with her."

"Because...you're her mother," Bridget said. "You can stay here and take care of her yourself. I love Stella to bits, but I'm only her aunt. The person she needs most right now is you. Besides," she added, "we have plenty of room to spare. It's not like the bed you used before isn't here anymore."

Marche swallowed roughly. She suspected this was Bridget's way of indirectly apologizing for what had transpired in the hospital room. *I need to reciprocate.* But she was too emotionally and physically drained to engage in a heart-to-heart talk right now. *Tomorrow. I'll clear the air with her tomorrow. After I've gotten some sleep.*

"I appreciate the offer, but I don't think Trey would feel comfortable sharing a roof with me right now."

"Don't worry about that. Regardless of whatever happens, we're still family. He wouldn't want you to check into a hotel. And I don't want that, either. Just stay here. It'll be better for Stella, too."

"I..." Marche hesitated. Maybe Bridget was right. And even if she wasn't, there were only a handful of hours left in the day to worry about it. In the morning, she could re-analyze the situation with a clear head.

"Okay," she said. "We'll both stay."

"Trey put her to bed as soon as they got back from the hospital," Bridget said. "I read to her for a little while, but I'm not sure that she was even listening."

Marche recalled the vacant expression on Stella's face and her chest constricted. "Did she speak at all?"

She set the suitcase on the guest room floor and unzipped it. After what she'd endured today, she couldn't, in good conscience, go near her daughter until she'd taken a piping hot shower. God only knew what germs she was carrying.

"A little," Bridget said, perching at the foot of the king-sized bed. "She was quiet until Trey brought Bianca into the room. Then she finally seemed to show some interest in her surroundings."

Marche sighed with relief. For once, hearing about the doll didn't bother her. It was just a doll. Nothing more. Stella was crawling out of her shell, and that was all that mattered. "What did she say?" Rummaging through the clothes, she pulled out a blue scoop neck nightgown and a pair of underwear.

"Something about Bianca taking care of her."

"That's a funny thing to say, isn't it?"

Bridget shrugged. "Toys are really important to some kids. I had a first grader last year who carried his favorite stuffed manatee to school in his backpack every day."

"Hmm. Did she tell you anything? Like about how she got injured?"

"No," Bridget said. "I didn't ask, though. I was afraid it might upset her. We just talked about what she might like to eat for breakfast. Then I read to her some more and she went to sleep. That was around six o'clock."

Marche nodded. She agreed with Bridget. It was better not to ask. Besides, there was no point in scratching at a healing wound. Whatever had happened wouldn't happen again. Squeezing the nightclothes in her fist, she determined that she wouldn't let Stella return to that house. Not ever.

"Would you like something to eat?" Bridget asked. "There's some leftover broccoli casserole from yesterday. I could heat some up for you."

"That's all right." Despite the fact that she hadn't eaten all day, she wasn't the least bit hungry. Knocking on Death's door had effectively killed her appetite. "I think I'll just wash up, check in on Stella, and call it a night."

"If you change your mind..."

"I know where the kitchen is," Marche said, forcing a tired smile.

"Okay. Well, I'll go discuss things with Trey. Maybe he can come up with a plan to help you sell the house quickly without taking a hit." Bridget pushed off the bed and headed for the door. "Enjoy your shower."

Marche did enjoy it. Never before had she been so grateful for Bridget's absurdly expensive hygiene products. Using a generous amount of both the scented soap and the shampoo, she scrubbed her skin until it tingled. She emerged from the shower twenty minutes later smelling like a bouquet of freshly cut flowers, all traces of the day's events washed down the drain. Patting herself dry with a fluffy towel, she dressed quickly and headed toward Stella's room.

Stella was sound asleep.

Marche left the door half open and tiptoed toward her. Light from the hallway spilled into the room, illuminating the cashmere pink walls and ecru furniture.

As she neared the bed, she noted the regular rise and fall of Stella's chest beneath the bedcovers. Bridget had tucked the seashell-patterned blanket snugly around her. Bianca lay on the bed beside her pillow, its porcelain gaze directed at the ceiling.

Marche kneeled on the carpet beside the mattress. Quietly, she studied her daughter's face. In sleep, Stella looked like one of the princesses she liked to read about in her picture books. Except that tonight she hadn't quite relaxed even in slumber; her eyebrows were drawn slightly together as though she were dreaming of unpleasant things.

A fresh pang of guilt pierced Marche like an arrow to the heart. *No more sadness.* From now on, she promised herself, she would do her best to make as many happy memories for Stella as she could.

Reaching forward, she gingerly folded back the sheets. A sob formed in her throat; she pressed her lips tightly together to choke down the sound. Both of Stella's hands had been wrapped loosely in gauze. Marche was tempted to touch the white mittens but refrained, fearful that the slightest pressure might cause Stella additional pain and jolt her into consciousness.

Pulling the sheet back up, she tucked it securely around Stella's shoulders. Then she pressed the backs of her fingers against Stella's forehead; her skin was warm but not feverish. Withdrawing her hand, she rearranged her daughter's hair on the pillow so that it looked neat and pretty.

"Just like a princess," she whispered. Then she planted a feather-light kiss on the tip of her nose, tiptoed back out, and closed the door softly behind her.

Thirty-Four

The latch!

Had someone whispered in her ear just then, or had she dreamt it?

Marche lay on her side, staring at the wall in the semi-darkness. All was quiet in the house—so quiet that she could hear an owl hooting from a nearby tree. The hushed atmosphere should have been comforting; the late hour should have lulled her back to sleep.

Instead, she was wide awake.

Kicking the sheets off her body, she sat up. Something was wrong. She lowered her feet to the side of the bed. The plush carpeting between her toes reminded her that she was not at home.

Yesterday's events came rushing back all at once—Stella with her burned hands, glazed eyes, and chalky cheeks; Agatha with the gun pointed at her; Vale's sudden appearance; and the old woman's brains splattered on the wall.

That's right. I'm at Bridget's.

Everything was okay now. She'd survived the ordeal, and Stella was safely recovering from her own injuries in the room next door. Yet a niggling voice in the back of her mind insisted that something was wrong.

She ran a hand through her hair—it wasn't that knotted. She rubbed her eyes, but they weren't crusty. Glancing at her watch, she was surprised to see that it was only one o'clock. She hadn't slept more than a few hours.

Digging her feet deeper into the carpet, she stood.

Moonlight peeked through the curtains, providing just enough illumination for her to see where she was going without needing to turn on the bedside lamp. She shuffled over to the closet. Peeling off her nightgown, she reached for one of the shirts she'd hung up before going to sleep. Then she slid into her jeans. She dressed slowly and calmly, without stopping to analyze what she was doing or why.

She turned to look for her shoes and saw the toes poking out from beneath the bed skirt. Hooking her fingers under the laces, she pulled them out.

As she slipped her feet into the sneakers, the house loomed before her in her mind. She thought about Agatha's letters. And the broken latch on the box. Something was missing. Though she didn't know what it could possibly be, she had an inkling of where she might find it.

"I have to see what's there," she murmured, knowing that she wouldn't be able to rest until she had.

Fishing through her toiletry items, she found an elastic band and tied her hair into a ponytail. Then she grabbed her purse and headed out.

The corridor was dark and silent. She passed the bathroom and a linen closet on her left, Stella's room on her right. Pausing, she opened the door and peeked inside. Saw her daughter tucked safely in the bed. "I'll be back real soon, kiddo," she whispered. Quietly, she shut the door. At the end of the hallway, she turned into the main foyer.

Ornate stained glass windows flanked the front door. The porch light filtered through the red and orange slabs, painting flame-like images on the floor. Unlocking the deadbolt, she stepped out into the hot, humid air.

Whoo. Who-whooo. Whoo. Who-whooo.

The owl's call was louder now; it seemed to be coming from a tree in the next-door neighbor's yard. Marche withdrew the keys from her purse. Metal jangled against metal as she locked the front door with the spare key Bridget had given her when she'd first moved to Egret Bay. The owl's song broke, then quickly resumed. Marche singled out the car key as she approached the Neon. She felt the smooth gliding sensation of the kinks falling into place as she slid the key into the lock. In another moment, she was in the car heading toward Victor Street.

During the drive, lengthened by only two red traffic lights, Marche pondered the possible meaning behind the broken latch. It seemed like the box had originally belonged to Agatha. But why would she break her own property?

"Unless..."

Someone without a key wanted to see what was inside? Maybe Charles had broken it? After all, some of the papers in there had belonged to him.

"She must have forgotten about the lock," Marche muttered. "Otherwise, she wouldn't have asked me to open it."

What was so important that Agatha was ready to kill to keep it secret? The longer she thought about it, the more confident she became.

It wasn't the letters Agatha was after. Something else had been inside that box. And someone—presumably her brother—had removed it. But what was it?

Slowing to a near stop, Marche steered the car onto Victor.

She turned into the driveway, killed the engine, and stared at the house. She'd never seen the exterior at this hour before. It was like a human face that a person had to look at twice. Once in passing. Then a second time, because the features—though conventional on their own—seemed "off" when assembled as a whole. With parts of the façade illuminated by moonlight, the structure's old age seeped through. The windows were like pockmarks on weathered cheeks, the white trim frown lines, and the gabled roof a toupee that didn't fit quite right.

Marche tucked her purse under the driver's seat and locked the car door. Stuffing the keys into her jeans pocket, she strode around the side of the house.

Street lamps on Washington flooded the yard with a pale, yellowish glow. The grass, slick with dew, shone like tinsel. A robust brown toad hopped on the ground to her left. It froze when she passed it, flattening itself into the earthy carpet. From one of the neighbor's yards came the spitting sound of a sprinkler system.

The shed, just a few yards up ahead, appeared more decrepit than ever. When she stared at it long enough, the rust looked like maple syrup trickling down a stack of pancakes—or blood dripping from a severed limb. Marche squeezed her eyes shut. When she reopened them, the blood became rust again.

The doors made a loud scraping sound as she pried them apart. Grabbing the ladder, which was propped up beside the extra paint cans, she lumbered back through the yard and rounded the house.

She set the ladder up against it and stepped onto the stoop. Singling out the house key, she unlocked the front door.

Slowly, she reached for the knob. Turned it. And then hesitated.

"You can do this," she whispered to herself. "Agatha's dead. There's nothing in there to be afraid of."

Opening the door, she entered the empty house. Forcing thoughts of the old woman out of her head, she switched on the foyer light. Then she trekked through the rest of the house and flipped every light switch she could find. When enough light blazed through the windows to alert the neighborhood that she was home, she went outside to get the ladder.

Reentering the house, she paused before the stairs.

Put it out of your head.

She was so focused on blocking out the memory of her death march that she became careless. Twice she banged the ladder against the wall. The second time she left a dent, revealing the wooden frame beneath the paint.

When she reached the landing, she rested the ladder against the wall and looked down the hallway. She hadn't opened the door to that room yet. She bit her bottom lip in uncertainty. Did she really want to go in there? Was she really brave enough? Maybe she should wait until morning. It wasn't a big deal. She'd just drive back to Bridget's, climb into bed, and return when the sun came up. What difference would a few hours make?

But if I don't do it now, I might lose my nerve altogether, she reasoned. *And then I'll have the mystery hanging over my head forever. No... It's best to do it now and get it over with.*

Heaving a sigh of determination, she approached the room.

As she twisted the doorknob, she imagined what she would find. Knowing that the death cleanup services had already scoured the room provided only a mild comfort. What if they'd missed something?

Pushing the door open, she envisioned Agatha's purple nails and the wild expression in her eyes. And she remembered the gun in the old woman's hand and her certainty that the Grim Reaper was about to cut her down with his scythe.

She paused partway, chewing her bottom lip; she had new demons to face. Rather than wake up six months from now slathered in a cold sweat, she preferred to conquer them in a single blow. Taking a deep steadying breath, she slowly peered through the entrance. "Ohhh," she exhaled, collapsing against the doorframe. The room looked the same as it had before the incident, except that someone had pushed the box against the far wall.

The latch!

Carrying the ladder into the room, she positioned it under the attic door, about at the spot where Agatha had stood when she shot herself in the head. Don't think about that. She shook the metal legs to test their sturdiness and then looked up.

"Flashlight," she murmured. No way in hell was she going to go rooting around up there in the pitch black.

The phone began to ring as she descended the stairs. She ignored it at first, heading straight for the storage compartment next to the half bath. After rummaging around for a few seconds, she located a medium-sized metal flashlight on the top shelf next to the hammer and nails. A second series of rings let loose as she stepped back into the hall.

"Oh, for crying out loud!" Marching into the living room, she lifted the receiver to her ear. "Hello?"

Silence.

"Nobody there?"

More silence.

"Right. Get a life, you little shit. I'm through with your games." Punching the "off" button, she unplugged the phone and returned to the spare room.

Staring at the panel in the ceiling, her hesitancy returned. Even with a flashlight, it would be dark in the attic.

"This is what you came here for, Marche Baker." Shaking the ladder once more, she set a foot on the bottom rung. "Up we go."

When she could touch the ceiling, she placed her palm flat against the panel. It was cold, much colder than the rest of the house, and colder than it should have been when it was so overbearingly warm outside.

She pressed against it, and it gave way easily under the pressure. Pushing the panel clear of the opening, she turned on the flashlight. Then, before she could let her cowardice get the better of her, she ascended the remaining steps and climbed into the attic.

The same odors greeted her as before. But there was also the cold. She crouched on her knees and rubbed her arms. In seconds, she was freezing, almost to the point of shivering. If she stayed there long enough, she felt sure that the perspiration on her forehead would turn into icicles.

Wait a second...

She sniffed.

She was wrong. The air smelled different now. Earthier. And somehow familiar. "Eww..." She tried not to gag as the stench intensified. *Onions. Mold. Rotten eggs.*

Grimacing, she swept the flashlight's beam across the attic.

The last time she was up here, she hadn't paid attention to the details. The space hadn't held interest for her. It had been Bridget's treasure hunt, and she had just tagged along to humor her. Now she had a purpose. With calm precision, she scanned the area again. This time she noticed something about one of the paneled walls that didn't look right.

"What—?"

Crawling closer to the wall on her left, she confirmed it. Hatch marks—about an inch long and etched closely together—covered the boards. They were black, as if they'd been burned into the wood with a hot chisel. As she touched them, an intrusive thought tickled like a whisper in her ear.

Two. Black and white. There are two of them.

Marche shook her head and continued to survey the wall. The scratches covered the entire length of it. Starting near the ceiling, they comprised several rows, the last of which terminated about three-quarters across, halfway from the bottom.

"There must be a few thousand or more," she murmured.

As she skimmed over the hatch marks, she imagined a prisoner in a locked room counting the days of their incarceration. *No*, the voiceless whisper insisted. *Hiding and planning. Waiting for the right moment. Waiting for the kill!*

Marche rubbed her earlobe, befuddled. Where were these odd thoughts coming from?

The cold in the room suddenly increased. A slight tremor sparked at the base of her skull and shot down the length of her spine. Her heartbeat increased to a rate that felt almost painful.

She gripped the flashlight tightly in her right hand and rested her forehead against the dusty wall. In the darkness, she pictured Dom straddling his motorcycle, both thumbs hitched through the belt loops of his jeans. He was carefree, but he hadn't been overly reckless. If only...

"Why did you have to leave us?" she whispered. And then she accidentally inhaled some dust and sneezed.

Wiping her eyes and nose with the inside of her shirt collar, she swallowed the fresh lump in her throat and straightened. *Now's not the time to reminisce.* She aimed the beam at the far corner of the room where she and Bridget had discovered the box—and nearly toppled backward through the attic door. "Oh, shit!" she squealed, the flashlight slipping from her fingers. It hit the floor with a loud thunk, rolled, and came to a rest with the bulb directed at her feet.

It isn't real.

It isn't real.

It isn't real.

Marche fumbled for the flashlight, her breath ragged. The metal was slippery in her sweaty grip, but she managed to lift it without dropping it again.

Everything before her was cast in blackness. Clamping her jaw shut, she steeled herself and raised the flashlight with both hands. The bouncing beam revealed what her rational mind tried so vehemently to reject.

It was the figure in white—the one that she'd seen on her very first day in the house.

It was still faceless, and still bleeding grossly from the abdomen. Loose threads from the ripped fabric, stained red, stuck out like whiskers. The skin hung open. A hand clutched tightly at the intestine-like mess to keep it from spilling onto the floor. The fingers were slender and long; pinkish flesh bulged through the spaces between them. In the midst of blood and guts, Marche detected a sparkle. Like a beacon of light at the end of a dark tunnel, a diamond on the specter's ring finger winked at her.

Marche closed her eyes. Where her fingers overlapped on the flashlight, she caressed her wedding band. *Is this my punishment for plucking our seed? Am I going to be cursed with this nightmare until the day I die?*

When she gathered the courage to look again, she discovered that the figure had changed its position. It now pointed to the floor.

A ribbon of red blood trickled down from the preternaturally white elbow to the wrist in a neat, thin line. From the wrist, the blood flowed to the first knuckle and down the entire length of the index finger. A steady stream dripped from the tip onto the floor.

Transfixed by the beautiful contrast of ruby on alabaster, Marche watched the blood land on the plank and gather into a puddle the size of a quarter. In the confined space, she thought that she could actually hear the soft *plup-plup-plup* of blood dripping into blood.

Covering her mouth with the back of her hand, she emitted a long, guttural moan.

As she watched, the figure began to fade in parts. Its bare feet dispersed and disappeared first. The slim legs and hourglass torso (with its exposed bowels) vanished next. Then the collarbone and neck, followed by the head.

Until only the cold remained.

Marche continued to stare at the corner. Determination overrode her fear. She had to see what was waiting in the dark. She had to know what had driven Agatha to madness. Flexing her limbs, she crawled forward.

As she crossed the floorboards, her hands collected and dispersed dust; she coughed and her eyes immediately watered. Tears streaked down her neck.

Finally, she reached the attic corner. Folding her legs underneath her, she scanned the ground. This part of the floor wasn't covered in the same heavy dust as the rest of the attic—the chest of letters had lain here for several years. But the planks weren't bare as they should have been. A single drop of dark red liquid shone on one of them.

Marche extended her hand to touch the spot. It was wet. She examined the tip of her finger; it was red. She lifted it to her nose. It smelled metallic, like blood.

Wiping her hand on her jeans, she examined the floorboards more closely. They were nailed tightly together, but an inch of space remained between the edge of the planks and the wall. Anchoring the flashlight between her knees so that the light hit the floor, she inserted her fingers into the narrow space. Securing them behind the plank, she pulled. The old nails were stubborn; her fingers ached as the rough wood bit into her skin.

"Ugh," she groaned. "Come on."

She yanked harder and harder, the pads of her fingers becoming raw. Just when she felt as though she would have to give up and go find the toolbox, a loud crack sounded and the board broke in two.

Marche tossed the wood fragment over her shoulder. Hastily grabbing the flashlight with her pulsing fingers, she leaned forward and aimed the beam into the shallow hole. To her surprise, she saw nothing.

"Damn it."

She rubbed the bridge of her nose with two dirty fingers. She thought of Dom again and her eyes threatened to well up with fresh tears.

While she sat there feeling sorry for herself, the temperature plummeted. She began to shiver; her teeth chattered. She extended her hand over the exposed flooring. A waft of cold air brushed against her fingers. Where was it coming from? A renewed sense of vigor enveloped her and, along with that, resolve.

Gritting her teeth, she leaned forward once more. It had to be there. Whatever it was that Agatha had been willing to kill for—it had to be there.

Lowering her face into the opening, she searched further under the floorboards. The area was small, no more than six inches deep and eighteen inches square. This time she spotted it, a coarse brown sack tucked off to the side that blended into the wooden frame.

Stuffing her hand into the hidden compartment, she wrapped her fingers around it.

"Ouch," she hissed.

Her hand burned as though she'd grabbed a fistful of ice. Instinctively, she released it. When the shock wore off, she reached for the sack again, ready to endure the intense discomfort. Fortunately, there was no reaction this time.

"Got it," she declared as she withdrew the item from the recess.

She crawled back to the attic opening with the sack clutched tightly in one hand. Then she descended the ladder and rushed from the room, shutting the door firmly behind her.

I am NEVER going into that room again.

She strode purposefully toward the stairs, comforted by the thought that she would soon be out of the house. As she lowered her foot onto the top step, however, an ominous thump stopped her. One sneaker suspended in the air, she turned. The sound—she was certain—had come from her bedroom.

"Is someone in there?" she called, her voice tremulous.

Turning, she tiptoed across the hard floor. She gripped the sack tightly to her stomach and held the flashlight in her right hand like a bat. Had she forgotten to lock the front door? Had someone snuck inside while she was exploring the attic?

She paused at the threshold and listened. Hearing nothing, she peered inside.

The room was as it should be. The soiled clothes remained on the floor where she'd left them. Not a picture frame was out of place. She neared the bed and peered cautiously around the other side. A wave of relief swept through her. Had she really expected to see that grotesque pulsating fetus again?

"Enough of this," she murmured. "It's time to go."

She turned to leave and stumbled at the doorway. The sack popped out of her hand, landing with a dull thud on the hard floor.

"Oops."

As she bent forward to pick it up, something moved within the bulging cloth. Whatever it was rose slowly and then fell back into place—like a baby's foot pressing against its mother's stomach in slow motion. Marche sucked in her breath, pursed her lips, and quickly snatched it up.

Feeling unsteady, she grabbed the doorknob for support.

It's shock, that's all. I'm in shock. None of this is real. There are no ghosts. Because ghosts don't exist. Just the ugly past. Get your act together, Marche Baker.

Then she stepped into the hallway.

And screamed.

Thirty-Five

Dom stood in front of Stella's room. Although reality dictated that he couldn't possibly be there, there he was. Just like Marche had yearned for—but not quite. This wasn't the Dom she'd known and loved. With his chin lowered to his chest and his arms dangling limply at his sides, he looked like a sinister exhibit at a wax museum. A slimy, clear mucus-like substance oozed down his legs and collected in puddles at his feet. Eyes made of oily black pools of nothingness stared at her. Gray lips peeled back in a ghastly, inhuman smile.

"Oh...oh...oh..."

Marche uttered the incoherent cry, squeezed her eyes shut, and counted silently to ten. *Please go away. You aren't my Dom.* She was not made of steel. She did not have an iron rod for a spine. She was still vulnerable. She *could* break. *Please be gone. Please disappear.* When she slowly cracked open her eyelids, however, the phantasm was still there, more menacing and repulsive than before.

Her stomach muscles contracted, tightening into knots of apprehension. The sensation was similar to what she'd experienced on a roller coaster at Busch Gardens, just before dropping seventy feet in the air at a forty-five degree angle. (Dom had laughed; she'd screamed.) Only now the excitement was absent, because there weren't any safety regulations to keep her from impending harm. This was a free fall, like jumping off a bridge without a bungee cord properly secured to her harness. Anything could happen and just about anything might. Except...this wasn't real. Or was it?

Marche never saw Dom's body after the accident. She'd identified his remains by his wedding band, which had both of their initials carved on the inside along with the date they had married. Scuffed and bent, that ring had remained imprinted on her memory all of these months—a haunting abstraction of his death, a vague hint of his corpse's condition.

But what she saw before her now surpassed her worst imaginings.

Shards of bone jutted out of one side of his exposed skull. Pieces of gray matter clung to the jagged edges; a portion the size of a marble dangled from his left earlobe. The tip of his nose was flat without the cartilage—it must have been scraped clean off between the moment he was thrown from the motorcycle and when he became lodged against the street sign that warned drivers of an oncoming bend in the road—and white bone glittered like clean beach sand in the hall light. Deep cuts ran down the side of his face where he had skidded along the pavement. In the areas where the skin sagged open, grains of dirt mingled with the exposed muscle and nerves.

It's not real, Marche reminded herself. This mutilated, soulless imitation of her husband did not have a conscience; it did not feel. *That's not my Dom.*

Stepping further into the hallway, she calculated how she might escape the second floor unscathed. *Keep to the wall and don't stop.* Taking a long, tremulous breath, she inched sideways, her eyes fastened on the grotesque wraith.

The grinning facsimile of Dom lifted a scuffed boot and shuffled forward, advancing in her direction. Its movement was mechanical, like the way a battery-operated doll might stiffly thrust one leg forward and then the other.

"You're not my husband!" Marche shouted. "You're a fake! You can't hurt me!"

She clutched the sack tightly to her chest like a shield. The stench of decaying flesh was stomach-churning; it nearly concealed the other odor that wafted to her nose—fresh earth and flowers. It smelled like a graveyard.

A scream lodged in her throat. Holding her breath, she swallowed it down and took another sideways step.

The figure continued to move forward.

Inch by inch, the gap between Marche and the ghoul was narrowing. Soon it would be close enough to make contact. And then what would happen? Could it actually touch her? Would it encircle her in its arms and suffocate her with death? Would she shrivel up and die like a desiccated jellyfish washed up on the shore?

Marche recalled Agatha, pointing the gun at her face as she trembled before the trunk of letters.

"I survived a crazy old woman," she said with a sneer. Anger—that this *thing* would try to pretend to be her beloved husband—boiled in her gut, quelling her fear. "You're just *air*. YOU CAN'T HURT ME."

Her gaze fixed on the grisly figure, she leaned to the left. Before she could lose her nerve, she stepped forward. The stench intensified, and she gagged.

As if pleased with her show of weakness, the grinning lips parted, revealing a horde of squirming, grayish-white maggots and slimy pink worms.

Gulping down the vomit that had risen to the back of her mouth, Marche took another tottering step toward the stairs. She pressed closer to the wall as the distance between her and the phantom decreased. *You can do this. You're almost home-free.*

Suddenly, the figure held out its deeply gashed arms to her. It wore the same sleeveless black shirt that Dom had died in. And the battered clothing revealed—with all too much clarity—the skinless elbows, the compound fracture of the radius and ulna, the laceration from the collarbone to the jaw, and the piece of scrap metal that had gored him like a rabid bull between two of his lower ribs.

The grinning figure beckoned to her with a pulpy index finger. For a brief moment, Marche went numb. The ring and pinky fingers were missing.

"Oh..."

She groaned, finally understanding what that distorted wedding band signified. Unable to keep the sickness at bay, she stumbled past the wraith and vomited. Clear yellow bile spewed onto the floor, making a wet *splat* as it landed before her feet. Marche sobbed and then retched again, her empty stomach aching with the spasms.

Don't stop! Go-go-go!

Sensing movement behind her, she scrambled forward. At last, she reached the staircase. In her haste to get away, however, she tripped over her feet.

"Whoa!"

Marche flailed wildly. Unable to latch onto the railing, she toppled forward.

The fall seemed to take forever. She tumbled down the first few steps on her side and felt pain swell somewhere in the lower region of her body. Then her torso twisted and she somersaulted. A gray haze misted over her vision, and she rolled—her feet banging against the stair railing and her head hitting the wall.

"Ugh."

Gradually the gray receded, and she realized that she was on the floor. How long had she been unconscious? Minutes? Hours? She was afraid to move. What if she'd broken something? Her head throbbed as though she'd been hit with a hammer. Or maybe a flashlight; she'd dropped it at some point during the fall. Her hip felt bruised, her right foot was bent at an uncomfortable angle, and her elbow burned. Slowly, she opened her eyes. She was on her back, her left heel resting on the bottom step.

Gingerly, she propped herself up on the elbow that didn't hurt. A quick visual scan confirmed that none of her bones poked through the skin. She flexed her toes, bent her arms and legs. All of her joints seemed functional. Despite her aches, she was alive and apparently still in one piece.

Whoosh.

A sound—like dead autumn leaves caught in a gardener's rake and hurled into the air.

Marche glanced upward. Dom's facsimile was gone. But something else stood in its place, watching her from the gallery balustrade.

A woman dressed in black.

Two. Black and white. There are two of them.

Scrambling backwards, Marche banged her shoulder against the door. Pain flared in the already-sore limb, shooting to her elbow.

The dark figure moved toward the stairs, its concealed face never turning from Marche's direction.

In a flash, Marche recalled Stella's nightmares. Thinking of them, she remembered her own chilling nocturnal episode; her lower back burned where the bony finger had dug into her skin. And then there were also Sarah's clippings. The unnatural succession of deaths. The curse that seemed to follow every woman who ever had the misfortune to live in this house—or versions of it. When had it started? Who was the first victim?

"Marietta," she whispered.

The phantom, hearing its name, hissed. The inhuman sound spiraled downward like a thread of smoke, filling both her ears and her nostrils. Marche coughed, choking on the putrid odor. As she struggled to catch her breath, the dark figure began to drift down the stairs.

The sack!

Marche searched the foyer and discovered it on the second step. Hastily, she reached for it and rose unsteadily to her feet.

With deliberate slowness, the figure progressed down the stairs. Whereas Dom's wraith had been a showcase of wrecked body parts, Marietta's figure was almost completely obscured by its heavy black dress. The vintage clothing was high-necked, the fabric fanning out just under its narrow chin. The long sleeves hugged its wrists. The hem bunched at the floor, spilling over each step like ink poured from a bottle. Whether it had feet, or whether it was gliding without them, Marche couldn't tell.

Halfway down, the figure lifted a gloved hand. The missing tips revealed fingers capped with black talons. Presenting Marche with a ghastly smile, it hooked its claws into the railing, gauging the wood as it continued its descent.

Marche stared at the half-veiled face, unable to move—as though her blood had literally frozen in her veins.

And then it hovered before her, only a few precious feet separating them. A prisoner in her own body, Marche fearfully awaited whatever horror was in store for her next. As the wraith's talons reached out for her, however, the sack became warmer. Waves of heat seemed to radiate from its center and roll outward, splashing across her fingers. As the tepid current flowed around her, the black figure dropped its arm.

In the next instant, it flew in reverse up the staircase like a kite yanked by its string. At the landing, it tilted back its head. The gray-lipped mouth opened, widening to an extent that was not humanly possible.

A howl erupted from its empty bosom. It was like a desert wind sweeping through a ghost town, a grainy sound full of desolation and hopelessness. All of the horrors of the world converged into that one cry and struck Marche like a physical blow to the chest.

Though she yearned to cover her ears—to block out this song of death—her hands were stuck like glue to the sack. Her mouth opened in unison, and she could feel the caliginous tune building up in her own chest, vying for release. Eternal despair reared on its hindquarters and threatened to devour her, mind and body.

When she felt that surrendering was her only course of action and that she would certainly join this thing in death, the figure suddenly vaporized. A rush of fresh air filled Marche's lungs. The doomful tune died in her throat and her jaw snapped shut.

The sack cooled in her hands.

What...just happened?

Her eyes were dry. Blinking several times, she stepped away from the staircase. Pressing the sack against her body, she cautiously stepped into the hall. Faint with discomfort, she carefully monitored each step.

"Ugh."

Standing free of any support, her head suddenly felt muddled. *I've got to get out of here. What if that thing wasn't finished? What if it comes back?*

In her current state, however, she couldn't possibly get in the car and drive back to Bridget's. What if she'd gotten a concussion during the fall? What if she lost consciousness behind the wheel?

I'll call for a taxi, she decided. *Then I'll wait in the car. I'll be safe outside.*

Stumbling down the hallway, she entered the kitchen and dropped the sack on the table. The baleful roar, replete with despair and ruination, had drained her of vitality. She felt completely dry, as if someone had squeezed all the blood out of her heart. Desperate for water, she pulled a clean glass out of the dish rack and filled it from the tap.

She drank long and deep. Then she reached above the refrigerator for the bottle of ibuprofen. Unscrewing the cap, she tossed two tablets into her mouth.

She washed them down with more water and then reached for the phone.

Carrying it with her to the table, she gingerly lowered herself into one of the chairs. Thankfully, she hadn't injured her tailbone in addition to everything else.

"Damn it," she muttered when she realized there wasn't a dial tone. She slammed the phone on the table and rubbed her forehead. She didn't want to get up again. Not yet.

The hands on the clock ticked steadily away. Marche stared at the sack while she waited for the pounding in her head to lessen.

She needed to leave the house; she needed to sleep.

Just as she was about to return to the living room to reconnect the phone line, a knock at the front door broke the silence.

Thirty-Six

KNOCK-KNOCK-KNOCK.

Marche jumped. Who could possibly be at her door at this hour? Checking her watch, she saw that it was half-past two.

KNOCK-KNOCK-KNOCK.

She plodded to the kitchen opening and looked down the brightly lit hallway. The knocking intensified. Whoever it was, it didn't seem like they were going to leave anytime soon.

KNOCK-KNOCK-KNOCK-KNOCK-KNOCK.

She hobbled down the hallway, favoring her right foot and kneading her head. She felt like a train wreck.

Entering the foyer, she was relieved to see that she had actually turned the deadbolt when she'd brought the ladder in earlier.

At least I don't have to worry about any surprise entrances.

She reached the door. Suddenly struck with lightheadedness, she swayed; worried she might be about to faint, she pressed her palm against the paneling for support. The door groaned softly under her weight. There was a pause in the knocking and then it resumed with renewed vigor. The wood vibrated beneath her fingertips.

When she'd regained her equilibrium, she leaned forward and peered through the peephole. She sucked in her breath. *You have got to be kidding me.* How much more insanity was she expected to contend with tonight?

Despite the poor illumination from the streetlamps, she had no difficulty identifying her visitor. It was the boy (no—young man) whom she'd confronted at the laundromat.

Impulsively, she backed away from the door. In broad daylight and in perfect health, she might deal with him. But not in the wee hours of the morning, with her body in such poor condition, and not another soul in sight.

"Open up, lady!"

Marche shivered. The young man's voice belied his gangly frame. Deep and emphatic, he sounded a bit like Vale, only with a touch of malevolence.

"I know you're in there!" he shouted, pounding his fist against the door even harder. "You killed my granny, you crazy bitch. You better show yourself!"

Granny?

"Oh, no," Marche murmured as the pieces fell into place. The staring, the hostility... She finally understood. It wasn't about *her;* it was about the *house.* The fact that she had moved into his grandmother's territory was all that mattered.

Taking a tentative step forward, she peeked through the peephole again. The stoop was vacant. "Where'd he go?" she whispered. She was tempted to glance through the living room curtains, but she didn't want to risk being seen.

She remained there for a few minutes, eye to the peephole, but saw nothing. Maybe he'd given up and left? She thought of calling the police, but quickly dismissed the idea. She didn't feel like the hassle. Besides, if the prank calls were any indication, he was more of a nuisance than a threat. And this was the last time she was ever going to be in this house alone, so whatever childish games he had planned from here on out didn't matter.

Turning from the door, she headed back toward the kitchen. She gave up on the idea of leaving. It was possible that Agatha's grandson might still be lurking around, and she had no desire to bump into him outside.

I'll wait an hour. By then, he should be gone. Maybe I'll be fit to drive by then, too.

Swallowing her feelings of discomfort and fear, she sat down at the table. *Might as well look at this now and get it over with.* Pulling the sack toward her, she withdrew its contents.

It was a book.

The cover was white with a large *A* (in blood red trim) embossed on the center. The surface was clean, without any dirt stains or scratches. Agatha had clearly treasured it.

Marche traced her fingers along the edge and opened it. No age-old perfume wafted to her nose, just the staleness of old paper. Agatha's name appeared on the inside cover, scrawled in faded black ink in the top left-hand corner. A single line had been struck through *Louis*, with *Vale* written beside it. Agatha's neat handwriting filled the unlined pages. Marche flipped through them to the back. Only the last ten or so pages were blank.

Returning to the front of the journal, she began to read. The first entries dated from 1951. This section was saturated with inane topics: what clothes she was going to wear to school to attract the boys, what new dish she'd learned to cook in her home economics class, the latest pranks she and her brother had pulled on one of their cousins.

Vale's name (or "Butch" rather) began to appear with regularity in 1952. By the following year, Agatha's all-consuming infatuation for him was clearly evident. She wrote of nothing but her undying love and unwavering devotion to him. If she wasn't professing these feelings, then she was wondering what he was doing during the hours they were apart. Gradually, however, the tone darkened. Agatha's protestations became more fervent, more desperate. And then Marche read the last entry for 1953—a single sentence laced with unveiled malice.

I'll make that harlot disappear.

Marche turned the page. The year jumped to 1969. *Staying with Chucky while Luther finishes up his business in New York. It's so good to be home! Found this old thing in the closet. What a sentimental brother I have!*

The next few entries detailed Agatha's plans for the house that she and her husband had purchased. She rattled on about paint colors and china sets, the upholstery fabrics she'd chosen for the parlor furniture, what local activities she should join to improve her status in the community. As Marche skimmed these passages, she wondered if she'd been wrong about the journal. It didn't seem like there was anything significant about it at all.

Then she came to the last entry. She read the paragraph carefully, taking care to reread every sentence so she didn't misconstrue any of it.

It was her. I saw Wilma in the house. She must have crawled out of her grave.

She was washing herself all pretty for Butch. The harlot. How could Chucky let her into our house? Is Butch more important to him than his own flesh and blood? Tomorrow I'll confront him about it. I'll make it clear to him that I couldn't let her have my Butch again. If I can't have him, neither can SHE. I made awful sure of that. I grabbed the butcher knife when she wasn't looking and cut the life out of her. She screamed and screamed and tried to hit me, and I laughed because she was not going to have my Butch again. Not now. Not ever.

I left part of her in Chucky's room for him to find. That should teach him not to betray his sister again. I kept a little piece for myself, too.

Marche closed the diary.

She thought of the letter, the one in which Vale had instructed Agatha to "get rid of it." Marche had assumed he was referring to an abortion. But hadn't he told her yesterday that Agatha wasn't pregnant? What was it she needed to get rid of?

She pressed her fingers to her lips as the answer came to her. *Wilma.* Vale said he loved her, but then he married Marlene. She recalled how the old man had spilled his cigarettes when she'd asked him about Wilma. Was it nerves? Guilt? Maybe it wasn't sacks that Agatha had shown Vale in the attic—but a corpse?

Why had Vale protected Agatha? Was it out of loyalty to Chuck? Or did he perhaps fear that he'd be considered an accomplice? But if Wilma had been dead sixteen years, then...who was the woman Agatha attacked with the knife?

"Betty," Marche breathed.

Agatha had murdered her sister-in-law. And Chuck had covered for her again. That was the only explanation.

"No wonder he became a recluse," Marche murmured. The pain in her head flared up, and she massaged her temples. As she applied the circular pressure, Agatha's words came back to her.

I kept a little piece for myself, too.

Was there something else in the sack? What had Agatha kept after brutally attacking her brother's wife?

Giving up on the massage, Marche fingered the frayed opening. Dare she peer inside?

Biting the inside of her cheek, she spilled the sack's remaining contents on the table. There was a soft *plunk* as something tiny clattered onto the surface. Marche stared wide-eyed at Agatha's souvenir.

"My God," Marche exclaimed, bringing her hands to her mouth. The truth was far more shocking than any spectral illusion she'd encountered in this house of horrors. "What did you do?"

A skeletal hand lay palm up on the tabletop. Each bone was white and shiny, like a carcass picked clean by scavengers and then bleached dry in the sun. The pisiform and scaphoid bones had serrated edges, as though someone had used a knife to separate the hand from the connecting arm. The crescent bone, which should have been located between them, was missing. Marche shivered violently. The hand was small enough to fit in the center of her palm. It was a baby's hand.

"Why did I need to know this?" she choked. "Why did I have to come back here?"

She remembered the moment she'd held Stella and her tiny fingers had clasped her thumb. She closed her eyes and fought back the urge to cry.

"Why did I have to come back here?" she repeated.

What difference did the facts make? There was no murderer to avenge for the crime. Agatha Marshall was lying stiff on a slab in the county morgue. If there were any surviving family members, would they benefit from knowing that Betty's death was murder and not suicide? Probably not. So what *exactly* was the point?

Marche searched for answers and found none. Bowing her head, she saw only the infant's hand and thought only of the unbearable pain that both Betty and her child must have suffered before death claimed them.

Horror and sympathy consumed her until the whole world consisted of nothing but those tiny bones on the kitchen table.

So absorbed was she that she didn't immediately react when an icy cold finger poked her between the shoulder blades. It took a moment for the sensation to pierce her thoughts, for her to realize that the cold she felt was not internal, but external.

And then she jolted upright as if she'd been electrocuted. The hairs on her arms and neck bristled. Her breathing became light and shallow.

A chill caressed her earlobe; a voiceless rush of air snaked its way into her head.

"Mine..."

Had she imagined it? Marche trembled. Leaning forward, she gripped the tabletop like a cat clinging to the side of a birdcage.

"Mine..."

"What do you want?" Marche whispered. Whose ghost was she addressing? Betty's? Marietta's? Or the mistakes in her past?

"Mine..."

Staring at the remains, Marche suddenly understood. There was a purpose to it after all. She *had* returned to this house for a reason. Everything that had happened had been building up to this single moment.

Give it to her. She needs it. She won't be able to rest until it's returned to her.

With trembling fingers, she picked up the cloth and draped it over the bones. Then she gathered it carefully in her hand, lifted the sack over her shoulder, and waited.

Her throat constricted until she couldn't breathe. Even her heart seemed to have ceased beating in the cloud of frigid air. Everything went still—the crickets outside stopped chirping, the house went dark—and then she felt it: bony, skinless fingers touching her own. Marche tried to swallow, but her mouth was too dry. The chill behind her ear increased and then the sack left her palm. Her fingers touched the last thread of cloth as it brushed across them, and then it was gone.

Marche exhaled sharply. The cold evaporated, and the kitchen light flickered back on. She felt alone. Turning in the chair, she saw that the kitchen was indeed empty. She scanned the floor, but the sack was nowhere in sight.

It's over, she thought. *It's really, truly over.*

She laid her head beside the journal. She felt peaceful—for the first time since Dom had died. But the throbbing in her head remained.

Standing up, she grabbed a fresh dish towel from one of the kitchen drawers. Then she filled a Ziploc bag with ice and wrapped the towel around it.

As she shut the freezer door, she reached for the cigarette pack and lighter on top of the refrigerator. Pressing the ice pack to her head, she cast one final glance around the kitchen. She gazed at the walls, the cabinets, the appliances—everything that she would not miss. Switching off the light, she padded slowly into the living room.

The sofa welcomed her with its worn cushions and old scent. She stretched out on it and focused on the coolness soothing her scalp. Opening the cigarette pack, she withdrew the last one.

"This is it," she murmured. "No more dragon's breath after tonight, Dom. I promise." Lighting the tip with trembling fingers, she inhaled.

Sayonara to this house. Sayonara to the past. When this is finished, I'm going to get in that car and leave this place behind forever.

She took another long drag on the cigarette. As she exhaled, her arm dropped over the side of the couch. Every part of her body felt heavy, as if she'd downed a bottle of cold medicine.

Sighing, her eyelids fluttered shut. She felt relaxed and weightless, her body slowly falling into itself. The towel began to slip down her cheek, but she didn't have the energy to put the ice pack back into place.

As sleep crept upon her, she visualized one of her happiest memories.

She was at the beach with Dom, Bridget, and Trey. Stella was in her pink two-piece bathing suit, smiling and chortling. The sun was bright and the baby blue sky was cloudless. The soft white sand swam over their toes and fingers as they worked. The five of them were building a sandcastle together. Laughing gulls waddled on the ground nearby, hoping for handouts. Stella was running toward the crashing waves, four years old and brown as a tree trunk. They all laughed as she dumped the pail into the water and then fell into the surf. Covered in saltwater and sand, she ran back to them, most of the water already spilled from the pail. Marche continued to laugh with Bridget, while Dom and Trey elbowed each other for authority over the construction of the highest tower. Marche looked from Dom to Trey to Bridget to Stella. Each one of them was smiling. Everything was perfect. And then it all suddenly slowed down, as if she was watching a video on television and had pressed the slow-motion button. Marche felt happy and content as her eyes rested on Stella's smiling, laughing face.

The doorknob rattled violently, but Marche didn't hear it. She was aware only of the *other* sound. An all-consuming sound.

As Stella puckered her lips and ran toward her to give her a wet kiss on the cheek, the chiming bells followed her into her dreams.

Beautiful sound! Oh, so beautiful!

Afterword

Repetition began with a true story.

From the ages of five to nine, my mom lived in Arlington, Massachusetts. The rented duplex on Whittemore Street looked normal from the outside, but it frightened her throughout the family's stay there. One night in particular has forever imprinted itself on her memory. Awakening in the darkness, my mom discovered flames leaping from the mattress. She backed up against the wall, petrified. "I put out the fire with my hands. I was sick with fear."

When morning came, the bed showed no evidence of what had occurred—but her hands were blistered. My grandparents never noticed—my grandma distracted with raising four other young children, my grandpa busy with schooling at MIT. The house was haunted, and my mom had to grapple with this nightmarish experience on her own. "I remember learning afterwards that two people had committed suicide in that house. One in the basement, and one in the attic. And both places gave me severe creeps."

This story would have captured my imagination, regardless. But knowing that my mom experienced this paranormal activity when she was a little girl, and that she was essentially alone in this frightening situation, made a stronger impression on me. I began to imagine what fateful acts or events might lead to such an occurrence, and I also wondered what domestic circumstances might contribute to a child having to fend for themselves in a waking nightmare. These ponderings ultimately led to the creation of Marche, Stella, and the house at 919 Victor Street.

—Crystal

Acknowledgements

Thank you, Mom. (For everything.) Thank you, Derek & Jennifer. (For the laughs.) And thank you to my friends, family, and fellow writers for your incredible support through the years. (You know who you are.) Lastly, I would like to express my gratitude to Kell, Hannah, and the editors at Dead Fox Publishing. Thank you for believing in Repetition and for giving it a home. And thank you for your dedicated passion. This book is creepier than ever because of you!

Tampa Bay native Crystal Sidell grew up playing with toads in the rain and indulging in speculative fiction. She holds a master of arts in both English and Library and Information Science, moderates creative writing groups, and has reviewed books for the Florida Library Youth Program. When she's not otherwise occupied, she's usually looking for ways to spoil her pets or stopping traffic to rescue turtles. A Best of the Net, Dwarf Star, Pushcart nominee and Rhysling finalist, her work appears in *34 Orchard, Apparition Lit, Baffling Magazine, Cosmic Background, Neurodiversiverse: Alien Encounters, On Spec, Sprawl Mag, Strange Horizons, Stupefying Stories, Trollbreath, Weird Christmas*, and others.

Thank you!

Your purchase helped support an indie author and a small press. We hope you enjoy enough to leave a review!

Want more Dead Fox books? Head on over to our website where you can purchase our titles cheaper than you'll find them anywhere else.

www.ingramcontent.com/pod-product-compliance
Lightning Source LLC
LaVergne TN
LVHW010645110826
845149LV00014B/2934